Praise for B[...]

NEMI[...]

"The most exciting book I have ever read."

—Arthur C. Clarke

SPLINTERED ICON

"It's hard not to get sucked into Bill Napier's incredible vortex. Truly an extraordinary tale, and one that throws the perfect bridge from England to the Americas . . . Sir Walter Raleigh's *Da Vinci Code*. More, it's smart as hell. It reads like an exploding brush fire . . . what a ride! *Splintered Icon* is a really terrific novel, head and shoulders above the genre."

—Jeff Long, *New York Times* bestselling author of *The Descent*

"Napier nimbly twists two separate tales into a thrilling novel of exploration, discovery, and, ultimately, survival. Fans of Dan Brown, take note, this is a one-sitting book."

—Jack DuBrul, *USA Today* bestselling author of *The Medusa Stone*

"Intriguing and imaginative. An inventive piece of storytelling."

—Steve Berry, national bestselling author of *The Amber Room*

"Deftly mixing history, science, and fiction, Napier keeps the action escalating toward a satisfying climax."

—*Publishers Weekly*

The Lure

Bill Napier

St. Martin's Paperbacks

This is a work of fiction. All of the characters, organizations, and events portrayed in this novel are either products of the author's imagination or are used fictitiously.

Originally published in Great Britain by HEADLINE BOOK PUBLISHING

Extracts from the *Marine Observer* reprinted by permission of the Meteorological Office

THE LURE

ISBN: 0-312-93681-8
EAN: 978-0-312-93681-5

Printed in the United States of America

HEADLINE BOOK PUBLISHING edition published 2002
St. Martin's Paperbacks edition / November 2007

St. Martin's Paperbacks are published by St. Martin's Press, 175 Fifth Avenue, New York, NY 10010.

10 9 8 7 6 5 4 3 2 1

For Bruce, Ailsa, Hazel and Jim.

Acknowledgements

In writing this novel I have benefited from many discussions with colleagues, friends and family. Dr Anna Gavin helped me with matters medical and biochemical; Martin Murphy advised me on computer matters; Tigran Khanzadyan and Georgi Pavlovski helped me with Russian, as did my son Bruce with Norwegian. Dr Peter Herring gave me insights into the mysterious glowing wheels sometimes reported at sea: the cited reports are from the logbooks, deposited in the Met Office, of numerous trained observers in the Voluntary Observing Fleet. I am indebted to the Met Office for permission to quote them and to Sir Arthur C. Clarke for pointing out that this strange luminescence has been given the evocative name 'Wheels of Poseidon'. The lyrics in Café Roland are from *The Beggar's Opera* by John Gay. I am especially grateful to my wife Nancy who assisted me in countless practical ways, not least in photography at various locations used in the book.

Contents

1

The Cavern

The Tatras in winter: a barren, snow-covered massif in Eastern Europe. Heavy, snow-laden clouds hid the tops of the highest peaks, and fingers of mist drifted down the valleys between them. And inside the massif, under the feet of the skiers and the mountain ramblers, another world.

Entrance to this other world was through a plain steel door set into a natural recess in the rock. There were no signs to proclaim ownership, or to say what lay behind it. It was reached by a steep, three-hundred-metre climb up a snowy path which zig-zagged between the conifers. The path was unmarked, and led off from a highway along which the skiers, ramblers and climbers came and went in their snow-chained cars.

The man approaching this door had a wide, turned-down mouth and narrow lips which made him look vaguely like a giant frog. Low gun-metal sunlight and white mountain peaks reflected from his bulbous sunglasses. The same sunlight was glittering off his companion's sapphire earrings. She was about the same age, taller, long-faced, with a naturally severe expression and long dark hair. She had light blue eyes. They were both puffing slightly from the climb.

The man fumbled for a key, pulled at the heavy door. It opened smoothly and they stepped through it, out of the cold sunshine and the snow, into the subterranean world.

Harsh lights, fixed at intervals in a rocky wall, lit up a flight of roughly carved stone steps. The man led the way down these, gripping a handrail. The steps ended at a small, flat concrete platform. Next to it was a metal cage, its wire-mesh sides painted a dirty yellow. It bobbed up and down alarmingly as they squeezed into it. He pulled the elevator door shut with a metallic *clash!*

The woman glanced up. In the semi-dark, twenty feet above them, she could make out what seemed to be miles of braided steel cable wrapped around a giant cylinder, and a confusing array of black-painted girders and steel pins driven into the rock. A rivulet of water was trickling down a rock face. 'Tell me, Charlie. Are these girders ever checked for rust?'

The man grinned, said, 'Nope,' and pressed a red button.

The cage plunged, reaching a brisk, near-silent terminal speed after some seconds. The woman's stomach settled back in place and she gave the man an embarrassed little smile. The overhead elevator lights revealed a coarsely cut tunnel of rock hurtling upwards, inches from them. The cage was held in place by black plastic sleeves through which four shiny metal tubes, squarely placed at each corner of the tunnel, were sliding with a faint, high-pitched whine.

She had done the cage hundreds of times, but still it left her feeling vaguely uneasy. Cold air was billowing around them, driven by the ram pressure of the plunging cage. 'By the way, I had a BBC producer on the line.'

The man took off his sunglasses. 'Really?'

'Yes, they'd like to do a documentary. But I put them off.'

The man's round face showed surprise and dismay. 'Hell, Svetlana, why did you do that? We can use all the profile we can get.'

'I didn't trust her. It was something she said, almost in passing. That we're not even sure these particles exist. That we could be on a wild-goose chase and all this public money could be for nothing. What use is this stuff, we could heat a thousand pensioners for the same money — that sort of thing.'

'All of which is true.' A lion snarled. There was a brief glimpse of a narrow ledge, and an illuminated tunnel, and fifty metres along it a cloud of spray from a roaring river; but in an instant image and noise had vanished upwards.

Now came the climax of the joyride, the bit she hated. The tunnel suddenly opened out and the cage was hurtling down from the roof of a cavern the size of a cathedral. She blinked at the sight of giant stalactites, and machinery scattered around a rocky floor rushing up at them. Then the black rings were gripping the metal tubes and there was a metallic screech and the elevator had slowed to a halt, and the grip of the rings loosened and the cage bobbed slowly up and down just above a concrete platform.

* * *

The room adjoining the cavern was small, brightly lit and bleakly furnished, with no more than a few grey lockers and a table on which sat a black box attached to a Geiger counter.

They picked up heavy yellow torches and made their way to another metal door. For a moment, they were in pitch black and there was a gust of cool air, but then the torchlight was showing a long, low, natural tunnel, curving out of sight. Overhead, millions of stalactites hung down like needle-sharp fangs. The man led the way along a rough path to a narrow rope bridge about twenty metres long. It swayed dangerously as he marched over it; blackness lay below. Then they were over it and turning into another tunnel, this one smaller.

Wavering torchlight, scattering off a pagoda-like stalagmite ahead of them. A man in a hurry. A deep Slavic voice echoed along the tunnel: 'Charlee!'

The torch appeared, dazzling their eyes, held by an immensely fat man dressed in a thick, blue one-piece suit.

Vashislav Shtyrkov, the Russian. He was waving urgently and there was tremendous excitement in his voice. 'We have a signal!'

They broke into a trot, following Shtyrkov. A short, final stretch of tunnel, and they were through another door and blinking in the fluorescent lights of a large, low-ceilinged, warm room.

The room was carpeted red, with light yellow wallpaper and a blue ceiling. It was furnished with leather armchairs and desks and computers. At the far end of the room, an open door led off to a corridor. The wall on the left was taken up with three panels, each about six feet by six, and labelled *XY*, *XZ* and *YZ* in black letters. The *XY* panel contained thousands of little red light bulbs, laid out in rows. The bulbs in the *XZ* panel were green, and the *YZ* bulbs were blue. None of them was lit. On the right, a large black blind had been pulled down; it took up almost half the wall. To the right of the blind was a wooden door, and to its left a digital clock labelled *UT* showed 07:17; below it another clock, labelled *Local Time*, showed 09:17. A long teak desk, cluttered with computers and printers, took up the centre of the room.

'Look at this,' said Shtyrkov, tapping at a computer terminal. Rows of numbers tumbled down the screen, most of them zero.

'Our first hit?' Charlie's voice was jubilant. 'We finally got a dark matter particle?'

'No, Charlee, not a hit. *Five* hits.'

'*What?*'

'And all within the last seven hours.'

Charlie stared at the Russian, open-mouthed.

'Charlee.' Shtyrkov's face was grim. 'That is not all.'

Charlie waited.

'The hits,' Shtyrkov said. 'They are arriving at regular intervals.'

'Regular intervals?' Charlie's tone was one of utter disbelief.

'Every one hour and twenty-four minutes.'

There was a long silence while Charlie assimilated this. Then: 'I'm sorry, but that's just lunacy.'

'Charlee. The particles are arriving at regular intervals.'

Charlie's voice was flat. 'Don't be absurd, Vashislav. That can't happen. It's impossible.'

'It has to be a bug. Some equipment failure,' Svetlana said.

Vashislav shook his head. 'It's your equipment, Svetlana, and you know it can't be that. The photodetectors work independently of each other. Each particle is being picked up by hundreds of them.'

'Vashislav, what's the alternative?'

Shtyrkov's eyes were staring. 'That it's real?'

'Don't be crazy. It has to be a bug.'

Shtyrkov shook his head like a stubborn child.

'When's the next one due?' Svetlana asked.

'The next particle will come in . . . forty-five seconds. It will arrive at seven twenty forty on the UT clock.'

'Are the speakers on?' Charlie asked nobody.

Svetlana was shivering. 'This is weird.'

'Weird?' Shtyrkov raised his voice. 'Svetlana, it is supernatural.' He looked at the wall clocks. 'You are just in time. We have thirty seconds.'

'It won't come.'

'It will come, Charlee, it will come. Ten seconds.' The Russian's eyes were fixed on the clock showing Universal Time.

'Time's up—'

A *click!* loud and clear, from all three speakers. Three streaks of light showed briefly on the panels, one red, one green, one blue.

'Yes!' the Russian shouted.

Charlie said, 'My God.'

A second *click!* Another trio of streaks.

They fell silent.

A third *click!*

And then the speakers roared.

Light blazed from the panels and Shtyrkov shouted something in Russian, his voice barely heard over the roar, and Svetlana shrank back in fear. Charlie ran to switches on the wall and they were momentarily in blackness. But then an electric motor slowly raised the big blind, gradually revealing another cavern, this one filled with a lake. The lake was a kilometre across and it was glowing, its rocky bottom visible in detail as if lit up by searchlights. The walls of the cavern were like a cloudy sky, reflecting the milky-white light from the water.

How long it went on Svetlana didn't know. She became aware of Charlie shouting, 'Come back, you idiot!' and then through the big window she saw the black silhouette of a man running towards the lake, arms spread wide. At first she thought Shtyrkov was about to jump into the water but then he was running on to a catwalk, jumping and pirouetting above the water, arms spread wide like a boy playing at Spitfires.

Then, suddenly, silence.

Blackness.

Svetlana praying quietly in the dark.

Charlie hyperventilating.

Shtyrkov singing, some Russian ballad, his voice echoing around the huge cavern, the song giving way to an outburst of insane laughter.

2

The Sign

Gibson was leaning over Shtyrkov's shoulder, a wild expression on his face. The Russian was typing at such a speed that the individual clicks were almost lost and there was just a steady machine-gun rattle from the keyboard. Occasionally the fat scientist would mutter excitedly to himself in Russian.

Svetlana was trembling. A solitary question kept pounding in her head: *What was that? What?* But she was too excited to think. *Vashislav will figure it out.*

And then a less noble thought intruded: *And he'll grab all the credit if I'm not careful. I'll be a glorified sparks.*

She saw the paper in the prestigious pages of *Nature* or *Science*: *Detection of a Swarm of Dark Matter Particles* by Vashislav Shtyrkov. And, buried amongst the footnotes: *With acknowledgements to Svetlana, faithful Tonto to my Lone Ranger.*

And she saw Shtyrkov and Gibson in Stockholm, bowing to let the King of Sweden drape the coveted Nobel medal around their necks, while she dutifully applauded in the audience.

She tried to put the ugly vision aside, but it kept gnawing. And she thought: *This will never happen to me again. Don't let them grab all the credit. Don't!*

For something to do she moved to a shelf and pressed buttons on a DVD recorder. The security camera played back the sequence of Shtyrkov running up and down at the edge of the lake, arms waving and singing like a drunk man. Then it showed him lumbering around on a catwalk, lying down and splashing water. Then he was running back to land, and for some seconds the camera showed only the white-glowing lake, and the iron catwalks and the cavern walls. Then a rowing boat appeared on screen, the Russian heaving at the oar as he headed for the centre of the luminous water. And then, suddenly, there was darkness, with only the digital clock in the corner of the picture to show that the camera was still running.

Shtyrkov's voice brought her back to the present. The Russian was looking at Gibson triumphantly. 'Done. It filled the DVD.'

'The whole disk? All ninety gigabytes?'

'There was more, much much more. But the SCSI interface can only absorb forty megabytes a second. We've lost a mountain of stuff.'

Svetlana turned from the DVD recorder and her dark thoughts. 'But you got something? You're sure?'

Gibson's eyes were shining and there was a light sweat on his brow. 'Yes,' he told her. 'One stuffed disk and a Nobel Prize. No question.'

Shtyrkov clicked his tongue in irritation. 'No doubt, but what was it, Charlee? What was it?'

Gibson looked as if the question hadn't occurred to him. 'Whatever it was, it's not in the book.'

Svetlana appraised her colleagues: 'Security. Until we've had a chance to look at this and make some sense of it, none of us breathes a word of this to anyone. Are we all agreed?'

'Absolutely.' Shtyrkov was still breathless from his lakeside exertions. 'This stays under wraps, as the Americans say, until we have understood it. Then we announce it to the world, whatever it is.'

Svetlana said, 'We analyse the data together and make a joint announcement. Nobody tries to steal a march on anyone else.'

Shtyrkov was still doing things at the computer. He swivelled to face them. 'It's no good down here. We don't have the computing power and the Net access. We need some office where we can work in secret. We should disperse to our institutes, keep our mouths shut and agree to meet up at some location, when something has been set up.'

Svetlana stared at the fat Russian. 'Disperse? Are you mad? One of us would let it slip. And who would hold the disk?'

Gibson bristled. 'As principal investigator here I'd have thought that's obvious.'

Shtyrkov managed to convey both surprise and injured innocence. 'We can surely trust each other.'

Svetlana's expression was bordering on the ferocious. She could hardly contain herself. She stabbed a finger at Shtyrkov as she spoke. 'Vashislav, I've spent twelve years of my life down this hole gambling that one day we'll pick up a dark matter particle. Well, we've done it. I've missed out on everything else including children to do it. This is our child – *my* child – and if you think I'm going to risk having it taken from me . . .'

'That's crazy talk. I don't want to take a child from its mother,' Shtyrkov complained.

'Vashislav, how do I know you won't make out I'm just the wiring technician and give yourself the lion's share of the kudos? You might even—'

'Be silent, woman!' Svetlana opened her mouth incredulously, but Shtyrkov's bass voice, when raised, had an arresting effect. He continued, 'There is no need for this. We are in this together, you madwoman. Of course we will announce this jointly.'

Gibson said, 'I'm the PI here. I make the decisions on that.'

Shtyrkov seemed not to have heard. 'But I understand your maternal instincts and we must respect them. I have an idea.'

'What?' Svetlana demanded.

The Russian touched the side of his nose with his finger. 'I have friends.'

Gibson said, 'Vashislav, like I keep saying, *I'm* the chief investigator here. It's my name on the application form.'

'Charlee, you're only the big chief because we needed your name up front for the British grant money.'

Gibson's face was threatening to turn purple. 'You have an idea, Vash? Tell me about it and I'll let you know.'

'Go to hell.' Shtyrkov glanced at the wall clock. He muttered to himself: '*On, vozmozhno, eschye spit.*' Then he picked up a telephone, turning his back to the others.

Svetlana translated Shtyrkov's Russian to Gibson. Gradually, as the phone calls were made, Gibson's worried expression gave way to a grudging satisfaction. By the time the fat scientist put the telephone down, Gibson was nodding agreement.

Svetlana and Shtyrkov picked their way along the narrow tunnels. The rope bridge was designed to take six normal people and in theory Shtyrkov could have joined her on it, but out of deference to human psychology he let her over first. The little bridge sagged and swayed dramatically as he waddled across, Svetlana lighting his way with shaky torchlight.

The elevator could take two individuals but the fat Russian counted as two. Svetlana disappeared from sight through the cavern ceiling, the cage sliding rapidly up on its metal poles. It always reminded Shtyrkov of an American movie he had seen once, with Batman sliding down a pole into his Batcave. He waited, alone in the big gloomy cavern, his mind racing.

Some minutes later the steel door opened and Gibson appeared, a woollen ski cap pulled down over his ears. He was holding a small plastic box protectively to his chest.

'The disk?' Shtyrkov looked greedily at the box.

'Ye-es.'

'I'm glad the rope bridge held,' Shtyrkov said. 'Imagine losing it.'

'And me.'

'A life is replaceable, Charlee.'

Gibson thought that was probably Russian humour. 'I've cancelled our rooms at the Tatra. We'll drive straight to the castle. If it's where I think it is we'll be there in four or five hours.'

'And?'

'You have influential friends, Vash, I'm impressed. We'll have the castle to ourselves. The administrator's setting things up as we speak. Three picohertz Alphas and a Sun workstation, though where they got these from in this neck of the woods I don't know. We'll be connected to the Net by the time we arrive, and they're giving us a video conferencing facility in case of need.'

'How long have we got?' Shtyrkov wanted to know.

Gibson made a face. 'Until next Sunday morning.'

'But this is Sunday,' Shtyrkov complained, his face

showing dismay. 'We need more than a week to get a grip on this.'

'They have some linguists' conference on the Monday after we leave. The staff will have to set things up for them the day before.'

'Seven days.' Shtyrkov's eyes were still glancing slyly at Gibson's little box. 'The most valuable disk on the planet.'

Gibson held it closer to his chest in a mock-childish gesture. 'I know, Vashislav, I know. And you'd like to take it up top with you, so that by the time I get there the van, the disk and the fat scientist have vanished into the Ukrainian steppes.'

'Charlee!' Shtyrkov had a hurt tone. 'We are colleagues. How could you even think such a thought?'

The elevator suddenly whined into view, sinking briskly down from the cavern roof. They contemplated the yellow cage. Shtyrkov said, 'I'll be waiting up top.'

* * *

Shtyrkov drove, Gibson navigated and they hammered over remote mountain roads, utterly lost. It was pitch black and pouring rain. As they began to climb the Little Carpathians the rain turned first to sleet and then snow, the roads worsened, and the Dormobile began to bounce and slide over the potholed surfaces. Svetlana managed to sleep in the back, stretched out on a seat.

Their first sight of the castle came after seven hours of unremitting grimness, and it took the form of a silhouette against a distant flash of sheet lightning. It was pure Gothic horror and Gibson, exhausted though he was, laughed with delight. Shtyrkov gave him a puzzled look.

A few lights were on and the administrator, a stooped, curly-haired man of about forty, was waiting just inside the door. He brushed aside their apologies and led them up endless stairs to a corridor with rooms off.

The scientists were now in a state of mental, nervous and physical exhaustion. With little more than mumbled goodnights they collapsed into their rooms. As she slipped between icy sheets, Svetlana could already hear Shtyrkov's heavy snoring next door.

* * *

In the morning, while a bleak dawn light was still creeping into her room, Svetlana dressed quietly in black sweater and jeans. An early morning sun was trying to penetrate heavy snow-laden clouds. The landscape was white.

The corridors were gloomy in the half-dark, but in spite of the sub-Arctic environment outside the big empty castle was warm. She wandered randomly through it, her trainers sometimes squeaking on the marble floors. On the ground floor, an oak-panelled door labelled *Administrator* was ajar. She pushed it open and switched on the lights. An impressive array of computers was sitting on the polished oak tables. She sat down on a chair embroidered with some royal crest, fired a machine up, and was gratified to find that an internet connection had been established. Then she left the machine humming, climbed back up the stairs, and listened at Gibson's door.

The door was unlocked and she slipped in. Gibson was still dead to the world, his mouth open and a hairy leg sticking out from under the covers. Clothes had been dropped on the floor. She noticed with amusement that he wore tartan boxer shorts.

On a table next to the bed were a wrist watch, spectacles, wallet and a little plastic box. She picked up the box and left, closing the door quietly behind her.

3

Celtic Tiger

A casual observer would not have distinguished him, as a type, from the students scurrying in the rain towards the Georgian façade of Dublin's Trinity College. He was thin, and wearing a worn black leather jacket and red and blue scarf. He carried a small blue rucksack, quite sodden. He was in his late twenties which would put him, most probably, in the category of a post-doc, or even a junior grade lecturer. He had short, untidy black hair, a two-day-old stubble and dark, intelligent eyes behind wet, round-framed spectacles which made him look slightly like an unshaven owl. The eyes were bloodshot and his skin was slightly pallid, as if he hadn't slept.

He passed under the sheltered archway of Front Gate and crossed Parliament Square, its cobbles shiny and slippery. Here the wind was erratic and buffeting, and he hurried under the bell-tower, past the Old Library, the museum and the mathematics department. He turned into a building with a 'Chaos Institute' sign and climbed steps, trailing water and puffing from his run.

Priscilla the Hun was typing at high speed, overcoat still on and door ajar. Her nose was red and she had a box of paper handkerchiefs to hand.

'Good morning, Priscilla. Did you have a good weekend?'

She gave him a frosty stare and the typing stuttered to a halt. 'Professor Kavanagh wants to see you right away,' she said with a malicious smirk.

Trouble. He went into the small office marked *Dr Tom Petrie*, switched on his computer, draped his sodden jacket over a radiator and wiped his spectacles dry.

- A conference announcement: *New Ideas in Quantum Cryptography*, to be held in Palermo in the summer. *Save.*
- A message from the Hun: three work-placement students arrive next week. You have been assigned to supervise them. *Delete.*
- A paper from a Sheffield colleague: *A Symplectic Approach to Chaos. Print.*
- Another message from the Hun, this one heavy with menace: you are three weeks overdue with your coffee money. *Delete.*
- Buy your Viagra here! Discounts for bulk orders. *Delete.*
- A lengthy message from a Brazilian he'd never heard of: I have proved the Goldbach conjecture. *A crackpot. Delete.*

The morning's e-mail done, he pulled a heap of papers out of his rucksack and spread them over his desk. Rain had seeped through the damp canvas and some of the sheets were almost illegible.

This isn't a good day, he told himself.

Having delayed as long as he dared, he left the office, walked reluctantly along the corridor and knocked nervously at a door.

'Come.'

The office was large, dark and smelled of stale cigarettes. The man behind the desk was near-bald, brown-suited with a trim moustache. The air of disapproval was a permanent feature; Petrie thought it might come with the moustache. A golf bag propped up against a bookcase reminded Petrie that this was Monday.

'Have you finished the PRTLI bid yet?'

Petrie's stomach flumped. 'I had intended to get it done this weekend.'

Actually, the intention only formed as he spoke; the assignment had gone completely out of his mind. Three nights ago, he had wakened up in the early hours of the morning with the solution – or just possibly the solution – to a long-standing paradox in quantum theory dancing in his head. Even the title of the paper had floated in front of him: *Quantum Entanglement and the Measure of Time.* As the dream-image began to fade he had jumped out of bed to write it down before it vanished for ever. In the gun-metal light of the winter morning, on a kitchen table cluttered with last night's takeaway and boxes of cereal, he had read through his pencilled scrawl and it still looked good. The outcome was feverish work, day and night, to write up a paper before the competition got there.

Kavanagh was talking; Petrie was hauled back to the present. '. . . expecting to see it on my desk by this afternoon.'

'It's not needed for a week.'

'Thank you for reminding me, although I was aware of the fact. Shall we say four o'clock?' The bald head went down to a paper.

'What's the time?'

Kavanagh glanced at his watch automatically and then looked up, lips puckered. He adopted a curt voice to

17

demonstrate his irritation. 'The time, Petrie? It's perhaps time you took your responsibilities to the Department seriously. Unless the PRTLI exercise delivers a top grade, our funding could suffer a serious cut.'

The Professor's telephone rang.

'I've written four papers in the last year, any one of which could bump us up to the top.' *And you haven't written one in twenty years, you old hypocrite.*

Kavanagh lifted the telephone. His eyes strayed to the young man, lines of disapproval giving way to a surprised frown. He handed the receiver over.

Priscilla. Her voice muffled, a mixture of heavy cold and awe. 'Dr Petrie, the Provost wishes to speak to you. Hold the line.'

Kavanagh tried to be subtle, leaning forward to catch both ends of the conversation, but Petrie – by accident or design the Professor knew not – leaned back in his chair, putting the Provost's words just out of hearing.

'Sir John? Petrie here ... Yes, sir ... No, nothing that can't wait. I have no lecturing commitments ... Yes, I have, Provost, it's my field ... The Royal Society ... I'll come straight over.' He handed the receiver back, paused briefly. 'I have to see the Provost.'

Kavanagh put the receiver down, pursing his lips once more. 'Well, well, the Provost. You do move in exalted circles, Petrie.'

It was a sweet moment. Petrie stood up. 'I'd better get going.'

'Yes, I suppose you'd better. We can't keep Sir John waiting. Are you able to tell me what this is about?'

'Afraid not, Professor.' Petrie closed the door harder than was necessary.

Petrie had rarely been in the Admin. building and never in the vicinity of the Provost's office. He trotted briskly across the quadrangle, entered the vast marble atrium and ran up broad stairs into a maze of corridors. A thin, elderly man was emerging from a toilet.

'Where's the Provost's office?'

'Straight ahead and first left.'

At the door marked *Office of the Provost* Petrie paused, brushed his wet hair back and then gave a tentative knock. He found himself in an outer office facing a surprisingly young woman with short wavy hair and a cheerful smile. She tapped on an inner door and waved Petrie into a room about twice the size of his Dublin flat.

The Provost looked somehow smaller and less imposing than when Tom had last seen him, swathed in academic gown and hoods, at a degree-awarding ceremony. At the side of the Provost's desk, on a high-backed chair, sat a man Petrie had never seen before. He was thin, urbane, fortyish and had Civil Service, UK style, written all over him, from the Balliol College tie, with its discreet lion rampant crest, to the well-cut grey suit. A careful man rather than a brilliant one, Petrie judged; someone whose career comprised a predictable, steady progression up the promotion ladder.

The Provost motioned Petrie to an easy chair and looked at him curiously over metal-rimmed spectacles. 'Dr Petrie, thank you for popping over. I dare say you're wondering what this is all about.'

'The PRTLI?'

'What?' The Provost looked surprised. 'No, no, this isn't a university matter at all.'

Petrie waited, mystified and nervous. The Provost's companion, he noted, was going unintroduced. Behind the man's brief smile, Petrie felt that he was being, somehow, *assessed*.

The man said, 'I can't tell you what this is about, Dr Petrie, because I don't know myself.'

'Right.' *So do we just sit here?*

'I'm just a message boy, you see.'

Petrie nodded. A message boy with a white silk shirt and Gucci cufflinks. The man continued: 'It's a request, really. Can you spare a few days to give some advice to Her Majesty's Government?'

'What about?'

'I don't know.'

In spite of the intimidating surroundings, Petrie laughed. 'Okay. Where do we go from here?'

The Balliol man said, 'It involves some foreign travel. To Vienna, I do know that.'

Vienna!

The Provost was leaning back in his chair, looking at Petrie thoughtfully. 'Is there a problem, Dr Petrie?'

'No, sir, I'm just thinking. My field is a bit off the beaten track.'

The Provost opened a buff folder in front of him. 'Yes, it does seem rather abstruse.' He peered at a sheet of paper. 'What does it say here? Non-periodic tiling algorithms and unbreakable codes.' The tone wasn't altogether approving and Petrie wondered what Kavanagh had written in the annual confidential report.

Petrie looked across at the Provost's mysterious companion. 'Does Her Majesty's Government want some decryption done? And if so, why don't they just get GCHQ on the job?'

The question caught the Balliol College man by surprise. 'It does seem odd.'

Sir John was strumming his fingers on Petrie's file. 'The request is that you be released from your university duties for the next two weeks. I have agreed to this.'

'But Professor Kavanagh needs the research assessment report by this afternoon.'

The Provost frowned. 'What? You're writing it?'

'Yes.'

The Provost scribbled on a memo. 'I'll drop Professor Kavanagh a note. He should perhaps be doing that himself.'

'In that case, I guess I'm out of excuses.'

Mr Balliol handed over a sealed envelope. 'Present yourself at the BA desk in two hours' time and give them this reference number. Have your passport and travel things with you. Give your name as Mr Craig. Treat the matter in the strictest confidence. My telephone numbers, office and home, are therein but they mustn't get into any other hands but yours.'

Petrie tore the envelope open, glanced at the numbers and returned the paper. 'Why should I want to contact you?'

The man raised his hands and adopted a mystified look.

Nervously: 'Are you asking me to get involved in espionage?'

'Espionage? Oh my goodness no, how absurd!' The civil servant quickly improvised a smile to emphasise this absurdity. 'You'll probably be back by the weekend, at which time I'll contact you. However, you should keep yourself to yourself. If anyone speaks to you en route, be noncommittal. Beware of inappropriate behaviour abroad. Always act as if there is a hidden camera. Be especially wary of any, aah . . .' – he squirmed slightly in the chair – 'approaches from strange women.'

Petrie's eyes widened.

The Provost cleared his throat. 'Of course this is only a request, Petrie. You're free to turn it down.'

'I can't wait.' Petrie stood up. He turned at the door, hand on the handle and a worried expression on his face. 'Forgive me, but this is pretty bizarre. Sir John, could this be some sort of elaborate hoax?'

A pink blush began to spread over the Balliol man's face. The Provost seemed amused. 'My colleague here is the genuine article. I was telephoned about him from London this morning.'

'But was the call genuine?'

'Oh, I should think so, Petrie. I know the caller well. The Prime Minister and I go back a long way.'

Petrie returned dizzily to his office.

* * *

Priscilla was sniffling in the corridor.

She looked at the young man with wonder. Dr Petrie was unimportant, lower even than her in the departmental food chain. In her own hearing he had heard the Professor call his research arcane and esoteric. She wasn't sure what these things meant but the tone had been disparaging. And yet here he was, the humblest creature in the hierarchy, summoned by God, or at least His earthly equivalent, the Provost. She could contain herself no longer. She blew her nose with a used tissue and asked, 'Dr Petrie, what on earth is going on here?'

Kavanagh walked into the office, trying to make it look like a casual encounter. 'Ah, Petrie. How did it go with the Provost?'

Petrie helped himself to a biscuit from a red tin on the filing cabinet. 'Very well, thank you, Professor.'

There was a pause. 'And?'

'I'm taking a couple of weeks off.'

Kavanagh stiffened. 'I don't think so, young man. You seem to be forgetting the PRTLI bid.'

'I'm sorry, Prof, but you have to write it yourself. Sir John's instructions.'

From the back of the taxi, Petrie looked out at the bars, the cafés and the bookshops lining the congested streets, but he saw none of them. His mind was elsewhere, grappling with questions.

And his stomach was churning.

4

Bratislava

Vienna!

Petrie had seen Vienna on TV. Some documentary about Mozart. Vienna was all crinoline-dressed ladies dancing with tailors' dummies, and prancing horses and elegant cafés.

But Freud and Turing are dead and the Vienna Circle is history and the real talent left for the States after the war. There's nobody in Vienna.

The mystery consumed Petrie all the way over the Irish Sea. *Why Vienna? The place is a desert!*

In Terminal Four at Heathrow, he was astonished to hear his name being called over the tannoy: 'Would Dr Petrie, on the British Airways flight from Dublin, please come to the information desk?'

At the desk a small fat woman in traditional Indian sari said, 'We've been asked to give you this.' The envelope she handed him was addressed to: *Dr Thomas Petrie, 158 Rock Walk, Dublin.*

'Who sent this?'

'The caller left no name, sir. She delivered it about ten minutes ago.'

'She?'

'It was a female, very English.' The woman was trying not to give Petrie a knowing smile; she was seeing secret assignations, lovers snatching time in exotic places.

'Okay, thank you.'

Petrie opened the envelope. It was empty. At a departures screen he checked his Vienna flight. He had a couple of hours. Back to the information desk. The sari lady directed him out of the airport, along a road near the bus stances and into a small, plain building: the airport chapel.

Petrie didn't live in Rock Walk. He'd never heard of a Rock Walk in Dublin. For all he knew, Rock Walk was the name of a pop group. But more likely the Rock was pietro, petra, Peter.

Down spiral stairs. A man in a long green gown was standing at a table covered with a white linen tablecloth and candles, engaged in some ceremony which had no meaning for Petrie. A handful of people stood around the pews. Petrie was in luck: there was a lectern at the back of the chapel, and on it was a large Bible. He turned the pages to the First Epistle General of Saint Peter, chapter five, verse eight.

> *Be sober, be vigilant; because your*
> *adversary the devil, as a roaring lion,*
> *walketh about, seeking whom he may*
> *devour*

Some sort of warning. Petrie felt a slight tingling in his spine, like a mild electric current.

He made his way to the departure lounge and sat with his back to a wall, surveying his fellow passengers with deep suspicion, at the same time feeling vaguely ridiculous. None of them showed the least awareness of his presence.

Beware of strange women. Petrie looked for unattached females. Maybe the blonde girl, in her early twenties, with the golden Scandinavian hair and long skirt and boots.

Petrie knew the type: Miss Lonely Planet, uncommitted and free as the wind, doing Europe and beyond on a shoestring. But she was too conspicuous, apparently attracting the attention of half the males in the lounge. Maybe the mousy little creature sipping from a paper cup and reading a paperback. She was so inconspicuous that she had to be a candidate. Or maybe it was the plump Hausfrau with the heavy-framed spectacles, the sandwich and the *Cosmopolitan* opened on her knee. She caught Petrie's eye and smiled; Petrie looked away in alarm.

It was cloud all the way until, over Germany, he glimpsed forested hills, covered with white.

Through the Customs at Vienna airport, not knowing what to expect. In the public area a lean, thin-faced man was holding up a white card with *Herr Craig* printed on it in red crayon. Petrie followed him to a silver top-of-the-range BMW with an Austrian registration. There was no conversation. The man took him along a motorway lined with high-rise flats and sprawling pharmaceutical factories, and on to a quiet, straight road leading away from town. The car was silent, its suspension smooth, and Petrie's imagination was becoming steadily wilder.

In an hour another city appeared on the skyline. There was a border. The policeman at the *Kontrolla* scarcely glanced at Petrie's passport. A long bridge took them over the *Dunaj*, which Petrie took to be the Danube. A sign said *Bratislava*. He looked out on tall grey buildings, buses and trams, cobbled roads, churches with an Eastern look. *Not Vienna, then*, he thought. *Bratislava*.

The driver stopped in front of a large grey-fronted hotel and opened Petrie's door without a word. By the time Petrie had reached the foyer, driver and BMW had gone.

Sir was expected.

His room was plain, wooden-floored with an embroidered rug. He tossed his holdall on a chair and left. On the first floor he navigated a crowded bar, its air thick with Turkish cigarette smoke, and reached a *restauracia*. It was pure *Belle Époque*, with oil paintings of Old Bratislava lining its walls and clusters of lights hanging like chrome and glass snowdrops from its high curved ceiling. Wooden partitions separated the tables, ensuring privacy for husband and wife, husband and mistress, businessmen making deals in the post-Communist market. Behind the nearest one, he heard snatches of conversation between a man and woman, in an unfamiliar tongue. The clatter of trams came through the window, and dark shapes like Lowry figures were crossing a slushy cobbled square. Wisps of the heavy tobacco smoke were drifting through from the bar.

By now Petrie was strung up like a cat. He felt somehow surreal, as if he was inside a dream; if a crocodile had slithered into the room it would hardly have seemed out of place.

A little waiter appeared. He had a dinner suit, bow tie, moustache and passable Slavic-tinted English.

'I'd like some fish,' Petrie said.

'What kind of fish?'

'What do you have?'

A shrug. 'Much fish.'

'What's local?'

'Štika. From the Danube this morning. It has sharp teeth.'

'I'll have that.'

'With cheeps?'

'Potatoes.'

'And to drink?'

27

'A white wine.' Petrie paused, and added: 'A carafe.'

'You can have zee house wine.'

'Fine.'

A borovička and a coffee later, he signed a chit and made his way, bloated, back to his room. He made sure his door was locked. He lay on the narrow bed and tried to analyse the sense of unease, anxiety even, which was now washing over him.

There was the sudden transplantation from the routine to the weird, from the familiar to the alien. There was the bizarre warning: *Be sober, be vigilant.* Beware of what? Roaring lions? Strange women? Slithering crocodiles?

But most of all, he realised, his tension was being driven by something else, by the conundrum still defeating his restless mind: *What am I getting myself into? And what happens next?*

* * *

Petrie wakened with a start. The telephone, its ringing tone unfamiliar. Disoriented, it was a second before he remembered he wasn't in his Dublin flat. He fumbled for a light switch, knocking over a tumbler. His watch said 5.30 a.m.

'Dr Petrie? Your car is waiting.'

5

The Castle

The icy air had a freshening effect on Petrie, even at twenty to six in the morning. It was the same silver BMW and the same wrinkled driver. The cavernous boot swallowed up Petrie's rucksack like a whale devouring a minnow. He kept a canvas bag with papers beside him, and settled into the back seat.

The car drove a few hundred yards along the road and turned into the front of the Hotel Europa.

Miss Lonely Planet.

The driver heaved her rucksack into the boot as if it was full of rocks. As she settled into the car beside him, Petrie saw that she was lightly made up. He caught a whiff of scent. She had an open, almost naive smile.

'I do planets.' Her voice was soft and curiously graceful. She wasn't a native English speaker.

The car took off, the driver muttering something under his breath.

Petrie said, 'I saw you at Heathrow.'

'I saw you too. I spotted you at Vienna airport and then on the streets here, last night. It was too much of a coincidence.'

'I've been warned not to speak to strange women.'

She gave a wicked smile, stuck her legs out and wiggled her feet. She was wearing walking boots and her slender ankles made them seem over-large.

'And then I got another warning. It was vague but I took it to mean I might be followed.'

She asked, 'How do you know I'm not a strange woman following you?'

'You weren't trying to look inconspicuous.' She was in fact extremely conspicuous but Petrie didn't want to mention that.

She gave a worried little nod. 'Should we be trusting each other?' Her voice had a slightly sing-song quality – Scandinavian, he thought. It fitted with the pure blonde hair.

'Who says I trust you?'

'This is like something out of a spy movie. Any idea what it's about?' She tilted her head slightly.

'No.'

'What do you do?'

'I'm a mathematician. Nobody understands me, I work on ferociously specialised stuff.'

'What sort of ferociously specialised stuff?'

'I suppose you'd call it pattern recognition. At the moment I'm doing knots.'

'You mean like in string?'

'Yes, only I do them in four-dimensional space.'

'I can't visualise that. No wonder nobody understands you. Anyway, it sounds useless.'

'Don't you believe it. I've found links with quantum theory and cryptography.' He patted his canvas bag as if it contained the secrets of the Universe. 'And you?'

'I'm a planetary scientist. Again a specialised area: extrasolar planetary systems.'

The car was warm and Petrie unbuttoned his jacket. 'Planets and patterns. I wonder how they connect?' He gazed out of the window at the dark mid-European streets and the unfamiliar skyline. Then: 'This is the car they collected me in from Vienna.'

'I had a Mercedes. But we were on the same flight. We could have shared a car, and even had the same hotel.'

'Exactly. Someone didn't want us seen together.'

The car had now taken them clear of Bratislava on to a broad four-laned highway. The dark sky was lightening to grey. After ten swift minutes, the driver slowed and turned on to a quiet side road, lined with snow-covered fields. Here the headlights lit up a wall of fog, limiting visibility to a couple of hundred yards.

'Do you think he speaks English?' Miss Lonely Planet whispered.

Petrie said, 'You've exposed a breast,' while looking at the man's eyes in the mirror. They didn't flicker.

'No, he doesn't. Sorry about that.'

She laughed.

'I'm Petrie. Tom, Tommy or Thomas depending on how you feel. From Dublin. So which part of Scandinavia are you from?'

'Freya Størmer,' she said, and they finally shook hands. 'From north of the Arctic Circle. Tromsø, to be exact.'

Petrie looked out uneasily at the fields and woods. In his imagination, he saw black bears roaming the forests. He wondered again what was bringing him out to these hinterlands. The trees looked black against the white snow and he had a brief, unsettling illusion of living inside a photographic negative.

Patterns and planets. Planets and prime ministers. Don't speak to strange women. A strange woman at his side. Beware of devouring lions.

How do they connect? How?

His new companion was smiling at some private joke. 'You do planets. What exactly?' Petrie asked.

'At the moment? I'm part of ESA's Darwin team.'

'Darwin?'

'A space-based interferometer. The European Space Agency are due to launch it next year. They're big mirrors with a long baseline which should be able to make out gross features like continents on Earth-sized planets round the nearest stars.'

'That's still not quite exact.'

'They want me to predict biological signatures for Darwin to search for.' They were into a village and running a gauntlet of neat, small houses, each one managing to be different from the others.

'Like what?'

'Like spectrum lines belonging to ozone or oxygen. Best seen in the ultraviolet. Oxygen is so reactive that if we see any at all on a planet there has to be biology at work producing it. Another . . .'

Suddenly, heavy metal blasted their ears from eight speakers. Startled, Freya shook her head and shrugged, and by mutual consent they attempted no further conversation. The driver switched off the big car's halogen beams.

Presently the road, now covered with compacted snow, began to climb steeply through a forest. The driver switched the heavy rock off and concentrated on a series of hairpin bends. Petrie found that his ears were ringing. He was now shaking slightly, whether due to nervous anticipation, or the driving, or the aftermath of the ACDC explosion, he couldn't say. On the next bend, the driver turned to the couple and said, '*Malé Karpaty,*' in a cigarette-hoarse voice.

The Little Carpathians. Dracula country. Petrie had a brief, movie-driven fantasy about isolated villages, Frankenstein monsters and grim, isolated castles.

The road levelled, there was a little lodge house and cables stretching up into the mist, and then the mountain pass was plunging steeply and Petrie's ears were popping with the swift change in altitude. At the foot of the pass the driver turned left on to a narrow lane.

Petrie sensed that they were reaching journey's end, realised that his fists were clenched with tension. By contrast, the young woman at his side seemed relaxed.

Past a tiny ochre church with a thin green spire. Something massive, dimly glimpsed through the mist and then lost behind trees. Another climb, and then a long, gently curving road through open parkland. A final turn, and through the mist there emerged a castle with conical turrets and low battlements. To Petrie's distraught imagination it looked like something out of a Bela Lugosi movie. The Dracula fantasies began to harden up.

Petrie and Freya stood with their baggage while the driver did a swift U-turn and took his car back down the hill. They watched it until it had disappeared through the trees, and then turned their attention to the castle.

Petrie knew nothing about castles or history but this one looked like some of the Austrian ones he had glimpsed in the distance on his drive from Vienna. He had a vague memory about the Hapsburg Dynasty and assumed that this had once been Austrian territory and that the castle dated from the eighteenth century. Two warriors, resting their hands on shields, sat on either side of a dark archway. To the right a circular tower was topped by a conical roof looking like a witch's black hat. Narrow, vertical windows were spaced around the tower giving,

Petrie supposed, a clear field of fire in the event of rioting peasantry.

They walked through the archway, which was about twenty feet long, and emerged into an acre of snow-covered garden lightly sprinkled with shrubs and conifer trees. To the left was a parapet looking over open, wooded countryside. To the right, and facing them, were tall grey walls surmounted by steeply sloping roofs, showing red where the snow hadn't covered them. Between the right and facing walls was a massive rectangular tower, jutting slightly out from the surrounding buildings and half as high again as them. Widely spaced pillars supported a steep roof atop the tower. The roof itself was covered with green diamond-shaped tiles and had tall thin chimneys and a lightning conductor. This tower, Petrie assumed, was intended as a look-out, and a small face was looking down between the pillars. It vanished quickly when Petrie looked up.

Someone had shovelled snow off the pathway and they walked along it, conscious of being overlooked by arched windows which, he noted, were double-glazed. Petrie inferred from this that the interior probably contained modern plumbing and central heating. Just past the tower, and hidden by it from the path, was a massive wooden door, covered with an iron grid and studs, and guarded by nothing more threatening than shrubs in huge stone pots. The door was in three parts and the centre one was an inch ajar. Petrie pushed this door open for Freya and followed her inside. By this simple act, he left behind his old world and entered a new one, more bizarre than anything his imagination could have devised.

His first impression was that of spaciousness. There was a high vaulted ceiling and a gleaming marble floor. A half-circle of velvet-covered sofa faced them. Potted palms and plants occupied odd corners. Broad corridors led off to left and right. There was nobody to be seen.

'What now?' Freya wondered.

They took to the right at random, and walked into another spacious area with another high vaulted ceiling, this one supported by tall pillars and with gold-coloured chandeliers suspended from it. Here their footsteps were softened by carpets and long strips of rug scattered around the marble floor. At the far end of this enormous space was a curved stone stairway, and trotting briskly down this stairway was a small, moon-faced man with large round spectacles and a grin.

Charlie Gibson. Last seen, half-drunk and upside down in Uppsala Botanic Gardens, trying to scale the tall gates after closing time with his fly caught on a spike and half a dozen equally merry colleagues offering ribald advice about his future sex life.

Gibson's handshake was firm and warm. 'Very glad to see you both. Very glad indeed. First let me take you to your rooms, and then I'll tell you what exactly is going on.'

Gibson led the way up the stairway, continuing past the first floor to an upper floor, ending up on a long broad corridor with a curved ceiling. Along the left of this corridor were recesses with potted plants and glass cabinets displaying stuffed animals and fossils.

He stopped at the fifth door on the right. 'This is yours, Tom. Freya, yours is the next one on. There are three of us, five now you're here, and we have the run of the castle for a week.'

The room was large, well-furnished with a double bed and a bright, substantial adjoining bathroom. Petrie dumped his holdall and jacket on the bed and crossed over to the window. Below him was a terrace with metal tables and chairs, all swept clear of snow. The terrace was bordered by a low parapet and more potted shrubs. The fog was lifting and he could see a village a couple of miles away. Then he went back out to the corridor where Gibson was waiting impatiently. Freya had replaced her boots with light loafers and was wearing gypsy earrings.

Gibson took them back down to the entrance area and they spread themselves around the semi-circular settee. He clasped his hands together and forced a brief smile. 'First things first. I apologise for the clandestine stuff.'

'I rather enjoyed it,' Freya said.

Petrie said, 'Especially the warning.'

Gibson looked blank. 'The warning?'

Petrie said, 'It told me to watch my back. Didn't you send it?'

Gibson stood up, and paced up and down, looking at the marble floor. Finally he turned to them, a worried look on his face. 'Christ.'

'I suggest that you start at the beginning,' Petrie said gently.

'What? Oh yes, Tom, yes of course.' Gibson sat down again. 'But before we go any further I need one thing more from both of you.'

'And if you don't get it?' Petrie wanted to know.

'Your air tickets are open returns.'

Freya gave an apprehensive little laugh. 'I can't wait to hear this.'

'For the next four days I want you to remain within the grounds of the castle. You are to have no communication with the outside world without my authorisation. After that, we review the situation.'

Freya and Petrie exchanged glances. Petrie said, 'Tell us more.'

Gibson looked worried. 'I can't. Not without your promise of confidentiality. If you knew what this was about you'd understand.'

Petrie turned to Freya. 'What do you think?'

She looked doubtful. 'It sounds military. Maybe a Star Wars thing that I wouldn't want to touch.'

Gibson's eyeballs rolled with alarm. 'I need you. There's no time to get anyone else.'

Freya smiled happily. 'You need us. We don't need you. It looks as if we're in a strong bargaining position.'

Gibson sat down across from Freya, and sighed. 'I hate all women.'

6

Patterns

Having just sat down, Gibson jumped up again. 'Follow me.'

He led the way round the bend of the left-hand corridor. At its end was an ornate door. He waved them dramatically through it.

The room was about fifty metres long. On its high barrelled roof was a fresco of cherubim. The little creatures were on a hillside, reading maps or turning hourglasses. One, its wings an aerodynamic impossibility, was flying through a star-spangled sky, holding a pennant bearing the words *Sapientissimi Opus*. The room was lined with books on either side and antique globes were scattered around.

'This is the theological library, folks. Take a look at this.' A single strip of perforated paper was laid along the full length of its polished floor and back up the other side. The numbers were upside down and the scientists bent double over them, walking slowly backwards.

'There's this big cave complex a few hours north of here, see? It has a deep lake half a mile across and we've built an aluminium scaffolding under it to hold light detectors. We have fifty thousand photocells, laid out in a cubic lattice. The numbers in the left column go from one to fifty thousand. They're just labels. The next column records light intensity picked up from each detector. As you see, there's nothing but zeros.'

'I'm not surprised,' Petrie said, moving backwards. 'How can you expect to record underwater light in a pitch black cave?'

Freya said, 'GUTS decay has been ruled out for ten years now. You have to be talking Çerenkov.'

Gibson gave her a look of open admiration. 'Ten out of ten. Funny things happen when you go faster than light. Çerenkov radiation is one of them.'

'I thought you couldn't travel faster than light,' Petrie said.

'Only schoolboys think that,' Gibson said smugly.

Petrie bristled, then decided the man was too absurd to be taken seriously. 'Thank you, Charlie, for treating me like an idiot.'

'Light moves slower in water,' Freya explained. 'In principle you could swim through water faster than the local light speed. If you did, you'd leave a trail like a sonic boom, only with light rather than sound. That's Çerenkov radiation.'

Gibson said, 'Fortunately you're not here for your physics.'

Petrie resisted the urge to punch the arrogant toad on the nose. 'Why *am* I here?'

'Patience.'

'I've always thought of Çerenkov radiation as faint,' Freya said, scanning the numbers.

'To the eye, yes. The retina needs sustained light for about a fiftieth of a second before it records anything. But our detectors have quantum efficiencies pushing a hundred per cent; they can track a single photon. Which is one good reason, incidentally, for being deep under the ground.'

'Okay.' Petrie was scanning the figures impatiently. 'So a particle tracks through the water and you pick up its trajectory from the trail of light.'

'We time it to a ten-millionth of a second – about the time it takes a particle to cross the lake top to bottom. That's the numbers in the third column. Now come over here.' A table, which in the eighteenth and nineteenth centuries had presumably hosted dinners for thirty or forty, was now covered by more computer printout, three inches deep, laid out along its forty feet. Petrie saw an incomprehensible mass of numbers. He moved along the table, flicking through the lists. 'Hey!'

Gibson nodded. 'Yes. No more lists of zeros. This is a single particle track, a cosmic ray. It's moving through the water at superluminal speed, so it leaves a Çerenkov trail.'

'It penetrated how far?' Freya's voice registered incredulity.

'One point seven kilometres of limestone karst.'

'Hold on. You're under a mountain.'

'Yes. Most cosmic rays are stopped by a metre or two of ground. Watch that chair.'

'That's awesome,' she said lamely.

'And it had the kinetic energy of a fast cricket ball. What sort of hell's kitchen it must have escaped from I can't begin to imagine. But that's not why you're here. No, folks, that's not even remotely why you're here. We can backtrack the trajectory, sort of. This particular particle seems to have come in a straight line from a galaxy called M104, about fifty million light years away.'

'The Sombrero, I know it,' Freya said, as if she'd vacationed there.

Petrie was still scanning the columns. 'So this particle had been travelling for fifty million years before it zipped through your lake?'

'Yes, but like I say that's not why you're here. By no means.'

Some Austrian prince, all haughtiness and whiskers, was glaring down at them from the panelled wall. Petrie continued, 'No doubt you'll get round to telling us.'

'We're trying to solve the dark matter problem.'

'What's that?'

'Groan,' Gibson said. 'Nothing special, just the biggest mystery in the Universe, that's all. Okay, let me do this in words of one syllable. We can weigh galaxies from their mutual orbits, knowing the strength of gravity. They turn out to be ten times more massive than we'd expect from their luminosities. That is, a typical galaxy has ten times more mass than the sum of all its stars. That's a big discrepancy.'

'You mean, out there, gravity's stronger than you think?'

Gibson looked as if he was fighting a sudden pain.

Freya laughed. 'You shouldn't say things like that, Tom.'

'Why not?'

'It's heresy. The law of gravity is sacred.'

'So what's the party line?'

Gibson said, 'The solution is obvious. There must be a lot of dark matter inside galaxies. It has gravity but it doesn't shine.'

'The problem's much worse than Charlie is telling you,' Freya volunteered. 'When you get to big clusters of galaxies, say hundreds or thousands of them, you find that they're flying around at speeds vastly in excess of what's expected from their visible mass. Something invisible is stopping these clusters from flying apart.'

'How do you measure their speeds? You don't *see* them moving?'

'No, but their light is shifted to the red or blue pro rata with their velocities, like the change in pitch of a train whistle when it passes. You find that the dark stuff in clusters has to be about ninety-five per cent of the total mass. What we're saying here is that the whole of astronomical science is devoted to only five per cent of what's out there.'

'Right. So rather than change the law of gravity, which is sacred, you assume that there's some exotic new type of particle. Invisible but with mass. If you find it, you have a handle on the missing ninety-five per cent of the Universe.'

'On the nail,' Gibson said. 'A subnuclear particle unknown to present-day science. There could be millions of them passing through our bodies now.' Gibson's froglike face had acquired a fanatical look.

'Where are these particles supposed to come from?'

'Hell, Tom, they were created in the Big Bang. They must have been.'

'Yes, all right, Charlie, I believe it. In fact, I believe everything you're telling me.'

Freya asked, 'Okay, Charlie, but why in the hinterlands? Why not someplace civilised like the Alps?'

'The Alps have been taken: a rival team got into the Mont Blanc tunnel long before us. Likewise the Gran Sasso in the Italian Apennines. And the karst limestone hereabouts has very little natural radioactivity. Anyway, our technique needs an underground lake. It's worth a little sojourn in the Carpathian hinterlands to solve one of the greatest scientific mysteries of the age.'

'And pick up a Nobel Prize in passing.'

'Provided we beat the competition.'

'You just did,' said Freya.

Gibson said, cryptically, 'Except that we got more than we bargained for. Follow me again.'

Gibson marched out of the library, half-ran back along the corridor and up broad stairs. He turned left and stopped at an oak door, puffing slightly.

He paused, his hand on its large wooden knob, and blinked. 'The stuff on the other side of this door will change your life. This is your last chance to walk away.'

'My goodness, Charlie, this is dramatic stuff.' Petrie's tone was light, but he was tense with excitement.

'Okay – you had your chance. Welcome to Wonderland.'

Gibson opened the door.

Petrie stared into a large room, almost bare apart from a square central table around which were half a dozen chairs embroidered with some royal insignia. On the table were six computer terminals. Windows on the right opened out to a snowy wooded landscape. At the far end of the room, wood panelling had been slid aside to expose a bank of television screens. Two people were standing at a screen, obscuring it. They turned, and Petrie formed instant impressions.

There was Miss Dominatrix. A long-haired female, mid-thirties, spinsterish, with a long thin face and an intense, dedicated look. She was dressed in black sweater and slacks, and fashionless trainers. She was devoid of make-up but wore sapphire earrings.

Gibson made the introductions. 'Well, at last we have our mathematician, Thomas Petrie, and our astronomer, Freya Størmer. The team's complete. Tom and Freya, this is Vashislav Shtyrkov and Svetlana Popov.'

Svetlana alias Miss Dominatrix had an unexpectedly warm smile. 'Cracow University, Poland. I just join up the wires.'

'Svetlana's modesty is out of place,' Gibson said. 'She's a first-class experimentalist.'

The two women were shaking hands. 'I know, Charlie, I just like to hear you say it. You must wonder what you're getting into, Freya.'

'It's all very clandestine. I think Tom and I are in the hands of paranoid lunatics.'

Shtyrkov approached and extended a powerful hand to Petrie. He had a deep bass voice, with a slightly breathless edge. 'Moscow State University. I do particle physics. Freya is right, I'm a paranoid lunatic. As will you be after a day or two here. So, you're our *Irlandets*?'

'*Anglichanin*,' Petrie corrected him. He turned to Gibson expectantly.

Gibson beckoned Petrie over to the terminals on the wall and pointed to the one on the left. 'What do you make of this?'

Petrie and Freya sat down on Hapsburg embroidered chairs and found themselves staring at an array of numbers, arranged into three columns. Petrie pressed the 'down' arrow on the keyboard and scanned the rapidly tumbling columns, his eyes trying to make out patterns.

The patterns were there. As the columns skimmed past, the numbers rose and descended in waves, some large, some small, some fast, some slow. They interacted like Bach fugues, sometimes merging into breakers, sometimes abruptly turning into columns of zeros.

Shtyrkov was looking over Petrie's shoulder. 'You saw the printout in the hall?'

'Uhuh. This is a lot more complicated. It must be more than one particle, which is impossible from what Charlie was saying. There must have been dozens of them.'

'Not dozens, Tom. Billions.'

Petrie stopped scanning. He looked at Gibson.

Svetlana was lounging back at a desk, playing with a pencil. 'At any instant each litre of water in that lake had a particle in it.'

Petrie turned back to the terminal and resumed the scan. 'But if a particle crosses the lake in a ten-millionth of a second . . . how long did this go on?'

Gibson spoke over Petrie's other shoulder. 'Thirty-seven minutes. There were about half a dozen leaders. They arrived every few seconds. Then it started. Two thousand, two hundred and twenty seconds of this, and then it stopped. No tail-off or fading away: there was just suddenly nothing.'

'The lake glowed.' Shtyrkov's eyes had a strange, almost insane gleam.

Freya turned to Gibson. 'Just what are we dealing with here?'

There was a brittle silence.

Petrie sensed something. 'So each detector was picking up light from all the particles passing through, and you have fifty thousand detectors each firing numbers into your hard drive ten million times a second, and you want me to turn these numbers into particle tracks through the lake.' He puffed out his cheeks. 'That's a mammoth job.'

Gibson shook his head. 'Oh no, Tom, that's not what we want from you at all.'

Svetlana said, 'You see, we've already done that.'

'I linked in to Moscow State University,' Shtyrkov said. 'It's the central node for a nationwide grid of computers. I was able to use idle time on every computer in Russia which holds hands with the Moscow link. No, we have computed the particle tracks. And the tracks through the lake are where you come in.'

Petrie looked around, bewildered. 'If this was a burst of particles from some source, surely they just came in on random parallel lines, like a stream of buckshot?'

Shtyrkov grinned. 'No again, Tom. Not at all. You see, the particles arrived in a pattern.'

'*What?*'

The grin became demonic. 'Yes, a pattern.'

Petrie felt his skin prickling.

7

The Shtyrkov Conjecture

'Hold on. You can't mean an intelligent pattern. You can't possibly mean that.'

Shtyrkov said, 'But I do, Tom.'

Gibson was peering at the mathematician through narrowed eyes. 'I have to apologise for Vash. He's clearly mad.'

Shtyrkov folded his arms and leaned back with a condescending smile.

'But you asked me out here anyway.'

'It's a million to one shot, Tom. No, it's a billion to one, a trillion to one. But suppose ... In a moment of fantasy, just suppose' – Gibson's voice was a strange blend of hesitancy, fear and greed – 'that he's right.'

'It would be the discovery of all time,' Svetlana said. Her voice was almost hoarse; Petrie suspected she hadn't slept for a day or two.

'A signal, coming from an intelligence beyond the Earth,' Petrie said to nobody. 'Jesus.'

'From Jesus?' Shtyrkov snorted. 'I doubt it, but you can never be sure.'

'Where do I come in?' Freya asked.

Gibson turned to her. 'If this is an intelligent signal, we need to know where it came from.'

'Imagine going to the public and saying, "Hey, we've

detected an ET signal but we don't know where it came from",' Svetlana pointed out. She was nervously tapping her pencil on the desk.

'The public would go ape,' Gibson said. 'So would our colleagues.'

'We know the direction the particles passed through the lake,' Svetlana said.

'Exactly?' Freya asked.

'No. Roughly.' Svetlana drew a box in the air with her pencil.

'How big is the error box?'

'We want you to tell us,' Gibson interrupted the conversation between the two women. 'And identify candidate sources, narrow them down to one if it's humanly possible. The home planet.'

'Why me for the decoding?' Petrie asked. 'There must be thousands of good cryptanalysts around.'

'This isn't code-breaking, at least I hope it's not. It's more a question of making sense out of patterns. I heard you in Uppsala last year. Making sense of complex patterns is your business. Me, I can only visualise things in two dimensions.'

The Russian's heavy frame stirred in the chair. 'There's an intelligent signal in there, Tom. But Charlee is too stupid to see this and I can only think in two and a half dimensions. We need a peculiar mind, like yours.'

Gibson nodded. 'It's down to you. Prove or disprove Vashislav's conjecture.'

'But you don't believe it.'

'Do you know what Charles Darwin said?'

'No, Charlie. What did Charles Darwin say?'

'He said that Nature will tell you a direct lie if she can. I think Vashislav is being lied to, and that there must be some natural explanation for this weird event.'

'So why did you ask us out here? Why alert the Prime Minister?'

'Because Darwin also said something else.' Gibson jabbed a finger at Petrie. 'Every scientist should now and then carry out a fool's experiment, something which nobody in their right mind would expect to yield a result. Because if it does work out, against all expectations, the payoff is fantastic.'

Petrie grinned. 'Well, you've got the fool.'

'Another thing Darwin said. He said maybe the people in the Gran Sasso or the Mont Blanc tunnel got the same signal as us, and maybe they're working like hell on it, and maybe they're going to beat us to it with an announcement, at which point Charlie Gibson will climb the tower of this frigging castle and jump off head first.'

'Charles Darwin said that?'

'He absolutely did. *Origin of Species* chapter three, paragraph three. One other trifling matter,' Gibson said, showing his teeth. 'This is Tuesday, in case you've lost track. We have the castle until the weekend. In the highly unlikely event of there being anything in Vashislav's conjecture, I'll need to know it by then. I'll want a public announcement made next week.'

Shtyrkov explained. 'Svetlana has some mad idea that once we've dispersed, one of us will try to steal the thunder from the others.'

'The announcement has to be made as a team,' Svetlana said in a determined voice.

Petrie turned to Shtyrkov. 'I see what you mean, Vashislav. You're *all* paranoid lunatics.'

Freya said, 'Tom, we'd better get started.'

'Can I work alone? I concentrate better that way. I can talk to myself, walk up and down and so on.'

Gibson said, 'You can have the theological library. In fact, you can have the entire Hapsburg Empire if it will get us the answer. Take one of the Alphas. What about you, Freya? Are you a social misfit too?'

Freya was already tapping at a keyboard. 'I'm a party-goer, Charlie. Here is fine.'

* * *

The Alpha was heavy but Shtyrkov shared the weight, while Gibson trailed behind with a terminal. After some fussing Petrie found plugs near a walnut desk. He cleared the computer printouts from the floor and the central table. Gibson disappeared and returned with a ream of A4 paper and a small disk. 'Watch out for the cleaners,' he said. 'Security!'

At last Petrie was alone. He took the time to absorb his amazing new office.

It was baroque, windowless, lined with gilded, carved bookshelves reaching to the ceiling and brightly lit with overhead spotlights. There was an upper gallery accessed by a spiral staircase in a corner of the room. The books were old, although many had been rebound. They must have taken centuries to collect and had no doubt been confiscated from some monastery by some thieving emperor, maybe the guy now looking down his nose at Petrie from his white horse. He browsed at random through some of the books. Most of them were in Latin, but a few were in some unfamiliar script which he assumed to be Czech or Slovakian. They seemed to span many centuries and many topics: there were illustrated herbals, travelogues, human anatomies, atlases, military manuals, alchemists' prescriptions, star charts and lists of wonders: two-headed cattle, serpents swallowing ships at sea, mysterious lights in the sky.

Then he sat down on a blue-upholstered chair, switched on, fed the contents of the CD into the computer's memory, and settled down to examine the cosmic blizzard which had briefly swept through the underground lake.

* * *

At first, Petrie made no attempt to analyse what he was seeing. Svetlana had a little three-dimensional picture of the lake, in blue, complete with underground scaffolding and little red spots to mark the positions of the light detectors. A white line appeared briefly through the far edge of the lake, at an angle, while $t = 00^m\ 00.000^s$ appeared at the top right-hand corner of the screen. Following Svetlana's instructions in the *readme* file, he tapped the return button a few times, speeding the movie up. A second white line appeared at $t = 03^m\ 40.414^s$ precisely, parallel to the first but nearer the lake's centre. At $t = 07^m\ 20.829^s$ a third line appeared, right of centre, making a neat right-angled triangle with the first two. It was followed a few seconds later by nine more, left to right across the lake. One-two-three near, one-two-three middle, one-two-three far; a neat rectangular grid.

It was as if the particles were being used to probe the lake, find its outline in the cavern.

Petrie dismissed the idea instantly; it was, quite simply, impossible. The apparent probing had to be luck.

He pushed the animation on a bit and was immediately faced by a white-out, the blizzard of parallel lines obscuring Svetlana's picture of the lake and its scaffolding.

He slowed it down to the point where he could just make out the ebb and flow of individual streaks. He was now looking at snowflakes in a blizzard. He let it run, still making no attempt to make sense of it. After an hour he pressed a button and the animation froze. Time elapsed read $t = 07^m\ 22.440^s$; in real time, the flow he had been looking at for the last hour had passed through the lake in just over a second and a half.

He went back to the beginning and started again. And again he saw the right-angled triangle, the rectangular grid, the sudden blizzard. Now Petrie ran the blizzard for three solid hours, staring at the hypnotic flickering lines, while a dull ache at the back of his neck spread up over his head and down to his eyes, which began to close up.

Yes, there was a pattern. But it was the pattern of any blizzard. Pauses, swirls, brief bursts, sparse areas and concentrations. Who was to say what realms the particles had passed through on their interstellar journey, and what forces had buffeted them on the way? There was no more reason to suppose the patterns were meaningful than there was to suppose that the wind was intelligently directed. What was that Elton John song? Something about a candle in the wind.

And yet . . .

Something about the patterns. Groups of four. Something trying to surface. An eightsome reel dancing in his head. No, a foursome reel. No, a room full of whirling reels, patterns dancing like Tam O'Shanter's witches. But, frustratingly, nothing that he could put into words or even formulate abstractly.

A knock on the door. Svetlana. 'Join us for lunch?' She saw the strain on the mathematician's drawn face and added, 'Have you found something?'

Petrie shook his head. Suddenly aware that his bladder needed relieving, he waved Svetlana ahead. He followed her along the corridor. She was trailing a whiff of perfume.

Or maybe it was shampoo – Petrie wasn't into the things women sprayed themselves with. She passed behind the curved stairs. Gibson, climbing them with a burger in one hand and a mug in the other, called down. 'Found anything, Tom?'

'Give me a chance, I've just arrived.'

In the kitchen, Shtyrkov was loading a dumb waiter with half a loaf of bread, butter, jam, biscuits and a plate piled with beetroot and what looked like a squashed octopus. Svetlana rattled a pot on to a big electric hob. 'I'm making myself some pasta, Tom.'

'No, thanks. I'll just get back to it.' Petrie poured himself a coffee from a bubbling percolator, helped himself to a couple of chocolate biscuits from Shtyrkov's dumb waiter collection and disappeared back to his baroque study.

This time he ran the animation for six hours. Apart from one visit to the bathroom, and one to the kitchen for water to relieve his parched throat, he never stirred from his chair. Gradually, as the swirling patterns saturated his brain, an unwelcome image kept forcing itself forward. He tried to reject it, concentrate on the patterns, but it kept coming back. It was a memory of Sampson-Kildare, his sixth-form English teacher, a vile old lecher. The man was thrusting his wrinkled, leering face into Petrie's, and he was croaking: '*The mirth and fun grew fast and furious,*' while the patterns danced like Tam O'Shanter's witches, and another image, incredible and malign, slowly crawled out from his unconscious mind.

8

Decode

'Look at you! You've got to eat.'

Petrie stared dully at Freya. It was some seconds before he brought himself back from his world of swirling blizzards. 'What's the time?'

She looked at the clock on his terminal. 'Just after eleven. The others have eaten.'

'I'm not hungry.'

'You are. And Vashislav's made something for us.'

'It's probably squashed octopus.'

'What?'

'Never mind. Okay, I'll be along.'

She took him firmly by the arm. 'Nice try, but you're coming now.'

'You remind me of my mother.'

Shtyrkov had been busy. Freya steered him to the first-floor canteen, if canteen was the word for the chandeliered elegance and gleaming silverware which greeted him. She sat him down at a table set for three, spread with a white tablecloth. He surveyed the bowls with brown bread, olives, gherkins, salad and fruit. A bottle of vodka took pride of place at the centre of the table. Through the windows, a flicker of distant lightning briefly lit up heavy clouds and forested hills.

'Where are Charlie and Svetlana?'

Freya poured the vodkas. 'Gone to bed.' She smiled mischievously. 'Separate beds, that is. Are you making progress?'

Petrie massaged his forehead. He felt as if his head was splitting in two. 'Maybe. I don't know. Where does the food come from?'

'There's a big freezer. And Vash tells me fresh food will come with the cleaners in the mornings. They'll be here for an hour each day. The castle administrator is keeping out of it but Charlie has his home number if we need anything.'

'An entire castle to ourselves. He carries some clout, does our Russian colleague.'

'And I can cook,' Shtyrkov boomed, appearing from a side room with a tray. 'A talent which I owe to my Great-aunt Lidia. First, we have caviar.' He set a large bowl of some chilled purée on the table and sat down heavily. 'Poor man's caviar, that is. A Georgian spread made of aubergines, tomatoes, garlic, sugar, lemon juice and pepper. Tom, tell us what you have found.'

'Nothing.'

Shtyrkov smiled sceptically. 'You are a bad liar. You can hardly keep your eyes open. Something is driving you.'

Damn the man. I'm not ready to talk about it. 'Maybe something.'

Freya's eyes widened. 'Maybe something? What exactly?'

Petrie spread the fake caviar on a hard, flat square of bread. It was his first taste of food since Shtyrkov's commandeered biscuits and he savoured the sharp, tangy taste. He wiped his mouth and said, 'Patterns. But no more than gusts of wind in a storm. Who knows what furnace these things came out of? I don't see evidence of an intelligence lying behind them.'

Shtyrkov seemed unperturbed by Petrie's negative comment. He smiled slyly and poured vodka to the brims of their vodka glasses. He nodded at Petrie's T-shirt. 'You play chess?'

'Sort of. Come on, Vash, what makes you think there's something in that particle burst?'

Shtyrkov raised four fat fingers. '*Yon. Tesera. Chetire. Cuatro. Quattre. Quattro. Vier. Four.*'

Petrie looked at the Russian with astonishment. Groupings of four, additions up to four, foursome reels, the bewildering fact had come to Petrie as the merest glimmer after hours of mind-breaking work. He said, casually, 'Okay. But I can't make sense of it. Not yet.'

Shtyrkov grinned but said nothing. Freya poured tea.

'People have always assumed that extraterrestrials, if they exist, would send out radio signals,' Petrie said. 'Nobody thought about weird particles.'

Shtyrkov sipped the vodka with satisfaction. 'Ice cold, as it should be. Extraterrestrials, however, may not feel bound by our limitations.'

'A Harvard/Princeton team are searching for laser pulses,' Freya said. 'They're using a modest telescope and they could pick up signals out to a hundred light years, maybe a thousand.'

'And let me tell you why, young Miss Freya, or has Anglo-Saxon angst spread to Norway and you prefer Ms?'

Freya laughed but didn't rise to Shtyrkov's provocative bait. The Russian continued, 'Bandwidth. Red light has a frequency thirty thousand times higher than microwave radio. In the time taken for a radio wave to arrive, thirty thousand light waves do so. Information is transmitted thirty thousand times faster. Equipment is smaller and more mobile: an intelligence could easily fire signals at ten solar systems a second if it was trying to make contact with other life forms. And one other thing. The Galaxy is awash with radio waves, from pulsars, nebulae, even stars. But I very much doubt if, anywhere, Mother Nature fires nanosecond laser pulses. Find one and there can be no confusion with a natural source.'

There was a rumble and lights flickered briefly. Petrie felt the icy vodka burning his lips and then warming his alimentary canal all the way down to the stomach. 'You mean, why use radio when you have lasers?'

'Why have cotton when you can have silk? Radio searches happen now because they happened first. They are an accident of history, a hundred-year slice of our technological evolution. Better means to communicate already exist.'

'If you're operating on timescales of thousands or millions of years, lasers may have a short shelf life too.'

Shtyrkov nodded. 'Exactly. To an advanced signaller, they would have the byte rate of smoke signals. You learn fast, young Tom. And because the higher the frequency the more efficient the communication, why stop at electromagnetic radiation at all? Weird particles, as you call them, carrying energy beyond even gamma rays, would be much more effective at transmitting information. A few thousand years down the line and we too will be firing them into space.'

'I ought to get back to it.' Petrie pushed back his chair.

Shtyrkov was heaping Georgian caviar thickly on to flat bread. 'Tom, bypass a thirty-year learning curve by absorbing the following truth, from Ecclesiasticus chapter 38, I think: "A scholar's wisdom comes of ample leisure." Did Plato rush to catch a bus? Was Socrates ever twitching to get back to his computer terminal? My chicken *tabaka* is flattened, fried, crisp and juicy, and it is ready. Ready, that is, to serve with a prune sauce, sour cream and red pickled cabbage. Now, do you propose to insult me by refusing my laboriously prepared feast?'

'If you put it that way.'

There was a bright flash, and this time the rumble of thunder was closer.

Freya spoke firmly. 'Look at you, Tom. You can hardly keep your eyes open. When we've eaten, I'm taking you to bed.'

Petrie thought that Freya's command of English was probably less than perfect.

* * *

Petrie needed sleep. He had to lie down, put his head on a pillow, shut his eyes and *sleep*.

Freya, it seemed, had adopted the role of a surrogate mother. After Shtyrkov's main course – a squashed chicken rather than a squashed octopus – exhaustion had overcome Petrie to the point where he could hardly stand up. Freya had taken him by the arm and led him up the stairs. Even in his exhausted state he had enjoyed the warmth, the scent, the animal femininity of this young Norwegian woman. She had gently eased him into his room and wished him a good night.

He threw off his clothes, pulled down the blankets and *flopped*.

But the blizzard was still swirling. Petrie could see it in the ceiling, and on the walls, and in all the dark corners of his room.

This was different from Bletchley.

In war, strenuous efforts were made to veil the message. Victory and defeat in battle, and even the outcome of a war, might nowadays depend as much on a contest between distant mathematicians as it once did between armies. If the Germans had known about Bletchley, they might have changed the course of the war with a single bombing raid. But if Shtyrkov's lunatic conjecture was right, nobody would be trying to hide anything. On the contrary, the signallers would be trying to communicate.

Even so, Petrie thought, his mind whirling, exhausted but unable to stop, how can they judge the mental level of the people they're trying to reach? He could still be an ape trying to understand a Fortran computer program.

He heard Freya's door closing next to him, visualised her taking her clothes off, sliding naked between sheets, just a few feet away.

As he drifted off, rain began to batter against the window. And once again Sampson-Kildare, the old horror, was croaking:

> 'The wind blew as 'twad blawn its last;
> The rattling showers rose on the blast;
> The speedy gleams the darkness swallow'd;
> Loud, deep and lang the thunder bellow'd:
> That night, a child might understand,
> The De'il had business on his hand.'

And now Sampson-Kildare was high on a ledge in the big cavern, shooting bullets through the lake. He paused to reload his machine gun, but only for a microsecond. The next burst of fire was somehow different from the one before. And then another tiny time gap, and another surge of bullets.

And the bullets were going through the lake faster than light and the lake was glowing and Sampson-Kildare was saying that's because the eye can't see flickering faster than a fiftieth of a second in duration, and he was sometimes firing millions of bullets through the lake in a microsecond, and at other times he was smoking and firing only a few thousands at a time.

And the bullet patterns were sometimes filling just one patch of the lake, or sweeping round it like a searchlight.

And yet not like a searchlight. It was more of a corkscrew or spiralling motion.

No, more like two searchlights, counter-rotating. And now there were two machine-gunners, the surface of the lake spitting as the stream of bullets danced around each other like a gunfighter's ballet, and Sampson-Kildare was leaping around grotesquely on the ledge and croaking:

> '*As Tammie glower'd, amaz'd, and curious,*
> *The mirth and fun grew fast and furious;*
> *The piper loud and louder blew,*
> *The dancers quick and quicker flew,*
> *They reel'd, they set, they cross'd, they*
> *cleekit . . .*'

BANG!

Rattling windows; a flash of light penetrating his eyelids. Petrie wakened with a gasp, staring into the dark. Heavy rain was battering on his window.

Impossible! Utterly impossible!

He threw back the blankets, groped for a light and dressed quickly. Shaking, he went out into the darkened corridor and felt his way along it. He could just make out the top of the marble stairs. Another flash momentarily lit them up and he descended cautiously, his eyes adapting to the dark. The headache had gone.

He hurried along to the theological library and groped for light switches. There were three of them and he switched them all on. He realised that he had left his computer running. To his relief, as he tapped at the keyboard, he found that the thunderstorm hadn't affected it.

He looked again at the particle storm on his screen. Parallel lines, and yet, not just parallel lines. The particles didn't like to crowd too close together. Petrie thought this might be down to their physics: maybe they repelled each other at short range or whatever. Nothing to do with aliens or similar rubbish.

There had always been a slightly mad streak running through Russian science. The Tunguska meteorite was a crashed flying saucer, or the innermost satellite of Mars was an ancient space station, crap like that. Maybe Shtyrkov was part of that tradition.

And in any case, order could be created out of chaos. Petrie thought there were maybe complicated force laws between the particles and that these forces had generated patterns during the long interstellar journey.

He rubbed his face with his hands and groaned with tiredness. Belousov and Zhabotinskii, more damned Russians. They'd mixed citric and sulphuric acids, added salts and chemicals, and within the mixture, as by a miracle, wonderful red-blue pulsations had appeared, and circular waves had come and gone, and spiral patterns had chased each other around the mixture. And it had all grown just from chaos, from the disequilibrium of the chemical mixture. They'd been beaten to their discovery by forty years, by William Bray, but his contemporaries hadn't believed you could get chemical reactions to oscillate, hadn't bothered to follow it up, and the man had died in obscurity, the Russians now collecting the kudos denied Bray by the idiocy of his colleagues.

Instead of looking at an indecipherable mass of lines, why not reduce each particle to a point? Imagine a flat surface, face-on to the flow, and record each particle's point of intersection with the plate. Like a telescope pointing to the signal source.

That would take programming. Hell, the Earth's rotation. Svetlana!

He ran back through the corridors and up the stairs. One, two . . . seven doors along. He knocked sharply. The sound of a body stirring within. 'Svetlana!'

A light switched on. Svetlana appeared, wearing an ankle-length yellow gown, curiosity and tiredness on her face.

'I need help.'

'What's the time?'

'I've no idea.'

She disappeared and reappeared in a moment, wearing sandals and putting her arms into the sleeves of a long, red cotton dressing gown. 'It's nearly two o'clock.'

He explained as they went. 'The flow of particles. I need to see them face-on.'

'You mean turn the trajectories into points?'

'Yes. Can you do that?'

She slipped a hand under her gown and scratched her shoulder. 'You're in luck, Tom. I can swivel the lake around.'

She took the stairs two at a time, leaving a faint trail of perfume. Or was it hair shampoo? In the computer room she fired up, typed, and over her shoulder Petrie saw an erratic, roughly oval blue shape appear on her screen. She flicked her hair back and traced the shape out on the computer terminal with a red-painted fingernail. 'That's the lake looking straight down from a great height. And you can spin it so that it's face-on to the particle flow. Look.'

A single frame appeared on the screen, the lake penetrated by thousands of straight lines. She clicked on a little icon and the picture tumbled and the lines shrank until Petrie found himself looking, not at a confusing jumble of lines, but at a pattern of dots.

Svetlana scribbled a few lines in a spiral notebook and tore the sheet out. 'Here are the instructions. You can take it a frame at a time, freeze it, run it forwards or backwards at any speed and so on, just like a video recorder.' She pressed the return key and a little cluster of dots appeared near the edge of the lake. In the next frame they had vanished, but a second cluster had appeared, near the far end of the lake. 'And here's the disk, you can copy it over.'

'Svetlana, I'll buy you summer roses.'

She screwed up her nose.

In the library, Petrie started again, but this time with dots rather than lines; and this time the patterns showed up with great clarity. He ran the frames like a slow-motion movie. Clusters of dots waltzed slowly around each other; but frame by frame, the number of dots in each cluster changed.

Then nothing – the particle flow had stopped – and then another sequence of changing patterns, looking completely different from the last.

He went back to the previous batch, the one with the waltzing clusters. And the thing which had been trying to crawl up out of his unconscious mind began to surface. A thing even crazier than Shtyrkov's rantings.

He put it aside, didn't dare to think of it.

He zoomed into the clusters. At higher magnification there were clusters within clusters: in each cluster in each frame, the particles were grouped. But one level of clustering was different; at this level, there were never more than four dots together. Sometimes a particle was solitary, sometimes it had a single companion or two or three, sometimes there were two pairs. But never more than four.

He wrote down the pattern on Svetlana's spiral notebook, and saw for the first time that his hand was trembling. He put them in order:

1, 2, 3, 1, 1-1, 1-2, 1-3, 2, 2-1, 2-2, 2-3, 3, 3-1, 3-2 . . .

Drop the dashes. Put them into an array:

	1	2	3
	1	2	3
1	11	12	13
2	21	22	23
3	31	32	33

What about zero? How would zero particles be recorded? Without worrying about that, Petrie put in zeros where they seemed to make sense:

00	01	02	03
10	11	12	13
20	21	22	23
30	31	32	33

He said, 'Oh God!' aloud.

Four-base arithmetic. A counting system. The one we'd have developed if we'd had only four fingers. Converted to the familiar ten-base, the same numbers read by a ten-fingered creature were:

0	1	2	3
4	5	6	7
8	9	10	11
12	13	14	15

He went back to the spirals. Here the signallers were counting up to three, no further. Here, if anywhere, he was going to crack the code – *if* there was a code.

He took a pulse at random, 7.34159 seconds into the particle blast. They had tracked across the lake in two counter-rotating spirals, a fact which he ignored. He counted the little clumps along one of the spirals, a frame at a time, converting them to four-base arithmetic: 210333223132212310 . . .

For the hell of it, he put $A = 0$, $B = 1$ and so on: CBADDDCCDBDCCBCDBA . . .

There were no E's or F's. It looked utterly random. All he could say was that they were using a four-letter alphabet.

A four-letter alphabet.

They.

Petrie had come across a four-letter alphabet before. His mouth was dry.

He went to the second spiral of particles, the one which had waltzed with the first one. The particles here too were bunched in little groups of up to four. He did the same letter substitution and asked the computer to line up the letters from each spiral, in two long columns.

A pattern.

The two columns were thousands of rows long, each one looked totally random, and yet no two rows had the same letter. In fact, A in column one was invariably matched by B in two. B in one was matched by A in two and so on. He wrote:

A	B
B	A
C	D
D	C

He glanced at the computer clock for the first time in hours. It was five past four. And now the excitement which had been growing inside him was at the point where he felt himself going faint.

He stacked the movie frames one on top of the other, starting at the beginning of the blizzard. The program took an hour to put together. He kept making elementary blunders and knew he could have done the job in a third of the time had he been fresh. Finally he had something cobbled together. The clock said 5.40 a.m.; it would soon be dawn. He was light-headed with exhaustion.

He stacked the frames into a solid, three-dimensional shape. He made the shape tumble slowly on the screen.

And he felt something like fear.

Now, at last, he took the time to sum up his night's work.

There were the rotating spirals: the double helix, now slowly tumbling on his screen, joined by rungs.

There was the four-lettered alphabet which ran through the rungs of the spiral ladders.

There was the complementarity, each letter on one half of the rung being matched by a consistent, different letter on the other half.

ABCD, an arbitrary choice of letters. Replace by *AGCT*.

Adenine, guanine, cytosine, thymine.

The building blocks of DNA.

9

Genome

Gibson spotted Petrie a couple of hundred metres away. The mathematician was wandering down the long path outside the castle; his head was bowed and he seemed to be muttering. His hands were waving as if he was addressing an imaginary audience. The path went towards the village but Gibson suspected the young man didn't know where he was going.

A light mist was clearing from the trees and the early morning sky was blue, but there was ice in the wind.

Gibson took a short cut over the snow and caught up with Petrie at the church. The mathematician's eyes were bloodshot and he had an overnight stubble. His face was drawn, almost as if he was in pain. He looked at Gibson vaguely, as if he didn't recognise the man.

'For Christ's sake, Tom, look at you. Get to bed.'

'What about the others?' Petrie asked. The words came out slurred.

'They flaked out hours ago.'

'What about Freya?' Petrie didn't know why he'd asked that; it just came out.

'She's up early, like me. She's reading a ton of downloads in the computer room.'

'Has she made progress?'

Gibson made a so-so facial gesture. He was now pacing

alongside Petrie; they turned left along a quiet road. A middle-aged man was sitting humped forwards on a hay-cart pulled by a small horse, sacking over his head and shoulders to protect him from the cold. There was an exchange of '*Dobryden*', and then the horse had clip-clopped past them. The smell of hay and horse lingered in the cold morning air.

'What about you?'

Petrie gave Gibson a strange look. He said, 'I have something to announce.'

Gibson stopped. 'Well?'

'Get them out of bed, Charlie. I want everyone to hear this together.'

'I run this outfit. Tell me what you've got.'

'This is for your team to hear.'

'Tom!'

Petrie relented; the man was like a starved dog waiting for a biscuit. He said, 'Okay, I tell the team but you get the preview. The signal is intelligent.'

For some seconds Gibson could have been a statue. He peered into Petrie's eyes, looking for clues. Then he gave a sort of moan, like a man in a trance. He performed a brief Zorba the Greek dance on the road, clicking his fingers and laughing. Finally his eyes widened, he shouted, 'God in heaven!' and sprinted back along the road, passing the hay-cart and swerving right up the hill towards the castle. Petrie carried on walking, humming to himself.

In a minute Petrie heard running footsteps. He turned. Gibson had reappeared at speed, arms waving to keep balance on the slippery road. His mood had swung from beatitude to desperate anxiety. He stopped at Petrie, his chest heaving with the sprint. 'Pulsars. Fucking pulsars. Bleep bleep bleep in the Cambridge radio telescope. A secretive lot, that group, they sat on it for six months because they thought they were detecting little green men only it turned out they weren't little green men, they were spinning neutron stars.' He glared fiercely at Petrie, looking for reassurance.

'Charlie, pattern recognition is my business. It's why you asked me here, remember? No natural process could produce what you detected. That signal is the product of a mind.'

Charlie smiled again, an enraptured saint. 'The discovery of all time. The Nobel for sure.'

'A Nobel Prize, Charlie, but that's the least of it. Think about it. We're not alone. There are thinking beings out there. What effect is this going to have on society?'

'Who cares? The effect on me is a Nobel Prize.' Then: 'The pattern really is intelligent? You're absolutely sure?'

'Absolutely.'

'You said a mind? A signal?' Gibson's face was distorted by a ferocious intensity. 'Are you saying it's a message?'

'I don't know what it is.'

Gibson took Petrie by the arm and they reversed direction, back towards the castle and the receding haycart. His eyes were lit with an evangelical gleam and his words came out rapidly, almost staccato. 'I'm very concerned about you, Tom, you need sleep, then you can waken up nice and fresh and crack the code, you'll do that, won't you, Tom? You'll wake up nice and fresh and crack the code? Then we'll all get big juicy Nobel Prizes, you for cracking the code and me for being the big cheese and we'll all be famous just so long as you get some sleep and then wake up and crack the fucking code for Christ's sake, please, just as quick as you can.'

10

Poet's Dream

After the penetrating cold, the warmth of the castle hit Petrie like a sleeping pill. Gibson, however, was in a high state of excitement. He now decided that the young mathematician could endure a little more sleep deprivation in the name of science. He took Petrie by the elbow, guided him upstairs to the common room, propped him in a chair and bustled through to the kitchen. Presently he came back with a mug of strong, sweet, black coffee. 'The cleaners turn up about eight,' he said for no obvious reason. Then he vanished, singing loudly and tunelessly.

Freya and Svetlana were first to appear, Svetlana in black jeans and sweater, Freya in the same long skirt and red blouse she had worn in the BMW. 'Good morning, Tom,' Freya said. 'You look terrible.'

'Like death warmed up,' Svetlana added, flopping into a couch. 'My great-aunt was a better cook than Vashislav's and she taught me how to make *pyzy* which have been known to revive frozen corpses.'

'Later,' Gibson said curtly. He popped out of the door impatiently, popped in again, and repeated the cycle twice before Shtyrkov arrived. The Russian sat down heavily on the couch next to Svetlana; the armchairs looked as if they would be too tight a fit. He grinned expectantly at Petrie.

'Tom has something to announce,' Gibson said triumphantly.

Petrie sipped at the over-sweet coffee. Exhaustion was blurring his words. 'Vashislav's suspicions were right. The signal can't be caused by any natural phenomenon. It's coming from an intelligent source.'

Freya gasped briefly, and then there was a long, stunned silence.

Shtyrkov muttered something in Russian, under his breath. Then Svetlana began to laugh and cry and Shtyrkov patted her shoulder. 'Stay calm, child.'

Svetlana produced a paper handkerchief, blew her nose and smiled sheepishly. 'I suppose the first thing is to be sure that Tom is right.'

'I can prove it. But the proof involves a bigger shock. I warn you, it'll blow your mind.'

'A bigger shock? Bigger than ET?' Alarm and greed mingled in Gibson's pale face.

Petrie put the mug on a table. 'Come through to the office.'

The office smelled slightly of stale sweat. Petrie threw up the cartoon picture of the lake and rotated it to orient his little audience in three dimensions. Then he fired particles through the lake, tapping at the keyboard to progressively slow down the flow. As the movie slowed, the stream appeared at first like a blizzard sweeping through the lake at a shallow angle. And then, with further slowing, individual trajectories became distinguishable, patterns began to appear, complicated and swirling, with blank periods in between.

And then Petrie explained about turning the lake so that it was face-on to the flow, and replacing each particle track by a point so that at any instant the lake was covered by a pattern of dots. And then he zoomed in on some of the fine structure and explained about the four-base arithmetic. And then he told them how he had stacked the microseconds of time on top of each other so that each slice of time became a thin slice in a jelly, so that the stacked slices defined a solid, three-dimensional structure. And then a century passed while Petrie tapped in a final set of instructions until, on the screen, slowly rotating and beyond any possibility of mistake or misinterpretation, was the double helix of DNA.

Shtyrkov sang, quietly. Gibson said, 'Oh man.'

Petrie left it on the screen, tumbling slowly, hypnotising them; even menacing them. He felt his limbs covered with goosepimples. 'I don't know whether it's even remotely human, but it's surely biological.'

There was a long silence, eventually broken by Shtyrkov. 'How much time does this represent?'

'The first minute of the transmission.'

'Meaning?'

'It's only three per cent of the message. We have another thirty-six minutes to analyse.'

Gibson said again, 'Oh, man.'

Freya said, 'They gave us this up-front for a reason.'

'Yes,' Shtyrkov said. 'They didn't want us to miss it. That's their starting point. They're saying, "Hey, we're life forms just like you." '

'Is this a hoax?' Gibson asked hoarsely.

Petrie looked up. 'If it is, you're not in on it, Charlie. You're as white as a sheet.'

'Look at us all,' Freya said.

'No, I mean someone monkeying with the equipment. Or something.' But Gibson's voice trailed off as the absurdity of his own suggestion got through to him.

'Hey, Charlie, the lake glowed.' Svetlana was speaking quietly, as if all emotion had now been drained out of her.

'An external input of some sort? From a satellite? Look – I know it's stupid.'

'No, no, you're right, Charlee. We have to think it through,' Shtyrkov said. 'We must eliminate everything, even stupid ideas. Keep them coming.'

'What sort of particles were these?' Petrie asked. 'Can you tell?'

Svetlana pointed to a far corner of the lake. 'Can you zoom into that?'

Petrie obliged.

'Now go back to the original trajectories, not the points.'

A cluster of parallel lines appeared.

'Now turn them. Look at the lines face-on.'

The lines shrank, turned back into points.

'Right. Absolutely straight, no curvature. In that corner, Tom, about twenty metres under the water, we have a dipole magnet that weighs half a ton and gives us forty thousand gauss. If we swam anywhere near it with anything metal we'd be pulled under. If the particles were charged their tracks would bend near the magnet.'

'And they don't.'

'Exactly, so they're not cosmic rays. Cosmic rays are charged, they'd be deflected. We have half a dozen magnets like that under the water and we can do more checks if you like.'

'Okay, Svetlana, if they're not cosmic rays, what then?'

'This time yesterday I'd have called them dark matter.'

'And today?'

'A neutral particle penetrating half a mile of rock? Unknown.'

'A vast surge of them,' Gibson reminded her. 'Double unknown.'

'Unknown to us,' Svetlana said.

'Which safely rules out some clown playing games with satellites.' Petrie was having trouble holding his head upright.

Freya said, 'The particles could have penetrated the lake from below.'

'You mean they came clean through the Earth?' Gibson asked.

'Or from some accelerator on the surface of the Earth. Therefore it still might be a trick.' Svetlana was saying the words with every sign of disbelieving them.

'Total fantasy,' Shtyrkov said. 'A flux of this magnitude is thousands of years in the future even if we were dealing with a known particle type, which we're not.' He struggled out of his chair. 'Ladies and gentlemen, we can securely eliminate both a natural source and a human one. Tom is right.'

'You were right, Vash,' said Petrie loyally. 'Your intuition saw this.'

Shtyrkov brushed the compliment aside. 'Lunacy has its compensations.'

'If that was just their opener, what about the rest of the message?' Charlie asked, his voice greedy. 'What's in it?'

Petrie said, 'If I don't get some sleep I'll crack up.'

'I don't care.' Gibson didn't seem to be joking. He was jiggling around excitedly.

'Ignore him, Tom. Go to bed,' Vashislav ordered. 'We'll play around with this. And, Tom – congratulations.'

Unexpectedly, Freya gave Petrie a hug. 'A signal from another world. This is the dream of poets.'

Petrie hadn't thought of it that way; but he thought the Norwegian woman had a terrific smile.

Svetlana said, 'I'll make you my great-aunt's *pyzy* when you get up.'

'The cleaners!' Gibson was suddenly horror-struck. 'They mustn't see this. They come at eight.'

'Okay, Charlee, don't panic. We'll keep the cleaning ladies out of here. We don't want them to look at the screen and say, "Hey, here's a picture of DNA sent by extraterrestrials." '

* * *

Petrie was wakened by sunshine in his eyes. His watch said 3.30 p.m. and his bladder was bursting. He relieved himself, stared at the unshaven hobo staring back at him out of the mirror. He ran a shower, shaving in the flow of warm water. Then he dried himself and rummaged in his holdall. He put on jeans and a white T-shirt emblazoned with a picture of pieces on a chessboard; to the *cognoscenti*, it showed the board at the moment the computer Deep Blue finally crushed Kasparov. When asked, he liked to explain that it symbolised the triumph of the machine over the human spirit; the reaction was always fun.

Svetlana was standing by the stairs on the floor below. She beckoned, and Petrie followed her along the corridor and into the refectory. A single place had been set with what looked like Hapsburg silverware. The *pyzy* turned out to be small, hot dumplings served with sausages. They were spicy and delicious, and had a warming effect which seemed to go beyond their heat capacity.

'I think Freya has found something,' she said.

Petrie washed down the last dumpling with hot tea.

'Come and see.' She extended her hand and Petrie took it; it was thin and warm. She led him to the corridor, down the stairs and into the administrator's office.

'Ah, the Kraken awakes,' Gibson said obscurely. 'Come and see what Freya has found.'

Freya was at a terminal. There was an empty chair next to her and she patted it. Gibson breathed garlic over them. Shtyrkov, taking up an armchair, waved at Petrie without looking up from a wodge of papers. Svetlana settled down at a terminal on another desk.

Petrie looked at the screen: there was what seemed to be a white shoebox traversed by parallel red lines. 'Tom, this is near the beginning of the signal.'

'Okay.'

She tapped at the keyboard. 'And this is a slice near the middle.' A set of parallel blue lines appeared. 'And here we have a slice from near the end of the transmission.' A third set of lines, in green. Petrie shook his head.

'Look closely.'

'I don't see anything.'

'Okay. Now let me take the average direction of the red lines, and then the blue ones, finally the green.' She tapped on the keyboard.

'Ha!' Petrie exclaimed in delight. Three large circles – red, blue and green – showed on the screen, red to the left and green to the right.

'Exactly.' Freya was unable to keep a touch of pride out of her voice. 'The direction of the source changed with time.'

'The source was moving?'

'No, we were. The lines stayed parallel in space while the Earth was turning. The rate and direction match the Earth's rotation exactly.'

Shtyrkov called over from his armchair. 'So, we can rule out a satellite as a source, or anything on the Earth. Whatever the source, it's in deep space.'

Freya agreed. 'Deep space it is.'

'And you now have the position of the source in the sky?'

'Two possible positions, depending on whether the signal came down or up through the lake.'

'And?'

'Give me a chance, Tom, I've only just discovered this. I need to carry out an error analysis to shrink these big circles to tiny spots. When I've done that I'll download star charts and catalogues and see what we've got.'

'Well, get on with it,' Gibson said impatiently.

Freya turned, smiled sweetly at Gibson and said, '*Dra til helvete.*' Then she returned to the keyboard.

Petrie turned to Gibson. 'Okay. We're all agreed that the signature is extraterrestrial, and the source is intelligent. What now?'

Gibson pulled up a chair and picked up papers from a desk. 'There's an outfit called the Institute for Aeronautics and Astronautics and they've set up a protocol. Vashislav's going through the small print now.'

'Let's hear it.'

Gibson waved the papers. A slightly pompous tone was creeping into his voice. He read: ' "*Declaration of principles concerning activities following the detection of ET.*" Principle number one. "*Any individual, public or private research institution, or governmental agency that believes it has detected a signal from or other evidence of extraterrestrial intelligence should seek to verify that the most plausible explanation for the evidence is the existence of extraterrestrial intelligence rather than some other natural phenomenon or anthropogenic phenomenon before making any public announcement." '*

'That's why I'm here,' Petrie proposed. 'Okay, so Freya and I have confirmed it.'

'And you can exclude any possibility of error?' Gibson said in an interrogatory tone. 'With such confidence that you are prepared to face the world and say, "These people have discovered ET"?'

'Yes.'

'Why "these people"? Why exclude Freya and Tom?' Vashislav called over, without looking up from his papers.

Gibson ignored the comment. 'Okay. Proceed to principle number two. "*The discoverer should inform his or her relevant national authority.*" '

'Our respective governments. But you must have told HMG already.'

'Yes and no. I naturally assumed Vashislav here was raving. You know, a lifetime of vodka. But yes, I did make a precautionary phone call.'

'To?'

'The President of the Royal Astronomical Society. I made it clear that it was an extremely long shot, not to be taken too seriously at this stage. My guess is he fired it up to the President of the Royal Society or even the Minister of Science.'

'My invitation came from Downing Street,' Petrie said. 'Did you ask for me specifically?'

'Yes, Tom. As I said, I heard you at Uppsala last year. All that chaos theory and pattern recognition. You were a natural, just the man to check out Vashislav's ravings. You're a rising star.'

'And being junior, I'm easily controlled. Less likely to steal the limelight than some big name.'

Shtyrkov gave a deep belly laugh. Gibson pouted.

Petrie continued: 'But they didn't route it through GCHQ.'

Shtyrkov said, 'The government would bring ridicule on itself if they got caught up in a false alarm.'

'Who cares? I asked for you and I got you.'

'Then I got this warning at Heathrow.'

'I don't understand that,' Gibson admitted. 'And I don't like it.'

'And Freya? Where does she come into it?' Petrie asked.

'We need to know where the signal's coming from. You'll find that out for us, won't you, Freya?'

The Norwegian girl carried on typing.

Petrie pointed to the paper on Gibson's lap. 'Okay, Charlie, what's next?'

'Principle number three. Wait for it, I love this one. *"A confirmed detection of ET should be disseminated promptly, openly, and widely through scientific channels and public media. The discoverer should have the privilege of making the first public announcement."* Since I'm the PI, that means me.' Gibson smiled a smile of great happiness.

'You'll be on CNN around the world within hours. I can see the flashbulbs reflecting in your eyes already. Even horsemen in Mongolia will know your name.'

Gibson continued to radiate beatitude. 'And that's about it, Tom. The rest is just stuff about protecting signal frequencies and distributing data.'

'Okay, Charlie. So the protocols say you first inform HMG and then Joe Public. How? Do you just phone up the Prime Minister?'

'I'll feed it through the RAS President like before. Let him handle the problem. What about you, Vash?'

'It's not a problem for me. Friends in high places.'

'And then we tell Joe Public straight away.'

'No, Charlie.' Svetlana turned round in her chair. 'Wait until we can name the source of the signal.'

'We can't wait for that. We can't risk some civil servant upstaging us.' Gibson's face was dark. 'I make the announcement today.'

Shtyrkov said, 'Our governments will not make any announcement without thoroughly checking out the story. That will take them days, maybe weeks.'

Petrie said, 'There's a message for humanity in that signal. We don't even know if that DNA is human. It's far more kudos for us if we, rather than some other group, tell the world what the signallers are saying.'

The argument had an immediate effect on Gibson. 'You know, Tom, I think you're right. If some other outfit interpreted the message it could draw attention from us.'

Petrie drove the point home. 'People would think we just hit it lucky but they were the real gurus. The high priests interpreting the sacred text.'

'My God, yes.' Gibson looked as if he had just stepped back from the edge of a chasm. 'What day is this?'

'Wednesday afternoon,' Freya said. 'I need as much time as you can give me.'

Gibson scowled. 'But the longer we delay, the bigger the risk of a leak.'

'So how long are you giving me, Charlie?' Freya asked.

Gibson counted up to three with his fingers. 'Okay. There's a balance. The longer HMG has this, the bigger the risk of a leak, but at the very least we need to tell people where the signal came from. However, with or without the source, I go public with this on Monday. We daren't delay any longer than that.'

Svetlana, at her terminal again, said in a startled voice, 'Oh, my goodness. What's this?'

11

The Bishop and the Chorus Girl

'It can only be a hoax. I mean, what else can it be?'

David Maddox, President of the Royal Astronomical Society, twirled spaghetti on to his fork. 'The genuine article?'

Lord Sangster, Minister for Science, gave a sceptical smile. 'David, let's keep our feet on the ground here. Let me look at it again.'

A red London bus roared noisily past the restaurant door. Maddox waited until it had passed, and handed the paper over. 'It was securely encrypted.'

'Not against our friends in the NSA, if they got to know of it.' Sangster put down his fork and read the e-mail, carefully, for the fifth or sixth time:

Dear Professor Maddox,

(1) In my communication of three days ago I fore-warned you that we may have picked up an intelligent extraterrestrial signal with our Tatras cave facility. I requested that cryptanalytic expertise be arranged in the form of Dr Thomas Petrie, whose abilities in this area are outstanding.

(2) He arrived yesterday, and after an overnight session confirmed my opinion that such a signal has,

in fact, been received by us. We are in the process of identifying the source of the alien message.

(3) We have so far decrypted only a tiny fraction of the signal. The information to this point is of a biological nature.

(4) In accordance with the SETI League protocol, paragraph 2, I request that news of this discovery now be passed on to HMG.

(5) Once we have identified the home planet, I will proceed to paras 3 and 4 of the protocol, hopefully within the next three or four days. As principal investigator, I claim the right to make the first public announcement.

Yours sincerely,

C.T. Gibson

Sangster looked up, glanced again around the shabby little restaurant, its walls studded with paintings of rural Tuscany, and dust-covered Chianti bottles along the shelves. Near the bar, at the far end, an old man was picking at a plate of fish soup. Two waiters – elderly men with grey waistcoats and faces, napkins over arms – were standing dutifully, looking like extras in *The Godfather*. 'What's your opinion, David?'

'A SETI signal? And from an underground dark matter facility rather than a radio telescope? It hardly seems credible.'

'Can we ignore it, then?'

Maddox wrinkled his nose. 'Suppose we ignore Gibson's message and the signal turns out to be real . . .'

Sangster said, 'The tabloids would crucify us.'

'And if we declare the signal to be genuine and it turns out a mistake?'

'The tabloids would crucify us, and come election time we'd be laughed out of office.' Sangster sipped at his Sicilian wine and made a face. 'Quite native, I would say. Tell me, David, this SETI League . . .'

'A league of respected bodies, the International Academy of Astronautics chief amongst them, but their SETI protocols have no legal force. They want the state that discovers the signal to inform the Secretary General of the United Nations as well as the public and international community.'

'But, as you say, the protocols have no legal force.'

'No, Simon. I looked into this. They would have to be endorsed by the United Nations and that hasn't yet happened.'

'So the game plan is still open.' Sangster finished his *spaghetti al sugo* and looked thoughtful. 'Biological information, David. I don't like the sound of that, not one little bit. What sort of information?'

'Maybe something about their life history, or panspermia. I really can't say.'

His lordship said, reflectively, 'Fee fi fo fum, look out humans here we come. Coffee?'

'No thanks, I ought to be getting back. I'm chairing a meeting.'

Sangster said, 'David, I think we have to be very careful with something like this. There are all sorts of things to be taken into consideration.'

The RAS President looked at Sangster with a tinge of apprehension. 'What are you saying?'

'Leave it with me. I'll get someone out there to check the whole thing from A to Z. Meantime, the tightest security is called for. Nobody – *nobody* – must know about this.'

'You're not going to keep the scientists in the castle quiet for long.'

'Quite, quite. Still, this dark matter operation is financed by my ministry through PPARC, which means that I have the ultimate say, even if I hardly knew the damn thing existed a week ago.'

'Simon, this is an issue for the whole of humanity. It's too big for the Whitehall secrecy mindset, standard issue. You cannot and should not put the lid on this.'

Sangster gave an urbane smile. 'You're out of date, David. We have an ethos of open government these days, haven't you heard?'

Maddox persisted. 'Try to muzzle this and the international scientific community will come down on you like a ton of bricks.'

'Unless we succeed in muzzling it, in which case no one will ever know.'

'I doubt if you have any legal authority for blocking this result.'

'Legal authority?' Sangster was still smiling. 'I'm talking about moral authority. Although governments do have other means of persuasion. Funding is always difficult these days.'

'Am I being blackmailed here?'

'Goodness, let's not get draconian. But if this discovery is real it touches on matters which go far beyond mere scientific interest.'

'Indeed, Simon. Such as whether we're here for a purpose, how the existence of other life affects the great religions and our views about God's purpose and where we fit into it, how our future would be bound up by a civilisation far in advance of our own . . .'

'Ask the Mayans or the Navajo what happens when the weak and strong come into contact.'

'That's human history. This could lift us out of that.'

'We will not rush to the media. Decisions about this will be made by HMG, not by some naive academics round a table at this Academy of Whatsit.' Sangster snapped his fingers, and one of the waiters jerked into motion. 'Security is the first priority. We'll probably have to bring MI6 into this.'

'What on earth for?'

'All sorts of reasons, David,' Sangster replied vaguely. 'Because we ought to make sure that communication with this castle is secure. Because we don't want our American cousins jumping the gun on this one. And after all, if these aliens exist, we are dealing with a foreign power.'

'But look at what Gibson says here. They're about to activate paras three and four of the protocol.'

'Which are?'

'They'll inform observers worldwide through the Central Bureau for Astronomical Telegrams, Commission 51 of the International Astronomical Union, and a dozen other bodies of that sort. And the Secretary General of the United Nations.'

Sangster's eyelids half shut; to Maddox, he was now looking positively reptilian. His lordship murmured, 'Will they, indeed?'

They made their way on to the pavement outside while the busy Piccadilly traffic roared past. An empty black taxi appeared and the Minister waved at it. It U-turned smoothly to a halt. Sangster opened its door and turned. 'Give you a lift?'

'No, thanks. I'm only going to Carlton House Terrace.'

The Royal Society, Sangster thought. Full of damned

chattering scientists. 'David, unless and until I say otherwise, you must forget about this whole business. Consider that to be an order.' In the back of the taxi, he wound the window down. 'And we never had this conversation.'

* * *

'Joseph? Sally Morgan here.'

Joseph Pembroke could never quite hide the surge of pleasure he felt whenever he heard her voice. He had known Sally Morgan from the remote past, when his hair was long and her skirt, he remembered well, was short. She was a cheerful, petite high-flier in Christ's College who could down a pint with the best of them. Her voice was twenty years older now, and its carefree tone was tinged with something he couldn't identify, but it still triggered distant memories – picnics by the Cam, dangerous winter climbs in Glencoe, the Flying Club, and of course that unforgettable overnight berth in the ferry to Dieppe . . .

'Good afternoon, Sally.'

'I'd like to speak to the PM, Joseph.'

The Prime Minister's PPS pulled a large black desk diary towards him. He glanced at his watch – it showed 3.40 p.m. – before running a manicured fingernail down the afternoon schedule, pencilled in by Anne Broughton, the Diary Secretary, with a couple of entries made by one of the Garden girls.

'But you saw him this morning.'

'Something's turned up in the interval.'

'And it can't wait until your next Wednesday session?'

'No, I must see the Prime Minister today.'

'You're an audacious little minx.' Pembroke said it lightly, but there was something in her voice. 'The PM's with Nicole at the moment, then he's straight into a session with Sir Crispin and the Foreign Secretary to discuss the Iraq campaign. There's not a gap in his diary.'

'What about the evening?'

'He's at the Guildhall dining with the Lord Mayor and the director of the new opera house, along with assorted actors and showbiz types. Then he formally opens the opera house and sits through an evening of modern ballet.'

'He doesn't strike me as a ballet lover, Joseph.'

'I don't know which he loathes more: modern ballet or the Lord Mayor.'

'Dear Joseph, who could take offence? Some day you'll be stuffed and exhibited in the Victoria and Albert.'

'Then he's back to Number Ten and, I assume, a stiff whisky and bed. I don't see how to squeeze you in.'

'You've never had any problem squeezing me before, Your Grace.'

Pembroke laughed. It was a reference to *The Bishop and the Chorus Girl*, a bawdy undergraduate play in which they had played the principal parts. The nicknames had stuck for years.

'I have to see him.' Again, that undertone in her voice.

'Maybe after he gets back. I'll have a word with him.'

'I'd be very grateful.'

'Consider it done. Be in the Private Office at ten o'clock tonight.'

'I'll use the Garden entrance.'

'By the way, Sally . . .'

Cautiously: 'Umm?'

'How grateful is "very grateful"?'

The Head of MI6 gave a deep-throated chuckle. 'Oh sir, Oi be a simple country lass.'

12

Icosahedron

'It must be their home planet.' Svetlana was waving them over impatiently, her face lined with excitement.

There was a rush to her terminal, and a collective gasp. Shtyrkov laughed, shouted '*Ne figa sebe!*' and clapped his hands. Petrie, looking over her shoulder at the image, shouted, 'Wow! Wow! Wow!'

The image was roughly spherical, like a dimpled ball. It was made up of thousands of tiny spheres touching each other. The little spheres were red, yellow or blue. Two enormous blue starry eyes stared at them, along with a big round blue mouth. The spherelets lining the eyes and mouth were yellow, making the face look as if it had yellow eyeshadow and lipstick.

'It's like the Man in the Moon,' Svetlana said. She pressed some keys and the round head shook slowly from side to side, then nodded up and down. Finally it turned slowly through a full rotation, showing an upside-down face on the far hemisphere.

The terrain was deeply sculptured with canyons and mountains, the cavities being filled with the blue spherelets, the mountain peaks the red ones; the little yellow spheres occupied the middle heights.

'How did you do this?'

'I just ran your program. I stacked the time slices as

far as the next big gap in the flow.'

'The little balls – are these my dots?'

'No, Tom, it's more complicated than that. There are hundreds of your dots inside each ball. But they were combined in just four basic ways, four patterns. So to simplify things, to get an image we could visualise, I replaced each pattern by a ball. Four patterns, four colours. I chose red, yellow, green and blue at random, and I expanded the balls until they touched and that's what I got.'

'Not bad for a wiring technician, Svetlana.'

She smiled happily.

'But there were four colours, you said. Where's the fourth? The green?'

'Inside the planet. You can't see the green spheres.'

'A planet with life needs water,' Gibson asserted. 'So the low areas are probably oceans. Blue was a lucky choice.'

Petrie said, 'Six oceans, regularly spaced, all the same size. It seems artificial somehow.'

'They've terraformed their planet,' Gibson suggested.

'Can you zoom in on it?' Petrie asked. 'Anywhere on the surface.'

A little wedge of lip grew until it filled the screen: a mass of coloured ping-pong balls.

'Now can you do a contour map on that? They must have given us a graph-drawing package.'

Svetlana created a fresh window on the screen and threw up a long list of programs. 'I don't recognise anything there.'

'*Mathematica*. I can work it.' Svetlana vacated her chair, which creaked slightly as Shtyrkov sat on it. He typed at the keyboard for a minute, then redisplayed the wedge of planet. Now the ping-pong balls disappeared and were swiftly replaced by an irregular, contoured surface.

'It's amazingly mountainous,' Svetlana said. 'Look at those cliffs.'

'Where is this planet?' Gibson wanted to know.

Freya moved back to her terminal. 'The zones are still narrowing down. At the moment they're constellation-sized. Okay, if the particles came through the lake from above, their source is somewhere in Ursa Major. If they came up from below, it's in maybe Tucana or Phoenix.'

'How long before you get a definite answer?'

'A couple of hours, Charlie.'

'Two hours?'

'It's a big job.'

'Is there anything interesting in the two zones so far?'

'Plenty. The Whirlpool galaxy, the 47 Tucanae cluster, Nubecula Minor . . .'

'I mean from the ET point of view, as well you know.'

'Charlie, I can't rule out anything right now.'

'Guess, will you?' Gibson's tone was exasperated.

'I suppose there's 47 Ursa Majoris,' Freya said doubtfully.

'Which is?'

She spoke while she typed. 'It's a G1 main sequence star, like the Sun only slightly hotter. It has two known planets around it. Too far away to see directly and we only know they're there because they make the star wobble. But the planets are gas giants, bigger than Jupiter, and they certainly won't look like that.'

'It could have other planets?'

'Yes, Charlie, but so could millions of other stars in the zones.'

'How far away is it?'

'Let me see.' A slender finger skimmed down the screen. 'Forty-six light years. Not too distant.'

'47 Ursa Majoris,' Gibson said. 'It sounds good. I have a gut feeling about it.'

'My gut is bigger than yours,' Shtyrkov said. 'And it tells me the odds are against this star.'

'Before I contact the government I want a positive identification of this planet.'

'And you'll want it for the press release,' Shtyrkov suggested. 'It will enhance the drama.'

'The press release, yes. I must put something together.' Gibson scurried towards a corner desk, leaving Petrie to wonder if the Russian had cunningly manoeuvred Gibson out of their hair.

Petrie sat at a terminal and hacked into the enormous file, randomly entering about halfway through. He ran the movie briefly; more swirling dots appeared, but now he knew, if not the mind of the signallers, at least the way they dumbed the message down. He sliced time, stacked it and this time it didn't work; there was no picture, no pleasing shape, just a haphazard swarm of dots.

'They're sending a different sort of message.' Shtyrkov was leaning over his shoulder.

'I think so, Vash. Something that doesn't lend itself to geometric visualisation.'

'Like something in four or more dimensions?'

'Maybe.'

The Russian laid a sympathetic hand on Petrie's shoulder. 'Back to the theological library, young man.'

'To hell with the theological library.' Petrie started to hack randomly into other points in the file, a small boy lost in an Aladdin's cave of mysteries.

After an hour he rubbed his face, stretched, and went out to the castle grounds. The sky was blue. Icicles of lethal size were hanging down from the high rooftops and he wondered idly if the warming air would send them hurtling down. He wandered across to the parapet, looked out over the countryside and almost immediately had a disturbing thought. He turned smartly back into the office. Gibson was scribbling; the others were doing their things at terminals and there was an air of quiet concentration.

'Svetlana, can you throw up those canyons and mountains again?'

She obliged.

'The regularity's amazing. Can you go back to the full view now?'

The Man in the Moon reappeared.

'Look at the edges. It's not exactly spherical. There are flattish plains, like continental plates, as well as bumps all over.'

'Obviously.' Gibson had rejoined them. 'It's a very mountainous planet.'

'There's more to it than that,' Petrie said.

Freya was looking at the screen with narrowed eyes. 'I've been thinking that, too, Tom. In fact, I'm way ahead of you.'

Petrie said, 'Yes! It's bizarre.'

'I don't want to interrupt your private telepathy,' Gibson said, 'but would either of you people care to let me in on the secret?'

Freya unconsciously flipped her hair back over her shoulder. 'Charlie, the Earth is eight thousand miles across and Mount Everest is six miles high. It's a tiny blip on the surface. That's because gravity is too strong to support a taller mountain. If Everest was pushed up much higher, the rock at its base would crumble.' She pointed at a couple of places on the screen. 'Look at the height of these mountains. They couldn't exist on an Earth-sized planet.'

'So gravity's weaker there. It's a small planet.'

'Yes, a very small one. It couldn't be more than a thousand kilometres across, say like a giant comet or an asteroid. That's your reasoning, Tom?'

Petrie nodded.

Freya continued. 'But an asteroid's gravity is too weak to hold on to an atmosphere. Any body of liquid water would long since have been lost to space. And you've been telling us that water is essential for life.'

Svetlana looked meditatively at the screen. 'How could any sentient being be content to live on a dry airless hunk of rock?'

Freya said, 'It's not a hunk of rock, Svetlana.'

Shtyrkov looked at the image, and then at Freya and Petrie. 'Is it possible?'

'Let me in on it,' Gibson pleaded.

Petrie squeezed Svetlana's shoulder. 'Make it tumble.'

Svetlana typed a few symbols and the Man in the Moon, mouth agape, tilted and disappeared, reappearing from time to time in random orientations.

'Look closely,' Petrie said.

Svetlana said, 'It's not a sphere.'

'No. It's an icosahedron.'

'A what?' Gibson was looking blank.

'It's made up of twenty triangular plates joined together. Look at it. See how it keeps coming back to the same shape. That's because it looks exactly the same from sixty different orientations. It's one of the Platonic solids.'

'Plato?' Gibson repeated in exasperation. 'Tom, are we on different planes of reality or what?'

'Charlie, an icosahedron is one of the most beautifully symmetric solid forms. Plato wanted to understand the world in terms of mathematics and harmony. He believed that tetrahedron, cube, octahedron and icosahedron made up earth, air, fire and water. It's all there in his *Timaeus*.'

'So what are you saying? That the signallers have read *Timaeus*? That they've shaped their planet like a Platonic bloody solid?'

Petrie shook his head. 'That's not a planet, Charlie. It's a virus.'

13

Moscow Chatline

Phone ringing.

Its rasp penetrated layers of sleep and merged with a bizarre dream in which she was floating above a TV quiz show. An uncomprehending eyelid dragged itself open; green numbers on a bedside clock read 2.10 a.m.

Phone ringing, at ten past two in the morning.

Dasha! There's been an accident!

She dragged herself fully awake. A sense of dread washing over her, she threw back the blankets and stumbled through to the tiny living room.

Phone still ringing.

The window was partially open and a black electric cable snaked through the gap down to the battery of a silver Niva five flights below: it was the only way to ensure that her car would start in the minus thirty degrees of a Moscow winter. But the night air from this Moscow winter was drifting in through the gap and she gasped as she opened the living-room door and hurried towards the telephone. The sound of traffic, still rumbling at this hour, came up from the street below.

Still ringing.

Don't stop!

She banged a shin painfully on the edge of a low table. *Keep ringing. I'm almost there!*

She found it, dropped the receiver, picked it up, trembling.

Professional voice, deep male: 'Tatyana Maranovich?' A doctor or a surgeon. Dasha was in some hospital bed. No. This was a policeman. Her daughter was lying on a mortuary slab somewhere.

Tanya's voice and hands shook uncontrollably. 'Yes?'

'My name is Vashislav Shtyrkov. I want to speak to Professor Velikhov. The duty clerk at the Academy referred me to you. May I have his home phone number?'

Relief and anger struggled in her head, and relief won: Dasha was all right, probably tucked up with Alexei somewhere. Suddenly the bitter cold, which she had ignored, became an issue. 'Vashislav Shtyrkov, it's two o'clock in the morning.'

'I know.'

'I can't give the Professor's name out to a stranger. I could lose my job.'

'Let me give you an assurance on that: you will lose it if you don't.'

'Can you tell me what this is about?'

'No.'

'At least tell me who you are.'

'A colleague, from the old days.'

Something stirred in Tanya's mind. 'Are you the one who called the Professor about that castle in Slovakia?'

'I am the one. Now will you give me his number?'

'No, I'm not allowed to do that. But if you give me yours I'll relay it to him.'

'That will suffice. But you must give it to him now.'

'At this hour? The Professor will not thank me for that.' She was now shivering inside her thick flannel nightgown.

'On the contrary, Tanya Maranovich, if you call him now he will bring you lilies from the Nile and sunshine from Mexico.'

* * *

Georgi Velikhov, as befitted the President of the Russian Academy of Sciences, had a villa in the Gorki-9 district of Moscow. The villa came with a maid and a cook, six bedrooms and government-issue furniture. His neighbours were diplomats, high government officials and, not two kilometres away, was the *fazenda* of Mikhail Isayevich Ogorodnikov, President of Russia.

And the central heating stayed on all night. Apart from anything else, the house was full of children: over the New Year, Velikhov was playing Father Frost to his wife Masha, his three daughters and their husbands, and nine grand-children.

So it was that, although it was three in the morning and the air outside was colder than a domestic freezer, the patriarch was warm and comfortable in a studded green leather chair in his study. A stove, which he had banked up with wood for an overnight slow burn, was burning brightly, and a green shaded lamp suspended from the ceiling was throwing a harsh light over a large leather-topped desk.

He was on the telephone for over an hour. Most of the time he listened, but now and then he would fire off a question in a staccato tone.

He didn't hear Masha come into the study, didn't notice his four-year-old granddaughter standing at the open door in a pink nightdress, finger in mouth and hand on the top of her head until Grandmother Masha picked her up and carried her back to bed.

At the end of the call he noticed the hot chocolate in front of him with surprise. It had gone cold but his mouth was dry with talking and excitement and he gulped it down.

Velikhov stood up, stretched briefly, and then paced up and down for some minutes. The Kremlin, of course, would have a duty officer.

Good morning, I want to speak to the President on an urgent matter.

Certainly. I'll rouse the President's Chief of Staff now.

Alexy? I believe we've been contacted by an alien intelligence.

Thank you, Academician Velikhov. I too find a few Stolichnayas quite heart-warming in this weather.

They have given us information of unbelievable economic, scientific, military and medical importance.

And I especially appreciate being wakened from my bed at three in the morning for a joke. A good New Year to you.

Velikhov smiled grimly and shook his head. *No, I don't think so.*

In any case, Ogorodnikov was unlikely to be in the Kremlin. More probably, he was five minutes' drive from here, tucked up with his little fat Katya; or he might be staying in his other *dacha*, the modest one in the Odintsovo district. Or no – didn't he go moosehunting in Sverdlovsk at this time of year?

Sensible to wait until waking hours.

Or a dereliction of duty?

* * *

Two miles away from Tatyana Maranovich's small flat, in a bleak basement in the Nevsky Prospekt, a young man listened to her conversation with Academician Velikhov.

The Professor had seemed a bit grumpy about being wakened up; perhaps the fact that it was three o'clock in the morning had something to do with it. The call was recorded automatically and there was little for the man to do but listen, which he did while idly filling in a jumbo crossword. Given the content of the call he was not surprised when, five minutes after it had ended, another one went out from the Academician's *dacha*.

The young CIA officer was alone, the Gorki-9 telephone traffic being light in the early hours. He had arrived only three weeks ago, full of enthusiasm about his Moscow posting, on the strength of his background in Van Eck monitoring. To his disappointment, he had been assigned to the 'chatline', the routine coverage of private calls to and from the *dachas*, private and government-owned, of the government officials.

Velikhov's name and address came up quickly on the screen, but there was a few moments' delay while the recipient's location was traced through a satellite.

Ninety-nine per cent of it was drivel – gossip between wives, teenagers talking to each other, remote calls to children in distant places. There was an occasional diversion, the Canadian diplomat's wife in particular: 'Ruth's on!' would bring a gleeful rush to the terminal, as the calls between her and her opera house lover became ever more steamy and inventive.

No name. Some castle in Slovakia.

At this hour. Interesting.

The phonetic translator threw up the words in passable English but the CIA officer's Russian was better than the machine's.

He listened with growing perplexity. This wasn't a conversation between two normal adults, it was between lunatics. He dropped the crossword and pressed the headphones lightly against his ear, frowning.

And then he smiled. Of course – he was on the receiving end of a joke, some ponderous Russian humour. They were saying, '*Merry Christmas, Amerika, we know you're listening in.*'

But there was no humour in the voices.

His smile gradually faded. If they knew he was listening in, why tell him this through a joke? Why not use this knowledge to transmit misinformation? Why tell a tale that couldn't be taken seriously, not for a second?

As the crazy exchange continued, it increasingly dawned on the young man that this was no joke and that if these were actors, they were damn good ones.

The call lasted over an hour. At the end of it, the CIA man took off his headphones with a sigh and scratched his head.

I've just intercepted this call about aliens.

Aliens?

The callers were serious.

Of course they were. How long have you been with us? Three weeks?

He shook his head. Three weeks in Moscow and either he had the coup of a lifetime, or he was the victim of a humiliating, career-damaging practical joke.

14

Kanchenjunga

'You people are nuts.' Little patches of damp have appeared under the armpits of Gibson's shirt. 'Am I supposed to go to the British government and tell them that aliens have beamed us a picture of a virus?'

Shtyrkov says, 'It's obviously a virus. They like to be icosahedrons.'

Petrie says, 'We can test it. Your little coloured spheres, Svetlana.'

'Yes. Each is a cluster of dots, hundreds of them.'

'These dots should be proteins.'

'Tom, I wouldn't recognise a protein if it hit me on the nose.'

'It's a string of amino acids.'

'That's all right then.' Svetlana is looking defiant.

'Right. We need a biochemist.'

Gibson says, 'No. There's no time. And we have enough outsiders.' He attempts a conciliatory smile at Freya and Petrie but it comes out as a leer. 'Nothing personal.'

'Svetlana and I will learn biochemistry tonight,' Shtyrkov says.

Petrie says, 'Will it take you all night?'

'Even genius has limits. Tom, you try to decipher fresh bits of the signal.'

'I'll try to identify the source,' Freya says.

'It's why you're out here,' Gibson reminds her. 'I'll get back to the press release.'

Shtyrkov warns Gibson: 'You and I contact our governments simultaneously, Charlee. No jumping the gun.'

Apart from a scowl, Gibson makes no response.

Petrie says to nobody, 'This is the biggest thing in history.'

Freya says, 'I'd kill for a coffee.'

* * *

6 p.m. Freya says, 'We can rule out 47 Ursa Majoris. It's way outside the error circle.'

A little later, Petrie takes to pacing up and down like a caged lion. There is a clear patch of floor near the centre of the room, and he criss-crosses this at random, looking over at the dancing patterns taunting him on his screen. From time to time he sits on the edge of his chair, still staring at the dots.

At random, he has cut into the signal about a minute down the line. Here the patterns are different. The biology was snowflakes in a blizzard, random swirls, sometimes a handful of dots, sometimes thousands. Random and yet not random. But here, further down the signal, things are in stark contrast. The salami technique, stacking slices of time to create a figure, doesn't work. Here the patterns are harsh and geometric. There are pentagons and pyramids, abacuses in three dimensions and jagged cliffs in four. And yet sometimes, as he pushes the movie on, the harsh geometry dissolves and the blizzard reappears.

An alien mind, reaching out to me. What are you saying? What are you telling me? What do you mean?

6.50 p.m. After forty minutes of sitting and pacing, Petrie mutters something about the theological library and disappears. He returns without explanation an hour later. The restless pacing resumes.

8.30 p.m.   Shtyrkov and Svetlana say that the virus theory is looking good. The little spheres look like proteins made up of amino acids, but they don't know enough to identify any of them or even to say if they are of a known type.

Close to midnight, they announce that the signal contains the codings for hundreds of viruses, maybe thousands. There is a brief discussion of what could possibly motivate the signallers to beam information of that sort. There are other structures of some molecular complexity, in their thousands, but they can make no sense of them. By this time Petrie, still doing the walk, is starting to mutter.

12.40 a.m.   Gibson leaves the room and returns with a tray of mugs and biscuits. Snow is fluttering down, the flakes catching the light as they pass the windows.

Petrie keeps disappearing and reappearing, muttering and sometimes walking up and down with his hands on his head, his face screwed up in concentration. Now and then he scribbles on paper and then, often as not, darts out of the room, sometimes with a groan of despair. Nobody pays him any attention.

2.05 a.m.   Freya's program runs to its conclusion. She tidies up some numbers and consults star charts. The signal has come from one of two small regions of sky, in opposite directions. One of them contains a few ordinary stars. The other is deeply disturbing. She looks around furtively; everyone is busy at terminals, except for Petrie, who is still pacing, lost in his world of patterns. She thinks he looks mad, like Rasputin or somebody. She decides to keep her finding to herself until she has searched the Net for every scrap of information about the candidate sources.

3.15 a.m. Gibson finishes the first draft of his press release with a sigh. He makes a show of walking up and down, holding the paper in front of him, and reading it with every sign of adoration. Petrie seems not to see him but somehow they avoid collision. Gibson puts his hands on Svetlana's shoulders, looks at her screen, and asks: could the double helix be human? On the face of it the question is mind-bogglingly silly, but after the day's surprises nothing seems too bizarre. Svetlana says they'll get on to it.

Petrie disappears again. He is beginning to look wild-eyed, but then so are the others.

3.20 a.m. Shtyrkov mentions that they haven't eaten. He is ignored. He says, my sugar level's going down. He gets the same response.

5.15 a.m. Svetlana turns her chair to face the centre of the room and gives a dissertation on genetics. She tells her bone-weary little audience that the human body contains a hundred million million cells, except for Vash who has twice as many as everyone else, and they're called cells because to the early microscope men they looked like the cells of medieval monks. And each cell contains a nucleus a tenth of a millimetre across and inside each nucleus are long strands that look like worms called chromosomes, which you can just see under a powerful microscope – not that I've ever seen them. There are forty-six chromosomes and they occur in twenty-three pairs.

With you so far, says Gibson, leaning back in his chair and rubbing an overnight stubble.

She says that these chromosomes are made up of a long folded molecule called DNA. This DNA is like a twisted ladder, the famous double helix, with the two spines of the ladder made up of sugars and phosphates; and each spine has letters sticking out from it, one letter on each rung so that each rung has two letters, drawn from Tom's set of four *A,C,G,T*.

Biochemistry sounds easy, Gibson declares.

This is how DNA turns baby food into a growing human, Svetlana tells them. The ladder unwinds and splits down its length to make two strands and the letters on the rungs are exposed. One of the strands, with its exposed letters, is active which means that each set of adjacent three letters along it attracts an amino acid but I don't want to overload your brain, Charlie, not at this hour.

But I'm still with you, Gibson insists.

Very good, Charlie. The way a strand gets its amino acids involves messenger RNA and transfer RNA and migration out of the nucleus to fish for the amino acids in the baby food, and lots of those three-letter words acting together create chains of amino acids called polypeptides, and lots of polypeptides combined make up proteins. Since biochemistry is easy, Charlie, I expect you're still with me and you now understand that the whole genetic code, the thing that defines you, is like a book written in three-letter words from a four-letter alphabet.

But you can only get so many three-letter words from a four-letter alphabet, Gibson says.

Sixty-four, she confirms. The book of Charlie Gibson has a vocabulary of only sixty-four words. The book of life likewise.

So how come life is so varied? Why don't you look like a zebra?

Because you can write a very long book with sixty-four words. I said the DNA ladder was folded. There are six feet of DNA in the nucleus of a human cell. The genome is the whole code, spread around the forty-six chromosomes.

There are three billion words in the genome. If I wrote the words of your genome out in normal book size it would stretch from here to London, like a thousand Bibles written out on a single line. You're really a wonderful human being in spite of everything, Charlie.

Why forty-six?

Who knows? Apes have more than us.

Okay, so there's this monk in a cell, and he's swallowed forty-six worms. And Lo! the worms turn out to be long twisted ladders, and these ladders have the Book of Life written upon them in three-letter words, unto the billionth degree. But where do you go from there, Svetlana? How can you tell if that thing – Gibson points to the double helix, still tumbling on screen – is human?

The human genome's been mapped, Charlie, all three billion words. Vash tells me the signal has clusters within clusters and so on, and if we go to the right order of clusters we're down to the atoms, like one dot for hydrogen, twelve for carbon, sixteen for oxygen and so on. He thinks if we look at the right hierarchy of clustering – not too deep, not too shallow – we'll be at the molecular level and we'll be able to match it against the human genome. The human genome exists on the Web and we can access it. We've already started on that. We're trying to automate the comparison to save ourselves a few centuries' work.

So why aren't you getting on with it? I want to know if that thing's human or not. Freya, what have you found? And where the hell is Petrie?

Shtyrkov: Stop! Charlee, calm down. It's six o'clock and we're played out.

Gibson: Are you people forgetting what day this is? Thursday! Saturday's our last full day here and I want to announce this in London on Monday. Freya, I want a progress report today. Twelve noon.

6.01 a.m.   Gibson staggers off.

* * *

In the theological library, the sound of a vacuum cleaner brings Petrie back to the real world. A middle-aged woman, with jeans, sneakers and a yellow sweater, gives him a friendly nod as she swings the industrial strength machine over the long carpet.

He has problems standing up. Into the corridor. The castle is crawling with cleaning ladies, polishing, vacuuming, dusting, swarming, dissolving. The door to the computer room is closed and a sheet of paper sellotaped to it has *Cizim vstup zakázán* written in big Biro letters. The room is empty, the computers switched off, and not a scrap of paper in sight.

At the foot of the stairs, swaying on his feet, Petrie finds himself staring up at the north ridge of Kanchenjunga.

15

The Observer

The angel had Freya's face and long blonde hair, and its wings spanned the sky. It was scattering counters at amazing speed in geometric patterns over the numbers on the roulette table. There was something behind the pentagons and butterflies and intersecting doughnuts, some unifying concept trying to get out, but as Petrie's dream faded, the idea slipped frustratingly back into his unconscious mind. A bedside clock told him he had been asleep for four hours.

The corridor was deathly quiet. There were no cleaners, and his colleagues, he supposed, were still asleep. He had the entire Hapsburg castle to himself.

He took the stairs two at a time down to the first floor. Icy air was wafting along the corridor and he saw that the door to the terrace had blown open. He walked along to close it and was surprised to see footsteps on the thin powdery snow which had settled overnight on the terrace. Someone had crossed to the battlement wall, walked alongside it and turned back to the door. He followed the trail, looking over the parapet. There was nobody to be seen and no vehicles other than the blue Dormobile belonging to Gibson and his colleagues, snow-dusted and tucked in a corner. Tyre tracks in the snow were probably from the cleaners' van.

Something flickered at the corner of his eye and he looked sharply up at the high tower, but there was nobody. He shivered in the bleak January sunlight, damned his imagination and turned back into the warmth of the castle.

Fresh bread, milk, vegetables and assorted groceries were piled up on the kitchen table. He filled a kettle and put a couple of slices of bread into an electric toaster.

Fed and watered, and faintly resentful of the time it had taken up, he walked along the empty corridor towards the theological library, anxious to coax back the conjecture which had come and gone in his angel dream. He was surprised to see the door to the computer room slightly ajar.

And even more surprised to see a stranger, his back to the door, tapping at Svetlana's computer. Her notes were on the desk; the man had clearly been going through them.

'What the hell are you doing?'

The man turned. He was in his thirties, with brown hair greying at the edges, and a tanned skin which told of years spent someplace hot. Brown, slightly watery eyes assessed Petrie through wire-framed spectacles. When he stood up Petrie saw that the man was lean and muscular, the sort who ran four miles before breakfast. His voice was English public school and surprisingly deep: 'Going through the signal. Mind-blowing, isn't it? But it can't be for real.'

Petrie, taken aback, asked lamely, 'Who are you?'

'Hanning, Jeremy Hanning. And you must be Dr Petrie.' The man gave a carefully judged smile. 'I'm an observer for the Cabinet Office. I have to see what you're all up to and report to Lord Sangster by tomorrow evening. It's that simple.'

Warily, Petrie asked, 'How much of a briefing have you had?'

'The story is that you've been contacted by little green men.' He nodded towards the terminal and gave an isn't-it-silly smile.

'And you don't believe it. Does Lord Sangster?'

Hanning ignored the question. 'There are five of you here, am I right? Two British, two Russians and a Norwegian.'

'Yes. The original team was one Brit and two Russians. Freya Størmer and I were co-opted.'

'How do you get on with the Russians?'

'Fine.'

'No, ah . . . differences?' The man was studying Petrie closely. One eye, Petrie noticed, seemed slightly larger than the other, but he thought that might be due to a cold.

'None – why should there be? Look, how do I know you're not a journalist or something?'

More laughter, a touch too brittle. 'We'll phone Lord Sangster up, shall we? Let's use the video circuit.'

'First let's get the team awake. Forgive me, but I think we have to make a communal judgement about you.'

*　*　*

There was a long teak desk at the centre of the administrator's office. A black computer sat at the head of this desk, and a large video monitor sat atop the computer, and a wide-angle camera sat atop the monitor. Sangster's face appeared on the screen, nearly filling it, against a background of books.

'Simon Sangster here.'

Gibson sat at the opposite end of the table, facing the screen directly. 'Lord Sangster, this is Charles Gibson, principal investigator on the Dark Matter Project. Good morning, sir.'

Sangster returned the greeting with a nod.

'I have a Jeremy Hanning here. He tells me that you've sent him out to oversee the proceedings.'

'Oversee is too strong a word, Dr Gibson.' Sangster's face was expressionless; he was making no attempt to be friendly or encouraging.

'First, would you confirm that this is in fact Jeremy Hanning.' Gibson played with controls on a keyboard and the camera swivelled round to Hanning.

'Well, of course it's Jeremy. Who else would it be?'

'Thank you, sir.' Back to Gibson.

'Jeremy will assess the situation and report to me at nine o'clock tomorrow evening by the British clock. The main thing is to confirm that this is not some dreadful error and that you really have received an extraterrestrial signal. Have you identified the source?'

'We'll be working on that today.'

'And I understand you say the message contains information of a biological nature.'

'Yes.'

Petrie had a momentary, startling vision of Sangster as a calculating lizard. He put it down to a slight exophthalmic goitre coupled with deep eyelids. His lordship was saying, 'What sort of information?'

Gibson hesitated. 'We'll be working on that too.'

'I look forward to hearing from you tomorrow evening. Meantime, of course, security is everything.'

'Agreed.' Gibson hesitated again, licked his lips. Then: 'But I intend to make a public announcement on Monday, whatever stage we've reached in our investigation.'

Later, and many times over, Gibson was to wonder why he had said that. Perhaps, he would wonder, he was unconsciously striking a blow in an ancient battle, defending a culture of openness against one of secrecy. Even as he spoke he sensed that something was wrong. Hanning cleared his throat. Shtyrkov, across the desk from Gibson, put his head in his hands.

Sangster was silent for a moment. His tone was icy. 'That's not your decision, Dr Gibson.'

Gibson swallowed. 'Actually, it is. I'm the PI here.'

'The facility is, however, financed by Her Majesty through PPARC, which falls within my department.'

'You may finance it, Lord Sangster, but I run it.'

Damn it, Charlie, shut up. This is a disaster.

'You may think so, but the fact that I finance it means that I also run it. HMG has ultimate responsibility for work carried out on its behalf. And there are assuredly dimensions to this discovery going beyond mere scientific interest.'

Gibson said nothing, but his face was showing open hostility.

'Let's not dig ourselves into trenches, Dr Gibson. We must talk through the implications of this discovery before we make it public. It's in everyone's interests to get this right. Jeremy, nine o'clock tomorrow.'

*   *   *

'I won't be done out of this.' Gibson's face was black with anger. 'I'm not having this discovery announced by some bloody government minister.'

Svetlana, next to him, touched his shoulder in a gesture of sympathy.

'That's what's behind this,' Gibson continued angrily. 'Sangster wants to pre-empt the announcement.'

'For once I agree with you,' Shtyrkov said.

Svetlana said, 'So do I, Charlie. The announcement has to be made by the discoverer.'

'Which is me. PI's privilege.'

'But I put twelve years into this machine,' Svetlana said. 'I get a slice of the cake.'

'You do, Svetlana, of course you do.' Charlie looked across at Shtyrkov. 'We all do.'

Nobody mentioned that Hanning was excluded from the 'we'; it was too obvious to need mentioning.

Petrie said, 'You guys have been on this for years; I turned up two days ago. I don't deserve an equal share.'

'Tom, that's not right,' Shtyrkov said. 'Your contribution deserves full recognition. Without it, where would we be? Your name goes on as part of the team. So does Freya's.'

'I've contributed nothing yet,' said Freya.

'But you will.'

'I agree with Vashislav,' said Svetlana. 'We're in this together.'

'I feel a bit of a lemon here,' Hanning said.

'Nobody asked your opinion,' Gibson said in a sudden outburst of fury.

'Charlie,' Svetlana chided him gently.

'Mr Hanning, I'm sorry about this . . .'

'Jeremy, please.'

'Jeremy,' Petrie continued. 'But I wonder if you would leave us for a few minutes?'

'I'm here as an observer on the authority of the Cabinet Office.'

Petrie waited.

'But I suppose in the circumstances . . .'

The moment Hanning left, closing the conference door behind him with a click, Gibson spoke quietly and rapidly. 'Monday morning we announce this jointly. We follow the IAA protocols. I send e-mails to the Secretary General of the United Nations, IAU Commission 51, et cetera.'

Shtyrkov said, 'We should put it out on the internet. It will be round the globe in minutes. Whatever your position, Charlee, the British government cannot claim jurisdiction over me. I am a Russian. But not Monday,' he cautioned. 'They'll be expecting that. Maybe pre-emption is their game. Spring a surprise. Do it sooner.'

'Maybe their game is suppression,' Svetlana suggested. 'Maybe they don't want this information to get out.'

The anger in Gibson's face became tinged with bafflement. 'Why not? Where's the sense in that?'

She raised her hands. 'Who knows?'

'How could they suppress the secret?' Petrie asked. 'We all know about it.'

There was a sudden, tense silence.

Petrie said, 'Let's not get into fantasy here.'

. . . your adversary the devil, as a roaring lion, walketh about, seeking whom he may devour.

A warning, but of what and from whom?

Shtyrkov tapped the table emphatically. 'Suppression, pre-emption, whatever. We must beat them to it. Make the announcement sooner, Charlee. Today.'

Gibson said, 'When I go public with this I want to say the signal has come from Planet X or Star Y. Freya, how goes the identification?'

'I may or may not have identified the source. It's weird.'

'How long will it take you to get one hundred per cent certainty?'

'Never. But I'm weeding out the implausibles.'

'With or without identification, this goes into the public domain on Monday.'

'Today, Charlee. Don't give them time for mischief.'

'It's a balance, Vash. Give Freya a chance to come up with something.'

'I might – just – be able to decrypt more of the message,' Petrie said. 'I'll work on it today.'

Shtyrkov said, 'Svetlana, your job is distraction. Spend the day briefing this man from Her Majesty's Government. Tell him everything. Tell him anything. But keep him out of our hair.'

Svetlana said, 'Shall I wear fishnet tights?'

16

The Whirlpool Galaxy

'Tom! Tom! It's Vashislav.'

The bedside lamp was shining in Petrie's face. He waved Freya ahead and pulled on clothes, slipping his feet into shoes without tying the laces. He wondered if he was destined ever to sleep again, but the urgency in Freya's voice said there were other priorities.

Until he saw the Russian, Petrie had always assumed that 'foaming at the mouth', as a description of a man gone mad, was populist nonsense. But flecks of white frothy foam were dribbling out of the corners of Shtyrkov's mouth. He was in the main hall, arms flapping, an idiot grin lighting up his face. He was running from one chandelier to the next, shouting and laughing in Russian, staring up at them in adoration. Svetlana was standing at the foot of the stairs, long yellow nightdress hanging under her red robe and her face screwed up in distress.

The Russian saw Petrie, pointed to the chandeliers and called up in English, 'Look at the pretty lights!' His eyes were starting to roll.

'How long has he been like this?'

Svetlana said, 'I don't know. I heard him singing half an hour ago but didn't think it was anything at first. I've been up for ten minutes. I've tried to stop him but he just keeps going.'

'He'll collapse,' Freya said. 'Nobody can keep that up.'

Tears of happiness were welling from Shtyrkov's eyes; his voice was enraptured but he was gasping for breath. 'Aren't they beautiful, Tom and Freya? Are we not in Paradise?'

'Vash.' Petrie stepped forward. 'Come to bed.' But Shtyrkov giggled and ran off like a naughty child, wheezing and foaming.

'Where are the light switches?' Petrie called back to Svetlana.

'Round here.' She switched them off.

In the sudden pitch black, Shtyrkov's footsteps halted, as if he too had been switched off. Petrie moved in the direction of the man's rasping breath, took him by the arm, and led him back towards the stairs. Shtyrkov was trembling, and whimpering quietly.

* * *

'Temporal lobe damage. It affects perceptions.'

'Are you sure, Freya?'

'Not even fifty per cent sure. All I can say is that it fits the profile I got on the internet.'

'Vashislav ran into the thick of the beam when it was hitting the lake.'

'Is it reversible, progressive or what?' It was just after noon but Petrie was at breakfast: a biscuit, which he was dipping into his second coffee. He hadn't bothered to shave.

'I don't know. Some people say Van Gogh had temporal lobe epilepsy, that it maybe even accounts for the intensity of his paintings. Colours are brighter, everything is seen more vividly. And Vashislav seems to love glittering things.'

'How can a particle beam do that? If it was disrupting cells it would surely have fried his whole brain.'

Freya said, 'It usually needs a lesion, but there were thin, concentrated pencil beams in the flow. And maybe it's more subtle than that. A powerful magnetic field applied to the brain can play tricks.'

'If you say so.'

'You don't understand, Tom, you're a creature of mid-latitude. Your body is synchronised with the rhythms of light. But in polar latitudes we're more sensitive to the effects of strong geomagnetic disturbances. We don't understand how, but there's a clear connection between things like Russian mine accidents and strong magnetic disturbances up top. It's been established by the polar geophysics people at Murmansk. They do upper atmosphere.'

Petrie said, 'The particles were surely non-magnetic, otherwise the underwater magnets would have distorted their paths.'

'Unless they carried so much energy that not even forty thousand gauss could divert them,' Freya suggested.

'That's surely incredible,' Petrie said.

'It's testable, Tom. The ionosphere is charged up. If you fired charged particles through the Earth you'd create a short-circuit between ionosphere and ground. At the very least you'd get disturbances in radio or radar. You might even get weird cloud effects through nucleation around the beam.'

'What about Charlie and Svetlana?' Petrie wondered.

'They were either on the periphery of the particle flow or they missed it altogether. I haven't seen anything odd about them yet, Tom, have you?'

'They're both odd. But what other symptoms might we see? Assuming it's this temporal lobe thing.'

'All sorts. Anxiety, visceral symptoms, feelings of fear or anger, destructive or aggressive behaviour, out-of-body experiences, you see tunnels, bright lights and so on. Sometimes you get an overwhelming sensation that there's someone near you. You might even see a face, and extreme character traits appear. Some people get religious hallucinations.'

'At least Vash isn't claiming to be Jesus or something. Will you tell him what you suspect?'

Freya said, 'Not until after the ET announcement. Let's not spoil his moment of glory.'

'We should keep an eye on the other two.'

* * *

Shtyrkov was last to appear, mid-afternoon. He showed no obvious after-effects, and made no mention of the trauma he had been through in the early hours. Petrie wondered if the Russian even remembered it. They settled themselves around a table in a bar next to the common room. Gibson stared greedily at a folder of papers Freya was holding.

Hanning said, 'Dr Popov gave me a very thorough briefing. I must say I'm having difficulty taking it in.'

Gibson ignored him; Freya was the focus of their attention. 'Friday afternoon, Freya. What have you got for us?'

'I've narrowed the source down to two possibles, depending on whether the particles came down through the lake from above, or up from below. Here's candidate number one.' She spread a large image on the table.

There was an assortment of gasps from everyone. Petrie's mind began to race. Two blue, feathery arms spiralled out of a reddish-white nucleus. The arms were lined with dark lanes. One of them, with little outcrops striking off, extended as a long bridge to a smaller, outlying galaxy. 'M51, in Canes Venatici, not too many degrees from the north galactic pole. It's just below the Plough.'

'M51? The Whirlpool galaxy?' Gibson's tone was awed.

'The Whirlpool. A bright open-arm spiral, part of a little group of galaxies. It's over thirty million light years away. Specifically, the signal came from this region here.' Freya used a pencil to circle a small area at the edge of the nucleus, where one of the spiral arms was just breaking away. 'It's rich in Population II stars, with lots of red and yellow dwarfs about ten billion years old. Twice the age of the Sun.'

'But that's—'

'If the signal came from here, Charlie, it set out thirty million years ago, long before Homo sapiens existed. Before there were even primates.'

'Don't be daft,' Gibson said. 'How could they signal us if we didn't even exist when they fired off their message? Anyway, no life forms could survive next to the nucleus of a galaxy. What's your second candidate?'

Freya spread out a second celestial image. The scientists gazed in bewilderment at a near-blank patch of sky. 'This is in a small constellation called Phoenix, in the southern sky. With the huge number of particles that flowed in I can place the source to sub-arcsecond accuracy. If the particles came up from below, they came from here.' She pencilled a small circle of black emptiness. A faint star sat just outside the circle.

'Empty space?'

'This chart goes down to magnitude thirteen. But we're looking at a very quiet bit of sky, well away from the Milky Way. In fact, almost in the direction of the south galactic pole.'

'What does that mean?'

'It means there are probably no more than a handful of stars within the sight cone. At a guess they'll be red and white dwarfs with very low luminosities, maybe a halo star or two. But basically we're looking at an empty region of sky.'

'What about this star?' Gibson pointed to the little dot near the edge of Freya's pencilled circle.

'Nu Phoenicis. A late F dwarf, F8 V to be exact, fifty light years from us.'

'That's close. Can you rule it out?'

'Not absolutely. But it's unlikely.'

'Excuse me,' Hanning interrupted, 'but what's a late F dwarf?'

'A Sun-like star,' said Freya. 'Just slightly hotter. It's likely to have planets around it. But as I say, it's just outside the error circle.'

Gibson sighed and leaned back. 'So what do I tell the world's press? And the Prime Minister and the Secretary General of the United Nations? That the signal came from empty space?'

'No,' Freya said, 'you tell them that it came from the Whirlpool galaxy.'

Hanning said, 'Forgive me, but I thought Lord Sangster had made it clear. You don't tell anyone about this without his clearance.'

Gibson didn't bother to conceal his hostility. 'You're here to observe, not lay down the law.'

Hanning bristled, but said nothing.

Shtyrkov said, 'It has to be the Whirlpool.'

Gibson shook his head. 'No. It's clearly the F star. I take your point about the error circle, Freya, but it's not that far beyond the edge. The star's a dwarf, Sun-like. It's practically our next-door neighbour. And another thing: it's at the right distance. Think about it. The first radio signals were leaked from the Earth a hundred years ago. As soon as the first radio waves from us reached them, fifty years ago, they knew we were here, knew we were technological. They immediately fired off their signal and it has just reached us now. It fits like a glove.'

Shtyrkov said, 'Two intelligence-bearing systems that we know of, us and them, a mere fifty light years apart? The Galaxy would have to be crawling with life.'

Gibson's thin lips crimped in annoyance. 'If that's what it takes.'

Hanning cleared his throat. 'I have a little experience in these matters and I must say I agree with Dr Gibson. In politics, you can't approach a minister with ifs and buts. An air of certainty counts. You need to present a united front.'

'Why?' Petrie asked. 'Why not properly reflect the scientific uncertainties?'

'It looks bad. It conveys an air of dithering, even incompetence. Given the bizarre nature of your claim, it might suggest to some that you are – forgive me – the victims of delusion or, worse, perpetrators of fraud.'

'That is outrageous.'

Hanning gave a cold smile. 'Welcome to the big bad world, Dr Petrie.'

Gibson said, 'That's what I've been saying all along. We'd lose the drama, and we could even lose credibility. We must agree on the source of the signal.'

'And if we can't?'

'Hell, Tom, we can at least look as if we do. We're about to enter a political arena and sniping at the margins will just cause damage. We need a united front for the announcement, even if you have to put on an act for the occasion, okay? As team leader I expect you all to back me up.'

'What, on the F star?' Dismay and scorn mingled in Shtyrkov's voice.

'It seems to me the evidence is crystal clear on this. The signallers are on a small, Earth-like planet orbiting the star. It's either that, or the signal was sent to us thirty million years before we existed.'

'We can't go public with the F star, Charlee. It's outside the error circle. You'll wreck our credibility.'

'What else is there? The Whirlpool? Do you expect me to face the press and tell them it's the Whirlpool galaxy thirty million light years away?'

Svetlana, who had been sitting quietly throughout the discussion, finally broke her silence. Hesitantly, she said, 'I'm sorry if this is a dumb question, but how could an alien civilisation possibly know about our underground lake?'

17

We Have a Problem

'I can explain that.' Gibson's voice had a triumphant edge to it. 'Vashislav said it himself. Two civilisations so close together can't be a coincidence. Well, let's follow the logic. If he's right – if I'm right about the F star – there must be a Galactic club out there. Millions, maybe billions, of civilisations talking to each other. That means a gigantic telephone network to go with it, particle flows criss-crossing everywhere. We just happened to drift across one of their lines of communication. The signal was just a lucky intercept.'

Shtyrkov put his hands on top of his head and frowned in concentration for some seconds. Then, 'Charlee, here are two experiments for you. Number one: let a fly loose in a cathedral, blindfold yourself, and fire a pistol in any direction, preferably not at your head. Number two: put Lake Tatras out there somewhere in the Galaxy, even just halfway to the nearest star, and fire a signal in a random direction. Let me tell you this: you'd stand a better chance of hitting the fly in the cathedral than the lake in the Galaxy.'

Petrie was scribbling on paper. He looked up and said, 'Vashislav is right. The chances of a random interception, even with a big galactic club, everyone chattering to everyone else, are too slim for words.'

Gibson said, 'Use your common sense. How can aliens know about an experiment in an underground lake?'

Freya said, 'I can prove that they do.'

The physicist gave Freya the floor with an ironic flourish.

She unconsciously flicked hair back over a shoulder and then itemised the points with her fingers. 'First. At the latitude of Lake Tatras we're spinning at fourteen hundred kilometres an hour round the Earth's axis. Second. The Earth's orbiting the Sun at thirty kilometres a second. Three. The Sun's drifting at thirteen kilometres a second through our neighbouring stars, us along with it. And Four. Our neighbourhood, millions of stars in it, is orbiting the centre of our Galaxy at two hundred kilometres a second.'

Shtyrkov said, 'Of course, Freya. Seen from even a light year away, the lake isn't just a tiny target, it's a fast-moving one.'

Freya nodded. 'And the signal corrected for all these movements. It matched the lake's speed through space with great precision.'

'What's your point?' Gibson asked curtly.

Freya tapped her calculations. 'Admit to error, Charlie. Whoever fired that signal knew about your underground cave and targeted it.'

'Oh yes, of course they did,' Gibson said, his face flushing. 'Naturally they have telescopes that detect underground lakes from light years away and they even know we've set up an experiment under the water waiting for a signal. In fact, they knew we were going to set it up before we knew it ourselves – and if you believe this M51 rubbish, they knew we were going to do that before we even existed!'

'I don't claim to have any sort of background in science,' said the Science Minister's envoy, 'but that would seem to be a problem.'

'Indeed, Jeremy. And here's another problem. How do I face the world's press on Monday and sell them a garbage tale like that without being carted off screaming to the nearest paddy wagon by men in white coats?'

* * *

'Jeremy?'

Petrie, in quiet conversation with Freya on a sofa, caught the unctuous tone of Gibson's voice. He glanced across. The physicist was leaning over Hanning, charm oozing out of his face and looking like a benevolent frog.

Hanning looked up from his scribbled notes in surprise. 'Yes, ah, Charlie?'

'Time is short.' The computer clocks were reading just after three o'clock. 'I thought you might lend us a hand.'

Hanning glanced down at his notes. 'Sangster is looking for a situation report at nine p.m. Still, I can spare some time. But be warned, I have no specialised knowledge, at least not in science.'

'We need help with Svetlana's viruses, if that's what they are.'

'There are thousands of them,' Svetlana said without looking up from her screen.

Gibson pushed his spectacles back to the bridge of his nose. 'There are also thousands of terrestrial viruses. I was wondering if you might like to try to match them up. There are pictures of them on websites.'

'It's a big job,' Svetlana said. 'For instance, there are things called pico-rna-viridae, and they're divided into five genera – entero-, rhino-, aphto-, cardio- and unassignedo-viruses. If you take the rhinovirus it's divided into human and bovine, and if you take the human it has a hundred serotypes. And these are just the small RNA viruses; there are thousands more.'

Hanning looked blank. 'RNA viruses?'

'Forget them,' Shtyrkov called over. 'They change by the year. Any signal representing them would refer to viruses which have evolved beyond recognition. In fact, this is a big problem, people. Any picture beamed to us from far away and long ago should refer to micro-organisms which no longer exist. E. coli reproduces so fast it can mutate as much in a day as humanity does in a thousand years.'

Svetlana sighed. 'There's another problem. We're all desperately ignorant about this and we're running out of time.'

Charlie said, 'So work harder. I want us to learn as much as we possibly can about this signal before we go public with it.'

'I've told you about going public without authorisation, Charlie.'

'I know.' Gibson's cheek twitched nervously. 'You're just being asked to match pictures. Any idiot could do it.'

Hanning said, 'Have you ever thought about a career in the Diplomatic Service?'

'I'm sorry, I—'

Hanning laughed. 'Of course I'll help. Let's see if these things are earthly.'

Gibson sighed with relief, and promptly exited from his unctuous mode. 'Svetlana, you still haven't told me if that thing is human.' He turned to Shtyrkov, who was lying back on another sofa, staring at the ceiling. 'Vashislav, are you a waste of space or what?'

The Russian waved a dismissive arm in the air. 'I'm meditating.'

'What the hell use is that? And what about you two?' Gibson wanted to know. Freya and Petrie were heading for the door. 'Don't tell me you people are meditating too?'

'I'll be in the theological library,' Petrie said.

'Good, good. More decoding, Tom?'

'No, I'll be looking for a Bible. I expect the theological library has one.'

Gibson's face showed bafflement. 'What in God's name has the Bible got to do with anything?'

18

Visions of God

Petrie heard the footsteps hurrying behind him in the broad corridor. Freya. She caught him by the arm and sat him firmly down on the velvet sofa. 'Don't be so secretive, Tom. What are you up to?'

He shook his head. 'It's too embarrassing to say.'

'Tell me anyway.'

'Look, it's too silly, Freya. Let's just say I'm off on some eccentric tangent and leave it at that.'

She nipped his thigh viciously. Petrie, taken by surprise, yelped.

'Tom!'

Petrie hesitated, then: 'Okay, okay. Look at the position. There's no way for others to confirm this signal – it's a one-off. Hanning's right, credibility *is* an issue. And if we make a wrong identification we'll lose it.'

Freya nodded impatiently. 'But we're all agreed on that.'

'Charlie's fixated on the F star. The timing's right, like he says.'

'But Tom, it lies outside the two-sigma error circle. There's only one chance in twenty that he's right.'

'You know that and I know that, Freya, but Charlie's an idiot and he's going to blow it.'

'So, what is this silly idea?'

Petrie hesitated again. Freya looked threatening, and he said, 'I might be able to disprove his timing argument. Suppose they've been probing us for centuries. Say they've been firing at us routinely, maybe even for thousands of years, to see if we've reached a level where we can understand and reply with our sticks and stones, like radio or lasers.'

Freya nodded.

'In that case there might be evidence in historical records.'

Another encouraging nod.

In a burst of bravado he added, 'Maybe even pre-history or mythology. Lights in the sky, things like that.'

Freya pursed her lips. 'That *is* embarrassing. It's unprofessional, like looking for flying saucers or something.'

Petrie flushed.

She grinned. 'But brilliant. History should have a record of glowing patterns in water, maybe even in heavy clouds. I'll join you.'

In the theological library, Freya made straight for the computer terminal and fired it up. Petrie started with an illuminated Bible on a lectern, its pages laboriously written in calligraphic script in some past century. Its preface began with an enormous letter, made up of little fantasy animals with a swastika-like cross in the middle. He could just recognise it as an uncial *D*, and barely make out the ornate lettering: *Dominus Deus noster Jesus Christus* . . .

He blew out his cheeks. This was going to take years. More prowling the shelves revealed more Bibles, all in Latin. His hopes rose with an illustrated book on *Mirabili*. Perusal showed that the book described miracles indeed, if two-headed babies, statues weeping blood and winged basilisks could be believed.

He clattered up the spiral staircase. After some minutes, tucked in a corner, he found a shelf of modest-sized Bibles, in assorted vulgar tongues-including English. He guessed this was the modern collection, grudgingly acknowledging the existence of the last three centuries or so. He pulled out a St James edition; its leather binding, he thought, was less than a century old, but the font and the feel of the pages told of something printed maybe three hundred years ago. It had a musty smell and he playfully wondered if the plague bacillus could survive for three hundred years.

Apart from the one at Heathrow chapel, Petrie hadn't looked at a Bible since his school days and had no more than the vaguest memory of the contents. He was dismayed to find that there were a thousand pages. He clattered down the staircase, sat himself at a table, and started on them systematically, speed-reading.

Two hours later, bleary-eyed and head spinning, he was practically through the Bible, and was beginning to think his memory had played tricks, when he came across the first nugget.

* * *

I was in the spirit on the Lord's day, and heard behind me a great voice, as of a trumpet.
Revelation 1:10

And immediately I was in the spirit: and behold, a throne was set in heaven, and one sat on the throne. And he that sat was to look upon like a jasper and a sardine stone: and there was a rainbow round about the throne, in sight like unto an emerald.
Revelation 4:2–3

So he carried me away in the spirit into the wilderness:
and I saw a woman sit upon a scarlet coloured beast,
full of names of blasphemy, having seven heads and
ten horns.
Revelation 17:3

* * *

'What are you getting at, Tom?'

'Don't you see? The prophet is describing celestial
visions, weird things in the sky. Okay, it's overlaid with
imagery but he sees them "in the spirit". What does it
mean, *in the spirit*? He repeats it all the way through the
Book of Revelation. Was he in some sort of trance? An
altered state of consciousness?'

'High on Ecstasy?' Freya suggested.

Petrie ignored the interruption. 'And look at what he's
raving about. Bright things, shiny things, glittering things
like emeralds. What does he mean, *a rainbow round about
the throne, in sight like unto an emerald*?' Petrie was still
flicking through the pages. 'Here's another one. Listen to
this:

And he carried me away in the spirit to a great and
high mountain, and shewed me that great city, the
holy Jerusalem, descending out of heaven from God.
Having the glory of God: and her light was like unto
a stone most precious, even like a jasper stone, clear
as crystal.
Revelation 21:10–11

'More shiny precious stones, more "in the spirit". This
guy's describing Shtyrkov's syndrome. Temporal lobe
damage. The signal makes you mad.'

Freya made a sceptical face. 'That is a monstrous speculation.' Her voice deepened by an octave at the word 'monstrous'.

But Petrie's eyes were shining with enthusiasm. 'No, it fits perfectly. The writer's an astral prophet. He has a cast of thousands, the Beast rising over the sea, the Dragon, the throne in the sky, the plague of celestial locusts, falling stars, centaurs, the abyss, the temple in the sky . . .'

'Tom . . .'

'The seventh seal marks the return of seven comets, trumpet-shaped. The four horsemen of the apocalypse are comets, streaming their manes across the sky. Don't you see? He's describing the sky and things that have taken place in the sky. And if that's right, Freya, if they're all celestial phenomena, then they include a glowing sky, complete with the temporal lobe stuff. You must see that!'

'No, Tom, I *don't* see it, not even remotely. In fact, I'm beginning to wonder if you've had a touch of the magnetic fields yourself.'

Petrie blinked in frustration. 'They've been sending us signals at least since the time of pastoral societies. They've been probing us for at least two thousand years.'

'Ruling out Charlie's F star?'

'Yes. But more than that, anyone watching the Earth would know there was no technological civilisation capable of understanding the message. Sending sub-nuclear particle messages to sheep-farming societies is not the behaviour of an intelligence.'

'What, then?' Freya's brow was furrowed.

'A probe. An automated probe. Something set up to run by itself. Something waiting for a response, maybe for thousands of years.'

'You keep talking about probes, probing us.'

'Charlie and you are both wrong. It's not the M51 galaxy and it's not the F star. I think it's empty space. Only the space isn't empty – it has a machine, something orbiting the Sun. Something that fires off bursts at us from time to time. It has to be close because it knows our geography and our rotation and all the rest. But it'll stay dormant until we send it a reply.'

Freya frowned. 'Tom, if that's right, it needn't be thirty million light years away or even three light years away. Its distance could be anything.' She stood up, and paced up and down in thought. Then: 'There's another clue. Whichever of the two directions it came from, it's well away from the ecliptic.'

'Meaning?'

'It's not orbiting in the plane of the planets, or the asteroids, or the Edgeworth-Kuiper belt. It could be out in the Oort cloud.'

'The what?'

'A cloud of comets orbiting the Sun far beyond the planets, where the Sun's gravity is very weak. The comets just barely hang on to the solar system. You could have something the size of the Moon out there and you'd never detect it.'

'What's the travel time of a signal from the Oort cloud?'

'A few months. A few weeks from the inner cloud.'

'Do you see what that means, Freya?'

Freya was tight-lipped. 'Of course. The galactic club isn't something for our distant descendants. We could be members by this summer.'

'An automated probe. An automated probe.' Petrie began to pace up and down, his head bowed.

Freya, struck by a sudden thought, cupped her hands over her mouth. 'There's more.'

Petrie stopped.

She paused to gather her thoughts. Then, 'Okay. If there's a probe targeting us then it's somewhere in the solar system otherwise it would just zip by. But if it's too close it wouldn't last. If you injected something into an orbit between the planets, the chances are it would be thrown around chaotically by the gravitational fields of Jupiter and Saturn and end up falling into the Sun or being thrown out of the solar system altogether.'

'How long would that take?'

'It depends on the orbit, but you'd be okay for typically a few millennia to a few hundred millennia. There are stable zones inside the asteroid belt but they're crowded and anything in them eventually gets hit by something moving at kilometres per second. If the signallers have put a robot probe well clear of the ecliptic plane – well away from the planets – they've been planning for longevity.'

Petrie's mouth opened and shut with astonishment. 'But you're talking millions of years.'

'It looks like it. We're so used to thinking in short time spans, I suppose because our civilisation is only a few thousand years old.'

To Freya, Petrie's round spectacles were making him look like a surprised owl. 'I'm beginning to understand this. In fact . . .' his voice trailed off.

'Well?'

'No, it can't be.'

'Do you want another nip?'

Petrie shook his head. 'I'm sorry, Freya, you just wouldn't grasp it.'

Freya gaped. 'You conceited . . .'

'No, no. It just needs a lot more thought. I can hardly take it in myself.'

136

'Tom, come down to earth. Ancient texts can be interpreted in a hundred ways. We need something more concrete.'

* * *

An hour later, Freya looked up from the terminal screen. Petrie was still at the table, reading the Bible and scribbling rapidly. There was an excited sparkle in her eyes. 'I think I've struck gold.'

19

The Wheels of Poseidon

Around 6 p.m., Svetlana walked into the library. She could hardly control the excitement in her voice. 'We think it may be human.'

Freya looked up in surprise. 'Are you sure?'

'It's not flatworm or fruit-fly, and it's not ape. So far we can't tell any difference from human DNA. But there's something odd. I don't know if there's an error in Tom's computer code – where is he?'

Petrie hailed her from the gallery.

'Tom,' Svetlana called up, 'if your code is okay, there's something extra. Vash is finding dot patterns that stand outside the mainstream. Some bits of the helix may be labelled.'

'Surely they're just stray particles?'

'Vash thinks not. Sometimes the patterns stand near particular genes and the same patterns are found next to other pictures, like maybe molecules. He thinks they're markers – he calls them flags. He reckons there's a breakthrough waiting to happen, and he says you need to get back to it right away.'

'Tell him I'm studying for the priesthood. He'll have to do his own decoding.'

'And I'm busy in the kitchen,' Svetlana told him.

'Making more *pyzy*?'

'Doing overtime as a femme fatale. Hanning and I are cooking. And Charlie has a plan. He wants to talk to you all in the bar, now.'

* * *

Shtyrkov was standing with his nose pressed up against the steel mesh grill which protected the bar. At first Petrie thought the Russian was wondering how to get at the dazzling array of bottles; but then he saw the little reflections of chandelier in the polished glasses.

'Vodka withdrawal symptoms?' Gibson asked the Russian. Gibson himself, Petrie noted, was showing no sign of mental abnormality outside the envelope of a stressed-out scientist.

Shtyrkov turned and sat heavily in a chair, and Petrie and Freya sat on either side of him.

Gibson remained standing, a general briefing his troops. He looked at his watch pretentiously. 'For those of you who've lost track it's now six o'clock, Friday evening. Here's the schedule. Tomorrow, Saturday, is our last full day on site. We're out of here at noon on Sunday. We drive straight to Bratislava: I've booked us all on a six o'clock flight to London. At nine a.m. Monday we hold a press conference in Burlington House. Vashislav and Svetlana then fly to Moscow. After that, events will sweep us along.'

'What about Hanning?' Petrie asked.

'I was coming to that. I don't trust him. He knows we'll be going for a public announcement but I want him told it will now take place next Wednesday. We just vanish on Sunday at noon.'

They had automatically adopted a conspiratorial tone, as if Hanning could hear through castle walls from the floor below. 'Wisdom comes with age, Charlee. Not always, and in your case probably not at all, but meantime you would be wise to listen to Papa. And what I say is this. *Don't wait*. Put the news out on the internet tonight – all the bulletin boards we can think of. And send a message signed by us all to the UN Secretary General. It will be midday in New York.'

'No, Vash, we need the press conference first. There'll be questions and we must be on the spot to answer them.'

'You're taking a grave risk, Charlee.' Petrie had never seen Shtyrkov more serious; he wondered what was lying at the back of the Russian's mind.

Gibson said, 'Come on, Vash, this thing's unstoppable.'

* * *

'Come through, children. Let us hear what Tom and Freya have found. Bring your coffees if you wish.' Shtyrkov was standing at the refectory door like a teacher summoning his pupils. There was a rattle of chairs.

Petrie had found a screen, an overhead projector and a heap of transparencies in a cupboard in the administrator's office, and had heaved them up to the common room. There was a large Bible next to the projector. The scientists spread themselves around armchairs, and Svetlana killed the lights.

Freya sat on the edge of a desk, holding a scribbled transparency. The projector threw her face into harsh contrast. 'They've been signalling us for centuries.'

Gibson gave a loud, sceptical snort.

'Most of this has come from a journal called the *Marine Observer*. Look at this.' She threw up the first transparency:

September 6th, 1977. The merchant vessel *Wild Curlew*, in the north-west Indian Ocean, approached

what seemed at first to be a white sea fog. On entering
the region it was found that the sea itself was glowing
with a milky light. This light seemed also to hover
above the surface of the water. It was so strong that it
illuminated the clouds overhead.
Marine Observer, vol. 48, p.118, 1977

'It's what you saw in your lake. There are lots of reports
like that.' She thumbed through some papers: '. . . like
sailing over a field of snow . . . gliding over the clouds . . .
an intense white glow not unlike viewing the negative of a
photograph . . .'

Gibson was shaking his head. 'Come off it, Freya!'

'I was in Micronesia once,' Hanning said. 'We went
swimming in the dark, which maybe wasn't a good idea in
those waters. But I remember it well. The water lit up as
we swam. We left a luminous trail. It was a wonderful
experience.'

'Exactly,' Gibson said. 'Simple bioluminescence.
Plankton firing up.'

'It's not plankton.' A stubborn tone was creeping into
Freya's voice. 'This is from the Captain's log, on board the
merchantman *Ebani*. He's in the North Atlantic at the
time.' She threw up the transparency:

March 18th, 1977. Spurious echoes have been appearing on the screen all day, like the echoes from small
groups of fishing boats. Their behaviour is very
strange. The echoes would close to within five
nautical miles of us and then disappear. None of us
has ever come across this before. Disappeared late
afternoon.

2200. The echoes have returned. They came back, closed to within 5.5 n.m., and then spread out around the ship in a circle. The entire sea has taken on a milky appearance and there is a fishy smell. We are all quite unnerved by this.

2400. After 45 minutes, the milky sea disappeared, and the radar returned to normal.

Petrie said, 'Plankton can't generate spurious echoes in a ship's radar.'

Gibson responded irritably. 'I'm not persuaded, Tom. The dodgy radar could have been a coincidence.'

Shtyrkov snorted from a dark corner of the room. 'Coincidence, the last refuge of the disappointed scientist.'

Freya said, 'There's more. Are you ready for this? August the fourth, 1977. In the Indian Ocean—'

Svetlana interrupted: 'Five months after the *Ebani* report.'

Freya read aloud from the big screen:

The SS *British Renown* sailed into a large area of milky sea, which was glowing from within. So great was the intensity of this light that the deck appeared to be just a dark shadow. During the display, the humidity seemed to increase and' – *Freya ran her hand along the text* – 'the radio operator reported a decreased signal strength at medium and high frequencies.

'Something is traversing the atmosphere, disturbing it electrically as it passes, and lighting up the ocean.'

'Charlee probably thinks it's another coincidence,' Shtyrkov called over from his corner. 'Right, Charlee?'

'The hell with you, Vash.'

'Throw up the *Wild Curlew* again,' Svetlana asked. Freya did so. Svetlana said, 'They're saying the phosphorescence was *above* the surface of the water.'

Freya nodded. 'That's a common feature in these reports.'

'Maybe Charlie's plankton have wings.'

Freya said, 'More likely there are enough water molecules just above the waves to glow when the particles pass through.'

Gibson said, 'Rubbish.'

Freya said, 'Explain this one, Charlie. This is from someone on board a ship in the Java Sea on May the twenty-ninth 1955. Ten past two in the morning.'

My first impression was that the ship was being attacked on all sides from different directions by pulsing light-bands, about 2 metres wide and 2 apart and moving at speed. The most intense activity was observed on the starboard side of the ship where the phenomenon stretched as far as the horizon. It was just a mass of high-speed interacting bands of light.

About this time, the ship passed a localised revolving system, distance off about 150 metres. My impression was that of a catherine wheel revolving and casting out waves in an angular motion. How many spokes it had I'm not sure owing to the speed of the pulsations. The system rotated in a clockwise direction wheeling itself along the ship's track.

'Maybe the plankton were disturbed by fish moving in tight circles,' Gibson suggested. There was a shriek of laughter from Shtyrkov's dark corner.

Freya picked up another transparency. 'What were the fish doing here, Charlie?'

October 13, 1996, Arabian Gulf. The tanker *Arabiyah*. Expanding phosphorescent rings were observed emanating from a single point. The rings were equally spaced and expanded outwards for about 500 metres before disappearing. Rings with spoke systems also formed, rotating clockwise. The observers had the distinct impression that the rings were above the sea surface.

'You'll find this report in the *Marine Observer* volume 67, page 192, 1997.'

'Freya, are you serious?' Gibson asked. 'Do you really expect me to believe these are ET signals?'

Freya gave Gibson the sweet smile which, Petrie was beginning to learn, preceded the verbal equivalent of a right hook.

'Okay, Charlie, I'd like to hear your explanation of this report. It happened on April the twenty-ninth, 1982, in the China Sea.' She threw up the transparency and read the words aloud.

The merchant vessel *Siam* encountered parallel phosphorescent bands rushing towards it at about 40 miles an hour. The bands were 50–100 cm above the surface of the sea. The bands then changed into two rotating wheels. The spokes stretched to the horizon. Then a third wheel formed. Then there was nothing for about 20 minutes and then the whole thing restarted with four systems of parallel bands which soon metamorphosed into four rotating wheels. Next, circular, flashing brilliant blue-white light appeared all around the ship out to about 150 metres. This system of patches flashed at 114 times per minute. Water samples revealed no luminous organisms.

The sea was calm, visibility excellent, but atmospheric electrical activity could be seen all around.

'You'll find that in the *Marine Observer* again. Volume 53, page 85, 1983,' she said. 'Now look at this. This is from a review paper by a couple of marine biologists. The reference is Herring and Watson, *Marine Observer*, volume 63, page 22, 1993.' There was a slightly triumphant tone as she read the text on the screen.

Most bioluminescent organisms flash briefly and cannot generate the strong steady glow of the milky sea. Marine bacteria glow steadily but unrealistic concentrations of bacteria would be needed to generate the observed light, and in any case samples retrieved from the affected waters show no such bacteria.

She turned. 'There's no known explanation for the glowing seas. It's an acknowledged mystery.'

'Put that in your pipe, Charlie,' Petrie said. 'And anyway, how could bioluminescence affect radio and radar? Given what you saw in the Tatras, what else can these patterns be but repeated probings of the Earth?'

Gibson grunted, an unwilling mule. 'How far back do these marine reports go?'

Freya said, 'I have them back to June 1854. South of Java, a Captain Kingman of the American clipper *Shooting Star* reported—'

'Okay. There were no subnuclear facilities to target in 1854. I guess that weakens the case for the F star, Freya and Tom.'

The relief was almost palpable. Freya mock-curtsied. 'A gracious acknowledgement, Charlie.'

'They're probing, but they don't know we're here,' Petrie said. 'Yet.'

Gibson nodded. 'But I still don't buy the Whirlpool. That leaves us guessing: where did the signal come from? What do I tell the media? That the signal came from empty space?'

'Not just the media, Charlie. Your scientific colleagues, your government and the United Nations,' Svetlana chided him.

Petrie said, 'I think they've been probing for thousands of years. Minimum.'

'Do you have evidence for that, Tom, or are you off on a flight of fancy?'

Petrie walked to the projector; the machine reflected brightly in his round spectacle lenses. Freya shared Shtyrkov's couch at the back of the room. Petrie opened the big Bible and cleared his throat. Gibson said, 'My God,' and Petrie started to read.

Now it came to pass in the thirtieth year, in the fourth month, in the fifth day of the month, as I was among the captives by the river of Chebar, that the heavens were opened, and I saw visions of God.

And I looked, and, behold, a whirlwind came out of the north, a great cloud, and a fire infolding itself, and a brightness was about it.

And out of the midst thereof came the likeness of four living creatures. And this was their appearance; they had the likeness of a man.

And every one had four faces, and every one had four wings.

Their wings were joined to one another; they turned not when they went; they went every one straight forward.

As for the likeness of the living creatures, their appearance was like burning coals of fire, and like the appearance of lamps: it went up and down among the living creatures; and the fire was bright, and out of the fire went forth lightning.

And the living creatures ran and returned as the appearance of a flash of lightning.

As for their rings, they were so high that they were dreadful; and their rings were full of eyes round about them four.

And when the living creatures went, the wheels went by them; and when the living creatures were lifted up from the earth, the wheels were lifted up: for the spirit of the living creature was in the wheels.

Then I looked, and, behold, in the firmament that was above the head of the cherubim there appeared over them as it were a sapphire stone, as the appearance of the likeness of a throne.

And when I looked, behold the four wheels by the cherubim, one wheel by one cherub, and another wheel by another cherub: and the appearance of the wheels was as the colour of a beryl stone.

And as for their appearances, they four had one likeness, as if a wheel had been in the midst of a wheel.

And their whole body, and their backs, and the wheels, were full of eyes round about, even the wheels that they four had.

This is the living creature that I saw under the God of Israel by the river of Chebar.

Petrie couldn't resist finishing with a dramatic flourish. 'Ezekiel's chariot. Four wheels, a moving pattern, in the sky over two thousand years ago.' He settled into a leather armchair. 'We've been targeted for thousands of years, long before we had the technology to understand the signals. It's possible they don't even know we're here.'

Svetlana switched on the lights.

There was a long silence as the scientists took this on board. Vashislav finally broke it. 'Why? Why should they do this? Indeed, why would civilisations millions of years old want to contact us at all? We are mice! Insects! Bacteria!'

'I've been wondering too,' said Svetlana. 'What's their motivation? And who are they?'

'And where are they?' Gibson chipped in impatiently. 'What do I tell the media on Monday?'

'Tom has a theory,' said Freya.

Attention swivelled to Petrie. Gibson leaned forward, his eyes alert.

Freya added, 'But he's not going to tell us.'

There was a chorus of dismay. Hanning snorted. Svetlana raised her hands to her cheeks. Freya grinned impishly. Shtyrkov sat bolt upright and rattled out something in Russian.

'Spit it out, Petrie!' Gibson ordered.

Petrie held up his hands in a defensive gesture. 'I need to think about it.'

Shtyrkov slapped his hand on a table. 'What? Are you a scientist or not? Open discussion, Tom!'

'Let me sleep on it. It's too crazy for words.'

20

Ogorodnikov

In line with long-standing practice, the paper folders were neatly laid out on Mikhail Isayevich Ogorodnikov's desk, waiting for his arrival. Red to the left, holding the files stamped with *Immediate* and *Urgent*: tomorrow's news headlines. White in the centre, for the internal files of office, the ministries and departments which comprised the sprawling monster of government: often these files were secret, usually they were self-serving. To the right, the green folder, for the enactment or veto of laws supported by the State Duma and the Federation Council.

The green folder also contained requests for clemency from condemned criminals. Men lived or died depending on where he placed his signature.

Ogorodnikov hated the green folder. It gave him insomnia.

He got the clemency requests over with first. A man of good character had stabbed to death his wife and three children for no apparent reason; another had raped and murdered a child and was now expressing remorse; a woman had hired a professional assassin to dispose of a troublesome husband; a gangster had done the same to a public prosecutor; three young men had murdered an American tourist for his wallet. He quickly skimmed through the catalogue of misery, spending no more than five minutes on each file, scribbling his signature after a few moments' thought.

A small man with a round, bald head topped by thin white hair came in carrying a red folder under his arm. The Russian President looked up with relief. The man wore a grey suit made of cheap material but, Ogorodnikov noted with approval, it was immaculately pressed. 'You're looking stressed this morning, Alexy. You should see the view from my side of the desk. What have you got there?'

'Good morning, Mikhail Isayevich. I thought you should see this right away.'

Alexy stood back nervously from the large desk. The red folder contained a single sheet of paper. Ogorodnikov read carefully through it, and then rubbed a hand over his face. 'Is this a joke, Alexy?'

The head of the presidential office gulped. 'No, Mikhail. It is serious.'

'Who else in Moscow knows about this?'

'Only the man who sent the message: Professor Georgi Velikhov.'

'Do I know him?'

'You appointed him. He's the President of the Academy of Sciences. The message came to him directly from this castle in Slovakia.'

'What about our own personnel? Who has seen this?'

'It came on to Olga's screen in the outer office. But I'm convinced she didn't see the significance of it.'

'Has it gone through our review procedure?'

Alexy shook his head emphatically. 'No. I brought it straight here.'

'Put it in the safe.'

Ogorodnikov pressed a button on the panel to the left of his desk. In the days of Yeltsin and Putin, the control panel had been clumsy, enormous. But now it had been replaced with a compact touch-the-screen monitor. It was much more modern and – he had to admit – *American* in style, but it had the same function: he could reach anyone in Russia within minutes. He picked up a telephone and pressed a button. 'Vladimir Vladimirovich, cancel my meeting with the Interior Minister. I want to see Academician Georgi Velikhov here at twelve noon precisely. Make sure he keeps his mouth shut – he must understand that the meeting is to be kept strictly secret.'

The Russian President put the phone down and turned to the head of the presidential office. 'Think about it, Alexy. This must be a clever hoax. But suppose – just for a moment – that it is not. That our people really have detected signals from some advanced civilisation. Do we reply to these signallers? What do we say to them? What rules do we apply? Are there international protocols to cover this event?'

Alexy said, 'On the last item, that is a question for lawyers. You should discuss it with Lebedev.'

Lebedev was the President's chief legal adviser and a former member of the Fatherland-All Russia faction. He was young, ambitious and good-looking in a TV presenter kind of way. Ogorodnikov didn't trust him an inch. The President had in fact been carefully preparing to dismiss the man, but he wasn't ready to reveal his intentions, not even to Alexy. He simply shook his head. 'We'll keep Lebedev out of it. Make quiet enquiries, Alexy. Find a top-class lawyer outside the political system. Someone with specialised knowledge in this area. Give me a name before the morning is out.'

* * *

Before the morning was out, Alexy caught up with Ogorodnikov in the long Kremlin corridor. The President was a small, heavily built man, but he was walking quickly and Alexy had to run to catch up. 'On that matter, Mikhail, I have two names. Professor Orlov of the Moscow State University is our most distinguished constitutional lawyer. And Professor Dobryshev is an expert on space law.'

'But this is not about our constitution, Alexy. And it is not about who pays for the damage when *Mir* falls. Are these the best names you have?' Ogorodnikov sensed Alexy's slight hesitation. 'Well?'

'Tanya Pleskov.'

'The woman who . . . ?'

Alexy gulped. 'Yes, formerly of the prosecutor's office. A brilliant woman. It happens she wrote a paper on' – he consulted a spiral notebook – '*The Legal and Ethical Implications of Contact with Aliens*. The story is she wrote it for fun one weekend but it's become the definitive treatise.'

'And where is this Tanya Pleskov now?'

Alexy shrugged. 'After the scandal, she just dropped out of sight.'

'Find her, and bring her here.'

Alexy's features were showing dismay. 'But the scandal . . . What about Katya?'

As soon as he had said the words, Alexy regretted them. Ogorodnikov's lips tightened. 'I think my forty-year marriage may just survive a professional contact with the notorious Tanya.'

Alexy's face paled. 'I'm an idiot. You should send me to a gulag.'

'I would agree, if we still had them. However, you may have a point. She should not be seen entering the office of the Russian President. And, on reflection, neither do I want curious eyes to see Academician Velikhov in the corridors of the Kremlin.' He tapped his fingers together. 'The meeting will take place in my Gorki-9 *dacha*. I want my limousine at the Borovitsky Gate in ten minutes.'

Apart from the two men, the long corridor was empty, but still Ogorodnikov lowered his voice. 'Alexy, either this is a bad joke or we are on the threshold of something. What that something is, and where it will take us, I don't know. But I have a bad feeling about it.'

21

Night Flight to Karkkila

6.00 a.m. Get up (wakened, usually, by the sounds of cleaning staff downstairs, sometimes by band practice in Horseguards). Finish off overnight boxes, make calls on a cordless phone (while still in pyjamas).

7.00 a.m. Pull on a tracksuit, put in five minutes of basic crunch, ten of skipping, five weightlifting (in a bedroom converted to a small gymnasium).

7.20 a.m. Shower.

7.40 a.m. Breakfast, thrown together in the cramped little attic kitchen.

8.00 a.m. Showered and breakfasted, plan the day ahead with three secretaries: Private Secretary, Diary Secretary and Personal Secretary.

Mondays Also plan the week ahead, with Chief of Staff, Personal Secretary, Press Secretary, Political Secretary and the Head of the Policy Unit.

For those wise to the routine, the Achilles' heel in the Prime Minister's iron routine was 7.20 a.m.: there is no lock on the door to the private apartments, and no place to hide in a shower.

So it was that on this particular morning Sally Morgan, the Head of MI6, was sitting on a lavatory lid with Edgeworth's naked, soapy form just visible a few feet away through the frosted glass. It was her second meeting with the PM within nine hours.

She read out the coded message from Ogorodnikov which had arrived at her desk in the early hours of the morning, via her Russian counterpart. Her voice was raised, to be heard over the splashing water.

'Prime Minister,

'You and I are aware of a certain breakthrough which has been made by our scientists working in a spirit of co-operation in an underground research facility in Slovakia. In mankind's long and troubled history there can be few more exciting discoveries than to find that we are not alone. Unfortunately, this discovery may also prove to be very dangerous. Information of a highly advanced scientific and technical nature has been received, which could benefit our species beyond measure but which may also carry enormous risks.

'I am advised that there are international protocols to cover this situation. This is surely a matter for all mankind, to be dealt with through the United Nations. However, I have also been told that if this information becomes public, we could do nothing to prevent a private individual or group from replying to the message, revealing to the signallers that we have reached a certain stage of advancement. Conceivably, the message could be a lure intended to sniff out civilisations which have reached this stage. The motivation lying behind the message could be far from friendly. We could find ourselves inside their test tubes.

'Prime Minister, you and I have been plunged into a strange and difficult situation. Do we use the new knowledge for all mankind, or for both our peoples, to create a pan-Europe far ahead of our American and Chinese friends? Or do we smother this dangerous discovery? And if so, what do we do about the scientists who have made it?

'This is not a matter for large teams of advisers and TV cameras. We must meet, you and I, and decide the matter face-to-face, in secret and alone. You will guess that time is very short. The scientists are to disperse in three days. If they do, so does the new knowledge. We must decide before then.'

The shower was switched off.

'Shall I leave?'

'No, just pass me that towel. That one. What's he getting at, Sally? Decide what?'

Sally Morgan handed over a large white towel, keeping her eyes averted. The Prime Minister appeared, wrapped in it, and started to blow-dry his hair, peering into a half-steamed mirror. She pretended to have misheard.

'A secret meeting with Ogorodnikov?' She made a clicking noise with her tongue. 'Not a trivial exercise, Prime Minister.'

'But there are precedents,' Edgeworth said. 'Kissinger told me he went in and out of China incognito in the seventies. He was supposed to be resting in a Himalayan retreat, and just slipped over the border.'

'And it's been done by a British Prime Minister,' Sally informed Edgeworth. The drier went off and she wondered how he intended to get his underpants on. 'Anthony Eden left England during the Suez crisis, spoke to the French Prime Minister and came back without anyone knowing he'd been away. But that was just a cross-Channel hop. To meet Ogorodnikov halfway in total secrecy would require clandestine flights over neutral territory and that's a different ballgame. Altogether different.'

Edgeworth was skilfully wriggling into blue boxer shorts, still wearing the towel. 'What's the halfway point between here and Moscow?'

She had anticipated the question. 'The Baltic Sea, give or take. Lots of islands, one of them owned jointly by Finland and Sweden.'

Now he was pulling on trousers. 'The Russian President and I have to meet, whatever the difficulties. I'll speak to Pembroke.'

At eight o'clock, showered and breakfasted, Edgeworth took the narrow stairs down to the large wood-panelled ante-room and turned right again through open double doors to the first-floor drawing rooms and the study. The latter, with its floral-patterned settees and soft cushions, its cabinet with the Bohemian glass collection and its deep carpet, had the air of a middle-class living room. Anne Broughton, the Diary Secretary, was sitting at an armchair with a pile of papers on the oval coffee-table in front of her. Joe Pembroke, the PPS, was leafing through a large black diary. Jean, the Personal Secretary, was pouring tea.

Edgeworth sat down next to Pembroke and loosened his tie. There was an exchange of greetings.

The PPS ran briefly through the day's events, Anne pencilling comments from time to time on her notes, Edgeworth interjecting here and there. He seemed distracted, impatient almost. Finally, with the day's schedule barely settled, he said, 'Ladies, I wonder if you would leave us for a few minutes?'

The Diary Secretary tapped her papers together neatly

and left the study, leaving a slight trail of perfume. Jean gave her boss a puzzled glance and followed.

Pembroke waited.

Edgeworth said, 'Ogorodnikov and I need to meet face-to-face.'

'When, Prime Minister?'

'Immediately. We should meet halfway.'

Pembroke said flatly, 'That's not possible.'

'No wagon train, no security and above all no publicity. Just you, me and a translator we can trust.'

'I'm sorry, Prime Minister, but it can't be done. And even if it could, I wouldn't allow it. You can't possibly dispense with security in this day and age, not even for five minutes.'

Edgeworth smiled grimly. 'I want to meet Ogorodnikov in the Baltic Sea area and return without anyone knowing I've been away. And I want to do it this week.'

'That's crazy. It can't be done.'

Edgeworth patted Pembroke's knee. 'Of course it can, Joe. If not by you, then by a PPS who believes it can.'

Pembroke frowned. 'You have this persuasive way, Prime Minister. Let me see.' He started to flick through the diary pages. 'This is Thursday. You've done the Queen, the Blair visit and the Young Inventor awards. This morning is Cabinet and Question Time, and tomorrow is the Kohl funeral. And then you have weekend guests at Chequers.'

'Cancel my weekend guests, Joe, and send Wentworth in my place to the Kohl funeral.'

'You can't. Chancellor Kohl was a good friend to us. You'll cause great offence.'

'I'll be indisposed. I'll head for Chequers tonight to recuperate. See if the medics can come up with something to make me look groggy this morning.'

'Prime Minister, I don't know what's going on here . . .'

'And join me at Chequers this evening. Arrive as quietly as you can and bring very warm clothes. By the way, Joe, you don't happen to fly a Tornado?'

Pembroke exposed teeth and grunted; after all, he thought, when the PM cracks a joke you're expected to laugh. The bit about the Tornado was, he assumed, a joke.

* * *

At weekends, with a hundred office staff gone, Number Ten was like a morgue, and Edgeworth liked to escape. The twenty minutes of grim body-building was replaced by a leisurely half hour in the covered swimming pool at Chequers. The daily planning session was replaced by a skim through the weekend newspapers over a breakfast of orange juice, yoghurt and banana, thrown together in a blender with a sprinkling of nutmeg. He made his own breakfast, lifelong bachelor's habits not being easily broken. Then he would set the log fire in the enormous great hall which occupied the centre of the Elizabethan house, and either read a novel or stroll round the gardens before dipping into Budget statements, communiqués or speeches. Weekend lunches were gregarious affairs, which he used to keep in touch with life outside politics.

At Question Time anyone could see that the PM was coming down with something, and it was no surprise to learn that this Chequers weekend was to be a long one. Pembroke cancelled the PM's Saturday guests, arranged for the Deputy PM to attend the Kohl funeral, and told his wife that he would be babysitting the Great Leader over the weekend. He then drove towards Chequers in his own Jaguar, an ancient red XJ which he liked to think made him in the image of Inspector Morse.

At 9 p.m. exactly, the PM's Daimler was driven round to the front of the big country house. Edgeworth and Pembroke, both dressed for the cold, sat in the back. Pembroke wore a black Cossack hat with ear-flaps; the Prime Minister thought he had last seen its like in a Christmas pantomime.

The Prime Minister pressed a button, and a sheet of thick glass rose to separate the driver from his passengers. 'Lighten up, Joe. I feel as if I'm riding with my undertaker. What's your beef?'

'You know perfectly well, Prime Minister. I've been saying it all day. This whole adventure is misconceived.' Pembroke had adopted an aggrieved tone to emphasise his displeasure.

'It had better not be. You planned it.' The Prime Minister patted Pembroke's knee. It was a habit which made the PPS cringe, but what could he do? Edgeworth said, 'Joe, I have full confidence in your logistic abilities.'

'What if we had to ditch in the Baltic? I'd like to see Carnforth spin *that* one away.' Edgeworth laughed. Pembroke scowled and continued, 'And what do we really know of Ogorodnikov's intentions?'

The driver was pulling out to pass cyclists, two abreast, no lights. Edgeworth said, 'Don't let your imagination run away with you.'

'But nobody will even know where we are. Anything could happen.'

Edgeworth looked out at the dark fields. He waved a hand dismissively. 'Go ahead, sweat the small stuff. I have bigger worries.'

At RAF Northolt, a black-bearded young man, on the promotion fast track at the Foreign Office, and said to be utterly reliable, was waiting nervously in the Commanding

Officer's office. The CO led them to a VC-10 which took them out over the dark North Sea.

Around 11.30 p.m., the aircraft tilted and slowed, and they found themselves approaching a short runway. Once landed, they taxied over to a big yellow Search and Rescue helicopter, the wind from its rotor making patterns in the grass. Pembroke held on to his Cossack hat as they transferred hastily over.

Two aircrew bundled the little group aboard and clambered up after them. The steps were pulled in and the door slammed shut. Pembroke, Edgeworth and the FO man buckled themselves into seats near the rear of the Sea King, and the aircrew joined two more RAF men up front. Then there was thunder and vibration and they rose sluggishly, the ground slipping under them. The lights of Lossiemouth began to dwindle. They passed over a cluster of red lights, an aerial farm. More distant lights marked out Elgin to their left, and Tain and Cromarty ahead; the inky black patch between them was the Moray Firth.

Then, over ghostly-white Highlands, away from curious eyes, the pilot switched off the navigation lights. Inside the big helicopter, it was suddenly pitch black apart from the subdued glow from the instrument panel. The pilot turned the machine north, and flew on for about thirty miles over the desolate peaks. Then he banked sharply and took them east, out over the rolling North Sea waves, past the Long Forties and the Great Fisher Bank, leaving the sovereign territory of the United Kingdom far behind.

* * *

To have landed on the deck of a Royal Navy warship, or to have been lowered into the bowels of a Russian Baltic Fleet submarine, would have been to tell a hundred or more sailors of each nationality that a clandestine meeting was taking place between the British and Russian Prime Ministers. It had taken three discussions over a scrambler phone between Joe Pembroke and his counterpart, Alexy Grigorivich, to solve the problem – if 'solve' was the word for the scheme they had hastily concocted.

By half past three the Sea King dropped to a hundred feet and flew along the Skaggerak. They passed low over an early morning ferry, its lights ablaze in the dark sea.

The helicopter banked left. The lights of a small fishing town drifted past to port, practically level with the Sea King. On a quiet promontory, the pilot lowered the machine noisily on to a stony beach.

The British Prime Minister and his entourage were now, illegally, in Norwegian territory.

The blades spun down, and the engine whined to a halt.

On another promontory, about five miles away, a lighthouse flashed every few seconds.

A truck driving on sidelights. Truck doors slamming; cigarettes glowing in the dark, illuminating two men jumping down from the big vehicle.

Pembroke and the pilot stepped out. Rough voices, in heavily accented English. The cigarettes were extinguished. In the near-dark, Edgeworth heard rather than saw cash being counted. He climbed out and relieved himself behind a wall, the whiff of fuel catching his nostrils. To the south-east, a sliver of light was beginning to touch the horizon. In another ten minutes rotors were beginning to spin up, and then the refuelled Sea King was once again flying out over the sea, just above the dark waves.

At five in the morning by their biological clocks, the helicopter once more approached a shoreline. The sky was lightening. This time they flew inland, over dense conifer forest, before landing in a clearing. Edgeworth, his nerves ragged, looked down on trees with snow being shaken from them as the big machine lowered itself on to the ground. There was a brief mini-blizzard, and then two crewmen jumped out; they were wearing holstered pistols. One of them lowered the steps. Pembroke left first, looking around warily. Then he shone a little flashlight on to a sheet of paper and set off along a track, followed by the Prime Minister and the translator.

Here the cold was sterner. It had hit them as soon as the door slid open; it was cutting through Edgeworth's woollen cap, and Pembroke's pantomime hat was turning into something to covet.

After ten minutes of trudging through deep snow, the path forked. Pembroke looked again at the little hand-drawn map. He grunted and led the way forwards along the right-hand path. Presently there was a frozen lake, stretching into the darkness, and at its far end a wooden cabin, brightly lit from within. They set out across the lake.

The man who opened the door was small, stout and white-haired, and wore a heavy polo-necked sweater. His voice seemed to come from the depths of his chest. The man from the FO translated Ogorodnikov's Russian in flawless Oxford English: 'Welcome to Finland, Prime Minister Edgeworth.'

22

The Frog

Petrie tried to convince himself that his random walk round
the castle was to clear the mental cobwebs.

He wandered into the theological library, dazzling with
baroque, shining with antique globes, but empty. He
strolled into the computer room. Svetlana and Shtyrkov
were at a screen filled with some weird, patterned shape.
She was pointing to something, and murmuring quietly as
if the room was full of ghosts who didn't want to be
disturbed. There was nobody else. Into the kitchen and
then the bar and the dining area: deserted.

He climbed nimbly up the broad stone stairs on to the
terrace. There was a blue sky and a nip in the air. At some
stage the overnight rain had turned to snow and there was
a thin covering everywhere. Hanning had cleared it from a
table and he was sitting at it with an early morning beer.
Nineteen sixties' pop was coming from an elderly transistor
radio on the table. The Cabinet Office observer was flicking
through sheets of paper and didn't look up.

Petrie strode over to the parapet and looked out across
the panorama. Trees, snow-covered fields, distant mountains. He walked to the south side and there she was at
last, in the courtyard. The collar of her long black coat was
turned up and she was pacing up and down, making a trail
of footsteps in the snow, hands in pockets and breath

steaming in the cold air. He wondered where she lived. Did she have a boyfriend? Was it possible such a good-looking girl didn't have a boyfriend? Or was she spoiled for choice, picking them up and putting them down on a whim? Or a partner. These days you didn't get married, you had a partner. Petrie ached to know.

Charlie Gibson came into view. He was walking stiffly, his head bowed, looking like a worried old man. There was an exchange of greetings and then Freya smiled and put her arm in Gibson's, and they walked slowly past the witch's hat and out through the front entrance.

A surge of black jealousy swept through Petrie. He crossed the terrace, ignoring Hanning's greeting, and took the steps two at a time. Out into the cold morning air, half-running. At the front gate he slowed down, breathing heavily, and told himself not to be an idiot. They were about a hundred yards ahead, on the path and deep in conversation.

Because of a couple of bad experiences, Petrie had never been comfortable with women. Just the presence of an attractive female made him nervous. It gave him a strange, contradictory surge of emotions, just seeing her smooth skin, long blonde hair and the outline of well-formed breasts underneath the coat. And sure enough, as he caught up with them, and Freya turned and smiled, he felt like a small boy caught stealing apples. Gibson's face, by contrast, was grim. Petrie wondered if the man saw him as a rival, but no, his expression was too overtly serious.

'Ah, Tom, just the man. Charlie's going through the tortures of the damned.' Freya's breath was steaming in the cold air.

'Me too. We're nearly out of time.' He felt his heart thumping in his chest.

Gibson's voice was harsh. 'It's not the time factor. I think maybe we should kill the whole thing.'

'What?'

'Erase all evidence. Pretend the signal never happened.'

Petrie was silent. For some seconds he wondered if the burst of radiation was beginning to affect Gibson's mind too. But Charlie Gibson, although upset, was still being Charlie Gibson.

The physicist said, 'How would you communicate with a frog?'

'I don't know. Why would I want to?' Petrie fell in beside Gibson, and they walked slowly across the snow.

'Exactly.'

'You mean, we're frogs?'

'What's bugging me is this: how can we ever hope to get inside an alien mind? Maybe they're wired up differently, maybe their minds work in some way we can't even imagine. Maybe there's no way to know what they're really thinking.'

'Charlie's worried that maybe they're sharks, not frogs,' Freya explained.

Gibson unconsciously cracked his knuckles. 'A Great White disguising itself as Kermit.'

'An intelligent Jaws, with malice in its heart?'

'Exactly. What's driving them to signal us?'

'Altruism, Charlie. We've reached the stage where we can be helped and they just want to do that.'

'So out there everybody holds hands and sings mantras round a big galactic camp fire? That's optimistic, Tom, very save-the-whales, very western liberal. Tell me, have you ever tried to do your own thinking?'

Petrie checked his temper; it was clear that Gibson was deeply upset. He settled for icy politeness. 'Are you saying they need us for food or what?'

Gibson said, 'Darwinian selection is ruthless. The strong survive. Why shouldn't that work out there as well as down here? Maybe the meek have been weeded out and the aliens go around on motor bikes with safety pins in their noses. Tom, maybe we have to suppress all this. It never happened, okay? Let's keep our heads down.'

Petrie stared, aghast. 'But Charlie, the Prize!'

'I know. I know. Why the fuck do you think I'm like this?' The snow was ankle-deep. Gibson kicked viciously at it.

Freya adopted a matter-of-fact tone. Petrie thought she was doing it deliberately to calm the excited physicist. 'Charlie thinks it could be a lure, designed to see if we've reached the stage where we might become a threat.'

'Freya, how can we possibly be a threat to creatures thousands of years ahead of us, maybe millions?'

Gibson said, 'We're not, not now. But give it a thousand years. It might make sense to zap us now while we're confined to a single planet. Give it a few hundred years and we'll be spread around and it will be too late to stop us. And a civilisation a million years old probably looks ahead at least a thousand years.'

'Are you seriously telling us we should keep quiet about this discovery? Kill it?'

'I'm beginning to think that way.'

'Oh boy,' Petrie said. 'Oh boy oh boy.'

Freya said, 'The critical issue is whether the signallers have a moral code, and if so what that code is.'

Gibson's voice rose an octave. 'Freya, how can we ever know about something like that? I just do Çerenkov radiation. I'd pull in a theologian except he'd come in waving a lot of religious crap and anyway there isn't time.'

Ahead of them, a couple of children were heaving a sledge up the road. A large Alsatian dog was jumping through the snow, its tongue hanging out.

Gibson continued, 'Look at our own evolution. It's been tooth and claw from the start. Human societies just continue in that vein. Whenever there's been contact between two cultures, the strong one has always overwhelmed the weak. This goes at least back to the Neanderthals. If we go public with this, someone on Earth will fire off a reply, guaranteed. It could be just what the signallers need: proof that we're into the subnuclear stage, where we need to be squashed before we get any further.'

Petrie said, 'Come on, Charlie, that's just a flight of fancy.'

'You think so? Do you want to risk humanity's future on it? And who are we to do that?'

'But that's the trap we're in, Charlie. We go public or we don't go public. Either way we make a decision that affects humanity's future.'

Freya changed sides with Gibson so that she was now between the two men. The Alsatian was leaping towards them, leaving an irregular trail in the pristine snow. A small child was pursuing it, shouting, '*Zlato! Zlato! Dâle!*' Come here!

Freya said, 'My brother has a husky. I put on skis and he pulls me over the lake when it's frozen.'

'Your brother?' Gibson asked.

'The husky, stupid.'

Petrie made a snowball and threw it at the boy. The Alsatian charged off, and the child managed to grab it by the collar.

Freya said, 'I know what's holding you back, Charlie. You're thinking there's one Universe, with one Big Bang, and it's transient. The stars will eventually burn out, the embers will cool and life will die out. You're thinking if life is just a spark in a bonfire then so are moral values. They're just a social glue. Right?'

'Right,' Gibson said, with a touch of aggression.

Freya continued, 'So you're thinking, if the Universe is just a big heap of burning ashes, okay, and there's no absolute morality, then maybe we do have survival of the meanest.'

'On the button.'

'Maybe this is a civilisation anticipating trouble and getting rid of it in plenty of time. I know you hate to think this, Charlie. I know you're terrified you'll have to shut up about this discovery. You're churned up because you want the fame, the Nobel, the immortality.'

'I do.' Gibson was in anguish. 'I want all of that.'

'But you're out of date, Charlie. The Universe isn't like that at all.'

'Not like that?' Charlie's tone was pathetic.

'Not at all. That's Victorian, it's yesterday's philosophy.'

'And today's?'

She squeezed Charlie's arm and Petrie's black jealousy resurged. 'Let me tell you about a big mystery. A huge mystery, a monster thing, the central mystery of the Creation.'

'Am I in for a Norse saga?'

Freya said, 'If only the epic poets had got hold of this story . . .'

Petrie said, 'I think my toes are falling off.'

She laughed. 'All right, Tom, I'll keep it brief. Hydrogen burns inside stars to give us helium.'

Gibson decided to take offence. 'Freya, I know I'm not a high-flier like Tom here, but credit me with knowing something.'

'It burns with efficiency 0.007.'

'What has double-o-seven got to do with answering the signal?'

'If it was double-o-eight the hydrogen would all have burned to helium by now and we'd have a Universe made of nothing but gas for balloons. If it burned at efficiency double-o-six we'd have a Universe made of nothing but hydrogen and just a little helium.'

As she warmed to the theme, Freya began to wave her arms dramatically. 'But you can't have life in a Universe made just of hydrogen or helium. For life you need complexity, you need to build up heavy elements, carbon, oxygen, phosphorus and so on. You cook them up inside stars and to do that, the hydrogen has to burn with just the right efficiency, point zero-zero-seven, neither more nor less. Somehow the atomic properties of hydrogen have been perfectly fine-tuned for building the heavy elements we need for life.'

Gibson was red-faced. Petrie wasn't sure if it was the cold air, or the physical exertion of ploughing through the deepening snow, or the mental exertion of following Freya's modern saga. 'That's remarkable, but where are you heading?'

'Patience, as you kept saying to us a couple of days ago. If gravity was even slightly stronger than it is, the stars would burn up so fast there would be no time for life to evolve. If the Universe expanded even slightly faster than it does, it would have dispersed before matter had a chance to collapse into stars and planets. If it didn't have just the right irregularities implanted in it, just after the Big Bang, we'd either be sucked into black holes or dispersed as a rarefied gas with no stars, no planets and no life. And so on and so on. There's a whole string of coincidences; get any one even slightly wrong and you'd have no life.'

'Freya, okay! But so what?'

Petrie cringed, but Freya continued, 'Charlie, don't you get it? The Universe has been fine-tuned to the nth degree to support life. Nobody knows how or why. Some things we may never understand. That's the monster mystery. One of the big questions.'

'That's quite something, Freya, in fact it's mind-boggling. But I don't see how it relates to the motives of the signallers.'

'Think about it, Charlie. For some reason the Universe is structured so as to be friendly to life. Maybe even life itself has built the Universe that way.'

'Now that's really pushing the boat.'

'Whatever. But the Universe isn't just dying embers with life getting a grip where it can. Life is central to it. The cosmos is a living entity.'

'Oh, man!' Gibson's complexion was an alarming red.

'This damn cold. It's getting to more than my toes,' Petrie volunteered.

'Some power, some force, call it what you will, has worked things this way. What's the sense in having a Universe built to be friendly to life but with no life in it? And whatever this force is, it couldn't allow one dominant life form anywhere to eliminate all others as they arise. It's just not consistent with the way the cosmos has been structured. Whatever's out there, Charlie, it's not tooth and claw. Not on the cosmic scale. The Universe is wild but it loves life.'

Stress was now flowing out of Gibson like water from a kettle, and he began to glow with such radiance that Petrie thought he might melt the snow around him. 'It's Kermit then. Not Jaws.'

Petrie pulled his collar up round his neck. He thought Freya's argument was more poetry than science but if it made Charlie happy he wasn't going to argue. He drove the point home: 'It's Kermit, Charlie. And that delicious weekend in Stockholm.'

The children were on the sledge, flying down the road at what to Petrie was a scary speed. The Alsatian was bounding behind them, tail flying.

Freya shivered. She linked arms with both men. The physical contact, even through the layers of clothing, gave Petrie a thrill. She said, 'It's getting cold.'

Gibson was now almost delirious with relief. 'Yeah. And when an Eskimo says that, you can believe it.'

They turned back, Petrie beginning to wonder if the physicist's outlook on life was, so to speak, politically correct.

23

Operation PM

The CIA Dining Room was elegant, the atmosphere restful. Even with a coating of snow, or maybe because of it, the view over the manicured grounds was lovely. But Melanie Moore dearly wished she was munching a bagel in the Food Court.

For one thing, there was her dining companion, the formidable John McLarty, Deputy Director for Operations. Not that McLarty was intimidating; in fact, he oozed friendliness. It was just that he was the Deputy Director for Operations, four grades above her, and all the smooth talk in the known universe couldn't alter the fact.

And then there was the awkward fact of her outfit. A white sweater, short white skirt and sneakers was carrying the smart-casual-as-appropriate code rather too far and might give the unfortunate impression that she had been planning an early get-away to a game of squash, which in fact she had. Under cover of the table, Melanie pulled her skirt as far down as it would go over her thighs.

She was relieved to see that the DDO, immaculate in grey suit, white shirt and Toc-H tie, was apparently unaware of her ultracasual dress. He smiled and said, 'I like the way you wrapped up the Olsen saga. You're running a fine Analysis team.'

'Thank you, sir.' *But that's not what this is about.*

A waitress, black as Melanie, approached with a smile and a pencil and pad. 'Are you ready to order?'

'Maybe in a minute,' the DDO said without consulting his companion. The waitress disappeared, and McLarty opened up. 'Something odd has turned up, Melanie.'

'Sir?'

'A communication from a guy called Sonny Karlsson landed on my desk an hour ago. You won't know him, he's based in London.'

'He's with the Company?'

'Actually not. He's a trade liaison officer or something like that in our Embassy. Anyway, Sonny has a regular Saturday golf session with a lady friend.'

'In London?'

'Someplace to the south, Virginia Waters. Only on this particular Wednesday . . .'

'Last Wednesday?'

'Last Wednesday, she phones him to cancel the session. She says she's been invited to Chequers by Alan Edgeworth, no less. Seems it's the British Prime Minister's thing, asking a few people along for the weekend. Have you eaten here before? I can recommend the clam chowder.'

'I usually just grab a bagel in the Food Court. What sort of people?'

'It varies enormously.' The DDO pulled a folded sheet of paper from his back trouser pocket. 'The guest list for this Saturday . . .'

'You mean tomorrow?'

'Yes, tomorrow, was Malcolm Dundee the *Sunday Times* editor, some English comedian called Ken Dodd, Alice Grissom from the Mars Corporation, Jack Nicholson who happens to be passing through London and so on. A complete mix. Anyway, the Prime Minister cancels, just like that. The story is, he has a bad cold.'

'So who's this lady friend?'

McLarty glanced at his notes. 'Susan Hope.'

'The fashion designer?'

McLarty showed surprise. 'Yes. You know her?'

'Not personally. My daughter wears her labels.'

'You don't say.'

'I do, sir. It's a small world.'

McLarty looked for nuances, gave up. 'Now at this point, Sonny shows the sort of initiative that makes me wonder if we shouldn't be employing him. He gets curious about this sudden cold. Yesterday evening he decides to do a little off-road driving in the woods around a village called Dunsmore, which happens to be close to Chequers. Sure enough, there's a ring of steel around the place indicating that the Prime Minister is in residence. Sonny waits. A car appears but he can't make out the occupants in the dark. An hour or so later, Sonny sees an entourage take off from Chequers in the direction of RAF Northolt.'

'An entourage?'

'A PM-sized convoy. The presumption has to be that it contained the PM.'

'And?'

McLarty gave a sort of a grin. 'Why do you think I'm giving you this lunch, Melanie? The Prime Minister of the United Kingdom has disappeared. If that don't ring an alarm bell I reckon you shouldn't be working for this Agency. I want you to find out where Edgeworth has gone.'

'I'll try, sir.'

'Of course I wouldn't want this to interfere with your busy social calendar.' McLarty smiled.

Melanie smiled back. *Damn racist male chauvinist Prussian pig.*

* * *

'Balmoral.'

'Huh?' Melanie leaned over the sandy-haired man's shoulder.

The sandy-haired man pointed to a small cluster of pixels on the screen. 'Edgeworth has no scheduled trips abroad. Domestic flights from Northolt are usually to visit the Queen in Balmoral.'

'Where did you get this? We don't spy on Britain.'

'As of this afternoon we do. This is a couple of hours old. We were lucky to get the cloud break.'

'What is this? A castle?'

An older male voice came from the far corner of the underground room. 'It's the summer *dacha* of the British Royal Family, or at least one of them.' There was the sound of pages turning, and then, 'Forget Balmoral. The Royals don't go near it in the winter, on account of it's like something out of *Dr Zhivago*. In the Scottish Highlands you spend winter indoors with a roaring fire, drinking whisky until spring arrives.'

'So who are these people?' Melanie asked. Sandy had zoomed the picture up until the individual pixels were visible. He was focusing on a group of people, black against the snow. They seemed to be throwing snowballs.

'Caretaker staff.'

'How can you be sure?'

Sandy clicked the picture back to its original size. Balmoral Castle, enclosed on three sides by a broad river, was throwing long winter shadows. A cottage and some outbuildings were scattered around. A hill to the south was partly obscured by cloud. There were patches of flat ground in the left and right foreground, like areas for sports like golf or cricket. 'No helicopters, no security worth a damn, no Prime Ministerial cars, and therefore no Prime Minister.'

Melanie nodded thoughtfully. 'So where the hell did he go?'

* * *

For this one, Sullivan did his own typing. He did it at an efficient, two-fingered speed, in a windowless office whose walls, underneath the oak panelling and the portraits, were imbedded with wire mesh.

Credibility, the CIA Director increasingly realised as he tore up one draft after another, was going to be the issue. After half a dozen attempts, he resigned himself to the fact that, whatever the words, it was going to come out sounding corny: there was a big giggle factor and no way round it. He ended up with a bald statement of the facts and a short section devoted to the possible implications for the USA, putting emphasis on the overwhelming advantage of the new knowledge for the countries which held it. It was slim stuff, and it had an air of hand-waving, exactly the sort of padding which he discouraged in his subordinates' analyses. He scanned in the telephone transcript from the Gorki-9 intercept; it made a fat appendix.

He sealed it, hand-wrote *For the President's Eyes Only*, and telephoned the White House. He asked for a twenty-minute slot alone with the President, and a space was found for him at 11 p.m.

He left the HQ at seven. A Secret Service man drove him to his home on Wisconsin Avenue, where Sullivan's little fat maid, following wifely instructions, served him boiled fish and boiled rice followed by a fresh fruit salad with fromage frais. All low cholesterol, low fat and virtuous; but just now and then, especially when he was under stress, he longed for a T-bone steak with deep-fried potatoes followed by a dumpling with double cream washed down with two or three beers.

This was one of those occasions.

At ten forty-five, his mind temporarily numbed with an evening of cable TV, he was collected, and ten minutes later he was dropped off at the West Wing security kiosk. A few minutes later he was at the door of the Oval Office, facing another Secret Service agent, this one with a crew cut and a clipboard. The man said, 'Good evening, Mr Sullivan,' and tapped on the Oval Office door.

A small, wiry man, with short steel-grey hair and a wrinkled skin, was sitting back in an easy chair, staring into flames. He wore an open-necked shirt, and a tie and jacket lay on the floor beside him. He waved Sullivan to the chair opposite the fireplace.

'Good evening, Mr President.' Sullivan took a deep breath. He leaned forward and passed over the sealed envelope containing his report. 'I got this from McLarty a couple of hours ago. It came in with the Moscow pouch. My people tapped an early-hours' call from a man called Velikhov, who's a big name in Russian science.'

'Never heard of him.' The President rested the envelope on his lap. His dark eyes stayed on the CIA Director.

'He's not high-profile like Sakharov was. In fact, he's more on the administrative side. But he does advise Ogorodnikov informally now and then on scientific matters. They're near-neighbours in the Gorki-9 district of Moscow.'

'The meat, Al?'

'Okay. We've been doing routine telephone taps in the Gorki-9 district for some time. We can only cover a fraction of the calls and it's nearly always low-grade stuff, wifely gossip and the like. But now and then it throws up nuggets.'

'So you got a nugget?'

'Mr President, we got a gold mine.'

The President leaned forward.

'The call went to a guy called Shtyrkov. Director of a radiation lab, lots of medals for academic distinction et cetera. He's respected.' Sullivan took another deep breath.

'Go on.'

'Mr President, according to Shtyrkov they've detected a signal from an alien intelligence.'

Bull stared.

Sullivan, the die cast, went on: 'It seems a huge flood of information came in with the signal. They're trying to work out what it means. *Inter alia*, the signal includes information about the human genome.'

'Our genetic make-up? How could aliens possibly know about something like that?'

Sullivan spread his hands wide. 'I – they – have no idea.' He pointed to the envelope in the President's lap. 'That's a transcript of the conversation. It's long, but you'll see I've added a three-page précis at the beginning. Mr President, if this is for real . . .'

Bull was looking at the CIA Director as if the man had gone mad. 'Is that it? A phone call between two guys purporting to be top Russian scientists?' He drew back his lips and gave a short, incredulous laugh. 'It's obvious! They've figured you're listening and they're feeding you a load of bullshit.'

The dreaded giggle factor.

Sullivan shook his head emphatically. 'The call was from Velikhov's home address. Just to be double sure, I got my people to run a voiceprint on a snatch of the conversation.

Not a significant part,' Sullivan added as the President opened his mouth. 'It matches old newsreel stuff we have on Velikhov. No question, the President of the Russian Academy of Sciences made that call. By inference, this Shtyrkov was the man he called.'

'And the place?'

'Some castle in Slovakia.'

'Slovakia? What in hell's name does a castle in Slovakia have to do with anything?'

'That's where we think the alien signal is being analysed. It's all in the report, sir.'

'We?' Alarm crept into the President's voice. 'Who else knows about this?'

'So far nobody. The Moscow intercept team, but they're passing on stuff which, so far as they know, is a hoax. They only put it in the pouch because they thought it meant the Russians had discovered they were being bugged.'

'I reckon they've got more sense than you. Why are you bothering me with this science-fiction stuff?'

'Sir, I've been in the game for a very long time: false flag recruitment, mission impossibles, stuff that makes James Bond look like Goldilocks. This doesn't have the right signature for a sting. For a start, it's impossible to believe. Mr President, according to this Shtyrkov, the signal may also turn out to contain recipes for creating enzymes to alter genetic structure in fundamental ways. What this means I don't know. Maybe it can be used to cure diseases, maybe to create a new kind of human.'

'For Christ's sake, Al.' Bull's tone was one of utter rejection.

'Yes, sir, I know.'

Bull put his hand over his mouth and looked into the

flames. 'The world's full of creeps who would love to see this nation humiliated.'

'Yes, sir, some of them within our shores.' Sullivan wondered what the old man was driving at.

'East coast editors especially. Now say this thing turns out to be a giant sting, which I expect it is, and the media get hold of it.'

Sullivan saw the point. He said, 'I see the point.'

'Exactly. This Administration would be ridiculed to hell, become the laughing stock of the world. What credibility would we be left with, say we used CIA analysis to warn of an imminent threat?'

And what would happen to you come election time, next November? Sullivan thought.

'You're right, Mr President. But let's say it's for real, which I believe. Uncontrolled publicity could be equally bad. We could have public panic.'

President Bull narrowed his eyes contemplatively. 'So. Either way you keep your mouth firmly shut. That includes talking to McLarty. Okay?'

'Agreed, sir. It's the only way to handle this.'

Bull flapped the envelope. 'I'll take it from here. And I'll read this with interest.'

Sullivan took his cue and stood up. 'Mr President, there's something else.'

'Hit me with it, Al.'

'Even without useful information in the signal, the implications of an intelligence out there need a lot of very careful thought.'

The President nodded. 'We'd be walking barefoot through broken glass.'

* * *

Fifty minutes after Sullivan took his leave, the President made one phone call.

The call was to a house in Fairfax County. It was a large two-storey dwelling with mock-colonial architecture, and it overlooked the Potomac River. The call was intended for Hazel Baxendale, the President's Science Adviser. Her husband took it sleepily, sat bolt upright, and handed the cordless phone over to his wife, mouthing *The President!* silently.

President Bull's voice was edged with tiredness. 'Hazey? I wakened you, I'm sorry.'

'That's okay, Mr President.'

'I need you in the Situation Room in a couple of hours. Can you manage that?'

'No problem, sir.' *Strange!*

'And then I'd like you to join me in Camp David tomorrow. Could use a little advice over the weekend. Unless you're otherwise fixed up.'

Baxendale's married daughter was due to arrive from Canada at Dulles, along with Husband Number Two and Alice, Hazel's six-year-old granddaughter. She had looked forward to this weekend for weeks, talked about a couple of days in the Poconos, maybe riding or even taking a canoe trip. 'No, Mr President, that will be fine.'

'Share my helicopter, Hazel. Be on the lawn after my morning briefing.'

It was now well after midnight, and silence had long since descended on the normally busy corridors of the White House. The President wrote a brief note, which he folded and put in an envelope carrying the presidential seal. He wondered grimly how the recipient would react to it. Then he called for an aide and asked for hand delivery. In the corridor outside the office, the aide looked at the envelope. It was an unfamilar address somewhere in North Carolina, and it was about eight hours' drive away.

24

Pandora's Box

The cabin was *hot* and already the Prime Minister could feel light beads of perspiration on his forehead.

The source of the heat was a glass-fronted stove, with logs glowing bright red and blue-white flames disappearing up a black flue. Logs were piled neatly on either side of it. On a mantelpiece above were beer glasses, books with German titles and a copper hod with long matches. The room was small; floors, walls and ceiling were pine-clad. A sideboard held an eclectic assortment of pottery and photographs. On the wall with the door, resting on hooks, were a long hunting rifle, two fishing rods, snowshoes, a row of heavy fur coats and Pembroke's hat. The smell of pasta and Mediterranean herbs drifted through from a half-open door and reminded Edgeworth that he hadn't eaten for twelve hours.

Ogorodnikov and Edgeworth were scarcely three feet apart, facing each other across a rough wooden table. Ogorodnikov's translator, immediately to the President's left, was a thin, near-bald man with a goatee beard, spectacles and a dark suit and tie. To Edgeworth, he bore a startling resemblance to a young Lenin. The far ends of the table were occupied by Velikhov and Pembroke.

The Academician's presence gave the PM an uneasy feeling that he had been manipulated. Now scientific input would be delivered by a man whose country's interests were not necessarily those of his own. And Pembroke would be as useful as a chocolate teapot. To judge by his slightly dismayed expression, Pembroke seemed to think so too.

Edgeworth glanced at Uncle Ogorodnikov, wondered if he had indeed engineered the situation. Ogorodnikov caught the look, but the man's face was impervious to scrutiny. He opened the exchange, looking directly into Edgeworth's eyes. The high-flier from the FO was sitting on Edgeworth's right – the PM's good ear. He translated Ogorodnikov's words: 'What are we to make of this, Prime Minister? Are we witnessing the end of mankind's childhood?'

Edgeworth replied warily. 'This discovery does change the way we think about ourselves, President Ogorodnikov.' Lenin turned his head toward his boss and spoke rapidly and quietly into his ear.

Ogorodnikov acknowledged the cautious response with a slight smile. 'I would like you to call me Mikhail.'

Edgeworth returned the half-smile but didn't reciprocate the offer of familiarity. 'In the short term this will be a major shock, Mikhail. Learning that out there is at least one intelligence probably millions of years in advance of ours.'

The Prime Minister sensed, rather than saw, his translator at his side freezing up, and remembered that the FO man had been given no inkling of the purpose of the meeeting. The man recovered quickly and delivered Ogorodnikov's reply, struggling to keep the astonishment out of his voice: 'An intelligence which wishes to communicate with us, and which is prepared to give us knowledge thousands of years ahead of our time.'

Edgeworth turned to the man seated at the far end of the table. There would be no keeping him out of it. 'What can Professor Velikhov tell us about this matter?'

Georgi Velikhov cleared his throat. There was a brief, three-way exchange in Russian between Ogorodnikov, his translator and the Academician. Then Velikhov was speaking in good English with a hint of Harvard American. 'Gentlemen, the idea of searching for alien life is centuries old. In 1822 the mathematician Gauss thought there were people on the Moon, and they could be contacted using a system of mirrors. Others thought to signal Martians or lunar dwellers by digging geometric ditches in the Sahara, filling them with oil and setting them on fire.'

'Can we skip a century or two?' Edgeworth asked impatiently.

Velikhov continued: 'The radio astronomers have been looking for extraterrestrial signals for almost fifty years. The pioneering work was carried out by an American called Frank Drake. He used a small radio telescope in Green Bank, West Virginia. Now, all the world's radio telescopes routinely look for meaningful chirps – signals in amongst the hiss of the galaxies and the echo of the Big Bang. Today's equipment is ten trillion times more sensitive than Drake's Project Ozma. And the Americans are using the world's largest radio telescope, the Arecibo in Puerto Rico, to examine a thousand nearby star systems. But all this effort has produced nothing. We have heard only a great silence.'

'The people inside the mountain weren't using radio,' Edgeworth pointed out.

Velikhov nodded. 'Perhaps we have been foolish. Perhaps we should have realised that the aliens might have discovered more advanced methods of communication than anything we could imagine. All this time we have been looking for smoke signals.'

The FO man translated Ogorodnikov's words. 'Are people prepared for this news? Will there be panic in the streets?'

'No. People see Captain Kirk fighting aliens on TV every day. And I suppose you know as well as I do, Mikhail, that there are ways of putting a message over to the public.'

'Aha! Your famous spin doctors! I too have my *"propagandisty"*. But the matter goes much deeper than spin, Prime Minister. Look what happened to the American Indians when Europe invaded North America. Look what happened to the Mayan civilisation when the Spaniards arrived. Whenever a strong culture comes into contact with a weak one, the weak is exterminated.'

'But we're talking about the transmission of information, surely not the prospect of physical invasion.'

Velikhov cleared his throat again. 'The distances involved in interstellar travel are huge. The technical problems even for an advanced civilisation . . .'

'How can you put limits on the capabilities of an advanced civilisation?' Ogorodnikov wanted to know.

Velikhov continued to speak English, while Lenin muttered into Ogorodnikov's ear: 'I don't, Nature does. Nature has set up a speed limit: nothing can travel faster than light. No civilisation, however advanced, can break that limit. Mother Nature has also arranged for the Galaxy to be immense. Given these factors, colonisation by aliens would take an immense span of time. Our species could be extinct by the time they arrived in their starships. But the real question is, why would they want to conquer us? Do we want to conquer an ant heap? We have nothing to offer and are of no conceivable importance to them.'

'This confirms my opinion,' Edgeworth said. 'There will be no panic. Intense interest, yes, but no blood in the streets. The Mayan and Native American civilisations were wiped out by physical contact. Disease and genocide did for them. What we have here is something different, a transmission of knowledge. Could that destroy our civilisation – mere knowledge?'

Ogorodnikov said, 'It came close, Prime Minister, in the age of the Bomb.'

Edgeworth showed a polite scepticism. 'Suppose that, in the time of Moses, there was a single telephone line, and that it connected him to our century. What would that have done to the pastoral societies of the day? Most of the knowledge would be so incomprehensible to them that they couldn't have used it.'

Ogorodnikov was studying Edgeworth closely. The FO man translated his words. 'So, what are you saying? That you agree with my Academician, here? That these aliens pose no threat?'

Edgeworth leaned forward across the table. 'The threat of new knowledge doesn't worry me. The threat of invasion doesn't worry me.'

'What then?'

'It's the threat of extermination.'

The room fell silent.

Edgeworth said, 'Mikhail, if we're of no importance to them, why are they signalling us?'

Ogorodnikov nodded grimly. 'Precisely. You and I have been thinking the same thoughts. The signal may be a lure. If we reply, they have a measure of our state of scientific literacy.'

'And are we still thinking the same thought, Mikhail? That if we reply, the next message from them might be our obliteration?'

Ogorodnikov clasped his hands together on the table. He nodded.

Velikhov interrupted in English. 'That is nonsense. I am sorry but I must protest. We are ants. We pose no conceivable threat to them. An advanced civilisation will long have climbed out of the mire of barbarism and warfare.'

Ogorodnikov spoke sharply. The FO man translated verbatim: 'You are here as a scientific adviser, not a policymaker.'

Velikhov ignored the rebuke. His voice was animated. 'Advanced societies will be altruistic. They are simply trying to contact young technological societies such as our own. They judge that we have reached a stage where we can be helped. Look at the information they have sent us already.'

Edgeworth said, 'We may be no threat now. When better to stop us, before we become one?'

There was an edge to Ogorodnikov's smile. 'A lure. A delicious bait. Perhaps the extermination requires no death rays on their part.' He turned to Edgeworth. 'The English have an author, Mary Shelley.'

'Had. She's a nineteenth-century figure.'

'She created the Frankenstein monster.'

'Yes.' Ogorodnikov's translator imitated the caution in Edgeworth's voice.

'We are being invited, are we not, to turn ourselves into monsters, for an unknown purpose, with a molecular code supplied to us by creatures about which we know nothing. What is this, Prime Minister, but a modern Frankenstein story?'

Velikhov interrupted his boss. 'Forgive me, President, but as your scientific adviser I must protest against such nonsense. Improving our minds and bodies doesn't turn us into monsters, it lifts us out of barbarism.'

'You miss my point, Professor. What time bombs may be hidden in these codes? What sort of monster will they yield?'

Edgeworth said, 'These are weighty issues, President Ogorodnikov. They're matters for extensive discussions by the whole international community, perhaps extending over many years. It needs input from philosophers, scientists, even religious leaders. How can you and I decide these things in a few hours in a log cabin?'

Ogorodnikov's brow wrinkled. 'If the genie is to be kept in the bottle – and I said *if* – then we dare not access the wisdom of our philosophers. Someone would talk.'

'Are you seriously suggesting that you and I reach an instant decision on a matter which needs to be thrashed out by—'

Ogorodnikov interrupted the translator forcefully, spreading his arms wide as he spoke. 'Prime Minister, don't you see? That is the tragedy of our situation. We have no choice. The scientists in the mountain will soon be dispersing and when they do, they will open Pandora's box.'

Edgeworth dabbed at the sweat on his brow. He wondered if some subtle psychology was at play; at any rate Ogorodnikov seemed unperturbed by the heat. The PM looked over at Velikhov. 'Suppose the home planet of the signallers was public knowledge. And suppose someone wanted to send a reply. Could it be done?'

'If the extraterrestrials have receivers no better than ours, a ten-kilowatt signal from us could reach anything out to a hundred light years from here. There must be hundreds of radar stations capable of firing off a reply. Yes, it could be done. It's not even difficult.'

'You see?' Ogorodnikov glared at Edgeworth. 'Once the knowledge is out, the situation is beyond our control. Someone in Cuba or South Africa or Baffin Island could decide to reply. There would be a race for the honour of being the first human to make contact with extraterrestrials.'

Velikhov said, 'In 1974 the Americans used the Arecibo telescope to send a message to a star cluster with over a hundred thousand members. If one of the stars happens to have a planet, and if someone on that planet happens to be pointing a powerful receiver at us for a few critical minutes in the future, they will know that we are here.'

Ogorodnikov spoke angrily. 'What right did these Americans have to do that on behalf of all mankind, without first consulting mankind about the possible consequences?'

'Mikhail Isayevich, the globular cluster is about twenty-five thousand light years away and it will be fifty thousand years before we receive a reply, if we do. They have handed the problem not to us but to our distant descendants.'

'And are these new signallers fifty thousand years away? Fifty years? Or five?'

Velikhov said, 'As of Wednesday the scientists in the castle did not know the location of the home planet. But you can be sure they are moving mountains to find out.'

'And what then?' Edgeworth asked.

'I believe that as soon as they know, they will shout their discovery from the rooftops. The news will be round the globe by e-mail in minutes. The public will see it on CNN within an hour. Every telescope in existence will point at whatever star system this signal comes from.'

Edgeworth said, 'You are telling us, Professor Velikhov, that the scientists in the castle will not willingly be muzzled.'

'Prime Minister, I guarantee it.'

Edgeworth said, 'And so, as you say, Mikhail, opening Pandora's box.'

The two leaders looked into each other's eyes across the table. Ogorodnikov voiced their thoughts quietly. 'This presents us with an interesting problem.'

'You mean . . .'

The Russian President said, 'What are we going to do about them?'

Edgeworth broke the shocked silence. He turned to his PPS. 'Joe, I'd like you to leave us for a few minutes.'

Pembroke, looking stunned, collected his hat without a word. There was a gust of icy air as he left. Edgeworth noted that the darkness outside had been replaced by a dull grey light; through the open door he had seen every detail of the trees and the lake.

Ogorodnikov, at last acknowledging the heat in the cabin, pulled off his heavy sweater. 'Prime Minister, I have a confession to make. Two days ago I asked our Slovakian friends to place a ring of steel around the castle where these scientists are working. They are not yet aware of this. I realise that I have illegally encroached on the rights of two British citizens.'

Edgeworth acknowledged the confession with a nod.

Ogorodnikov added, 'And I have a team of specialists standing by. They can fly there, without fear of detection, at a moment's notice.'

'Specialists?'

'Should we decide to suppress the secret permanently.'

Edgeworth sighed. 'They're not necessary. I've had a man inside the castle since yesterday. He will carry out any special tasks we decide on.'

'Whatever we decide, Prime Minister, we must at all costs keep the Americans out of this. That will not be easy.'

Edgeworth took a deep breath. 'Meantime, you and I have to make some hard decisions.'

25

CIA

For this one, Sullivan himself was carrying out the morning briefing. The CIA Director was flanked by McLarty and Melanie Moore, and the trio faced President Bull across a coffee-table. A Marine unpadlocked the briefcase on the table and left smartly. Sullivan pulled out a buff folder.

Sullivan had bags under his eyes, as if he hadn't slept. 'Mr President, I want to make you aware of some very unusual movements by Prime Minister Edgeworth over the last day or so. It may be relevant to the other matter which I brought to your attention yesterday evening.'

The other matter. Melanie wondered about that.

'Ms Moore here is one of my bright young analysts and I think I should just let her tell the story.'

Melanie Moore had never been inside the White House, let alone sat in the Oval Office in the company of such powerful men.

After the embarrassing memory of her tennis outfit, she had dressed in a well-cut, dark-grey suit, touched her eyelashes with mascara, used a little bronze eye-shadow and a muted plum lipstick which went well, she believed, with her black skin. Her hair was straightened and sleek. She finished the effect with small, plain pearl earrings and she was wearing spectacles with the heaviest frames she could find. ·

But still none of it was quite obliterating that embarrassing memory.

> *Melanie Moore*
> *Should be demure.*

The stupid rhyme, having popped into her head in the Lincoln on the way over, would not go away. She opened the folder Sullivan had laid on the coffee-table. 'Mr President, Prime Minister Edgeworth left Chequers on Thursday evening on a domestic flight, having abruptly cancelled his appearance at the Kohl funeral in Germany and a weekend social engagement. There's no comment on it by the British press. We know, or think we know, he was driven to RAF Northolt which isn't too far from Chequers. Now Edgeworth normally uses a VC-10 on domestic flights and one took off from Northolt soon after his ETA there. This was at twenty-two hundred hours Greenwich Mean Time.'

'So far so good,' Bull said encouragingly.

'Now we don't monitor Royal Air Force communications.'

'Okay.'

'But there are people who do that sort of thing for a hobby. Enthusiastic amateurs.'

'Like trainspotters?' Bull suggested.

'Exactly like trainspotters, except that these people use VHF and UHF scanners, HF radio and so on which are able to pick up military communications. They cover Western Europe and they swap "sightings" on the Net. It's murder on military security, especially if there's, say, a Middle East operation on the boil, but there's nothing any of us can do about it. Anyway, all we had to do was log into their records to find where the Prime Minister's aircraft landed. Here's their record of arrivals at RAF Lossiemouth on the evening in question.' Melanie passed over a sheet of paper with a shaky hand.

aircraft type	serial	squadron	homebase	callsign
2 RAF Tornado OR4	–	9 sqn	RAF Brüggen	Batman 51,52
US Navy P3 Orion	161128	–	Keflavik, Iceland	Navy 61128
1 RAF VC-10 c1	xv104	–	RAF Brize Norton	Gauntlet 62

Bull's eyes skimmed over the sheet. 'The VC-10?'

'Yes, sir. It's based in Brize Norton as you see, but it stopped off at Northolt. Unquestionably the Prime Minister was picked up there and taken on to Lossiemouth.'

'Lossiemouth . . . the name rings a bell.'

'You landed there last summer, sir. The British have a strong strike/attack Tornado complement up there, and it's also where the Royal Family sometimes land when they want to go to Balmoral Castle. That's the Queen's summer house. You've been there too, at the Queen's invitation, that's why you flew to Lossiemouth.'

'I remember the damned castle. Nothing but tartan carpets.'

'But the Prime Minister didn't go to Balmoral. First off, the Queen is in the Bahamas at present. Secondly, the castle just has a few caretakers in it at this time of year.' Melanie passed over a couple of DSP photographs. 'No security, as you see.'

Bull nodded. 'So? Where *did* he go?'

There was a hint of satisfaction in Melanie's voice. 'Lossiemouth also has two Search and Rescue helicopters.' She passed over another cluster of photographs. 'And this is one of them. This particular reconnaissance satellite works in the infrared, Mr President, and the resolution's not too good. But if you look at the second picture – that one – you'll see one of the two Lossiemouth choppers, a Sea King HAR3.'

'I'll take your word for it.'

'We've put it through image enhancement, sir. It's a Sea King, all right. Fifty-six feet long, a hundred and forty miles an hour at sea level, normally a crew of four. This was taken halfway between Scotland and Norway.'

'And you say the British Prime Minister was in this helicopter?'

'There were no ships or aircraft in distress in the area at that time. There was no recorded radio traffic between the Sea King and Lossiemouth. It was flying late at night, almost at sea level, without navigation lights. Why would it be doing this? It has to be connected with the Prime Minister's arrival at Lossiemouth. My analysis to this point is that Edgeworth was heading for some secret destination.'

'Okay, I buy it so far,' said Bull. 'You say it was halfway to Norway?'

'The Sea King's radius of action is just under three hundred miles. That's barely enough to get it to southern Norway and back from north-east Scotland.'

'What's in Norway, Ms Moore?'

Melanie passed over another batch of satellite reconnaissance pictures, each about a foot square. 'We lost coverage for nearly three hours, but here we've picked it up again.' A helicopter, bright in the infrared, was flying over a white background. 'Sir, this is a Sea King. It has to be the same one; there are no others in this part of the world. That being so, it's flown beyond its maximum range. It must have stopped to refuel somewhere in Norway.'

'Which part of the world are we talking about?'

'Finland, sir.'

'Finnish radar would have picked it up.'

'No, sir. This is flying at treetop level through densely forested country. An operation not without risk.'

'The whole damn thing sounds perilous to me.'

'Finally, Mr President, we got this on a DSP pass last evening. The blow-ups are image-enhanced.' The view had been taken looking directly down. A frozen lake and a little cluster of cabins were plainly visible, surrounded by trees. Two of the cabins were shining brilliantly in the infrared. There were two clearings separated by about two hundred yards. 'This is an almost impenetrably remote part of Finland. There are lots of mosquitos in the summer, and just a few trappers and hunters in the winter.' A sharp red-painted nail circled a helicopter in one of the clearings. 'And that's the Sea King.'

'And what the hell's that?' Bull tapped a finger at the image of a much larger machine in the other clearing.

'An Mi-26T from the Moscow Mil helicopter plant. It can incorporate passenger carriage for VIPs in highly comfortable conditions and it has a range of 1300 kilometres if extra fuel tanks are added.'

'VIP carriage?'

'Almost certainly President Ogorodnikov, in our view. He was supposed to be in his Moscow *dacha* at the time.

We asked Ambassador Wilson to confirm this but they've been giving him the runaround.'

'He must have had his nuclear suitcase with him,' Bull observed. 'Where are the communications?'

'We don't know. Maybe in the Mi-26.'

The President shook his head sceptically.

'That's it,' Sullivan said.

Bull leaned back in his chair and steepled his hands thoughtfully. 'What are you telling me, people?'

McLarty decided it was about time to be heard. 'Mr President, this Finnish place is about halfway on the direct route between London and Moscow. Melanie's evidence leads me to believe that the Prime Minister and the Russian President left their respective countries for a clandestine meeting without anyone being aware of their absence.'

'Um-huh. And where are they now?'

'Visibly back in their respective capitals, as if they'd never gone.'

Bull looked at McLarty. 'Any clues?'

'None at all, Mr President.'

— The President sighed. 'John, Ms Moore, thank you both. Good to meet you, Ms Moore.'

Melanie glowed. She followed her boss out of the door, the words:

> *Melanie Moore*
> *Was quite demure*

skipping through her head.

The President waited until the door had closed. Then he swivelled his chair round to face the CIA Director.

'So what's going on, Al?'

'Two crazy things within a day of each other. First the conversation about an ET signal, then a secret head-to-head between Edgeworth and Ogorodnikov. They have to be connected.'

'Where does Edgeworth come into it?'

'Go back to that conversation between the Russian scientists, Velikhov and Shtyrkov. This Shtyrkov is part of an Anglo-Russian experiment in a cave a few hours' drive from the castle. It's an experiment to detect exotic particles from space.'

'Exotic like signals from extraterrestrials? Is that what you're trying to say?' Bull's face was expressionless.

'They could have picked them up by accident.'

'This is getting beyond a joke.'

Sullivan tried to keep his frustration in check. 'Mr President, with respect, they didn't meet up in Finland to catch salmon. Whatever is going on, it's deadly serious and we've been excluded from it. In the interests of national security, it's vital that we find out about that signal.'

Bull strummed his fingers on the table for some moments. 'Al, use your common sense. They're cooking something up over the Iraq crisis.'

'There's no evidence of that, sir.'

'There is now. I want to see an analysis of the options if the Brits changed sides on that one. What's the balance of risks and opportunities for them? What does it mean for us? That's what I need, Al, not this fantasy stuff about alien signals.'

26

Shangri-La

The road was narrow and wet and lined with snow, and the driver took it with care. He glanced in the rear mirror. His passenger was asleep and he took the opportunity to appraise the man. He was in his seventies, white-haired and white-eyebrowed. His mouth was turned down at the edges, giving him a slightly dogmatic look. The man had dressed for the cold: a grey woollen scarf, hand-knitted, poked up above the fur collar of his winter coat, and a pair of fur gloves rested on his lap.

'Much further to go?' the passenger asked, his eyes still shut.

'We're nearly there, sir. We're past Hagerton, going along Hunting Creek.'

The road was climbing steeply, approaching a one-in-ten gradient. The fog was thickening by the yard. The twin halogen beams of the limo lit up a sign for *Catoctin Mountain Park*, and the driver slowed and turned right. Two deer, startled in the headlights, leaped nimbly into the dark.

Logie Harris gave up on his nap. He sat upright in his seat, pulling at his safety belt.

The road levelled. Lights were piercing the fog and an indeterminate shape resolved itself into a metal gate, like the entrance to a high-security prison. A handsome young

Marine took a document from the driver, examined it carefully and peered into the car. 'Welcome to Camp David, sir.'

* * *

Red Oak, like the other guest cottages, was a simple two-bedroomed wooden cabin with a lounge, all wood panelling and timber beams, and an open fireplace. Someone had lit a fire and he was enveloped by a comfortable warmth. The call from the President had come at midnight and he had frantically scoured his library until the car had come to collect him at 2 a.m. It was now 5 a.m. and he had barely slept. He threw off his clothes and put on pyjamas. He kneeled briefly by the bedside and murmured, 'Lord, forgive my sins. Help the President in his troubles, and give me the wisdom to guide him. Amen.' Then he slid between warmed sheets and listened to the silence. His mind drifted back, to the goosepimpling midnight call from the President, to his weird question, and to his closing words: '. . . above all I need someone I can trust.'

Seth Bull, the evangelist deduced, was falling back on his reserves, summoning up the unique bond that half a lifetime of friendship produced. But if the President of the United States couldn't trust the people around him . . .

He was wakened by a powerful roar. He jumped out of bed and drew back the curtains just in time to glimpse a large blue and white helicopter sinking amongst the snow-covered trees a few hundred yards away. The early-hours fog was gone and the sky was blue. A chipmunk scurried over some rocks in front of the cottage. The air was pure and scented. He dressed quickly in casuals and sweater and put on the blue windcheater a steward had given him. He was just pulling on his shoes when he heard a tap on the door. 'Logie, glad you could make it. Come over to my place for breakfast.'

* * *

In the sun lounge of Aspen, at a table with orange juice, Granola and toast, Bull waved his arm towards the window. Beyond the patio was a snow-covered lawn and beyond that a frozen pond. Flurries of snow drifted down from a tree, tracing the route of some creature jumping from branch to branch. Light mist floated up from the Monocacy Valley.

'I can see why Truman called this place Shangri-La, Mr President.'

Bull's tone changed; he became businesslike. 'A good place for clearing out the cobwebs. And believe me, I need a clear head for this one. Finish your breakfast while I change, Logie, and then we'll get down to it.'

Harris strolled on the patio, the President's *Berchtesgaden*. This was indeed a wonderful place for rejuvenation. Here a President could go for a solitary walk, listen to the birds and watch his dog chasing the squirrels. The last time he'd stood here, the patio steps had been bordered with flowers, courtesy of Nancy Reagan. 'Of all the things Ronald misses about the Presidency,' she'd told him, 'his Camp David weekends come top.' Now the flowers were gone and there was ice in the air: at eighteen hundred feet up it could be rough. He turned up his collar. A pristine blanket of snow covered the roof of the lodge, the lawn and the trees, and thin ice coated the hour-glass swimming pool over to the right.

The President appeared wearing a navy-blue wind-cheater and casual trousers to match. White hair protruded under a baseball cap with a badge showing the Presidential yacht. The word *Titanic* was emblazoned beneath the vessel. The men went down the steps and strolled past the pond and the little artificial stream on the west side of the lodge.

'Logie, I need answers in a hurry.' They were in step together, a slow, rhythmic pace. There was nobody else in sight. 'What is the theological position on life out there?'

'Read up on it as soon as I got your call, Seth. But I already knew that the Scriptures give clear guidance on the issue, as they do in so much else in life. But I also looked into the writings of the great thinkers of the past, to see how they handled the question.'

'So what does the Bible say?'

'The Bible is silent on the question of extraterrestrials. I believe the silence is significant. God created Man in His own image. The Bible says nothing about creatures beyond the Earth because there's nothing *to* say about them. They don't exist.'

'Well, that's simple enough.' Bull's tone was sceptical. 'Is that it?'

'The heavy hitters in this area were the medieval thinkers. Nobody has surpassed them for depth of thought, even in modern times.'

'I guess if you're a monk with nothing else to do all day but think . . . Sometimes I wish I was a monk.'

'They were against the idea of life out there on grounds that are still valid today. They were thinking about it before we even knew the Earth is a planet.'

'Incredible,' said the President.

'Incredible. Saint Augustine opposed the alien concept in his *City of God*, likewise Thomas Aquinas in his *Summa Theologica*. They said that mankind, here on Earth, is the focus of God's love. Creatures on other worlds wouldn't have the Creator's love and there would have been no point in creating them.'

Bull's mouth twisted in annoyance. 'Logie, I can't take executive action on the basis of stuff like that. Are medieval monks all you've got?'

'I have all I need, namely the Word of God. If there are people on other worlds, have they sinned as Adam sinned? Would the Saviour have to go from planet to planet, dying again and again? Do we expect this of a God of Love?' The evangelist waved an arm. 'Only a God of Love could create beauty like this.'

'He had a little help from Roosevelt.'

The evangelist seemed not to have heard. 'Are we to believe that Jesus is some sort of travelling redeemer? There just can't be men out there in need of salvation. This has been pointed out over the centuries from William Vorilong in the Middle Ages through Melanchthon in the Renaissance to Thomas Paine in the Age of Reason.'

'Maybe aliens don't need salvation.'

'Mr President, all men need salvation, and it can only be attained through Divine Incarnation. That's core Christian doctrine.'

The valley mist had reached them and snowflakes were beginning to drift lightly down. They were into the trees: maple, birch, hazel and dogwood surrounded them.

Harris went on relentlessly. 'Look, Seth, if there were men on other worlds, then men here on Earth wouldn't be of unique importance to the Creator. You just have to open a Bible to see the absurdity of that belief. The Bible tells us that man was made in the image of God. We're special to Him, like children to a father. God so loved the world that He gave His only begotten son . . .'

'Turn left here. It'll take us back while our ears are still attached to our heads.' The President was frowning. 'Logie, how far do we go back?'

' 'Nam.'

'Right. And as Christians go, would you call me a lousy one?'

Harris grinned. 'You want a sin list? I've picked you up legless from the sidewalk a few times. There was the drink driving charge which the media have miraculously overlooked. There was that business with the Saigon hostess . . .'

'Before Beth, bless her memory.'

'. . . but as old sinners go, you're no worse than me.'

'Well, old habits die hard. I still pray at night, and I try to grab a few verses of the Book in the morning.'

'What are you on now?'

'Psalm 72. *Give the king Thy judgements, O God, and Thy righteousness unto the king's son.*'

'You have more power than any king ever had.'

'Sure. The people gave and the people can take away. I have a duty to do my best for them. But I also have a duty to God. So far, the two have coincided. My dilemma is that in the present situation I can't find a path that embraces the two without compromising either.'

'Render unto Caesar . . .'

The President interrupted impatiently. 'Logie, I'm being given hard evidence that advanced beings are out there and have signalled us.'

Harris stopped. He stared disbelievingly at the President. 'You've been given wrong information, Seth. Intelligent life beyond the Earth is just plain unBiblical.'

Bull shook his head in irritation. 'I'm getting no concrete help from you. Frankly I'm becoming frustrated by your evangelical fantasies. You're telling me there's a flat contradiction between my Christian faith and the evidence my people are bringing in to me.'

'I am.' Harris's face was set in an expression of righteous determination familiar to millions of television viewers.

'But for once in your life, suppose you're wrong. This is what I want to know from you: what would these aliens be like? Would they share our moral code? Would they be well disposed towards us? I need answers to that like a man in the desert needs water and I don't need any fucking medieval monks.'

They were back at Aspen. They climbed steps. Harris turned to the President, his face grim. 'You're looking for something concrete, Seth? I'll give you something concrete.'

'I'm listening, for Christ's sake.'

'If these creatures exist – if you have hard evidence, which I gravely doubt . . .'

'Well?'

'There's only one remaining possibility.'

The President waited.

'Think about it. We're God's beloved. Here on Earth, not scattered around the stars. Therefore any message reaching us couldn't come from creatures born of God. What's left? Angels, yes. But angels born of Satan before the Fall.' Harris paused. 'The message would have to come from the spawn of the Devil.'

'What are you saying?'

'Say you truly received a signal from space, Mr President, a phone call from some advanced intelligence. On no account answer the phone. Keep quiet. Keep very, very quiet.'

27

Siege

A scrawny hand, all skinny grey talons and sharp nails, was stretching over the castle, and black clouds were rolling down the hills on the horizon like an advancing army. But even at half a mile, in the dull light, there was no mistaking Shtyrkov's oblate form. He was moving at a fast waddle, as if trying to escape from the approaching claw.

Svetlana, looking out over the parapet, watched his approach curiously, but with a touch of alarm. He cut across the grass, puffing and wheezy, his eyes fixed on the ground ahead of him, and toddled briskly under her before disappearing from sight round the corner. She went into the building and stood at the top of the marble stairs. In a moment he appeared at the foot, breathless. He looked up at the stairs helplessly. Anxiety showed in his eyes.

'Stay down there,' Svetlana called to him. 'I'll get the others.'

A few minutes later she had herded the scientists into the computer room. Gibson entered carrying a tray of coffee and biscuits. Petrie was unshaven and his eyes were red-rimmed. He was carrying a bundle of papers as if reluctant to let go of them.

'Where's Hanning?' Gibson wanted to know.

'I can't find him,' Svetlana complained.

Gibson poured coffees. He looked at Shtyrkov, who had collapsed into one of the blue armchairs. 'What's the problem?'

'I go for a walk, to think. I meet soldiers in the woods. They turn me back. Ladies and gentlemen, they will not allow us to leave the castle. They intend us to die here.'

Gibson said, quietly, 'That's a bit dramatic, Vashislav.'

'But I tell you, they turn me back!'

'Maybe there's some military exercise going on in the woods,' Petrie suggested.

'Not an exercise.' Shtyrkov shook his head vigorously. 'An operation. To keep us here. We are prisoners in the castle.'

'Prisoners?' Freya giggled nervously. She was stirring coffee with brisk little movements, the spoon jangling in the china cup.

Petrie stood up. 'We can test this.'

'Spoken in the best scientific tradition,' said Gibson. 'Take a walk in the woods. I'll give you five minutes and then stroll out the front gate.'

'I tell you we're prisoners,' Shtyrkov said. 'We will die here.'

* * *

Into the woods.

The black clouds are now overhead and the light is fading by the minute. Petrie tries to look like a man out for a stroll, tries not to peer into dark corners.

Stop, stretch, glance behind. All very casual. The castle is still visible in outline through the trees, a dark silhouette against a white misty patch of sky. The air is damp. Rain will come at any minute. The witch's fingers are at ground level now, little tracers of mist creeping through the trees on either side of him. In Petrie's imagination they are purposeful, enclosing him in a pincer movement.

And there are shapes, lurking in the shadows.

Tricks of the light: be rational. He turns up the collar of his fleece jacket and walks further into the forest, his mouth dry.

Somewhere ahead, a dog barks. It's a big dog, heavy on the low frequencies, and it's more of a howl than a bark. Maybe a mile ahead, maybe less. His breath is misting in the cold, and his footsteps are muffled; the acoustics remind him of a tomb inside a pyramid.

The path still easily visible, but dark shapes are now everywhere. More tricks of the light. Of course.

A low whistle, off to the right, on the limit of hearing.

Nonsense. Just a sound in his head.

Petrie feels his nerve going. He thinks he must be a mile from the castle. He wonders where the path ends: at a lodge house? Or does it wind into . . .

'*Stůj!*' Stop!

The voice, all Slavic intonations and deep-chested, cuts into the stillness. He freezes. Suddenly, half a dozen soldiers in camouflage gear are emerging from the trees. They look like sixteen year olds. They are carrying rifles which resemble black plastic toys. Petrie thinks a burst from one of them would probably cut you in half.

One of the soldiers approaches to within a couple of feet of Petrie. He is older than the others, maybe in his late twenties, with a grey, thin face. He smells of stale nicotine. 'You are not allowed here, Englishman. Get back to the castle.'

Petrie knows the answer but he tries it anyway. 'Why should I? These woods belong to the Academy of Sciences. I'm their guest and I have every right to be here.'

The officer's expression becomes one of amazed disbelief. He gives some order without taking his eyes off Petrie. Two of the teenage boys step forward. They are plainly nervous, but their expressions are heavy with truculence. Then: 'Turn back now while you can. *Rozumíte mi?*' Understand me?

Somewhere, in some magazine, Petrie has read about the best response to an armed opponent: don't discuss, don't argue, do what you're told. He shrugs, says, '*Rozumím*,' understood, and turns back on the path. A simple fact fills his mind: he has his back to half a dozen nervous teenagers with rifles. His mouth is parched and his shoulder-blades ache with tension.

Stroll. Don't run.

A light glimpsed through the trees; lights have been switched on in some of the castle rooms. He glances back, casually. The path is empty; he is alone in the woods. Petrie wonders about another experiment: leave the path, take off at some angle, run clear to God knows where. But then his imagination sees dogs unleashed, the chase through the woods, kids with nightscopes and black plastic toys that cut you in half. Rain starts pattering on leaves.

The dog again. A lot closer, maybe half a mile behind him, maybe a couple of hundred yards. The castle is half a mile ahead. The temptation to break into a run is becoming irresistible, but he keeps strolling, his nerves at breaking point and a light sweat inside his gloves. His ears strain for the sound of running dogs but the rain is now battering noisily on the leaves.

By the time Petrie reaches the glorious front door of the castle it is dark, the rain is teeming down, and he is shaking with fright.

* * *

'They intend to kill us.'

Shtyrkov was putting together something which he had described as 'monastery stew'. A handful of finely chopped carrots went into an outsize frying pan. It sizzled as it hit the oil, and he stirred it with a big wooden spoon.

It fitted.

'You can't mean that.' Worry lined Svetlana's face, but she had clearly followed the same logical route as the fat Russian. 'I mean, governments don't do things like that. Not nowadays. Not in civilised Europe.' She turned to Hanning as if for reassurance. The civil servant was draining water away from diced potatoes and pretended not to notice her anxious gaze.

'Pass me the mushrooms, Svetlana, and don't be so naive.'

'You can't be right,' Petrie said, but he had already made the same deduction. *It must have been a multi-national decision, taken at the highest level.*

'Why not? It fits like a coffin.' Shtyrkov was now waving a big pepper mill over the frying pan.

'But why?'

'Now the onions and the olives, please. Fear of the unknown, Svetlana. The fools think the signallers are trying to flush us out, to see if we have reached a level of technology where we might threaten them in a century or two.'

Svetlana brought two Pyrex bowls over to the Russian. She seemed close to tears. 'Why don't we confront them?'

Hanning, at the sink next to Shtyrkov, emptied a big saucepan of water and rice into an orange colander. Steam was rising. 'You really are being absurd.'

'We have to give it fifteen minutes.'

'How can you think of food?'

'We need to keep our sugar levels up. This is no time for slow thinking.'

Potatoes and rice were transferred over to the brew. Shtyrkov sprinkled salt, and then half a bottle of wine was going into the mixture. Back at the kitchen table, he poured the remaining wine into glasses. He seemed almost euphoric, as if he was involved in some sort of game. Then Petrie caught him looking in the wine glass, reflecting light from the overhanging chandelier.

Freya broke the tense silence. 'What now?'

Petrie said, 'We have one advantage. They think we don't know.'

She swept long blonde hair back over her shoulders.

Gibson rubbed his chin. 'The fact is, we don't know. Maybe we're getting steamed up over nothing.'

Automatically, the scientists looked over at Hanning, the insider in the counsels of government, the man who would know about things like this.

'This place must be getting to you. These things just aren't done.'

'How would you see it from Lord Sangster's chair?' Petrie asked.

Hanning sighed. 'If, as a matter of policy, it was decided that knowledge of the signal poses an unacceptable risk to humanity – or even to the country – then yes, we pose a problem. An awkward problem.'

* * *

'All present and correct?' Gibson said to nobody in the administrator's office. The office was brightly lit with standard lamps commandeered from alcoves and corners.

The video camera atop a computer terminal stared at them from the polished teak table.

He tapped at a keyboard. Snow appeared on the terminal. 'We're cut off?'

'Nonsense, Svetlana.' Hanning typed in a string of numbers again slowly, with one finger. Then a mature, white-haired female, all cashmere sweater and pearls, appeared. 'Lord Sangster's office.'

'Sandra? Jeremy here. I'd like to speak to Lord Sangster, please, on the video conference circuit.'

There was a hesitation. Then: 'A moment, Mr Hanning.'

The face disappeared. They sat in silence, watching the background of bookshelves on the monitor. Shtyrkov started to strum his fingers noisily on the table. Hanning gave him a look and the Russian finished his strumming with a defiant roll. Then suddenly a round face appeared on the screen. Sangster's smooth, plummy voice came over clearly: 'We're secure, Jeremy?'

'We are.'

'Who is with you?'

'Just the scientists.' Gibson panned the camera around the little group. Petrie, at the corner of the table, studied Sangster's face closely; it was serious, sagging, his cheeks tinged a little red which might have told of an outdoors life or an excessive love of alcohol. The expression gave nothing away. Hanning, on the other hand, had just a touch of anxiety in his expression. Or so Petrie thought; it was hard to be sure.

Hanning said, 'Simon, we have a strange situation here.'

Gibson swivelled the camera slightly to centre on Hanning. Sangster's face had acquired a grim look. Petrie felt his own face going pale, began to feel nauseous.

Hanning was saying, 'We can't get out of the castle,

Simon. The Slovaks have put a brigade of soldiers round it. Do you know anything about this?'

'Yes. Yes, I do.'

Petrie's nausea intensified. He wondered if he would have to flee the table.

'I think you owe us an explanation.'

'It's a simple security precaution.'

Shtyrkov muttered, '*Yob tvou mat.*' Svetlana gasped. Then, unaccountably, Shtyrkov laughed. 'They want us to die and the secret with us. That is what they want for humanity. To live in slime for ever.'

'Who is that?'

Gibson swivelled the camera.

Hanning said, 'Vashislav Shtyrkov. A Russian citizen.'

'You do not intend to let us leave the castle. We are to die here and the signal with us.'

Sangster's expression was one of incredulity. 'That really is nonsensical of you, Mr Shtyrkov.'

'What about my country?' Shtyrkov asked. 'Was Ogorodnikov consulted? Did he push for it?'

Sangster's head was shaking at the absurdity. 'Please, be realistic. Perhaps the isolation is doing things to you. We are dealing with civilised governments, not gangster states.'

Shtyrkov giggled. 'You are a very simple organism, Lord Sangster. You want the knowledge about an intelligent life form out there to be buried. You know that we won't be gagged. The conclusion is inevitable. And of course you lie to us, to keep us pacified.'

Petrie was startled to find that he was daydreaming, fantasising about Colditz-like escapes from the castle. He forced the absurdity out of his mind, dragged himself back to reality.

There was silence round the table. Then the camera lens was zooming to give Sangster a panoramic view. He adopted a sorrowful tone. To Petrie, he was hamming it up like a third-rate actor. 'I'm deeply sorry that you are suffering from this delusion, Mr Shtyrkov. All I can do is repeat that the Slovaks have kindly agreed to put soldiers round the castle as a simple security precaution. The stakes are just too high for, let us say, agents of another state getting hold of the signal you are deciphering.'

Gibson's tone was despairing. 'The signallers are extending the hand of friendship. And we're too steeped in barbarity to—'

Sangster interrupted. 'Possibly, even probably. But decisions on such issues are not your domain and further discussion is pointless. We shall require additional progress reports from you. I suggest we make contact at noon tomorrow, your time, and then again at midnight.'

For a moment uncertainty was flickering across the face on the screen, as if Sangster wanted to add something. But then he gave a little nod of finality and his image dissolved into snow.

Svetlana rushed out of the room.

Gibson dived over to a computer and started tapping briskly. Then he slapped the keyboard angrily. 'I can't get out.'

In a minute Svetlana returned, out of breath. She was holding a small mobile phone. 'It's dead.'

Petrie buried his face in his hands. Then he heard:

'My oh my oh my oh my
Here we stay until we die.'

He looked across the table at Shtyrkov. The Russian caught the look, grinned ghoulishly back. 'My temporal lobe damage, it progresses, does it not?'

28

Where Are They?

For an incredible second, she thought she glimpsed Logie Harris, the famous evangelist, through the trees. *What is this, Jurassic Park?* the Science Adviser asked herself. *Surely Bull isn't taking advice from that old dinosaur?* But then the figure had gone and she carried on towards Laurel.

Hazel had always thought that the word 'cabin', applied to a building with three conference rooms and a mass of communications to the outside world, was stretching the English language a bit. Maybe, she surmised, it had been a cabin in the days when it had housed the Head of the Secret Service detail. But at least, unlike the Oval Office, the President's office in Laurel Cottage was small and workmanlike.

The Chief sat behind his L-shaped desk with a computer and a clutter of papers. A man – a stranger – faced him across this desk, sitting uncomfortably upright. He was thin, intense, and looked as if he had slept in his cheap suit. He glanced briefly at Hazel and then looked away. Hazel thought that someone invited to the desk of the world's most powerful man might at least have made an effort with the suit. Probably a bachelor, she guessed, living in some enclosed little world of his own.

The President waved in the general direction of the man. 'Hazel, I want you to meet Professor Cardow, from

Stanford. He's with some think-tank which tries to predict future trends. He's made a special study of the alien question – whether some day we'll meet up with little green men.' The thin man grinned nervously, stood up, touched Hazel's extended hand briefly then sat down again. Hazel groaned inwardly. *Another high-powered genius who couldn't boil an egg.*

'Sit yourself down and listen to what the Professor has to say.'

Cardow glanced uncertainly between the President and his Scientific Adviser. His voice, when he spoke, was nasal and high-pitched. Hazel found it irritating almost from the first word. 'I've been asked by the President to give an opinion on whether there's intelligent life out there. My answer is No.'

'And he can prove it with mathematical certainty,' the President stated. 'Sorry to interrupt, Stanford University, don't let me do it again.'

Cardow resumed. 'The problem is this, ma'am: where are they?'

Bull said, 'That's what I've been saying all along. Where are they?'

Hazel waited patiently. It occurred to her that Cardow, although addressing both the President and her, was avoiding eye-contact with both.

Cardow cleared his throat. 'Given enough time, space travel is easy, Ms Baxendale. If we take the modern scientific age as having started with Newton's law of gravity, we're only four hundred years old. From the first Model T Ford to the International Space Station was only a hundred years – a human lifespan. It's doubtful if there will ever be a time from now on when there isn't a human being in space. And who knows how long our civilisation will last? Maybe another ten thousand years, maybe a million . . .'

Hazel shifted impatiently in her chair. 'What's your point, Professor?'

'My point is that given a few million years, you can colonise the Galaxy easier than you can fall off a log. We've already sent the *Pioneer* spacecraft clean out of the Solar System. In another thousand years – in maybe a hundred years – we'll have probes heading here, there and everywhere in interstellar space. Now there are a hundred billion stars out there and half of them are older than the Sun. Suppose there are civilisations out there millions of years old. Suppose there's even one. It would have colonised the Galaxy long ago. We'd see plenty signs of it. The aliens would be here amongst us now. So where are they? If there was any intelligent life at all out there, the galaxy would be humming with radio signals. But all we hear is silence.'

'You're saying there's nobody else in the whole Galaxy? We're totally alone?'

'Totally. We're at the very beginning of our evolution as an intelligent species. Any other civilisation out there would be millions of years old, maybe tens of millions, maybe hundreds of millions. It would have taken over long, long ago.'

'Did I hear you say hundreds of millions? Civilisations *hundreds* of millions of years older than us?' the President asked.

Cardow, still avoiding eye-contact with Hazel, turned to the President. 'Mr President, any civilisation which takes the science route will explode in power. Look where we've reached in four hundred years. Where will we be in four thousand years? Or four million? And there are stars like the Sun four *billion* years older than us. Any intelligent life forms out there would have taken over our planet long ago, before there were even humans. But where are they? There's no sign of them.'

Hazel tried a line she'd read somewhere: 'So you said. But absence of evidence isn't evidence of absence.'

'But we have evidence,' Cardow countered smoothly. 'They're not here.'

'Let's not get too smart,' Bull growled.

Hazel felt her jaw tightening. 'There's got to be something wrong with that argument. We know the Sun is an ordinary star. We know planetary systems must be common. There must be Earth-like planets out there in their billions, lots of them with water. And where there's water there's every prospect that life will evolve.' As soon as Hazel mentioned the word 'evolve', she remembered that the President was a creationist, almost felt his negative body language. *Shit*.

'That's the NASA line,' Cardow was saying. A slightly peeved tone was creeping into his voice; Baxendale suspected the man didn't like being contradicted. 'They push sub-surface oceans on Europa and permafrost on Mars, make out you're a screwball if you don't believe that's a recipe for life, and use the prospect of finding it to squeeze megabucks out of Congress.' He turned to Bull again. 'The fact is, Mr President, there's every reason to believe we're alone. Take the idea that life was created out of a primordial soup.'

'Soup? Life created from soup?' Bull looked incredulous.

'A primordial soup, formed by a chance combination of molecules. Now we're made up of proteins and a protein molecule is made up of dozens to hundreds of amino acids, put together in a particular order. Suppose the soup is full of these amino acids. If we were to randomly shuffle these amino acids to get the full range of proteins that life depends on ... well, the odds against getting it right first time are one in ten to the power forty thousand.' Cardow looked triumphantly across at Baxendale. 'That's a one followed by forty thousand zeros.'

'Thank you, Professor, but as a past Vice-president of the National Academy of Sciences I have some familiarity with power notation.'

'Can you put that in layman's terms?' Bull asked.

I thought I had, the Stanford man thought. 'Ah, what it means is that there's absolutely no chance that the process has been duplicated anywhere in the Galaxy or even anywhere else in the Universe. The odds are far too great.'

The President opened a drawer and pulled out a cheroot. 'That's pretty persuasive to me, Hazel. We're one-offs, God's creation. His little fallen angels.'

Cardow, having found his tongue, was becoming eloquent. The President leaned back and puffed in the air, letting the Stanford futurologist talk.

'Even if life did develop somewhere, the odds that it would evolve to an intelligent state are astronomical. Evolution has more twists and turns than you can imagine. It took three billion years even to get to the stage of sponges. Compound the improbabilities and you see it's a miracle that we're here at all. We're alone in the Universe. We've been brainwashed, not just by NASA, but by Hollywood. There's no drama in Star Trek movies where the crew never meet an alien.'

'No drama equals no bucks,' Bull observed.

Cardow turned the knife: 'The public has been duped into the expectation that the Universe is teeming with life, and it suits a lot of people, from movie producers to Californian scientists, to feed that expectation. But it's a falsehood. Otherwise the aliens would be here.'

Hazel looked over at Bull. The President had a satisfied look, as if he'd just had a big poker win. 'Mr President, the world's full of cranks with axes to grind. I've never heard of this man. I'm your Science Adviser, dammit. It's me you listen to.'

A little wisp of smoke was drifting up from the President's cigar towards the ceiling. 'But I think you just lost the argument. Stanford here has given us a two-pronged, watertight case. First, even if you believe in evolution which I don't, the odds are billions to one against intelligent life emerging from primitive bugs. Second, if there was alien life it would be everywhere including here and it's not. The arguments fit like two gloves.' Bull leaned back in his swivel chair. 'There are no aliens, not anywhere. But you see, Hazey, I already knew that. Little green men with pointy heads are unBiblical.'

'Mr President, the seabed's littered with ships that were thought to be watertight. I don't know what Professor Cardow's hang-up is, but he's just fed you some very bad advice.'

Cardow's lips tightened like a prim old woman's, and he blushed an angry red.

'Uhuh?' Bull gave his Science Adviser a long, thoughtful stare. With his slightly hooked nose, she had the disconcerting feeling of being watched by an owl. 'You need to unwind a bit, Hazey, that's what this place is for. Come over about ten, and you and I'll watch a movie.'

'Why thank you, sir. You know that as a woman I can't deal with the heavy issues. But I do appreciate a nice pat on the head.' Baxendale said it with a big smile to show that she was joking. She gave Cardow a look of pure venom as she left, and the futurologist blushed again.

THE LURE

* * *

Big snowflakes were drifting down when Hazel trudged her way through six inches of snow to the Aspen Lodge. Footprints had preceded her.

Warm air and Latin-American rhythm enveloped her as she stepped inside. Along the corridor to the living room, Jet, the President's black Labrador, sniffed at her trouser legs.

'Come on in, Hazey, you're just in time.' The President, tieless and with his shirt hanging out, was dropping ice cubes into a cocktail shaker. Logie Harris was leaning back in an armchair, Coke in hand. He gave a tense little nod to Hazel.

'Cha cha cha.' Bull was nodding to the beat while expertly rattling the cocktail shaker over his shoulder. 'Paid my way through Harvard doing this. Law student by day, barman by night. Never forgotten how to do it.' He added the contents to tall ice-filled glasses, carefully trickled a red liquid into the drinks and delivered a multi-coloured liquid to Hazel. 'Tequila sunrise. Guaranteed to put a smile even on the grim face of my Science Adviser.'

Hazel took a sip and smiled. Bull wagged a finger and gave an I-told-you-so grin. 'Hell, you look beautiful when you smile. You know Logie?'

Harris stood up and extended a hand to Hazel. 'I hear you crossed swords today.'

Hazel said, 'Yes, with another backwoodsman.' Harris's face froze.

Bull crossed to a light switch and to Hazel the room fell dark for a few seconds, until her sight adapted to the gentle red glow of reflected firelight. Now a screen was coming slowly down from the ceiling, and the President was removing a painting to reveal a small alcove with a projector. A white-haired steward built the fire up with seasoned logs, and Jet stretched out in front of it. Hazel shared a settee with the President, while Jack Lemmon and Tony Curtis shared misadventures with Marilyn Monroe on an overnight sleeper. Bull and Harris chortled through the movie, the President occasionally laughing out loud and slapping Hazel's thigh.

As the closing credits rolled, she said, 'I ought to go, Mr President.'

'Have a nightcap, Hazey.'

'No, thank you.' She stood up. What made her say it she didn't know; it just came out in a surge of anger. 'Mr President, I see this alien message as a turning point for mankind. You can't handle the issue by cutting yourself off, surrounding yourself with these people.'

'These people?' Bull's tone was suddenly frosty.

Harris, on his feet, adopted a combative tone. 'I for one thank God for the President's wisdom. I don't doubt your erudition, Ms Baxendale, but only arrogance can make us believe that infinite knowledge is given us.'

She said coldly, 'I can't argue with that.'

'Then surely you can see that the origin of life is a domain that belongs to the Creator, not to man? And surely, unless you are godless, you must accept that God's intentions are revealed to us through revelation?'

'Now it gets complicated.'

Harris pounded on, a preacher with a congregation. 'And the Scriptures are clear: only Man is made in the image of God. Therefore the only possible life forms beyond the Earth cannot be creatures of God. We must pay no heed to their siren message. We dare not.'

Hazel sighed. 'I'll wish you both goodnight.'

She turned at the door, said, 'Jesus H. Christ,' and slammed it shut.

* * *

Despair was settling over her like a cloak.

The snow had stopped, and between the clouds were stars, sharp and crystalline. Her ears were beginning to hurt with cold, and her fingers were tingling. She trudged down the steps and made her way on to a path between the trees. As she walked she looked up at a cold and alien sky, utterly unlike the haze which overlaid Washington D.C., orange like the cheeks of a pantomime tart.

Somewhere up there. *Somewhere up there.*

Maybe that bright star, or that one, maybe one of the thousands of lesser ones, going as faint as the eye could see and no doubt beyond. Maybe, even, the signallers came from someplace between the stars, from some dark interstellar realm.

There were animal tracks in the snow; small, clawed creatures. Her breath was steaming.

Someone had lit a fire in Maple Lodge; she saw its flickering light, and the smoke curling up from the chimney. Again she looked up at the myriad lights between the trees, each one a prodigious nuclear furnace, many with planets orbiting around them.

Where are you? Who are you? What do you want of us?

She shivered, and turned into the cabin. Inside, she paced up and down the corridor, baffled.

You have a Harvard law degree.

Sheer popularity swept you into your second term. You won support for the Poverty Bill against the conservatives, and by some miracle you even got the Environment Bill through while keeping the oilmen on board.

You're handling the Iraqi crisis like a maestro.

You're a miracle-worker, Seth.

She tossed her coat, hat and gloves on to the bed and marched angrily through to the small kitchen.

So why are you taking your advice on this paramount issue from screwballs, nuts and hillbillies?

She filled the kettle with icy water.

Is it conceivable that something deeper than Bible Belt fundamentalism is holding you back?

An incredible thought leaped into her head:

Is it conceivable, by any stretch of the imagination, that Cardow and Harris are right?

She paced up and down some more, looked at her watch, and picked up a telephone.

29

Freya

'I wonder what it will be like?' Shtyrkov wanted to know. The metal grid protecting the bar had proved impenetrable but the men had used an antique stool as a battering ram on the door. Both stool and door now lay in splinters and an impressive array of bottles was spread over the coffee-table in front of them. He was cradling a tumbler of some green liquid.

'What?' Gibson, having downed four large J&Bs, spoke the word with exaggerated care. The hands of the big clock were pointing to just before midnight.

'The slaughter. How will they do it? Will they smother us? Shoot us? Slit our throats?'

'Cut that out. Think of the ladies.' It came out chauvinistic but Gibson was too far gone to care.

Svetlana giggled. From time to time she rubbed her nose, as if the bubbles from her champagne were tickling it.

Hanning said, 'I really don't know what's got into you people. Sangster went blue in the face telling you the soldiers are there as a simple precaution. To keep unfriendly people out.'

Shtyrkov finished his tumbler of green liquid and reached for the half-empty bottle. 'But they're keeping us in.'

Petrie looked round at his drunken companions, sunk in the blue armchairs: Shtyrkov, Gibson, Svetlana, Freya,

Hanning and himself. *Six of us.* 'Can we go over it again? The escape possibilities?'

'What's the point?' Hanning asked.

'The point is survival.' Freya's voice was tense. 'There must be some way out of this. Didn't you say the place reminded you of Colditz, Jeremy? Well, people escaped from Colditz, didn't they?'

'You're clutching at straws,' Gibson said, pouring his fifth whisky with immense care.

Hanning spoke gently. 'Say I go along with this ridiculous fantasy for the sake of argument. Colditz was master forgers, tunnelling engineers, teams of specialists. Colditz was months of planning. Above all, Colditz was before night-vision optics.'

Freya waved an arm around. 'Look at the brainpower in this room. We can think of something.'

Hanning shook his head. 'You're imbeciles in these matters. You have a few hours and we're surrounded by a brigade of troops. There's clear grass all the way around the castle and no way whatsoever of crossing it undetected. There are no tunnels. You can't disguise yourselves as cleaning staff. You can't hide in the trash cans. And you can't fight your way past a hundred Kalashnikovs with kitchen knives. I'm sorry, Freya.'

Something wrong. Something about Hanning.

Through his alcoholic haze, Petrie analysed Hanning's words. *You have a few hours. You're imbeciles in these matters.* Not *We have a few hours. We're imbeciles in these matters.* Was Hanning excluding himself from the imminent killings? Was it a slip of the tongue, or a case of *in vino veritas*?

'There is no prospect of escape.' Shtyrkov said it with emphasis, almost with a tone of triumph.

Petrie listened to the Russian's words and his heart sank. *Come on, Vash, you're the sharp one. Think of something!* Until now he had hoped, even believed, that Vashislav would find a way out. If there was a way out, some lateral thinking to be done, some trick, Vashislav would have come up with it. A sense of nausea washed over him. He said, 'Still, "It is a sweet and seemly thing to die for one's country." Seneca. Right, Jeremy?'

Hanning raised a tumbler unsteadily. 'Right. To Seneca.'

Petrie added, 'Oh, God.' Nobody paid any attention.

'What's that green slime?' Gibson nodded at Shtyrkov's glass.

'Charlee, it is alcohol. It is called Green Slime and when I have finished this bottle I will start on another one.'

'Well, you may have given up, pal, but I'm thinking survival . . .'

'To the British!' Shtyrkov raised his tumbler ironically.

'. . . and I can't do it with a spinning head. I'm for bed.' Gibson stood up, steadying himself on an armchair.

'Me too,' said Petrie.

Gibson turned at the door, swaying. 'Would any of you ladies care to join me?'

Svetlana giggled again. It was that or burst into tears.

* * *

A tap on the door. Petrie, his head still groggy with wine, dragged himself into a sitting position. He switched on the bedside lamp.

Freya, carrying an opened bottle of white wine and two glasses. She put them down on the table and sat on a chair, pushing Petrie's clothes to the floor. 'I can't believe things like this happen.' She was wearing her red sweater and long dark skirt, and was bare-footed.

'All the rules are off,' Petrie said, pulling his knees up. The headboard was cold on his back.

'We think, when the cleaners come in the morning, we'll take their van and ram our way out.'

'Don't be silly. Anyway the cleaners won't come.'

'How can they not? There's a conference on Monday. But if that doesn't work, we'll hide until the conference people turn up. The castle is full of hiding places and we only need to hide for a day.'

'They'll sniff us out with dogs.'

Freya blew her nose. 'I love dogs. Have you given up, then? The great pattern finder, the man who boldly goes where no problem solver has gone before?'

'No way have I given up. I just need to sleep on it. So you love dogs?'

'And life. I don't want to go at age twenty-three. I want to go when I'm ninety, drinking and smoking a cigar and watching the northern lights. So sleep well, Thomas, and waken up with an idea.' She moved over to Petrie's bed, and sat on the edge. He caught a light whiff of eau de cologne, felt a sudden, sharp pang of attraction. *Bloody hormones!*

She asked, 'Have you seen the aurora?'

'Not yet.'

'*Oy! Oy! Oy!* To die before you have lived! When you see them from the roof of the world, in their full glory, then you will believe in Thor and Odin.'

'You're a poetic sort of creature, Freya.'

'And you're a miserable, disembodied computer, a pale imitation of a real man.' She poured two glasses. Petrie took a sip; the wine was cold.

'Freya, I'm a bundle of inhibitions. I can't sing or dance. But I'm in love with your hair.'

'I see you have hairs on your chest.' She touched his chest; Petrie wondered if she could feel his heart hammering.

'They go all the way down.'

'I wonder if the signallers dance? And what they would sound like, singing?'

'I didn't see any music in their signal.'

'I wonder if they make love? What about you, Thomas, have you ever made love?'

'Freya!'

'Ha! I thought not.' She snorted scornfully and sipped wine. 'Do you know where the name Freya comes from?'

'Of course not.'

She put her glass on the table and smiled again. 'My little inhibited computer, Freya is the goddess of love and fertility. And we could be dead tomorrow.'

We could be dead tomorrow. 'What a wonderful chat-up line!'

She touched his chest lightly again. 'They go all the way down, you say?'

* * *

At first, Petrie thought they had come for him. He was being shaken roughly by the shoulder. Then he smelled the green slime on Shtyrkov's breath and saw his massive bulk in dark outline. 'Tom! Tom!'

He felt Freya's leg taut over his own. She was stretching. A bedside lamp clicked on and then she was hiding under the sheet, only the crown of her head visible on the pillow.

Petrie sat up. The Russian's face wore an intense expression and he had a finger to his mouth. 'Get dressed. Come and see this. Be very quiet. No shoes.'

Suppressing his embarrassment, Petrie stretched out for underpants and in a moment was dressed in plain T-shirt, jeans and socks.

'Freya. Put the light out.'

A slim arm appeared from under the sheet and groped towards the bedside lamp, and then they were back into darkness. Petrie followed the Russian to the door, sensing rather than seeing his frame.

Along the narrow carpeted corridor and down the broad staircase. A faint light was coming from below. Shtyrkov's wheezy breath was loud in the silence and there was an occasional *crack!* from his arthritic knee.

Into the atrium. The light was here; it was blue, and it was coming from under the door to the administrator's office. They crept past the armchairs and settees, and stopped at the oak door. Shtyrkov tapped Petrie on the shoulder. He whispered in his ear. 'The keyhole!'

On his knees, Petrie had a good view of half the room. He looked, and was appalled.

Hanning was talking quietly. The light was coming from the monitor he sat at. The screen was edge-on to Petrie and he could neither make out the face on it nor hear the words. From Hanning's body language the conversation seemed to be coming to an end. Suddenly the civil servant leaned towards the monitor. He switched it off.

In a near panic, Petrie jumped up and collided with Shtyrkov. They set off quietly and as fast as the near-blackness would allow, Shtyrkov gasping for air. They reached the marble stairs but it was too late, the door was opening. Petrie pulled at Shtyrkov and they were down, crouching, behind a chair a few feet past the steps.

The door to the library closed, very quietly. Hanning

was padding straight towards them. He was making almost no sound. At the foot of the stairs they heard him stop.

Dead silence.

Hanning no more than six feet away.

Shtyrkov holding his breath.

A distinct *crack!* Shtyrkov's arthritic knee.

Somewhere in the distance a dog barked.

Shtyrkov still holding his breath.

Petrie wondering if they had been seen: two figures, one of them bulky, trying to hide behind an armchair.

Silence, except for the dog going wolf and the hammer-hammer in Petrie's chest. And Shtyrkov still holding on, his eyes beginning to pop.

Green slime! Shtyrkov was reeking of alcohol. It had to be a giveaway. Hanning could surely smell their presence.

Then footsteps were padding quietly up the stairs and Petrie was mentally saying, *Hold on, Vashislav, don't blow it now, don't breathe, just seconds more.*

The footsteps were gone and Petrie was shaking all over and Shtyrkov was taking in air in deep, shuddering gulps. He was trying to do it quietly but without much success.

They made their way slowly up the stairs, following Hanning's direction, with the Russian bent double and gripping the balustrade. After every few steps he would pause and wheeze. Back to the corridor. Petrie counted the doors on the right. *One, two, three, four, five.* He turned the handle and the door was unlocked. Good for Freya: she'd had the presence of mind to keep the room dark. So far as Hanning knew, the condemned scientists were sound asleep.

Shtyrkov found a switch and they blinked in the sudden light. Freya had pulled on her skirt and sweater but Petrie thought there was no bra underneath it. She was sitting on the broad window ledge, hair tousled and her face showing strain and tiredness. Eau de cologne lingered in the air.

Petrie sat on the edge of the unmade bed, and they waited, wordless, while Shtyrkov leaned against the door, slowly regaining his breath. Finally: 'Hanning is a traitor.'

'He was on the conference circuit just now,' Petrie told Freya.

'What does that prove?'

'That he was communicating without our knowledge.'

'So? Maybe he was trying to bargain for our lives.'

'No.' Shtyrkov's voice was quiet but emphatic. 'I heard him earlier. He was talking to Sangster. He was informing his lordship that we are deeply suspicious, that we would like to flee the castle but can see no way out and that we are nevertheless continuing to work on the signal.'

Freya said weakly, 'That makes him a traitor? It's no more than the truth.'

'Oh, young Freya, I love you for your innocence.' Shtyrkov managed a grin, but his face showed pain and there was a purple rim round his lips. 'If I were thirty years younger ... But no, Hanning's tone was that of an informant. He is reporting back to Sangster and that has only one interpretation. The man is what you call a mole.'

Petrie said, 'Damn. *158 Rock Walk.*'

Shtyrkov looked bewildered, and Petrie continued: 'Somebody sent me a warning. It reached me in London on my way here.'

'I remember. It worried Charlie.'

'It was lightly encoded, I cracked it in minutes but it wouldn't have made sense to a casual reader. Vashislav, it can only have come from someone in the UK government who had access to your ET suspicions.'

'More than that, my friend, someone who anticipated the possible reaction of your government. Someone close to your Prime Minister.'

'That settles it,' said Petrie. 'Hanning's a traitor in our midst.'

Freya asked, 'Does it matter now?'

'It matters very much, my dear, if we think of a way to escape. He tells your fine English lord, the lord tells your Prime Minister, he tells the President of Slovakia and then . . .' Shtyrkov made a throat-cutting gesture.

'But even if you're right, what harm can he do? We have no way out. You said it yourself.'

'I gave a good performance, did I not? "There is no prospect of escape." I spoke with such bravura, such conviction!'

Petrie's heart lurched. 'What are you saying, Vashislav?'

'Englishman, your life may depend on keeping your voice down.' Shtyrkov flopped down next to Petrie on the bed. The mattress sagged under his weight. He took some breaths before continuing: 'There is a way out, just possibly. Very likely to be terminal, and only for the desperate.'

'Vashislav, stop playing games.'

'Games, my friend? With the signallers waiting for our answer?'

Freya said, 'Vashislav, for God's sake, we're condemned prisoners. A desperate plan will do nicely.'

'Yes, young Freya. But listen, here is the word on my escape route. One. It is very dangerous. Two. It cannot work if Hanning knows we suspect him. And Three, the worst bit.'

They waited while Shtyrkov once again caught his breath. Then, 'The route can only be taken by two of us. We will have to decide who goes and who stays.'

'Well?' Freya asked.

'In the morning, young lady. This must be discussed by all of us together.'

30

Hanning

Sunday morning brought a blue sky with a light trace of high cirrus. The air was cold. Shtyrkov, Gibson and Petrie climbed the stairs to the high tower, slowly out of deference to the Russian. They looked out over the panorama. Hanning was already on the terrace below. He had his back to them and was handling two piles of papers, weighed down by books to keep them from fluttering away. It was impossible to believe that they were in their last hours, perhaps their last hour. Impossible to believe they couldn't just walk away from the castle, across the sunlit fields.

'What's he doing?' Petrie asked.

'Still trying to match our downloads with pictures of known viruses,' Gibson said. 'That should keep him occupied for hours.'

'Not outdoors,' Shtyrkov suggested. 'It's freezing.'

'He's a public school type,' Petrie said. 'Brought up on cold showers and running around naked at sunrise.'

Shtyrkov looked at Petrie with some wonder. 'Sometimes I think the English are a strange people.'

'Where can we talk?' Gibson asked.

'Here,' Shtyrkov proposed. 'We can keep an eye on our English gentleman while we do so.'

'I'll bring the ladies up,' Petrie said, making briskly for the door.

Petrie found the women in the kitchen. The air of normality was weird, even surreal. Freya was pouring herself cereal, and Svetlana was bringing a pot of water to the boil. His invitation to join the others in the tower was delivered quietly, as if Hanning was listening at the door.

'I wondered where you'd all got to,' Freya said.

'Why the tower?' Svetlana asked. 'And what about Jeremy?'

'We're keeping him out of it and we don't want him to know we're having a meeting.'

Svetlana looked puzzled. Petrie added, 'We don't trust him. I'll explain as we go.'

To reach the tower from the kitchen, they had to pass French windows leading to the terrace, in full view of Hanning. Petrie took Freya's arm and they strolled past as if in conversation. Hanning looked up and nodded. They waited at the steps. A minute later Svetlana walked purposefully past, head bowed and looking neither left nor right. 'He didn't notice me,' she said quietly on the stairs. 'What's this about?'

'Vash will explain.'

Shtyrkov explained. They stood back from the edge of the tower, speaking in low, conspiratorial voices although there was no chance of being heard from the terrace below. Petrie glanced out from time to time, but Hanning was single-mindedly concentrating on his papers.

As the Russian talked, Gibson occasionally shook his head in disbelief, and once had to suppress a derisive laugh. Then he turned up the collar of his jacket and paced to and fro for a minute. Finally, he seemed to reach a decision. He stared from Shtyrkov to Petrie and back to the Russian again. 'I guess it's all we have.'

The Russian spoke the words they had all been thinking. 'Now we have to decide who goes.'

Petrie added, 'And what we're going to do about Hanning.'

Shtyrkov's face became ghoulish. 'I have no problem with that.'

* * *

'Something's missing.' Petrie was coiling pink mustard on to his plate from a tube, next to a broken-up boiled egg. He was unshaven and haggard. Svetlana sipped at her tea and looked at the mixture with distaste.

'I agree with Thomas,' Vashislav declared. 'He has decoded a big hunk of energy desert, somewhere between the X and W bosons. It is wonderful. What people have called the Higgs particle turns out to be just one point in a spectrum of – I can't even call them particles, they are entities . . .'

'Maybe we just didn't record it,' Gibson suggested. He was adding milk with microscopic care to a coffee.

The Russian said, 'No, we picked it up all right. It must still be on the second SCSI drive, in the cavern.'

Hanning looked up from a mug of tea; his voice was tinged with surprise. 'What are you saying, Vashislav?'

'Didn't you know?' Gibson said, taking a sip. 'Yes, we have a second hard drive as a matter of course. One stays behind while we remove the other for analysis, in case particles come in, in the meantime. Clearly so much information came in that some of it was automatically shunted over to the number two drive.'

'We need to get hold of it.' Vashislav was being assertive.

'With the time we have left – forgive me – surely you have more than you can handle here.' Hanning was being casual.

Vashislav smiled tolerantly. 'You don't understand, Jeremy. There is a critical area beyond the energy of our particle accelerators and short of the unimaginable energies of the Creation. We know it only as a desert, but its span is immense, over thirteen powers of ten. There must be oases in this desert, new force fields we know nothing about, new forms of energy beyond anything we can visualise.'

Petrie was scooping up the pink gunge with bread. 'If we had the hard drive here we could analyse it in a few hours. The decipherment pattern's been cracked.'

'Centuries of knowledge in a few hours.' Vashislav turned to Gibson, appealing. 'What do you say, Charlee?'

'It's the biggest gap,' Petrie said. 'We've enough genome stuff on site to keep the biochemists busy for a generation.'

Gibson pretended to count. 'We're three hours from the Tatras, another three back, say half an hour to penetrate the cavern and another half to dismantle the drive. Seven hours.'

'I could be back late this evening and work overnight on it.'

'This is our last full day,' Gibson lied.

'The bastards.' Svetlana was looking down at the table.

Hanning was smooth. 'Not that I go along with your paranoid fantasies, Tom, but it could be an opportunity for you to escape.'

Petrie shook his head. 'A fact which will occur to my military escort. It's not even worth thinking about.'

'Still, if an opportunity should arise.' The civil servant's voice was still casual, but he was peering closely at the mathematician.

He suspects something. Petrie shrugged dismissively. 'Sure.'

Gibson turned to Hanning. 'Jeremy, can you explain to his lordship that there is vital information still stored in the cave and that we need to retrieve it in short order. Might give particle physics a jump start of a few hundred years, with God knows what outcome.'

'Take someone with you,' Shtyrkov said to Petrie. 'You'll need an extra pair of hands to dismantle the drive.'

'Can I come?' Freya asked. 'I want out of here, even for a few hours.'

'Sure.' Petrie thought, *Everyone's being so bloody casual.* Svetlana was playing her part, sitting quietly, still staring at the table. At that moment Petrie was overwhelmed by her quiet courage, felt utterly inadequate against it.

'You know how to do it?' Hanning asked, turning at the refectory door. 'Get this drive thing out?'

'Of course,' Petrie lied, with a grandiose wave of the arm.

Hanning looked around at the scientists, then left.

'Did he buy it?' Gibson asked in a low, urgent voice.

'He was suspicious,' Freya suggested.

'I thought so too,' said Svetlana.

'Who cares?' Vashislav said. 'So long as it gets Tom and Freya to the cave. Remember the count, Freya and Tom.'

'Fifteen.'

'It's critical. Not fourteen, not sixteen. Apply the brakes fifteen seconds into the fall. If that works, if it stops you at the entrance to the Styx, then you have a chance.'

'Split up as soon as you get away,' said Gibson. 'Take different routes. That way you'll double the chance of success.'

Svetlana's face was ashen. Petrie stretched over to her and held her hand, without saying a word. She looked at him, managed a smile. 'You'll make it, Tom? You'll do it for us?'

He returned the squeeze of her warm, small hand. 'If it's humanly possible.'

Something about Hanning.

Petrie climbed the stairs to his room, locked the door and pulled out a sheet of paper from his rucksack.

Arthur Jeremy Winterman Hanning. Eldest son of Edward George Hanning, gentleman farmer, and Agnes Strathairn née Forsyth. Education Leatherhead, Winchester, Greats at Oxford. Began career as HEO in the Agricultural Research Council. Transferred to Central Office, attained Grade 6, transferred over again to MAFF. At age forty became Secretary to the Minister for Science, in which capacity Lord Sangster was the second minister he had served.

That much he had pulled down from the Net within an hour of Hanning's arrival at the castle. No woman in the man's life, no interests or hobbies, no recorded scandals or peccadillos; just a bog-standard Civil Service career route.

But now, without warning, something jumped into his head. He had no rationale for it, but it was suddenly, obviously, blindingly true. *That man isn't Hanning. He's our assassin.*

31

Tatras Ride

Up the stairs, running. Petrie stays at the foot.

Freya, gasping, reaches the top first, followed by Gibson and Svetlana. She stops at the corner of the corridor, waving them past, looking back down the stairs.

Gibson and Svetlana run to the far end of the corridor, turn right. Hanning's door first left.

Locked.

Gibson has the master key. In his excitement it jams. Svetlana impatiently pulls his hand away, takes the key out, starts again and opens the door.

Unmade bed. *The Fifth Miracle* by Paul Davies on the bedside table, next to a bottle of pills. Suitcase on wooden table, lid zipped shut. Gibson opens it, rakes through the contents; Svetlana rakes through the wardrobe of clothes.

Gibson shakes his head, heads swiftly for the bathroom.

'Here!' From between the folds of a spare blanket in the wardrobe, Svetlana pulls out an automatic pistol, heavy and shiny.

'Jesus!' Gibson takes it, looks at it incredulously.

'More!' She pulls out a box, opens it. A hundred cartridges, it says so on the lid, and there they are, sinister little messengers of death.

Freya is whispering urgently at the door. 'He's coming!' She sees the gun, gapes in open-mouthed horror.

Gibson shoves it into the belt of his trousers, the box of cartridges into a pocket. The pocket bulges. He pulls his casual shirt out, stretches it down.

Out of Hanning's room. Svetlana locks the door and they run quietly along the corridor.

Petrie is at the foot of the steps, waving them down in an agitated manner. They take the stairs two at a time. Back into the refectory. Into their seats, Shtyrkov looking at them with alarm and curiosity. Hanning saunters in. Petrie is pouring tea and Svetlana is spreading toast, a picture of normality. They are trying not to pant.

Hanning sits down, stretches for toast, leans back in his chair. His manner is relaxed, almost insolent. He lacks the strain showing on the faces of the others. 'I've spoken to Sangster. A truck will come for Tom and Freya at twelve o'clock. So, the pair of you should be back here by this evening.'

Freya, behind Hanning, is looking out of a window. She turns and puts a finger to her lips.

Gibson seems to be looking for a handkerchief in his pocket. Under the table, he puts the gun on his lap. 'Will we need to make any more arrangements with the soldiers?'

'No. Freya and Tom should just walk out of the castle.'

Gibson nods. 'That's it, then. I think it only remains to see whether we can escape from here.' He looks directly at Hanning. 'Do you have any suggestions?'

Hanning senses something. 'You don't need to escape. I think we've been over that.'

Gibson speaks quietly. 'I think you should try harder, Jeremy.'

Something in Gibson's voice. Hanning looks round the scientists, suddenly wary. 'You people are up to something. Is it Tom and Freya? Do they have an escape route?'

Silence.

Hanning's face grows pale. 'I think I'll go to my room. Not feeling too good.'

Freya turns from the window in alarm. '*Herregud!* Soldiers in the grounds.'

'Are they coming in?' Shtyrkov asks.

'I don't think so.'

'We must not alert them with gunshot.'

There is a moment's shocked silence, then Hanning quickly pulls his chair back. Gibson clatters the pistol on to the table. Hanning freezes.

'Like I said, Jeremy, try harder.'

Shtyrkov stands up, wheezes his way through to the kitchen.

Hanning, grey-faced, looks down at the table, his hands clutching each other. 'There's never been anything personal in this. I was hired to do a job in the service of the Queen.'

'There's nothing personal in any of this,' Gibson says.

Svetlana says, 'Speak for yourself.' She moves away from Hanning, round the table, and sits down next to Gibson. Her face is paler than Hanning's but her lips are thin with determination. Freya comes back from the window and joins them.

Petrie says, 'Actually it was Horace, not Seneca. A real Oxford Greats man would have known that.'

Gibson's voice is calm, almost conversational. 'I'll get no pleasure out of an execution, Jeremy.'

'I'll bargain with Sangster.' Hanning's voice is now hoarse.

Svetlana asks, 'Is that the best you can come up with?'

'Do we have to do this?' Freya asks. She is biting her lip.

'Think of something quickly, Jeremy,' Gibson says.

Svetlana's voice is trembling. 'That cave is my child. I

gave it twelve years and it rewarded me with the greatest discovery in history. And you and the system you represent want it all destroyed, and us along with it.'

Gibson lifts the pistol and examines it curiously, snapping the safety catch on and off. 'You see our problem, Jeremy. When Tom and Freya go, there will only be three of us left to keep you under control. Vashislav is too slow, which makes it just Svetlana and me. But you've thought all this out already, haven't you, Jeremy? You're two moves ahead of us, and working out move number three.'

Svetlana says, 'You're too dangerous to have around. You could finish us and everything we've achieved.'

'But you've achieved nothing. You will find that you no longer have access to the signal. I changed the password. And the original disk is now on its way to GCHQ, where it will be examined by others subject to the Official Secrets Act. They will have no information about the place or time of the signal, and so no way to work out where the signal came from. But they will know what the disk contains. It may put the Great back into Great Britain.'

Gibson grows pale, looks as if he might hyperventilate. 'You've denied us access to the message?'

Hanning nods. 'So far as you are concerned, it's gone.'

'I'll check.' Svetlana disappears quickly from the room. They hear her running downstairs. She returns after two long, silent minutes. 'I can't get into the computer.'

'What? Have you tried Tom's?' Gibson is almost croaking with tension.

'Yes.'

A despairing groan comes from Gibson. He hunches forward, puts the gun on the table. Hanning sits very still; only his eyes move, flickering between Gibson and the pistol.

Svetlana flops into her chair. 'Jeremy, does your government's treachery extend to double-crossing my country too?'

Hanning shakes his head. 'I don't know. But think of the advantages to any country which has sole access to the secrets of the signallers.'

'And the hard drive in the cave?' she asks.

'The intention was, and is, that it will be taken from you as soon as you have it. So you see, even if by some miracle you escaped from here, you would have no hard evidence to back up your story. It would just be a fantasy thing.' Hanning's body language is now defiant. 'There's absolutely no purpose in getting rid of me. You're already defeated.'

Svetlana breaks the brittle silence. 'Charlie.'

'What?' Gibson's head is on the table, and his arms are cradling it as if to keep out the world.

'I didn't trust you when we came here. I thought you might disappear with the disk and try to grab all the kudos for yourself.'

'So?' His voice is indifferent.

'So I made a copy of the disk. It's in my room.'

Gibson is like a man rising from the dead. He sits upright, visibly swelling. He looks at Hanning as if the man is Satan incarnate, then laughs harshly. His hand goes to the pistol. He takes a deep breath and says, 'Do it, Vash.'

In the fraction of a second it takes Hanning to understand Gibson's remark, Shtyrkov is bringing the fire axe hard down, as if he is chopping wood.

* * *

Petrie had first fainted, then vomited on and off during the following hour while Svetlana and Shtyrkov had wrapped

Hanning's body in a grey blanket. Gibson and Freya had then seen to the scrubbing down of the kitchen table, chairs and floor, while Shtyrkov had taken Petrie by the arm, led him gently to a settee in the atrium, and described some of the things his grandparents' generation had had to do in the Patriotic War. Petrie had listened to the horrors with his face buried in his hands.

Freya had then appeared with tea and biscuits, looking as if she had just been baking scones. The cosy normality of this had sent Petrie slightly mad. After a fit of hysterical laughter, he had calmed down sufficiently to drink the tea, giggling and spluttering into it now and then. He got to his feet and staggered apprehensively through to the refectory, while Shtyrkov headed up the stairs to change his blood-spattered clothes and have a shower.

It was impossible to connect the clean, polished refectory with a grisly murder. Petrie looked round in bewilderment. 'Where is he?'

'Don't use the kitchen freezer,' Gibson advised. He looked at Petrie closely. 'I don't think you're up to this. Maybe Svetlana should go in your place.'

'I'll be fine. You need a tough, aggressive male to see it through.'

'In that case Svetlana should definitely go.'

Svetlana shook her head. 'There's nothing I'd love more. But we've made the decision. Tom's the expert on the decipherment.'

'He'll be fine,' Freya said.

'I'll be fine. Thanks, Svetlana.'

Gibson adopted a businesslike manner although he was visibly shaking. 'Okay, we have about ninety minutes. Let's go over the maps again while Vashislav prepares the copy disks.'

* * *

Freya and Tom stood just inside the door they had entered five days earlier.

'Final check-list,' Gibson said.

Petrie unzipped his inside pocket. 'Two disks. One with a sample, the other with the full works. Encrypted.' He tapped a side pocket. 'Purse with cash and all your credit cards. Pin numbers memorised.'

'Freya?'

'Two disks. One the full signal, the other a message from Vash to his friend in Murmansk, to prove authenticity.'

'How will he know the message is really from you?' Gibson asked.

'It has things on it which only he and I know about.'

'And Vashislav's mobile,' Freya added, feeling a side pocket.

'With which you can send and retrieve e-mail on the move,' Vashislav reminded her. 'I'm sorry that there is only the one between you.'

'Remember your passwords?' Gibson asked. 'One for decrypting the disks, the other for deleting them if you're loading up under duress.'

Shtyrkov said, 'I've used Blowfish encryption and put a compiled C program into the DVD. Insert the duress password and the program will flash "decrypting" on the screen while it's busy writing zeros all over the disk.'

Gibson smacked his forehead. 'I nearly forgot! The screwdriver!'

Freya fiddled with the waistband of her jeans. 'It's here, Charlie.'

'Remember, Tom: fifteen. Not fourteen, not sixteen. Fifteen seconds precisely.'

'We never did get that game of chess, Vash.'

Gibson said, 'That's it, then.'

There was a long, long silence. Shtyrkov eventually broke it. 'I'd have slaughtered you.'

'Never. I do a good endgame.' *Damn!* Endgame was the wrong word.

But Shtyrkov smiled and said, 'A good endgame won't save you, Tom. It needs to be devastating.'

Freya's eyes were moist.

'Do this for us.' Gibson's voice was strained.

'Either we'll get you your immortality, Charlie, or we'll die trying.'

Svetlana said, 'It's probably as well I never married, never had children. Maybe if you have a child some day, Freya . . .'

'If it's a girl she'll be called Svetlana.'

Gibson said, 'I think you'd better go.'

There was an exchange of handshakes. Petrie held Svetlana briefly, and then Gibson was opening the door and she was pushing him towards it, and they were out, Freya first. Cold air met them. As the door was closing Petrie looked back and glimpsed Shtyrkov, smiling at him. Then Freya was taking his hand and they walked along the path towards the archway.

Beyond the archway, an army truck was waiting, steam coming from its throbbing exhaust. The canvas flaps were back and there were about a dozen soldiers inside. Most were grinning in the direction of Freya. A bulky Sergeant directed them into a Land Rover. Freya sat next to a dark-skinned, swarthy driver in battledress. The driver nodded curtly. The vehicle grumbled into life and set off down the hill, the lorry following about thirty yards behind.

Past the little church, they turned left. The look-out

tower, still snow-capped, was visible over the trees. Then the driver picked up speed on the narrow road and the castle was out of sight and they were heading north, towards an uncertain future.

32

The Madonna

In 1921, in the Demänovskà Valley in the northern part of the Czechoslovakian Low Tatras, a spelunker called A. Král penetrated a cave. The cave, or rather system of caves, turned out to be in four levels connected by steep passages, and to be over eight kilometres long. Bones showed that, long ago, the cave had been penetrated by some bear, which had no doubt wandered in the dark until it died of starvation. Over the years the cave was made accessible through a system of walkways, stairs and galleries, and the public could now visit the sinter waterfalls, the stalagmites and stalactites, the caverns, pools and streams of this Tolkien-like underworld.

In 1951, thirty years after it had first been penetrated, a connection was discovered to another cave system. Thirty-two years on again, in 1983, a speleo-diving team discovered yet another connection, and three years after that the system, now named 'the Demänovskà Cave of Liberty', was found to be connected also to 'the Demänovskà Cave of Peace'. The limestone mountains, it seemed, were honeycombed with tunnels.

In the early twenty-first century, a young German caver by the name of Armin Tyson explored a long, deeply descending passage. After many kilometres this opened out to a cavern of curved and banded curtains, flowstones like melted wax, ten-metre stalagmites rising out of rimstone pools and – most amazing of all – a cavern with an underground lake almost a kilometre across and, it would later turn out, two hundred metres deep.

Vashislav Shtyrkov, of Moscow State University, heard of this lake by chance from a speleo-fanatic student. Himself physically incapable of squeezing through the discovery passage, now known as 'the Wormhole', he sent the student to Slovakia with Geiger counters. The student reported back that the radon, uranium and carbon-14 levels in this deep hole were satisfyingly low. The lake was wonderfully inaccessible to the public, and the opportunity was too good to miss.

There was just one problem: the Russians had no money.

The British, however, had. Charlie Gibson was soon enticed from the Rutherford-Appleton Laboratory's Yorkshire mine experiment by the prospect of leading a new dark matter team. He fronted the paperwork necessary for the British funding.

At a cocktail party in Warsaw, Shtyrkov also approached Svetlana Popov, a Russian woman at Cracow University with a rising reputation as a careful experimentalist. On the basis of a conversation over lemonade and canapés, she agreed to join Shtyrkov's little team: dark matter was a powerful lure, the quest for it hard to resist.

The newly discovered lake was part of the Tatras National Park but Shtyrkov, as he liked to say, had friends in high places. Nevertheless strict conditions were imposed for the use of the lake as a laboratory. Diversion of an underground stream, nicknamed 'the Styx', was permitted. A narrow shaft could be sunk. Everything – scaffolding, chairs, cables, electromagnets, computers – had to be brought up and down this shaft. Desks were assembled underground. Doors were welded on site out of steel panels. Svetlana knew every piece of wire in the cavern.

From then on, it was a question of maintaining and improving the apparatus, and waiting. Waiting for a dark matter particle to zip through the lake, trailing light, on its endless cosmic journey.

Tyson's Wormhole was the way out.

Tyson and his team had used ropes, bobbins, gunlocks, Gibbs ascenders.

Between them, Freya and Petrie had a screwdriver.

* * *

The driver maintained a sullen silence and chain-smoked along a twisting, narrow road. Petrie, having retched his stomach contents out a few hours previously, began to long for an early death. That the wish might be close to fulfilment was something he couldn't quite take in.

Visions of Hanning kept recurring: an axe splitting the man's skull like a log; blood and grey matter squirting up; face becoming a non-face, something hideous and non-human; the cadaver sliding, trembling violently, under the table. It added to his sense of unreality, of detachment from the real world. Freya smiled thinly at him from time to time but he was too miserable for conversation.

Svetlana's sketch had been too dangerous to carry and he tried to go over it in his head.

'First the Styx, then the Madonna. First opening left, along the phreatic tube. A high vertical chimney to the grotto with the white flowstone; first left again and a long narrow crawl to a boulder chamber. Over this to a broad sloping highway, like a motorway with a rocky roof, marching steadily and steeply up for a kilometre. Then the dreaded sump, a long underwater tunnel which Tyson's

team had traversed with aqualungs and which you probably won't survive. Use the guide rope left in place by Tyson's team. Finally, if by a miracle you aren't lost or drowned to this point, you arrive at Piccadilly Station. Take the fourth entrance round from the big orange stalactite; you will find walkways and lights and human society. Slip in with a tourist group and leave the mountain. What follows then is up to God and you.'

After an hour a sizeable town, or at least rows of Identikit high-rise flats, appeared ahead of them. They joined a motorway, its surface wet but clear of snow. The jeep speeded up, turned north. The *Malé Karpaty* receded to the horizon. The driver maintained his silence and kept up his chain-smoking. Now and then he would hum something tuneless, strumming nicotine-stained fingers on the steering wheel. Petrie wondered about heaving the wretch out of the jeep, taking off with the lorry in pursuit, finding a helicopter in the wilds, flying to an airport and jumping on a plane to Rio de Janeiro. He laughed and Freya gave him a look.

After another hour the lorry behind them tooted and the driver pulled over to a small roadside restaurant. A young officer opened the jeep door and guided Petrie by the arm to a table. Freya was led to a separate table. A dozen soldiers spread themselves noisily around and Petrie ate what was put in front of him without knowing or caring what it was.

It was late afternoon, with the traffic getting dense, when the jeep began to run alongside sterner mountains. A white fluffy cloud in the distance turned out to belong to a chemical works. They passed by mysterious assemblies of fat pipes, and big cylinders painted blue or yellow, and tall chimney stacks, all enclosed within wire-topped concrete fencing and not a human being in sight. Petrie thought it could be run by aliens and nobody would ever know.

At last, just past a large lake, the driver left the motorway, took a side-road, turned off at a roundabout. Almost immediately they found themselves on a narrow road, covered with compacted snow, heading towards massive peaks. The ski-laden cars were here in force, streaming away from the mountains with snow chains on their wheels and snow on their roofs.

Petrie began to tense. He sensed that Freya, next to him, was the same.

To their astonishment, the driver finally spoke. '*Nizke Tatry.*'

Petrie said, 'Drop dead.'

They drove into a car park deep with snow. There was a little row of wooden shops with postcard stands at their entrances, and windows filled with tourist junk. They stepped out and stretched. A path from the car park led over a wooden bridge and disappeared into a conifer forest hugging the mountainside. A chain barred the way over the bridge, and next to it there was a notice. Petrie guessed the path was closed because of avalanche risk.

The army truck was just turning into the car park and Petrie momentarily wondered about running into the trees. He caught Freya's glance; she was clearly thinking the same. But then the truck had stopped and soldiers were jumping out and the moment had passed.

An officer was shouting orders. Then he pointed at Freya and Petrie and snapped something, waving his hand towards the path. They followed him along it. The soldier unhooked the chain and they passed over a stream of icy water and then they were climbing a steep, slippery path, soldiers strung out behind them on the trail. They had rifles, a fact which excluded any prospect of running away through the trees.

Stick with the Russian's plan.

* * *

A steel door. The officer had a key. A push from behind, from some teenage soldier enjoying a sense of power. A dark atrium, the indefinable smell of old air, and steps going down to blackness. Lights flickered and came on, and there was the yellow cage, just as the others had described.

The steel door clanged shut. More orders, and the scientists were hustled down the stone steps. Two soldiers squeezed into the cage. With rifles and combat gear, it was almost impossibly tight. There was some chatter and then someone pressed the red button and they dropped from sight as if through a hangman's trapdoor. The overhead drum whined smoothly and the braided metal cable vibrated tautly. Freya and Petrie stood close and shivered.

Presently the whine stopped, and then the cable began to move in reverse, more slowly. When the cage appeared two more soldiers were ordered into it and the shaft swallowed them up.

Fifteen seconds. That was Shtyrkov's figure. Not fourteen, not sixteen. Fifteen precisely. Get it wrong by a second and you miss by ten metres.

The officer's game plan was clear. At least four soldiers would be waiting for them down below. That left eight up above or, if he sent two more down, an even split between the top and bottom of the shaft. Freya and Petrie would each be under the guard of at least two, and possibly three, armed men. The cage reappeared and two more soldiers were sent down to Hades; the officer was going for a fifty-fifty split.

This was the crunch moment, or rather the first of several. The essence of Shtyrkov's plan was that they go down the shaft together. The big worry was that Freya and Petrie would be split, each being sent down with a single soldier. In that case, the contingency plan was to insist on going back up together, on the slender grounds that two were needed to tend the delicate equipment. If that too failed, the outlook was bleak.

The officer snapped his fingers and waved them towards the cage. Petrie tried to look impassive, and Freya was putting on a good act. The cage closed. Freya pressed the red button and they plunged out of sight.

In an instant Freya produced the screwdriver from her waistband and Petrie started the count. 'Fifteen – fourteen – thirteen – twelve . . .' while she frantically unscrewed the black cowling protecting the circuit box. It came away easily and she was faced with a mass of wires. Rockface was hurtling past and the buffeting wind was blowing her long blonde hair in her eyes.

To stop the cage they only had to press the emergency button. But the plan was to destroy it. To do that, they had to kill the circuit which told the winch far above to stop unwinding the cable. They had to pour a ton of steel cable down on to the cage. And they had to be out of it.

'The green wire,' Petrie shouted. 'Nine – eight – seven . . .'

'No, the yellow. Svetlana got it wrong. The yellow feeds up to the cable.'

'Five – four – *Do something!* – two – one.'

Freya wrenched fiercely at a thick green wire. There was a vicious spark of current, she yelped, and then a nerve-shattering *screech!* as electromagnetic clamps tried to strangle the metal shafts and the cage juddered to a halt, its overhead light flickering.

Petrie found that his eyes were level with a roughly hewn floor. He scrabbled up and out of the cage, his nose catching painfully on a sharp rock.

Up top the big winch, unaware that the elevator had stopped, was still unwinding its steel cable, which was now raining down on the wire mesh above them. The noise was deafening. He turned and to his horror the cage lurched down. Freya, halfway out, fell back into it with a frightened cry, landing on her backside. For a ghastly moment he thought it was headed down the shaft but it stopped, groaning, inching down in little jerks as the overhead cable poured down.

And now, steel was beginning to tear. The screeching was painful on Petrie's ears. He had a brief, claustrophobic fantasy: he was trapped inside a ship on its way to the sea floor.

And Freya was on her toes, arms extended, her face white with fear. She was now out of arm's length.

If we both go down the shaft the project is finished.

And thick metal cable was still pouring down.

Two corpses rather than one. Leave her.

She was reading his mind, pleading with her eyes.

I can't risk the project for one individual.

Freya's hands were stretched up, but Petrie, hanging halfway into the elevator, could only touch her fingertips.

The wire mesh was buckling. The elevator was now juddering down more rapidly, inches at a time.

Any second now.

She jumped. Petrie grabbed her wrists but the lift lurched suddenly and she slipped from his grasp. She jumped again, and again he made contact with her hands; desperately, he dug his nails in, but Freya's hands were slippery with sweat, and again he lost them and she fell back on the elevator floor with a despairing cry.

Oh, what the hell! He scrambled back down into the elevator. He cupped his hands. She clambered, there was a painful heel on his collar bone, and then their positions were reversed; Petrie was in the cage and Freya on her knees in the tunnel and turning to catch him.

The foot of the tunnel was now about nine feet above him. The gap between tunnel floor and sagging elevator roof was now about eighteen inches and shrinking. Petrie leaped up, aware that he had only this one chance. His fingers clutched at the rim of the tunnel floor. It was wet and slippery. Freya leaned down, grabbed his hair and pulled. Slowly, he bent his arms until his elbows reached the tunnel floor. Then he levered himself up by the elbows and rolled on to wet, freezing ground and pulled his feet clear just as the wire roof of the elevator gave way with a *crash!* and tons of thick metal cable clattered on to its floor and started to spill into the tunnel mouth.

They leaped away from the mortally wounded elevator. In the confined space of the tunnel the thunder of the falling cable was like hammering on a steel drum. They scrambled back just as the elevator gave way with a final scream and the cable which had been overflowing into the tunnel started to accelerate swiftly down the shaft after it.

The tunnel lights failed.

Petrie cursed, and waved his arms in the dark like antennae. The cable was now whipping the air and he had another brief fantasy, that of decapitation. The noise seemed to come from all directions and he broke into a sudden sweat with the realisation that he had lost his sense of orientation.

A voice in the dark, surprisingly faint. 'Where are you?'

Seconds later there was a *bang!* from below, like an explosion, but by now Petrie had found the damp tunnel wall and was feeling his way along it – away, he hoped, from the elevator shaft. From somewhere in the distance he began to hear another sound, the thunder of a torrent. He edged towards it.

'Over here!' Freya shouted. Again her voice came over faintly, and Petrie thought his hearing had temporarily gone. There was a scraping sound, like metal on wood, as if she was struggling with a metal clasp on a box. Petrie stopped, trying to locate the direction in the pitch black.

And then there were four pinpricks of green light, making a rectangle before Freya's body interposed itself on the line of sight. Petrie quickly crossed the twelve feet to the lights. He bumped into Freya and she gave a startled little scream. Four torches, each charged up: the beams were dazzling. And four yellow helmets. They selected helmets and clipped the torches into place.

'I wonder how long we've got?' Even at a couple of feet separation, Freya's voice was faint, and he understood her more by lip-reading than by the sound of her words. The torchlight from her helmet was painful, and she was screwing her eyes up.

Petrie tried to calm down, collect his thoughts. His whole body was beginning to shake. 'Depends,' he said. He noted with surprise the calmness of his own voice, which contrasted with the turmoil in his mind and body. 'If the officer thinks it was an accident, we have a good start. If not, he'll know we must have an escape route in mind and he'll start finding out about the cave system . . .'

'Let's hope he's stupid. Hold it.' She clicked her torch off and Petrie did the same, following her alarmed gaze to the tunnel mouth.

Little specks of dust were wafting up from below. They were visible because, far above, someone was shining a powerful light down the shaft.

'Surely they couldn't abseil down?' Petrie wondered.

'Or climb down the cable?'

'Let's get out of here.'

The tunnel was broad and flat and the torchlight showed a spray of water about two hundred yards ahead of them. Freya led the way towards it at a brisk trot. The end of the tunnel was marked by a black metal railing with a red and white lifebelt attached to a long coil of rope. They found themselves inside a much larger, natural tunnel, about thirty feet wide and as high. Water below them was surging, tumbling, roaring along this channel; Petrie felt the ground vibrating. Their torches made rainbows in the cold spray, but showed only that the subterranean river curved out of sight on either side of them, piling up steeply at the corner.

Petrie said, 'The Styx,' but his voice was lost in the roar.

He felt an urgent tug on his arm. Freya was pointing to a flight of stone steps on the left, going down to a concrete path running alongside the river. Just before they took them, he glanced back. It might just have been the dark adaption, but the light shining down the elevator shaft seemed stronger.

'Tyson's entrance is two sixty metres along,' Petrie shouted.

'I can't judge distances.' In the torchlight, Freya's face was glistening wet. 'I'm relying on you.'

Petrie said, 'Hell. I was relying on you.'

They hurried along, gripping the handrail. Here and there the river was almost level with the concrete path, and in some places they had to wade knee-deep, the force of the water threatening to knock them off their feet.

'The water level must be up,' Freya shouted. She was shivering.

'And it's rising.' Petrie didn't try to hide the fear.

After two hundred metres the path seemed to dip into the water. Their torches picked out the railing for another twenty yards or so before it, too, vanished under the waves.

He looked along the tunnel wall, searching for footholds. About fifty metres ahead, his helmet light picked out a natural recess about seven metres above the river.

'What do you think?' he shouted. 'Tyson's Wormhole?'

'There's nothing else. We'll have to swim for it, try to grab that ledge in passing. Think you can do it?'

Petrie was appalled. 'You're mad. What if we miss?'

'We drown.' The river was thundering round the corner, heading for an uncertain destination.

'I can't swim,' Petrie confessed.

'You idiot! Why didn't you say so at the castle?' She turned away from him, her light scanning the recess and the smooth tunnel wall. Then: 'Go back for the lifebelt. And be quick.'

Petrie waded back along the path. Without question, the river had risen, and the concrete was now almost wholly under water. To Petrie, the journey seemed to take an hour. He climbed the steps, gasping. To his horror, he saw that a light was still shining down the shaft but that it was much brighter than before. And it was swaying rhythmically, as if it was attached to a descending human. Hastily, he hoisted the lifebelt on his shoulder and put the coil of rope in the crook of his elbow. With a last fearful look at the light he ran back down the steps.

By the time he reached Freya the water was up to her chest and she was gripping the handrail, under the surface, with both hands. She was shivering violently and Petrie thought she looked ready to faint.

'They're coming.'

'Put your arms and head into that,' she ordered in a shaking voice. Petrie obliged. 'Wait until I'm on the ledge and then float. Let's hope the rope's long enough.'

'What if it's not?'

She ignored the question, tying the end of the rope crudely round her waist before wading along the path. In a moment she was caught up in the surge and bobbed along, seemingly helpless in the flow of freezing water. More than once her torchlight shone underwater, but then she was climbing on to the ledge and waving at Petrie.

The next ten seconds were amongst the most frightening in his life, but Freya was pulling the rope in as fast as the distance between them was shortening and he found himself gasping and spluttering face-down on a big slab of rock.

Freya was saying, 'Look!' Set in the natural recess about seven metres diagonally up was a gnarled pillar of rock, vaguely resembling a faceless woman wrapped in a shawl or cloak. 'The Madonna!'

With an effort, Petrie got to his knees, his clothes heavy with icy water. Freya was already skimming up the smooth rockface instinctively, like a spider. Water was pouring off her clothes. Petrie couldn't see what she was gripping but forced himself to follow. He found he could hardly grip the rock for shaking. He inched his way along, the torrent roaring angrily below. Once he glanced down and saw that the ledge was no longer below him: the helmet light showed only swift churning water.

Freya was shouting something. It took all his nerve to look up. He had passed under the Madonna, but now he was only a few metres from the recess. He warily edged towards it; and then Freya was gripping him by the elbow and at last he was being pulled behind the pillar of rock.

The recess went in about five metres, and their lights showed that it narrowed to a crack about six feet wide and barely a foot high. Over it, someone – it could only have been Tyson – had scraped a *T*.

She pointed triumphantly. 'We've found it! The Wormhole!'

The beam from Petrie's helmet lamp shook from side to side. 'I'll never get into that.'

Freya was looking up the river. 'Douse your light. Quickly.'

The first time it might have been an illusion, but not the second. Far upstream, torchlight had reflected briefly off the swirling waves of the Styx.

33

Rapunzel

Bull was taking time off for the Iraqi crisis and she had three hours at the most.

There was a harsh cry and she almost jumped with fright. A large, long-legged pink bird with a yellow head fluttered past at eye-level and settled on a palm frond about six feet away, eyeing her curiously. Hazel Baxendale began to wonder if the Baltimore aquarium, even in the depths of the Baltimore winter, had been such a good idea.

She stepped carefully past the bird and carried on through a winding path, surrounded by lush greenery. An emerald-green iguana blocked her way. She moved respectfully past it and, a little further on, sat down on a wooden bench.

The tropical house was *hot*. And humid. Hazel draped her synthetic fur coat over the back of the bench, but kept her sunglasses on. She waited.

The MIT engineer, Professor Gene Killman, was first to arrive. He was overweight, bald, with a gaudy yellow tie and dark glasses. He was licking his thin lips nervously, and looking around. He was almost comically furtive. The President's Science Adviser rubbed her forehead in despair and groaned inwardly. The man spotted her, looked around again, and sidled up to the bench, sitting down without once looking at her.

Something rustled in a tree. A small creature with long golden fur peered at them. 'What the hell is that?' she said.

'They call it a tamarin, ma'am. Cute, isn't it? So many have been taken for pets that it's now an endangered species.'

The Harvard philosopher, a small, cheerful, grey-haired woman in her forties, appeared a few minutes later and sat down on the other side of Hazel. The woman was dressed for the winter, in a heavy coat and scarf. It was ninety degrees hot and ninety per cent humid, but the philosopher kept her winter clothes wrapped round her. Just looking at her put the Science Adviser in a sweat.

Hazel said, 'Rosa Clements, meet Gene Killman.' There was an exchange of cautious nods. 'I'd like to emphasise again that this discussion is off-the-record and highly confidential. You won't understand what's behind it and all I can tell you is that it involves a matter of national security. Don't tell a living soul that I've approached you for advice, not even your partners. Especially not your partners.'

'I'm between wives,' Gene Killman volunteered.

'You have my full attention, ma'am,' said Rosa Clements.

'Okay, here we go. I'm going to ask three questions and I need the best answers going. You mustn't go jumping to any goddam conclusions; treat them as hypothetical. Number one. Is there life beyond the Earth? Or are we just a mega-fluke? Professor Killman.'

The MIT man replied. 'In my opinion the Universe is teeming with life.'

'I thought the odds against life forming by chance from simple molecules were super-astronomical. There are more ways to combine amino acids than there are atoms in the Universe, but only one way forms them into proteins.'

'That's a problem,' Killman admitted. 'I don't have the answer except to say here we are, and life got established down here just as soon as the meteorites stopped smashing our crust. Take a walk over Slave Province in Canada and you're walking over micro-organic sediments a hundred feet thick and two and a half billion years old. In bits of West Greenland you're walking over iron-rich layers just as thick but four billion years old laid down by primitive microbes. If life was some sort of mega-fluke, how come we're here and how come it got started so early?'

'But what about intelligent life? I've been told that's a quadrillion to one chance.'

Killman said, 'Again, as soon as the conditions were right on Earth, there was a transition from single-celled life forms to multi-celled ones. Once you've done that, there are selective advantages all the way from the formation of nerves, then synapses, then cerebral ganglions and all the way to brains, intelligence and societies.'

Hazel studied the man closely through her dark glasses. 'Are you saying intelligent life should be common out there?'

'It should be everywhere.'

'So why don't we see it everywhere?'

'That's a problem too,' Killman admitted frankly. 'There have been lots of suggestions but I don't believe any of them.'

But Hazel had stopped listening. The message had come home loud and clear: *ET is on the cards.*

'Okay.' She sensed that something was slithering in a branch above her. 'Question number two. Say we receive an intelligent signal from space. Say that all sorts of information, including genetic recipes to improve ourselves and our children, is in this message. That's all the information you have to work on. I need the answers to the following questions. What sort of creatures would send it? What are we dealing with? Could it be on the level, or some sort of trap?'

'Ms Baxendale, at MIT we've developed a doll. We call her Rapunzel on account of her long hair. She uses sensors to pick up movement and sound. She feels heat and she has a sense of touch. We have a couple of hundred facial expressions programmed into her and a few billion sound combinations. Would you believe she has moods? That she needs attention? Rapunzel can fool a child into believing she's a real baby.'

'Call me Hazel. What's your point, Gene?'

'This, ma'am. Rapunzel is just a dumb machine made of plastic and wire, programmed by a few silicon chips. We're still in the steam age.' Killman leaned forward. His voice was beginning to carry a zealous edge. 'But give it fifty years. A hundred at the outside. By then we'll have molecular and even quantum computers a billion times faster than anything on the market today. We'll have dolls that fool adults, not just kids. They'll be more mobile, smarter, and more imaginative than us. We're moving into the age of intelligent machines.'

'But they're still just machines. They can't think.'

'Ma'am, I'm a machine and I can think. What am I but a collection of atoms, every last one obeying the laws of physics? Same as the doll.'

'So a hundred years down the line we'll have robot slaves. I still don't see what you're driving at.'

'Hazel, these slaves as you call them will be smarter than us. A lot smarter.'

Hazel Baxendale peered into the MIT man's eyes. 'Rapunzel will take over?'

'As surely as night follows day. It goes further than smart robots, ma'am. We'll have so many implants to boost us, neural circuits inside our heads, networked into grids, that we'll be hybrids ourselves. The need to outstrip rival nations or even just rivals will drive this. Eventually the carbon-based part of us will be redundant. Organic life – carbon-based – is on the way out. This is inevitable whenever intelligence develops technology. Sooner or later the technology takes over, supplants the primitive organic life. Therefore the signal – this make-believe signal – hasn't come from a life form like us. It's been sent by a machine.'

Hazel puffed out her cheeks. She took a few seconds to assimilate this amazing new thought. 'Humanity will disappear?'

The MIT engineer was scrutinising her. 'It'll merge with our smart machines. Not that there has been a signal, ma'am.'

Hazel blessed her upbringing with three brothers on a Montana farm: her poker face was impenetrable.

Rosa Clements broke the silence. 'I think I can anticipate your third question, ma'am.'

'Go ahead.'

'You want to know what would motivate a machine to contact us. More to the point, whether it would go by a moral code and if so, would that code be malign.'

This is one bright cookie, Hazel thought with some alarm. 'As we keep telling each other, this is all hypothetical,' she said. 'But if it wasn't, I'd say this goes far beyond anything any Administration has ever had to handle.'

Rosa nodded. 'You know what Truman said when he became President? He said, "There must be a million men better qualified than me to take on this job." '

'Truman was wrong, Professor Clements. The American people didn't elect a million highfliers, they elected Harry S. Truman. It's the only qualification that counts.'

The woman acknowledged the rebuke with a slight bow.

Killman stabbed the air with a fat finger. 'We couldn't relate to machine aliens. There's no reason to assume they'd have anything like human compassion built into them. They'd be programmed only to survive. Any philanthropy, any knowledge being fired at us, could be a mask. There's no way to tell what's really lying behind it. So don't take a chance, don't respond. Don't even use the genetic recipes. There might be something hidden in them.' He added, 'But as you say, this is all hypothetical.'

Rosa smiled and said, 'Hazel, this is the sort of ill-informed rubbish technocrats come away with from time to time. They think because they can make machines that are brighter than humans, therefore these machines are *conscious* beings. The technocrats don't begin to grasp the subtleties. Will their dolls feel pain? No. Will they be conscious? No. They'll never be more than mechanical zombies. I would say that no machine is *ever* motivated by philanthropy or malice or anything else. It just obeys a program. Any signal comes from a thinking, feeling intelligence. Or its proxy in the form of a tape recorder. Whatever, there will be an underlying moral code from a living creature. Intelligent machines will share the values of their creators. And these values will be benign.'

Benign? It was the crucial issue. 'Convince me.'

'As soon as Homo sapiens acquired intelligence we also got the concept of sin – in other words, a sense of right and wrong. The ability to make moral decisions emerged along with intelligence.'

'Tell that to the victims of the Hitler gang, or the Bin Laden creeps,' Hazel said.

'Sure there's moral failure everywhere you look. But that's because we're just out of the caves. Already we help others because we instinctively feel it's the right thing to do, even if it's of no advantage to us. A few thousand years down the line and it'll be so ingrained in us we won't know any other way to behave. Okay we're still apes, but cultural evolution is directing us towards a complete moral altruism. The signallers must have arrived there long ago.'

'So moral capacity comes with the central nervous system. I buy that, Rosa, I really do. But what morality? How can you be sure the signallers have the same moral outlook as us?'

'Because of ruthless Darwinian evolution. It works on societies. And that's why I believe the signal – this make-believe signal – is motivated by a genuine wish to help.'

Hazel looked bewildered. 'You're losing me.'

'It's simple. In Nature you have survival of the fittest. In a primitive tooth and claw society you have the same. But as technology progresses it makes the killer instinct so destructive that you eventually have survival of nobody at all, except maybe a few cave men. Either evolution weeds out the killer instinct or everyone ends up dead. Either moral evolution goes hand in hand with technological evolution or we're doomed.'

Hazel was saying, 'You mean, the meek will inherit the Galaxy?'

'Precisely. What we'd get from the signallers would reflect the moral altruism they'd evolved into.'

It was precisely the answer Hazel had been praying for. She stood up. Her head was dizzy with unfamiliar concepts, or maybe it was just the jungle heat after Camp David.

The pink bird flapped its wings and took off to a safe height.

'Would you like to visit the sharks, ma'am?'

'I'd have loved to, Gene, while you tried to persuade me that the human race is about to let itself be obliterated by a clever doll, and Rosa here told me that if it speaks and acts like a human to the nth degree it's still just a doll with no feelings and no consciousness. But I have to get back.' Hazel Baxendale gave a lopsided smile. 'I'm swimming with bigger sharks.'

34

Wormhole

Freya's upper half disappeared, followed by her soaking jeans and finally her boots. A little cascade of rock dust sparkled briefly in Petrie's lamplight.

He took a last look at the Styx. The river had definitely risen, and its thundering was louder, but it was the lights which attracted his attention.

Two of them.

No, three.

Petrie switched off his helmet lamp, his feet wedged against the Madonna. He was breathing heavily and aware of his heart thumping in his chest.

Four. Moving in single file.

And now he was seeing black silhouettes, moving swiftly along the pathway: wild dogs hunting.

Five of them.

Six. Seven. They must be deploying the lot.

Petrie stopped counting. His mouth dry with fear, he edged himself towards the entrance, on his knees, seeing by Freya's receding lamplight. A final glance: eight, at a minimum. He forced himself into the crack, his breath noisy in the confined space.

Freya was out of sight. There were three entrances, none of them more than two feet high. He kept his lamp off and sure enough, light was scattering from the wall of the left-hand tunnel.

On to his elbows. Petrie had never caved in his life. He quickly found himself sweating with exertion.

The light from Freya's lamp was getting fainter. Of course. She was smaller, slimmer.

Along the phreatic tube to a high vertical chimney.

How far along? He experimented with different ways of crawling but none of them seemed any better than the others. Freya's light was becoming a flicker, sometimes seen, sometimes not. He turned his own lamp on; the sight of the rock enclosing him accentuated his claustrophobia. He wanted to scream and push the walls away.

What the hell is a phreatic tube anyway? It sounds Greek, he thought, trying to keep the panic demons out of his mind. Maybe to do with frenetic? Frantic? It made sense; the tube was round, as if it had been formed by water under pressure.

Water under pressure. Petrie thought about the melting snow half a mile overhead, percolating down through a million cracks and fissures in the limestone mountain. He wanted out of the phreatic tube more than he had ever wanted anything.

He pushed himself harder, fearful of losing his way in a subterranean labyrinth, of dying of cold and exhaustion, of stumbling into the enemy. After about five minutes, the roar of the Styx had vanished. The scrabbling of his boots and his own gasping breath cut into an unnatural silence, tomb-like.

The tunnel wall was closing in on him. A million tons of overhead rock were settling down. He was an insect, about to be crushed under the boot of the ancient Tatras. He found himself taking big, gulping, frightened breaths. The demons were now inside his brain, poking, grinning, gibbering.

Cut it out!

Twenty minutes into the climb, the tunnel was opening up and acquiring a steep upward slope. At last! A high vertical shaft: *Tyson's chimney*.

He looked up, gasping with exertion. The chimney was a narrow, smooth-sided shaft. It rose almost vertically and it was higher, much higher, than he had visualised from Svetlana's sketch. He could barely make out the top with his torchlight. Water was trickling down its walls. And there was no sign of Freya, no light reflecting from her lamp.

He scrambled up a vertical face and then eased his head into the shaft. There would be no room to spread arms in the chimney, and he switched off his lamp. He inched himself up by holding himself in place with his elbows, bending his legs and thrusting against the shaft wall with his feet. A spray of cold water kept him soaked.

He slithered, lost about six feet, scraped his face, twisted his wrist, cursed aloud. After some minutes the chimney broadened marginally and he was able to grip its sides with icy fingers. He clambered up quickly, the iron taste of blood on his lip. There was a ridge; he waved his hands in the dark and found he could now hoist himself into a crouching position. He switched on his light and looked around.

He had reached a little chamber: the grotto, its floor covered with the white flowstone, a congealed river of rock. Three narrow tunnels led into it, discounting the one he had climbed up.

Freya, where are you?

Petrie remembered Svetlana's scribbled sketch. He now had to take the left-hand tunnel. He wriggled into it, crawled frantically along. It rose gently but he was making good progress. The tunnel was dry, but it smelled of damp and ancient air. The cold was intense now, into his bones, and Petrie thought it might be slowing him down mentally.

A long, narrow crawl, she had said.

A right turn and the tunnel narrowed to a mouth-shaped channel three feet wide and six inches high. Petrie stared. This wasn't in the map.

Stay calm.

Back out, inching painfully; now the demons were attacking in force, claustrophobia washing over him like big waves. Back into the little grotto with the flowstone, half-expecting soldiers. He switched off his lamp once more.

Pitch black. Not just any pitch black, like a country lane on a dark night. Pitch black somewhere inside a mountain; and lost.

How long would the battery last? A couple of hours? One?

Switch on again. The light hurt his eyes for a few seconds. He looked at the tunnel entrances. Maybe 'first left' was ambiguous; there were two entrances sharing a larger one. He said, 'Oh God!' and crawled swiftly along this other tunnel, using his elbows to wriggle along like a lizard. Why not gamble when you have nothing to lose?

A random walk in two dimensions will eventually take you where you want. It may take a very long time, depending on the number of choices, and the distance to cover, and luck. But you will always, sooner or later, emerge from a maze, provided you haven't died of cold or thirst in the meantime. In two dimensions, all roads lead to Rome.

This tunnel was even narrower than the last one. It went on for ever.

A random walk in three dimensions is different. In a three-dimensional maze, the probability that you'll end up where you want is about – Petrie tried to remember the exact figure – 0.35, that's it, one in three.

I'm going to die here, right inside one of my knots.

McCrea and Whipple, that was it. *Proceedings of the Royal Society of Edinburgh, 1940.* The Nazis were about to invade Britain and these cool dudes were calculating random walks, like playing bowls with the Armada on its way.

After ten minutes he thought to give up, crawl – backwards! – back along its length. Something stupidly jumped into his head:

> *It may be proper likewise to mention to the benighted traveller, that when he falls in with bogles, whatever danger may be in his going forward, there is much more hazard in turning back.*
>
> R. Burns, footnote to *Tam O'Shanter*, 1710

The tunnel curved slightly to the right, giving him a ten-metre line of sight. He would crawl that distance and then give up.

Ten metres on, the tunnel seemed to be opening out. He gave it another ten, and then twenty, and then the torchlight was showing a large chamber strewn with boulders. Reaching it, he found it was about nine feet high and adorned with thousands of little needle-like stalactites and stalagmites. He stood up and stretched.

Leading off from this chamber was a curving man-sized tunnel. If he wasn't lost, and if Svetlana's map was right, this would lead to Tyson's Autobahn.

It did, and Petrie almost wept with relief. He shouted,

'Yes!' and, '*Yes! Yes! Yes!*' echoed back at him, fading into silence.

The Autobahn, an ancient bedding plane uplifted by whatever forces had created the Tatras, was a lot steeper than he had expected it to be. It was about twenty metres broad and ten high, patterned with stony icicles on floor and roof, many of them as thick as tree trunks. It stretched beyond the range of Petrie's lamp.

Again he momentarily switched off; again, pitch black. *Freya! Where are you?*

A kilometre, Svetlana had said. He set off smartly, his breath echoing in the long chamber. Gradually, as he climbed, the roof became lower. He thought he glimpsed . . .

Voices!

Petrie froze, switched off his helmet lamp and stood in the pitch black. Not pitch black. Lights, at the foot of the Autobahn. Half a kilometre away, but it was hard to judge distances.

A candlelit procession. Skiers gliding down a piste, torches lighting the snow. A Viking funeral.

None of these. Men with guns, hunting him.

He switched on his lamp, turned to run.

Men shouting, the tunnel efficiently transmitting the voices so that they seemed only yards away.

Bullets would follow. Petrie began to swerve, keeping big stalagmites between him and his pursuers when he could. The ground levelled and sloped down; another fifty metres and he would be out of sight. A smattering of gunshot and little chips of limestone buzzing off stone icicles. One of them hit him hard on the cheek, drew blood. A last swerve and he was running downhill and there it was, seven metres down a shaft, the sump, a turquoise pool of infinite depth with a red nylon rope descending into it, attached to the vertical rock by pitons, and demons waiting for him under the smooth surface.

Petrie stared, horrified, at the water, still as death. Nothing was going to induce him into that pool.

> *Ah, Tam! Ah, Tam! thou'll*
> *get thy fairin! In hell,*
> *they'll roast thee like a*
> *herrin.*

A shouted command. They were much closer. Or was it the acoustics? Petrie scrambled down, gripping the rope, slipped, cried with pain as the friction burned the palms of his hands. Then his ankles were into the icy water, and his waist and his chest. He took a deep breath and then his head was under and he was hauling himself along clumsily, upside down, water getting into his nose.

He made no attempt to time the underwater journey. He didn't try to estimate how far the sump went down. But it levelled at some depth and he was pulling himself along frantically, his helmet bumping against the rock. He wondered if Freya had gone much further along the sump, whether he would bump into her drowned body. Stars began to explode in his eyes. Random walks, knots, soldiers, Freya, Hapsburg castles, alien signals, all went from his mind and were replaced by a single, burning focus: the red nylon line, winding through branching tunnels. And then the rope was curving upwards and there was light and he broke the surface, whooping and gasping.

Freya was perched on a boulder, looking like a sodden elf. Her helmet torch dazzled him.

'You took your time,' she said.

He heaved himself on to a ledge, flopped out on it for a few seconds. Then he sat up, still gasping. 'They're on the Autobahn. They shot at me.'

Freya scrambled around, picked up a fist-sized rock and started to hammer at a piton. Petrie, weak at the knees, scrabbled around for another stone.

'Tom, someone's on it.'

The rope had gone taut, as if a fish had been hooked on it.

Petrie said, 'Jesus.'

But now the piton was loose and in a minute they had the grim satisfaction of seeing the guide rope spiral down towards the bottom of the sump. Petrie felt a surge of guilt at his own hope that the soldiers using it would drown.

And now they were in a cavern with limestone stalagmites the size of tree trunks and branches leading off like exits from Piccadilly Underground.

'I know the way,' Freya said. 'I've been along it.' She led Petrie, streaming water, along a high tunnel, through a knee-deep stream. Ahead, faint light was scattering off the tunnel wall. They switched off their lamps. Human chatter began to echo. And then there was a short, dry shaft, brilliantly lit from the other end. Freya put a finger to her mouth and crawled along it. Petrie followed, and found himself looking down into a vast natural cathedral with flowstones, fountains and millions of stone icicles, frozen in brown, white and orange limestones. The cathedral was glowing from the spotlights scattered around its walls. About twenty people were clustered round a guide.

'This is the second party I've watched,' Freya whispered. 'I think the woman at the left is there to pick up stragglers.'

'Wait until they've moved off, then catch up, with

apologies. If anyone asks about our clothes, we've been scuba diving.'

But Freya, scanning the cavern, seemed not to have heard.

'Freya, we can't hang about. There could be strong swimmers amongst the soldiers. We may only have a couple of minutes' start.' He looked back fearfully at the black hole of the sump.

'I hope they all drown,' she hissed. Then she cuddled into him like a little wet kitten and whispered, 'Isn't this beautiful?' and Petrie tried to suppress a fit of giggling hysteria.

35

Death Squad

Gibson shambled reluctantly into the refectory. The entire team was present and the table was laid with toast, hard-boiled eggs, butter and jam. The croissants looked and smelled fresh, but only Shtyrkov was eating. Gibson's face twisted in tension, but only for a moment. Svetlana poured him a coffee.

'Can't be long now, Charlee.' Shtyrkov was grinning and Gibson believed that the man had finally lost his mind. 'Not once they find Hanning has failed to deliver.'

'I looked further down the signal, about two minutes into it, using Tom's algorithm – and found another genome, would you believe it? Another billion bytes or so.' Gibson was speaking without enthusiasm. 'It doesn't match anything in the *snp* database.'

'Meaning?' Shtyrkov asked.

'It's definitely non-human. Not even primate.'

'Drosophila? Nematode?'

Gibson shook his head emphatically. 'It's far more complex. Whatever it is, it's biologically more advanced than anything on Earth.'

'More complex equals superior?'

'Put it this way. Until I knew more about this entity, I wouldn't want to meet it on a dark night.'

Svetlana pushed her uneaten egg away, an angry gesture. She was close to tears. Shtyrkov squeezed her hand.

Gibson said, 'I know. Here we are, frantically working to the last minute for the good of all mankind, and mankind is about to squelch us.'

Shtyrkov asked, 'I wonder how they'll do it?' He seemed detached, almost cheerful.

'Why don't we just open the door and run out?' Svetlana asked.

'Calm yourself, child.'

Gibson sipped his coffee. It was the best he had ever tasted. Every sense was tingling. He wondered if this was what Shtyrkov was feeling, or whether the temporal lobe stuff was finally getting to him, or whether it was just his impending execution. 'They don't give the Nobel Prize posthumously.'

'Charlee Gibson. For once in your life forget earthly baubles. This discovery is beyond any prize.' Shtyrkov raised his coffee cup to Gibson. 'You are a very imperfect man, Charlee, but you have done something wonderful. Your reward is immortality.'

'I hope Tom and Freya make it,' said Gibson. 'I want my immortality.'

36

Pursuit

Sibelius filling the cathedral, scattering off a million stalactites, echoing along a hundred tunnels. A pool glowing blue from hidden underwater lighting. The tour guide had stopped and was talking to his audience. Freya edged her way forwards. A mother with a child said something in German; some joke, Petrie inferred, about their sodden clothes.

And the guide was still talking, over the music.

Petrie looked behind, trying to hide the fear, make it seem like a casual glance. The path they had come down was a giant orange throat lined with needles. There was no sign of pursuit. Not yet.

And the guide was still talking.

At last there was a flurry of laughter, and a little applause, and the inspirational music had risen to a shattering climax and stopped. Now the crowd was shuffling with infinite slowness towards concrete stairs which headed up towards the roof of the cavern.

Freya was well ahead, just a few bodies behind the guide. Petrie was almost taking up the rear. In a minute she had vanished from sight. And then at last Petrie was at the top of the steps. If the Slovak army was waiting there was nothing to be done. Along a short corridor, and out, and blinking in the white glare of snow. A hairpin path plunged steeply down towards roofs far below, just glimpsed through trees. There were no soldiers to be seen. Freya was waiting, letting the crowd flow around her, wet blonde hair over her shoulders. At that moment Petrie believed she was the most beautiful woman on Earth.

The path was slippery and people linked arms or gripped the steel handrail as they started the descent.

The guide locked the exit door. It was sheet metal.

Freya put her arm in Petrie's and they started slowly down. The snow had compacted to a shiny, hard surface. The guide and the tail-end Charlie were soon ahead of them, striding down the slope with practised ease.

And now the fugitives were alone.

'What now?' Freya wondered.

'We're alive.'

She was gripping his arm. 'I wonder about Charlie and Vash and Svetlana.'

Petrie looked back at the door, still only metres from them. 'It's solid steel. The soldiers are entombed. Even if they found their way back through the Wormhole, they'd never get upstream against the Styx.'

'They have guns. If they get through the sump they'll shoot the lock, like they do in movies.'

Petrie looked again at it, wondering. 'They'll never get through the sump.'

Freya said, 'You're shaking. Are you cold?' She held him. For a few glorious seconds he felt her breasts, warm and wonderful, against his chest.

Then he gently disengaged himself. 'No, I'm terrified. Let's clear off. By now the army have worked out that we're either trapped inside the mountain or we've found a way out of it.'

They clambered down the path, gripping the handrail,

and then left it, ploughing through the snow-deep woods in case of soldiers at the foot of the path. A big fluffy snowball loped down through the trees and passed them at a leisurely pace, gathering speed: a gentle warning that they were at risk from avalanche. On the flat, they crossed a wooden bridge and an icy stream. A large yellow notice told them they had left the Demänovskà Cave of Liberty. And they were now on an ice-covered road winding perilously through steep-sided mountains.

There was a general exodus in progress, cars with snow-chains and skis on their roofs moving slowly down the valley to their right, heading for home after the weekend skiing.

Right was motorway, and the road to towns like Popov and Levoce where you could lose yourself.

Right was the border with Poland, not too far to the north, with big cities like Cracow and Wroclaw in easy reach.

Right was the only sensible way to go.

They looked at each other, and without a word turned left, against the flow.

* * *

Nerves taut and chilled to the bone, they spied the land from trees at the edge of a car park. The nearest humans were two hundred metres away, but still Petrie spoke quietly. 'Are you thinking what I'm thinking?'

Freya gave a tense little nod.

Petrie watched the activity quietly. 'Want to chance it?'

At five in the morning, the big foyer of the hotel was buzzing with life. Two blue tourist coaches stood outside the entrance, engines throbbing steadily, steam coming from their exhausts. Bleary-eyed people, dressed against the cold, were boarding them in twos and threes. The driver was heaving skis and suitcases into the bowels of the first coach, showing every sign of a short temper.

'We can't do this,' Freya said.

Petrie murmured, 'What else is there? Climb over the mountains?'

'We have no luggage, no skis. And there's bound to be a tour operator.'

'We'll just have to slip past.'

Freya shook her head. 'Tom, that's crazy.'

Petrie looked at the tousled blonde hair, the scratched nose and cheeks, the stained and torn jacket, the Levis stiff with ice and the heavy boots, and felt an overwhelming urge to protect this vulnerable creature while knowing that she was tougher than him. 'We've no choice.'

She took Petrie's arm, teeth chattering with cold. 'In that case we'd better get a move on.'

The driver of the lead coach had slammed the luggage doors shut and was climbing into it. Petrie was seized with a sudden dread that they'd left it too late. They picked their way through snow-dusted cars. An overflow of weary passengers was clustered round the second coach. A few others were coming out of the hotel.

They emerged from the car park, passed the first coach; a thin-nosed elderly woman looked down and smiled wearily. Petrie smiled back.

Merge casually. Don't be noticed.

The driver, a small, wiry man, was muttering to himself. They nudged their way through a group of young people with bags and skis and little blue boxes. Nobody was paying attention. Petrie was beginning to think they might get away with it. Freya put her foot on the coach step, gripped the rail. The driver looked up sharply, said, '*Ne!*'

Petrie's heart lurched.

The driver approached Freya and jabbered something. She shrugged. Petrie wondered about taking her arm and saying something about the wrong bus, when a tall, bespectacled man behind Freya said, in German, 'What about your boxes?'

'Sorry?'

'He won't let you on without your breakfast boxes. Otherwise you could be anyone.'

'Of course!' Freya replied in German, put her hand to her head. The little blue boxes.

'Better be quick.'

Into the hotel. A fat, surly woman behind a trellis table was handing out boxes, and keys were being handed in at the desk. They joined a little queue. The receptionists, two girls nearing the end of the overnight shift, paid them no attention. The fat woman handed Petrie and Freya little blue boxes without looking up. They boarded the bus, the driver glancing at them with an air of suspicion.

The coach was half-empty, and wonderfully warm. They took a seat near the back, Freya at the window. There was a trickle of ski people, and then the driver finally climbed on board and sat heavily down in his seat, and the doors closed with a hiss. There was no tour operator, and nobody counted heads.

The coach moved smoothly away. They looked at each other, too exhausted even to smile, the sudden warmth draining away the last of their energy. Freya leaned her head on Petrie's shoulder. Her voice was slurred. 'Colditz was easy.'

'Alcatraz was a joke.'

Now she was whispering, and Petrie could hardly hear her. 'As for Devil's Island . . .'

He tapped her nose. 'Now for the hard bit.'

* * *

Colonel Jan Boroviška sighed.

The hand-rolled Don Tomas cigar was carefully placed in the crude ceramic ashtray – a treasure made by a younger daughter at the Gymnasium in the remote past – and he leaned back, his hands clasped on the desk in front of him.

Lieutenant Tono Pittich, standing rigidly to attention at the Colonel's desk, knew the signs, and longed for a quick release.

'Tono, how long since you gained your Lieutenant's badge?'

'Four years, sir.'

The Colonel nodded thoughtfully but made no comment. 'And you had an entire platoon at your disposal? To guard two civilians?'

'That's true, Colonel, I had a platoon.'

'And you allowed the two down together in the elevator shaft? Not one at a time, each accompanied by one of your men?'

'I put four of my men down the shaft ahead of the scientists, and the rest stayed up top. I didn't see how they could possibly escape.' The Lieutenant was aware that he was beginning to jabber, but couldn't stop himself. 'I didn't know about the side tunnel.'

The truth was otherwise; the Lieutenant *had* known about the side tunnel. It simply hadn't occurred to him that the scientists might stop the rapidly falling elevator at its entrance. The young man wondered fearfully whether the

Colonel believed him, thought that the story had come out sounding like the lie it was.

'Did you not have a map of the cave complex?'

Desperately, the Lieutenant wondered if he should compound the lie with another one, and deny that he'd had access to a map. But no, it was too easy to check, and in any case his failure to acquire something as fundamental to an officer as a map could be seen as dereliction of duty. But to admit that he had a map would be tantamount to admitting that he knew about the side tunnel. He was beginning to feel entangled in a web.

'I had, sir.'

'I know you had.' Boroviška took a contemplative puff. 'We shall go into the matter of your amazing dereliction of duty in due course, Tono. Unfortunately, or perhaps fortunately from where you are standing, it will have to wait. We will shortly be having a visitor.'

'Sir?'

'Yes. General Kamensky, no less.' Boroviška spoke softly. 'What am I to tell the General, Tono? Do you have any suggestions?'

37

Flight by Coach

Between Petrie and Freya, and the Austrians, were several rows of empty seats. This made it gratifyingly difficult to engage the strange, wet young ones in conversation, and in any case nobody seemed inclined to make the attempt. Such desultory chat as there was soon died out, and in the soporific warmth of the coach people dozed or stared morosely out of the window. The countryside was dark and mountainous, the hills barely lit by a crescent moon.

Petrie was too exhausted, too frightened and too wet to sleep, but Freya snuggled into him, shivering, and within minutes she was snoring slightly, her head on his shoulder.

He tried to think it through, but the freezing wetness of his clothes and the awful stress of the past few hours combined to keep him in a sort of stupor. He opened the breakfast box and found himself staring at a small bottle of mineral water, a hardboiled egg and a sandwich filled with some indeterminate gunge. He slid the lot under his seat.

All they could do now, he reckoned, was wait.

The coach took off, and trundled carefully down the narrow, ice-packed road, past the ski hotels, past the Demänovskà Cave. In the lights of the bus Petrie glimpsed a couple of soldiers, tucked away in front of a tourist shop and invisible from the steep footpath leading down from the cave. One of the soldiers, a red-faced farm boy from oxcart country, looked at the passing coach. He stared directly at Petrie, their eyes meeting momentarily; and then the image was gone and Petrie's hands were clenched into fists and his mind was filled with a simple question: *was I recognised?*

Nobody stopped the coach. It took a left at a roundabout and picked up speed on a broad road. The snow had gone and there was a pale sliver of dawn to the east. No headlights were pursuing them in the dark. Petrie unclenched his fists. He saw the chemical works, all aluminium pipes and orange smoke stacks catching the dawn light. Freya's wet hair tickled his nostrils. Suddenly, Petrie was overwhelmed with exhaustion.

Shortly, the bus slowed and turned on to a motorway, and then accelerated to a satisfyingly brisk speed. The countryside here was flat and bleak. In the distance, shortly, Petrie saw a forest of high-rise buildings, shimmering, floating on water and flamingo pink in the light of the rising sun.

He stared stupidly at the distant mirage, mumbled something about a socialist paradise, and flaked out.

* * *

'Tom!'

Freya was poking his thigh.

Memory flooded back. Petrie looked out in sudden panic. They were in the suburbs of some big city. 'Is this Bratislava?'

'I think so. The bus is going to Austria.'

'What? But the border!'

'We must get off now.'

Now Petrie definitely recognised the city as Bratislava. They made their way to the front of the coach. Freya said something in German. The driver shook his head.

She turned to Petrie in alarm. 'He's not letting us off.'

'We have to. It's life or death.'

She spoke to the driver again, sharply this time, but the man simply gave a surly shake of the head. Petrie wondered about punching him.

'I could start to take my clothes off,' she suggested.

'He'd just get the police.' Petrie tapped Freya on the shoulder and they made their way to the back of the coach.

'What now?'

'Wait till it stops. Then we'll get out of the emergency window.'

Down a broad street, every set of traffic lights turning green as the bus approached. Glorious congestion loomed ahead. Petrie recognised the area. The big Tesco store appeared on the left. The bus stopped. A blue tram pulled up a few feet behind the bus. They pulled open the window and clambered out, in front of the astonished tram driver. Freya's boot caught Petrie on the cheek. The coach driver was shouting angrily.

They held hands and dodged their way across the busy street, not daring to look behind. On the busy pavement, they ran.

A couple of hundred metres on, they slowed down to a trot. And then they stopped at a little cluster of market stalls.

'Where are we?' Petrie asked, his chest heaving. A red and white tram clattered past them, jammed with commuters.

She pointed. 'There's the castle. Let's head for the Old Town.'

'I've dried off. How about you?'

'Yes, but I'd kill for a shower.'

* * *

General Kamensky sat with three telephones. Two of them were on the Colonel's desk and the third was a mobile which he produced from a deep army pocket. For his first call he cleared the Colonel's office. Boroviška and his Lieutenant stood in the outside corridor while tantalising snatches of phrase came through the door. Then the General was at the door and waving them in while he made a further call.

This second call was to the Chief of Police in Prague. The Czech Republic being an independent state, the call was in the nature of a request. Equally clearly, someone had made sure that this 'request' was backed up with all the necessary authority. A third call, identical in content, went to Bratislava.

At last he turned his attention to the officers facing him nervously across the desk. 'Colonel, I won't emphasise the magnitude of your failure as I'm sure you are already aware of it. The fact is that your task force had a special assignment, an unpleasant duty but a simple one. In fact, it could hardly have been simpler.'

'Sir . . .'

Kamensky waved a hand dismissively. 'I don't want to hear it. I turn up here to supervise the – how can I put it? – the terminal arrangements, to find that you have lost two of your charges. Untrained civilians bottled up inside a castle surrounded by a brigade of regular troops!'

He helped himself to one of the Colonel's cigars, he struck a match on the underside of the table and took a few puffs. Then he sighed. 'The position is that for this operation to be successful, *all* the enemies of the state have to be removed. One survivor equals total failure.'

'Sir . . .'

The General banged his hand on the table. 'I told you I don't want to hear your excuses! Now, thanks to your incompetence, we have to involve the regular police in the recapture of these people. Do you have any idea how much that complicates the operation, Boroviška?'

'I do, General.'

Kamensky stared at him. 'I hope you do, Colonel. You now have to liquidate these people out of the public eye, and before they talk to the police, but at the same time we need the police manpower if we are to have any chance of finding them. We may also have to operate in the territory of a neighbouring state.'

Boroviška finally got a word in. 'They can't have gone far. They had no transport. The only railway stations within reach are at Mikulas and Benadikova. I have posted men at both, in plain clothes. The hotels within a ten-kilometre radius of here are being checked now.'

'And if you were fleeing for your life, would you put up in the nearest hotel?'

'No, sir. It's too stupid to be worth checking. Which is why I'm checking.'

Kamensky nodded approvingly. 'We may indeed be dealing with a couple of clever foxes.' He stood up and moved over to a map pinned on the wooden wall. 'We are very close to the Polish border.'

'Very close indeed.'

'What are you doing about that?'

Boroviška pointed. 'There are only two crossing points, here at Trstena and possibly over here at Cadca. I have informed the border police and faxed through photographs of the criminals.

'There's a rail crossing into Poland at Cadca.'

'I expect the border police . . .'

'You *expect*?' The General rubbed his forehead in an anguished way. 'Colonel, move some of that idle brigade at Smoleniçe, and have them waiting at Cadca before the first train arrives.'

'Yes, sir.'

Kamensky's eyes roamed over the map. 'Border crossings, away from roads? What about Narodny Park here?'

'At this time of year, General, without specialised equipment? Survival is impossible.'

'Another of your impossibles, Boroviška. However, I agree. It can't be done.' Kamensky paused.

Boroviška picked up the cue. 'I'll speak to the Park Rangers.'

'You will. You will also check the local hotels, and find out what transport has been leaving from them, and whether anyone fitting the descriptions of the targets has been seen in the area.' Kamensky looked at a photograph. 'The Størmer woman is strikingly beautiful. What wonderful blonde hair. So distinctive, would you not say?'

38

The Chess Player

Café Roland was pure 1920s' kitsch, all palm fronds and Art Deco. Somewhere a husky-voiced chanteuse was half-singing a bittersweet lyric to a background of violin, cello and flute.

Near the front door a man was resting his arm on a red velvet cushion, which was as well because the clay pipe he held was about three feet long. He was dressed in a golden tunic lined with thick white fur, and he was wearing a hat which looked like a giant Liquorice Allsort. His free hand was hovering over a chessboard on a polished black cabinet.

The café was big on black: polished black granite floor, square black tables and chairs, a big black clock over the bar, shiny black panelling everywhere. But it was light and airy, with a high vaulted ceiling and tall windows, and delicate green marble pillars decorated with rustic scenes in colourful mosaic.

Freya sat dreaming about the daughter she might have one day.

She was the perfect baby. Toughened against a host of diseases, she had a likely life span of three hundred years. At age three, she had a two-thousand-word command of the English language. By five, she spoke Norwegian, English, German and French fluently, and had a good grasp of history, geography, mathematics, physics, chemistry, English and Russian literature, and biology. By six, Mozart was easy and by age nine, when her physiology allowed it, she had mastered Soradji's Clavicembalisticum.

She got her doctorate in molecular biology at age sixteen. By then she was both sexually precocious and surprisingly mature. Having taken a 'year out', she started a small pharmaceutical company at age eighteen. Its expansion matched her own amazing rate of development and within a decade the young woman, incredibly beautiful by Western standards, was listed in Forbes as well as attracting, and rejecting, a long list of suitors.

A young man wearing a bow tie and waistcoat interrupted her dream. He was dressed in black. Freya ordered hot chocolates in German. Petrie watched the waiter anxiously as the man sauntered behind the bar, heard him give a curt order and then saw him disappear behind an enormous palm; in a moment cigarette smoke began to drift through the fronds and Petrie sighed briefly with relief.

The agreed plan was to split up, but being only flesh and bone, they were postponing the moment, desperate to stay in each other's company for a few extra minutes. Freya's fantastic Superbaby receded from her imagination, but the concept left her vaguely uneasy. She looked at the big clock, unconsciously biting her lower lip. 'Five to ten.'

The chanteuse sang in melancholy vein:

> 'Let us drink and sport today
> Ours is not tomorrow
> Love with youth flies away,
> Aye is naught but sorrow.'

'I know.' Petrie rubbed his face.

They both knew. By now, at the castle, a coachload of linguists would have arrived. Some of them would be in the conference room, sorting out viewgraphs; some would be having coffee on the terrace, greeting old colleagues, nodding at rivals; others would be spreading clothes and coats around their little bedrooms. Of the video room or the computers, there would be not a trace.

And Vashislav, Svetlana and Charlie would be gone.

Vashislav the Terrible with his brilliant mind and childish sense of fun; Svetlana the Timid with her there's-nowhere-else-to-be dedication; Charlie the Gloryseeker with his thirst for the Prize. By now, at five to ten on this cold morning, they no longer existed.

'If we get through this, Tom . . .'

> *'Dance and sing,*
> *Time's on the wing.'*

'They'll get full recognition.'

Freya was still cold and her hand kept straying to a central heating ventilator. 'Tom, we're fugitives in a foreign country. We stand out. I don't have a bean and neither of us speaks the language.'

A silver salver arrived bearing little glasses of water and two hot chocolates which had the consistency of melted chocolate bars.

'You're right. That Scandinavian blonde hair. Any cop will spot you from two hundred metres.'

Freya was stirring her chocolate. Her face was strained and worried. 'I don't want a perfect baby.'

Petrie looked at her in surprise.

'I want a messy baby. One that I can nurture and love.

One that needs its nose wiped and its diaper changed.'

'Carissima, have you finally flipped?'

'Are we doing the right thing, Tom? Maybe this knowledge *is* better buried. Maybe the species should muddle through without help from the signallers. If the decision-makers want that, do we have the right to say no?'

'We do, because we're responsible for our own decisions.'

'If we voluntarily handed the disks over, it would prove that we intend to keep quiet.'

'Hand them over?' Petrie's surprise turned to bafflement.

'If we did that we'd never be able to prove that there was a signal. They'd leave us alone.'

'Betraying Svetlana, Vash and Charlie while we're about it.'

'Who are we to make decisions on behalf of the entire human species?'

'Not so loud, Freya.' Petrie leaned forwards, speaking quietly. 'Burning the disks is doing just that. How can we deny humanity the knowledge that there's something out there? And you've picked a fine time to get steamed up about the ethics of germline therapy.'

'We shouldn't fix the aging genes. Imagine an eight-hundred-year-old Genghis Khan running our lives. We need death to get rid of monsters and we need young people to question and challenge.'

Petrie shook his head in disagreement. 'Why should life be brutish and short if we can make it beautiful and long? Anyway, babies will always be horrible messy little critters. And if you want one prone to all the diseases, don't drink the enzyme juice. Just don't expect it to thank you when it's an adult.'

Freya whispered fiercely, 'I'm a female, have you noticed? It's my reproductive role you're playing with. As the goddess of fertility I reserve the right to say No.'

'Fine. But don't deny others the chance to say Yes.'

'Maybe the signallers want humanity dead. Maybe there's a time-bomb hidden in their DNA-repair instructions.'

'If what I think about the signal motivation is right . . .'

'Ah yes, the famous X-theory, which you don't deign to reveal to us lesser humans.'

'And we don't know what the politicians want, except that one or two of them want us dead, but two don't make a quorum.'

Petrie looked around. A bearded character three tables away was smoking a strong cigarette. Two five-year-old girls with Turkish fathers were tucking into enormous, cream-laden cakes. Two hatted, elderly ladies were exchanging scandals. A sultry girl with a short black skirt was sipping an espresso and scanning the menu. A cork popped noisily somewhere behind the bar. Through the windows a wide cobbled square scattered with gas lamps and trees showed a toddler, well-clad and looking like a Russian doll, chasing a pigeon. A girl in her mid-twenties, with jeans and red hair, was crossing the square briskly, behind the child. At the far end, a party of tourists hovered around the archway of the *muzéum*. 'Our first lovers' tiff.'

She didn't respond to Petrie's smile. 'Do we sit here until closing time?'

'If I could only get to a cybercafé . . .' Petrie touched his chest, felt the reassuring presence of the disks.

'Don't be an idiot. They'll be watched.'

Petrie reluctantly nodded his agreement. He looked at the menu, not understanding a word.

'Where do we go? Do you head south and swim the Danube while I walk back north and climb over the High

Tatras? Or maybe I'll walk to the Ukraine and hide in some haystack while you stroll over open fields to the Czech Republic?' She spread her hands in a gesture of despair. 'This is a small rural country, Tom, and we're bottled up in it. And your credit card will set off bells if you try it out.'

Petrie was frowning. 'Wolfgang von Kempelen.'

'What?'

'The chess player.' Petrie aired his knowledge. 'Hero of Bratislava, born in 1734. He travelled Europe with his little cabinet, which was a chess-playing machine, which beat all comers. Von Kempelen was the original cybernetics man.'

'If the police catch us they'll hand us over for special treatment. Tom, I can't visualise it. We were speaking to Vashislav, Svetlana and Charlie yesterday. Are they really dead?'

'So naturally the Slovaks don't want to tell you that the cabinet was a fraud. It couldn't have been anything else.'

'I can't take it in. That we could be dead before the day is over.'

Petrie shrugged. 'It must have had a chess-playing dwarf inside it.'

'A chess-playing dwarf?' Freya's eyes were moist. 'Tom, would you like to come back to planet Earth?'

'Maybe. I'd think more clearly if I didn't have this woman going on at me.' Petrie was riffling through his wallet. 'Nearly three thousand slovaks. At seventy to the pound we have forty quid between us.'

'Wonderful. I might get a change of knickers.'

In the square, there was a sudden flutter of pigeons. The toddler was being pursued by its mother and moving at surprising speed. Petrie said, 'And another thing you don't know is that during the Second World War, some of the caves in Slovakia were hideouts for partisans.'

'That's about as useful as your chess-playing dwarf.'

'I'm full of gems like that. For instance, the Domica Cave was formed in the Middle Triassic; it's twenty-five kilometres long, and you can take a rowing boat through it all the way to Hungary.'

Freya paused, her hands wrapped round the mug of chocolate. 'Twenty-five kilometres? All the way to Hungary?'

'All the way to Hungary.'

> *'Dance and sing,*
> *Time's on the wing.'*

Petrie continued: 'The bit open to the public is a four-kilometre round trip, of which only four hundred metres is rowing boat.'

'So we hide away in the cave after the tours have gone and pinch one of their boats? Thanks, Tom.'

'The caves are near a town called Plešivec, about a hundred miles from here. A couple of hours by bus.'

'That's desperate.'

'Or you could just walk across the border a couple of miles from here.'

But Freya had stopped listening. Petrie followed her alarmed stare. Three policemen had appeared at the far end of the Hlavné Namestie. They were sauntering in the way policemen do the world over, looking around as they did. They were heading towards the café.

'Take off. I'll get the bill.'

'What about you?'

'No time.' Petrie was on his feet. He handed her a wodge of banknotes. 'Get out of it, Freya.'

'Will we meet again?' She stood up, white-faced.

'No.'

'Life never knows the return of spring.'

One of the policemen, fat with a red beard and untidy hair down to his collar, was looking in the direction of Roland's Café; he seemed to be staring directly at them. Petrie turned away, spoke in a low, rapid voice. 'Listen. Steal a bike. Go to the high-rise apartments south-west of the castle. There's a wood below them, and a cycle-track going through the wood. The track goes straight to the border post but if you turn off it when you're in the woods and keep going west you'll end up in Austria.'

The waiter was eyeing them curiously. Petrie waved banknotes at him and left them on the table. The trio of police were halfway across the square. Whether they had been seen he wasn't sure, but their direction of approach was unmistakably threatening. 'Go, Freya!'

She kissed him, holding him in a brief, desperate clutch. Her lips were wet. She whispered, 'Unur Arnadottir, Reykjavik Seafood Centre. An old friend and an e-mail drop you can trust.'

Then he was pushing her away and she was out of the door.

The Scandinavian blonde hair.

There was a look of surprise from the red-haired policeman and a brief, sharp word to his colleagues. Freya took to the left. The policemen moved quickly, then broke into a trot. Petrie gave it a couple of seconds then sprinted off to the right. He had time to glimpse their hesitation, a moment of confusion about who should chase whom. One of them shouted, '*Stůj!*' in a deep, authoritative voice but Petrie, bogles at his heels, wasn't about to *stůj* for anyone, least of all a policeman with a deep, authoritative voice.

39

Embassy

'So what do we do? Send in the Marines?' Bull turned to a thin, bird-like woman in her fifties. Behind thick spectacles, her eyes were like blue pebbles. 'What have we got out there, Ms Rothwell?'

'Miss Rothwell,' she corrected the President. 'An Embassy, sir.' Her diction was precise and there was a slight nervousness in her voice. It was the first time she had spoken to the President, and the first time she had been to Camp David. 'In Bratislava, as it happens. It has the usual offices, commercial services, public affairs, Defense Attaché. They run a few Peace Corps volunteers.'

'So where do you hide the CIA?' the President asked impatiently. 'In the Peace Corps?'

'No, sir. We front a travel agency, mostly for handling commercial information. And we have a well-placed source in their Foreign Office. Regional Security harvests economic intelligence. Our military liaison team – five Americans in the Slovak Ministry of Defence – has the full blessing of the Slovak government.'

The CIA Director, Al Sullivan, interrupted. 'None of which is useful to us in the present situation.'

'What about our Defense Attaché?' the President asked.

Miss Rothwell flicked through some sheets of paper. 'A Lieutenant Colonel Herschel, seconded from the Indiana

National Guard. We have a bilateral military programme with the Slovaks. We help their Mig-29 pilots with specialised English, we gave their rapid reaction battalion a couple of million dollars' worth of communication equipment and so on. Herschel's responsible for the whole spectrum of our military interest out there.'

'Which means he almost certainly runs some people,' Sullivan interrupted again.

'I wouldn't know, sir. But they wouldn't be useful to us.'

Sullivan gave Miss Rothwell a look. She coloured slightly.

Bull grunted. 'So, in a nutshell, your little nest of spies isn't worth a diddly.'

The State Department lady agreed. 'They're not geared up for a dragnet.'

'Right. Right. So the Embassy are out of it.' The President looked over at the DCI, who was sitting across from him, hunched forward. The CIA Chief had a worried frown. 'Al, can you get a team out there?'

'To find Petrie and Størmer?' He shook his head. 'The manpower lies with the Slovak police and they know their own country. We can't compete with that.'

Judith Rothwell coughed. 'If we mounted a manhunt on Slovak territory, and the Slovaks found out, which they probably would, there'd be diplomatic hell to pay.'

'Yeah.' Bull clasped his hands and looked meditatively across at the CIA Director.

The DCI said, 'Look, these missing scientists have no money and no contacts. They're in a foreign country and they don't even speak the language.' He spread his hands expansively. 'They haven't a hope. The Slovaks will have them in days.'

The President wrinkled his nose sceptically. 'Maybe. So

what happens to them when they're caught? What does the East Europe desk have to say?' He looked at the State Department woman with raised eyebrows.

'The Slovak Constitution prohibits arbitrary arrest and detention.'

'I'm talking real life, Miss Rothwell.'

'If the scientists are arrested they'll have to be given a hearing within twenty-four hours and either freed or taken to a court for remand. If they're remanded, they can get a second hearing within twenty-four hours. After that, it's due process all the way, with the Supreme Court stepping in if—'

Bull raised a hand to stop the flow. He sighed. 'I'll try again. What I'm asking is this. What's the Slovak government's record on human rights? Have there been, let's say, disappearances? Maybe even extrajudicial killings? Hell, the country was Communist for fifty years.'

'I see.' She pursed her lips primly. 'The Department gives Slovakia a clean bill of health on human rights.'

'Uhuh?' Bull waited.

Miss Rothwell took the cue. 'Of course we do carry out a lot of business there. Manganese ore, pharmaceuticals. The country's expanding, post-Communism.'

'And we wouldn't want to rock the boat by getting oversensitive,' the President suggested.

'No, sir. Then there's the political aspect. It's in all our interests to stay friendly. And the Slovak government does respect its country's Constitution.'

'Uhuh.'

'But there are some little problems.'

The wait was longer.

'Mostly racial. The Romany population complains of occasional police brutality, followed by threats if they try to press charges. Skinhead attacks against racial minorities don't get investigated.'

'And we can't let a few gyppos with a persecution complex get in the way of a good commercial thing.' The air was heavy with the President's sarcasm.

'It's not like that, sir. The Slovak government are trying to deal with it.'

Sullivan said, 'Hell, Seth, I wouldn't want to be black, vagrant and under arrest two blocks away from here.'

'There was one possible extrajudicial killing,' Miss Rothwell said, warming to the theme. 'That was Jan Ducky, a former Economy Minister, and Head of the National Gas Distribution, a state monopoly. He was bumped off in the lobby of his apartment in January 1999. He was under investigation for financial shenanigans and the speculation is he was killed to keep him quiet.'

Sullivan said, 'Could have been anyone. Not necessarily the government.'

'And then there was the kidnapping of the President's son.'

'The what?' Bull stared.

'Kidnapping and torture. He was abducted to Austria. The Interior Ministry was heavily influenced by the SIS – the intelligence service – and the intelligence service was out of control. Their boss, Ivan Lexa, was charged along with about a dozen SIS people.'

'What happened?'

'Lexa pleaded immunity but Parliament removed it in 1999. He fled the country and there's an international arrest warrant out for him. But the point is this, Mr President. If our fugitives are arrested, I believe the Slovak government will respect their rights.'

'But you've just given me torture, kidnapping, judicial killings,' Bull pointed out.

'Not by the government,' Miss Rothwell insisted. 'By renegade elements within it.'

Sullivan said, 'The message is clear. The odds are against us but it's imperative that we capture this pair before the Slovaks get to them. We'll have to mount a covert operation.'

'Renegade elements within the government. I'm glad I don't have that problem.' The President grinned at Sullivan. 'I don't have that problem, do I, Al?'

* * *

The rattle of a passing tram startled Petrie. He was still out of breath. He had sprinted along a narrow lane, with the fat policeman's footsteps in his ears. At a corner he had glanced quickly behind and with a surge of terror saw that the man had drawn his revolver. Dodging frantically through the passers-by, he finally reached a busy, cobbled pedestrian street. He recognised an archway – St Michael's Gate – ran towards it and turned sharp right on to another lane. An old lady shouted something at him. There was a restaurant, closed for business. A van driver was heaving a tray of bread into the front door. The keys were in the ignition. Petrie leaped into the van and crashed into gear. In the mirror he saw the van driver rushing out of the restaurant and the policeman colliding with him. Then he was round the corner of the lane and back into the Roland's Café square. There was no sign of Freya or the other policemen. He had driven through the pedestrians-only square, swerving to avoid someone half-hidden under a pink frilly umbrella, and on to another road. On a busy main road, with traffic crawling, he had lost his nerve –

the bright red van would be picked up in minutes – and he had turned into a side road, ditched the van, and sprinted off in a random direction.

Running attracts attention. Now he was walking, although his chest was still heaving. The embankment was too open, and there was nobody on it but himself. A hundred pairs of eyes looked at him from the Danube Hotel across the road, plainclothes police were spotting him from every passing tram, and men with binoculars were watching him from the high concrete tower which straddled the flyover bridge.

Cut the panic. Get a grip on yourself.

He walked, smartly but not conspicuously so, past a floating hotel and a moored restaurant: the Cirkus Barok, flying the skull and crossbones and festooned with coloured lights. It looked closed. Further along he came to the Café Propeler; he climbed down a wooden gangplank.

The waiter waved him to a seat overlooking the river. Now that he was sitting, Petrie found that he was shaking with fright. A small Turkish waiter approached and Petrie ordered a coffee. He looked around. A middle-aged couple sat a few tables away. He had black hair, bushy eyebrows and unhealthy grey skin; he was immaculately dressed in a cheap grey suit, cheap shirt and nondescript tie, and he was smoking a cigarette. She had shoulder-length hair and was talking animatedly to him over her spectacles. In a corner a heavy man of about thirty, with designer stubble and an over-large blue shirt hanging out of his trousers, was staring at a sheet of paper. There was an occasional click of a Biro as he scribbled.

A haven, for the time it took to drink a coffee. Get your breath back. *Think.*

The coffee arrived. He tried to stop shaking but he

spilled some into the saucer. Alarmed, Petrie read a world of suspicion in the waiter's glance.

The truth was that, in focusing on the escape from the castle, the scientists had paid almost no attention to what they would do once they were out of it. The goals were clear: get out of the country, fire an answering signal, and tell the scientific community and the world about the shattering discovery. But how to achieve these goals?

Petrie found himself drifting into fantasy, one with sensational announcements to packed press conferences, worldwide CNN broadcasts, intense debates at the United Nations, the carefully prepared response to the signallers, the plaudits, the prizes. Again he dragged himself back to harsh reality. HMG, in its wisdom, had decided the knowledge was too dangerous, had decided to kill it – was trying to murder one of its own citizens.

The border was by now sealed, he was nearly out of money and there was a manhunt in progress. He didn't speak the language and had no friends here. His own Embassy was a hostile place.

His probable survival time was minutes or hours, depending on luck. Maybe stretching to a day or two.

Solution: none immediately occurring.

Petrie looked at the snow-covered woodland across the river, but his mind's eye saw Freya.

Freya with the long hair, glowing golden in the way that no peroxide could quite reproduce. Freya, who chattered and laughed infectiously and whose charming, knowing smile could reduce him to a jelly. Whose slender body carried that heavy rucksack as if it were filled with paper. Whose every movement and gesture was filled with life and happiness, in stark contrast to his own introverted gloominess. And the first girl he had shared intimacy with.

He preferred to forget that ghastly encounter as a teenager ('Come on, duckie, shoot your load, I'm losing business here').

And now she was gone and Petrie was suffering pangs of longing and anxiety. He wondered whether she was now on a bus to Plešivec, to attempt an even more desperate underground escape to Hungary and points beyond; or whether they had caught her in that frantic sprint from Café Roland. Maybe she was even now being interrogated in some police basement or an army barracks.

Petrie finished his coffee. He glanced at his watch; it was mid-morning. He looked up at what he could see of the embankment traffic. He half-expected to see police cars trawling the streets but at the moment there were no signs of unusual activity.

Forget Freya. Survive, damn you! Find some way out of this trap!

Maybe she was even now dead.

* * *

At that moment, Freya was shampooing her hair a few hundred yards from Petrie, in the cloakroom of a large department store.

She had lost her police pursuers almost immediately. The forty metres' start, along with an athletic build and a fast acceleration, had taken her into a busy pedestrian precinct adjoining the square in seconds; rather than run along the lane she had instinctively turned into a chemist's shop. The cash Petrie had thrust at her was still in her hand. As she closed the door, trying to look calm and return the female assistant's smile, the policemen ran past, almost within arm's length.

The blonde hair!

She had bought a colour shampoo, eyebrow pencil, a dark lipstick and dark glasses, and had picked out a pink frilly umbrella from a rack. At the door of the shop she was in full view of one of the policemen. He had stopped running and was looking around. She had put on the glasses, put the umbrella up and sauntered back towards the square. Then she had crossed the square with nothing more eventful than a near-miss from a red van driven by a maniac; then she was through an archway with decorated windows and into a small courtyard. Into the museum, where she spent an hour investigating Slovakian viniculture through the ages before daring to emerge into the streets. She had recalled seeing a large department store, and had found it after an increasingly nervous half-hour of wandering the streets. She had bought some underwear, a smart dark skirt, a black sweater and a long black coat. In the store's cloakroom she had applied the eyebrow pencil and the lipstick and shampooed her hair. Finally, with the depleted supply of cash, she had bought a cheap briefcase and re-emerged in the icy streets as a dark-haired businesswoman.

Now all she had to do was sleep, eat and stay at large. Without money.

* * *

'May I speak English?'

The voice was female, Midwest. It said, 'Sure.' To Petrie, it summoned up a movie-inspired vision of log cabins and feisty homesteaders.

'My name is Petrie. I'm British and I need help.'

'This is the American Embassy, Mr Petrie. Your people are on Panskà Ulice, just round the corner from us.'

'I have information which may affect the interests of the United States.'

Silence.

Petrie, heart still thudding in his chest, turned the screw: 'I'm talking vital interests, national security, major league.' Petrie didn't know a thing about leagues, major or minor; just so long as it impressed.

Another long silence. Then: 'Hold the line a moment, Mr Petrie.'

'What's your name?'

'Brenda. Why?'

'I'll call you back, Brenda, I don't want you tracing me. Make sure I'm put straight through to someone relevant.'

Petrie put the receiver down and stepped out of the Pizza Hut. He wandered round a corner and was met by a forty-foot woman, dressed in white and carrying a packet of Persil. Water from the verandah above had created a streak of discolour down the side of the tenement mural but it had apparently been stopped by her hat. The broad streets were busy and there were queues for the trams and trolley buses. He hovered around a little street market for some minutes. There were no security cameras but he felt increasingly exposed. He took off past a taxi stance into an enormous Tesco – a sure sign that capitalism was here to stay – and lost himself amongst the cheeses and baked beans and strange meats for half an hour. Then he went back to the busy pizzeria.

Brenda, her voice a little cautious. 'Yes?'

'This is Petrie.'

A momentary silence, a faint click which could have been anything, and then a deep male voice came on the line, vowels drawling slightly. 'Dr Petrie. We need to meet.'

Dr Petrie. How did he know? 'You've been sold some story about me.'

'Yeah, it's a beauty. Want to hear it?'

'No, you might trace me.' A dark-skinned waiter shouted something. Petrie recognised the word 'peperoni'.

'Okay, Tom, but we can't assume this line is secure. Just imagine we're shouting at each other from the treetops, okay?' The man's drawl was suspiciously slow.

Petrie was having to raise his voice above the buzz of the restaurant. 'You're trying to trace me.'

'Hell no, Tom, I know exactly where you are. That was Darko. They're doing an eat-all-you-can promotion just now. Stay put, I'll be along in a few minutes.'

'How will I recognise you?'

'I'll be wearing a grey Cossack hat and I look mean.'

40

Kamensky

The first call reached Colonel Jan Boroviška in the early morning. A couple answering the description of the criminals – the blonde hair was an especially strong indicator – had been seen in Bratislava. Enquiries in local Tatras hotels had also revealed that a young couple behaving oddly had boarded a coach for Vienna, but had jumped it in Bratislava.

With this observation, the search area, fifty thousand square kilometres of Slovakia, shrank to the fifty or so square kilometres of Bratislava.

Boroviška felt reasonably satisfied with the morning's progress.

* * *

The face under the grey Cossack hat was podgy, American, and alert rather than mean. A grey scarf was tucked under a double chin. The man wore a long brown coat the likes of which Petrie had last seen in a movie about Wyatt Earp, and his hands were thrust deep into his pockets. From a doorway across the road Petrie watched him look around the tables, exchanging a brief comment with Darko. The waiter shook his head. Then the American disappeared briefly into the men's toilet before reappearing and heading out on to the freezing street. Petrie judged that the man

320

really was alone; he dodged across the busy street and intercepted him on the pavement.

The American had a strong, sincere handshake, as if he'd just read an article on *What Your Handshake Tells About You.* 'Dr Petrie, I presume.'

'Mr CIA?'

The man scowled and Petrie thought yes, he did look mean after all. 'Actually, Joe Callaghan. Phone lines aren't too secure and the first thing is to get you the hell away from here. The way you're blundering around you won't last the day.'

Callaghan turned and walked smartly along the broad street. He took Petrie across a broad square criss-crossed by trams.

'This isn't a hostile city like Moscow was fifteen years ago. I've no reason to expect we're under surveillance.'

'That's reassuring,' Petrie said. 'You mean I'm safe for the moment?'

Callaghan ignored the anxious question. They walked past a little row of market stalls. An old woman, dressed for the Arctic, tried to sell them a bag of hot chestnuts. Callaghan turned into the Tesco, still walking smartly. A security man watched them incuriously. Petrie followed the American through to a café and out a side door; they turned left on a quiet street, walked about fifty yards and then stopped. The American looked around. Then: 'You're on your own.'

'What?'

'At least for the next few hours. I'm waiting for instructions about you from Washington.'

'A few hours? Look at me. I won't last that long.'

'By rights I should hand you over to the Slovak authorities, Dr Petrie.'

'Why?'

Callaghan put a world of meaning into a sniff. 'Spoken as if you didn't know. You're wanted for murder.'

Petrie took a second, aware of the American's eyes assessing his reaction. Then he said, 'I've been set up. They want to kill me.'

Callaghan said, 'Uhuh?' in a neutral tone of voice. *And by the way, I've landed from a flying saucer.*

'I won't last a few hours,' Petrie repeated desperately.

'Sure you will. Look, take in a movie. And call the Embassy at seven o'clock. Hey, this is like the good old days.' The man turned back towards the Tesco.

Petrie, feeling exposed, walked off in the opposite direction. He gave serious thought to clearing out of Bratislava altogether, finding his way across the Austrian border only a few miles away. But what then? Would he be any safer there? Wandering the exposed streets at random, he came across a cash machine. Money! In his present situation, it was water in the desert. He inserted Vashislav's card. After an uncomfortably long delay a message came back: *refer to your bank.*

He visualised a warning message coming up on some terminal somewhere: *card belonging to wanted criminal being used at the General Credit Bank, Gorkého 7*; the terse message going out to the nearest police car; the swift U-turn in the street; the arrest.

Get a grip. They can't have anticipated I'd have Vashislav's card and pin number. He tried Svetlana's card, inserting it wrongly twice in his haste. Again the delay; this time agonisingly long. And again the message: *refer to your bank.*

Petrie cleared off smartly.

It was half past four when he joined a short queue outside the Kino Istropolis. The poster outside showed a group of youths obliterating the entire Yakutsa by leaps, kicks and punches against a background of skyscrapers and exploding cars. *Blood of the Tiger*, it turned out, was in Japanese with Czech subtitles but Petrie followed every word. When he emerged from the cinema, warm but hungry, it was dark, snowing heavily, and time to phone the Embassy.

'Is that Brenda? Joe Callaghan, please.'

'A moment.'

A couple, in their thirties, appeared outside the phone booth, hats flecked with snow.

Petrie thought there was a coolness in Brenda's voice, and then he thought he was being paranoid, and then he thought that in his present fix maybe paranoia was his best friend. He waited. The man outside the booth made a big thing of the cold, stamping his feet and flapping his arms. Then a stranger's voice, male, came on the line. 'Dr Petrie? Be at the Zámočnícka Ulica at nine o'clock.'

'Where the hell is that?'

'It's in the Old Town, just off St Michael's Lane. I can't talk any more.' The line went dead.

Petrie glanced at his watch: eight-forty. He had a vague idea that the big castle overlooked the Old Town. He set out, using the orange-lit Bratislavský hrad as a beacon.

He wandered along cobbled streets, shiny and wet. Past an Irish bar, all Guinness and green and full of chatter. Couples passed, sometimes single people; there was a 1920s' elegance about the fur coats and hats. In the dull light, the East European architecture seemed bleak and unwelcoming. Away from the main thoroughfares, the narrower streets were almost deserted; windows were shuttered or heavily curtained. It was a good night to be indoors.

He found the Zámočnícka Ulica within fifteen minutes. It turned out to be a narrow cobbled lane. Feeling vaguely uneasy, Petrie turned cautiously into it, peering into dark corners. Wonderful smells drifted out of a *crepa*, reminding him that he was out of money to buy food. Something moved but it was only a shadow passing behind a heavy curtain; the lighting inside the room was dull. The lane had a blind bend and light from a café flooded the cobbles at its curve. Petrie stepped into the shadow of a doorway, and waited.

* * *

By mid-afternoon, another call reached Colonel Boroviška, this time from the Deputy Governor of the General Credit Bank: an attempt had been made to use two of the credit cards belonging to the criminal gang, on the Gorkého, right in the city centre. A swift convergence of plainclothes policemen and anonymous cars drew a blank, as did saturation coverage of the surrounding streets.

Still, the news was good: they had no money. Hunger, and the rigours of sleeping in the open in this weather, would soon force their hand. Bratislava was so close to the Austrian border that, Boroviška felt, they would try to cross it in desperation.

He gave them a day, two at the most.

* * *

At ten to nine a police car stops at one end of the lane and a small policeman steps out. Two uniformed colleagues go over and start chatting to him. Petrie tries to sink into the shadow, wonders if he should clear off; but they are just laughing and talking, one of them leaning on the car. It has to be coincidence.

At nine o'clock a church bell begins to strike. At the other end of the lane, two men appear in silhouette. They walk unhurriedly into the lane.

Suddenly, irrationally, Petrie is overcome by panic. There is something implacably *hostile* about their body language. And the policemen have stopped chatting; they are peering into the lane.

He dives for the café and almost collides with a woman of about thirty, dressed against the cold in a long fur coat and hat. She says, 'Darling!' and gives him a squeeze, puts her arm in his and guides him along the lane towards the police. He wonders about pulling free and running but the men, both in their fifties, are about twenty yards away and approaching smartly. 'Put a smile on your face.' The accent is American. Terrified, he tries to grin. 'That's horrible. You look like Hannibal Lecter.' He giggles like a teenage girl, feels the woman's arm tensing in his. They pass within feet of the policemen. They watch them pass, a couple enjoying an evening out.

Up St Michael's Lane, under the archway, breaking into a trot. The two men are now half-running; they are drawing the attention of the policemen. At the top of the lane there is a black Merc; they climb in. Now the men break into a sprint. The car takes off. One of the men manages to grab a door handle. He is white-haired, about fifty. But then the car accelerates clear. Petrie says, 'Oh Jesus.' Callaghan, at the wheel, says, 'Don't worry about the number plates.'

The woman is holding out her hand. 'I'm Alice, Joe's assistant,' she says in a conversational tone. She is long-faced, with gypsy earrings and lots of bangles. Petrie begins to wonder if he has strayed into some alternative reality, like Alice in Wonderland.

'So,' says Callaghan. Petrie waits, but Callaghan has nothing to add.

'Who were they?' Petrie asks Alice.

She shrugs. 'Don't worry about it.'

* * *

The car moved quietly north on the Stefanikova. They stopped at traffic lights, next to a blue tram. Faces looked down at him, people who rode trams every day and lived in cramped apartments where you could hear your neighbour snore, and who wondered what it was like to drive an E-series Merc with soft lights, sweet music and red leather seats no doubt convertible to a bed.

Callaghan looked at Petrie in the rear mirror. 'You're quite a guy, Tom.'

'I committed murder?'

'Uhuh.'

He kept his voice level. 'Why did I do that?'

The traffic was lightening and Callaghan put his foot down. The car surged forward effortlessly. 'Nobody's saying, beyond the fact that state security is involved. The cops have clear instructions: find you, fire you over to the army, and forget you.' Callaghan looked over at Petrie, strummed his fingers on the leather-padded steering wheel. 'State security,' he said thoughtfully.

Petrie nodded. 'Find, fire and forget.'

'And the media are being kept out of it.'

'What did I do exactly?'

'You took a hatchet to some guy. You and your girlfriend both. Split his skull in half.'

Alice said, 'I can tell you're a dangerous psychopath just by looking at you.'

Callaghan added, 'Your girlfriend has such a sweet

innocent face I think she must be the axe lady.'

Petrie looked out at the grey streets. 'What was our motive?'

'The uniforms aren't privy to that. State security's a wonderful blanket.'

'So what happens now?'

'Alice and I are taking you someplace safe. We listen to what you have to say, and then people in Washington make a decision about you.'

'There's a limit to what I can tell you.'

Alice said, 'There's no limit to the time you can spend in a Slovakian prison.'

'I wouldn't get the length of the courthouse.'

Callaghan sounded as if he was in pain. 'Tom, the Cold War's long dead. Extrajudicial killings and poisoned umbrellas are for spy stories.'

Petrie allowed himself a brief, sardonic laugh. 'Mr Callaghan, you haven't a clue. Not even the beginnings of a clue. In fact, you have absolutely no bloody idea.'

41

High Tatras

They were on a motorway. It was dark and the traffic was thin, but Callaghan was clearly taking no chances with the speed limit. The big estate car was warm and Alice slipped out of her fur coat. Soon Petrie recognised the road as the one which Freya and he had taken with the soldiers. Callaghan turned off at a sign for Zilina and they drove into a middle-sized, underlit town. Callaghan trickled the car round dark cobbled streets until he found a quiet café. They sat on rickety wooden chairs in a corner.

Petrie had forgotten when he had last eaten. The Czech for spaghetti turned out to be *spagety* and the proprietor, a small man with Turkish features and a filthy apron, served him a satisfyingly large plate. The Americans settled for coffee and cakes.

Petrie asked Callaghan what he did.

'I'm a trade adviser. Been on the trans-Caucasian desk until now.'

'You're CIA, of course.'

'I strenuously deny it.'

Alice said, 'And I deny it too. I'm a freelance travel agent. I travel between Bratislava, Budapest and Prague, arranging package deals for regular tour companies.'

'How do these cities compare?' Petrie asked her, although he was too fraught to care.

'Bratislava and Budapest are cities in transition. They're exciting places to be. I'm not so fond of Prague these days. It's still beautiful, still the Paris of the east, but it's become too fashionable for me and there's too much organised crime. You can't walk alone at night and the Mafia control the taxis.'

Callaghan nodded his agreement. 'Getting like LA.' He was beginning to twitch restlessly and kept glancing towards the door. 'We ought to move on, people. The less exposure the better.'

Beyond Zilina the road was poor. An ocean liner in the distance turned out to be the chemical works from his earlier trip and Petrie wondered if he was being taken back to the cavern for some reason. But Callaghan drove past the turnoff without comment, and presently they turned left.

They were heading north. From his memory of a map Petrie knew they were approaching the triple point between Slovakia, Poland and Russia. It was gratifyingly far from Bratislava.

'The High Tatras,' Alice said.

'Real mountains,' Callaghan added. 'Not the toys you people have been under.'

The warmth of the car, and the events of the day, were driving Petrie towards sleep. He fought it.

A side road, and a long, winding climb. At just after 1 a.m. by the Merc's clock, the headlights swept round a large white-painted building.

The stars were bright in a crystalline sky and the air was bitter. Callaghan was playing with a flashlight, and then he had turned a key and was pushing open a green-painted metal door.

Petrie found himself in a cavernous living room with a

sloping, wood-lined ceiling. Wooden shutters took up the far end of the room; at the other end was a fireplace seemingly large enough to take small trees, and next to it a set of wooden steps went up to an unfenced balcony from which doors led off. The house was icy.

'This is a safe house?'

'I guess so,' Callaghan said. 'At least until I turn you over to the authorities. We don't have much call for safe houses these days. It's actually my holiday chalet. Come on up and I'll show you to a guest room. Maybe I can rustle up a toothbrush.'

They left Alice pouring herself a remarkably large Martini.

'This do?'

'Fine, thanks.'

'See you in the morning, then.' The door was heavy ash and it closed with a satisfying clunk. There was a lock and Petrie turned it. More wooden shutters took up a wall but Petrie left them shut. He felt cocooned and safe after the exposure of the city streets, and he knew it was a dangerous illusion.

He emptied the contents of his pockets on to the bed.

A few notes and coins. Six credit cards. A Swiss army knife. Two compact disks which could change the world, and Vashislav's mobile phone, which Freya had handed him in the coach.

He adjusted the mobile to be mute and put it under his pillow. There was a small bookcase and he slipped the disks into *Wildlife of the High Tatras*, somewhere between the Tatra marmot and the Ural owl. He told himself, as he slid into a dream, that Freya was safe and well somewhere in Europe and that the Americans would pluck them out of the cauldron and that in the land of the Burger King they would, like so many before them, find refuge from a hostile world.

* * *

Low sunlight was finding chinks in the solid wooden shutters. Petrie pulled them open and looked out over a panorama more Swiss than Slovakian. A French door led directly on to a wooden balcony and he stepped out.

As safe houses went, this one would be hard to fault. A scattering of chalets lined a hairpin road up through the mountains. Anyone approaching would be seen for maybe fifteen minutes. Here and there, in the distance, sunlight glinted metallically from mountain tops, pink in the morning sun, and he thought there might be radio antennae or military radars on the summits.

The early morning cold was breath-catching, and he was wearing only boxer shorts. Shivering, he turned back to dress.

He checked the mobile phone. A message!

Crossed border through woods near Bratislava, stole bicycle and cycled to Gyor in Hungary, fifty miles. Lift to Romania – don't ask about border crossing.
  How are you? Reply through Unur.
  Freya.

Relief surged through Petrie's body. He looked again at the snowy needles bristling all the way to the far horizon, topped with sun-pierced fluffy clouds like pink and yellow knickerbocker glory, and he thought it was the most beautiful sight on the planet. He re-read the message, bubbling with pleasure.

Freya! Still alive!

* * *

'Who is he?'

General Kamensky was enjoying another of Boroviška's cigars. There was a No Smoking sign in the police chief's office but nobody, least of all the Chief of Police, was daring to point out the fact.

The screen showed a security camera's view of a busy street. The time resolution was poor, and Petrie and the other man were shown as walking in a series of jerks.

'Where's his companion? The girl?'

'We're working on that.'

'You mean you have no idea.'

The Assistant Chief of Police said, 'Here it comes,' froze a frame and zoomed in on Petrie's companion until the face was a mosaic of little squares. 'We've smoothed it out,' he said, and the image sharpened.

'Who is he?' the General repeated in an irritated tone. So the little country was proud of its expanding IT, but Kamensky had less interest in this display of electronic virtuosity than he had in the results.

'Our cameras tracked him as far as Hviezdoslavova Square.'

'So?' Kamensky thought, *The fool can only spin out his moment of glory for so long*.

Another picture came up on the screen. The Cossack hat was gone, and the man was grinning at some social function, but it was recognisably the same individual.

'Hviezdoslavova Square houses the American Embassy. This man advises American businessmen on trade opportunities in our country. His name is Joseph Callaghan.'

There was a pause. Then Kamensky smiled, and the others round the screen smiled too.

42

The X-Theory

Bull had loosened his tie and was tapping his chin meditatively with an unopened can of beer. Across from him, the CIA Director was sipping froth from the top of a glass.

Hazel Baxendale started the DVD rolling and settled back in an armchair next to Professor Gene Killman.

The picture was in colour and its quality was good, although the sound had an echoey quality. The camera had been set up in a room decorated with yellow embossed wallpaper. Shutters had been opened at a large window through which there was what looked like an Alpine view. Petrie sat in a swivel chair, at a desk with pewter trays, blotter and pen holder. A desk lamp had been swivelled to light up his face and there were little beads of sweat on his brow. Occasionally a hand would appear on the right, when the questioner was gesturing. Otherwise the only sign of the interrogators was cigarette smoke and two voices off-stage, both American, one of them female. In the event they had little interrogating to do: Petrie was pouring it out like a man unburdening his soul. He was visibly shaking.

Petrie: First, the starting point. You're not going to believe a word of what I say. Not a word.

Callaghan: Not even one?

Petrie: But that's okay. The important thing is not whether you believe it, which you won't, but that you transmit what I say to people in Washington who can evaluate it.

Callaghan: Okay, Tom, that was a good opening line. You've softened me up nicely and now I'm ready to buy whatever you tell me. Now, just so there's no misunderstanding between us: you're wanted for murder and I ought to be handing you over to the Slovaks. I haven't yet done so for one reason only. You claim to have something – you haven't said what – that affects American interests.

Alice: Big league.

Callaghan: Now I don't give a toss if you're the Boston Strangler. All I want to know is one thing: where do big league American interests come in?

Petrie's voice is low and rapid, matching the tension apparent in his face: First you have to understand about the underground facility in the Tatras. It's designed to pick up exotic particles of a type we might know nothing about.

Callaghan: Is this a secret laboratory or what? I've never heard of it.

Petrie: No, it's a joint British-Russian experiment, unclassified and open. It's under a mountain, but that's because they need to shield the equipment from ordinary particles, cosmic rays and the like. Only particles of a new type can get through. Apart from the odd neutralino from the Sun. I won't bother you with them.

Callaghan: Why should we care anyway?

Alice: American interests, Tom?

Petrie: They picked up particles all right. For twelve years there was nothing and then there was this terrific storm, billions of particles shooting right through the

334

mountain and probably right through the Earth. It was something totally new, and it was Nobel Prize stuff.

But then they saw something else. The particle storm wasn't like a spray of buckshot: they arrived in a pattern, there were rhythms in space and time of arrival, that's when they asked me in, I'm a mathematician and I specialise in pattern recognition, that's what I do, I do patterns, I look for order inside chaos.

Alice: When you say patterns . . .

Petrie: Intelligent patterns. The signals were arriving from deep space and they were intelligent signals.

There is a long silence. The camera is fixed on Petrie's face, but he adds nothing to his incredible statement.

Callaghan: Intelligent signals? Like from Klingons or something?

Alice: You were right, Tom. We don't believe it.

Petrie: What? No no, that was the bit you're supposed to believe. This is the bit you won't believe. I decrypted some of the patterns and it turned out I was looking at the human genome, all thirty thousand genes, redundant DNA insertions from ancient bacteria, the lot. Then there were chemical formulae, thousands of them. So far as I can see they're enzymes, they target the aging genes, the cancer genes, the Alzheimer genes, everything. Lots of them do things we don't understand and it will take a generation or two to work them out.

You see what this means? Your girlfriend drinks some enzyme juice, gets herself pregnant and nine months later she's produced a superior little baby.

Callaghan: A genetically modified baby? Are you serious?

Petrie: One which will never suffer disease. When we've worked through the enzymes, my bet is we'll have a means to boost our intellects, live three hundred years, maybe three thousand. We'll have transformed humanity but that's just scraping the surface. There's a mountain of stuff I couldn't understand but it related to particle physics. I saw some of the easier subnuclear patterns – Gell Mann's eight-fold way and stuff like that – and I thought I glimpsed a Calabi-Yau space, but most of it I hadn't a clue about, and I think we're being given knowledge of physics centuries ahead of where we are now. We can't handle the real stuff because it's so advanced we'd have no basis for under-standing it – it'd be like giving calculus to an ape – so they're making it easy for us, giving us stuff a few centuries ahead instead of thousands of years ahead. We don't need to think that far ahead anyway since what they've given us is enough to transform all our lives and we're still just skimming the surface of it. There's an intelligence out there which maybe holds all knowledge and it knows more about us than we do about ourselves.

Alice: Whoa, Tom, slow down for us. What do you mean, an intelligence out there? You know the source of these signals?

Petrie: I do, yes I do. I absolutely know where they're coming from and it's absolutely incredible.

Callaghan: Well?

A sly grin momentarily breaks the tension on Petrie's face: That's a bargaining chip. I'll keep it to myself for now.

Callaghan: Okay, Tom. You said something about still skimming the surface. What do you mean?

Petrie: Yes, there's more, far far more, but this next bit will blow your mind. I can't take it in myself, it's just fantasy ... Can I have some water or something, please?

Off-screen muttering. A chair scrapes on a hard surface. A door bangs.

Petrie stands up: I don't think you'll grasp the next bit.

Callaghan: Tom, don't be so bloody insulting. I have a degree in law.

Petrie: We're being invaded.

Callaghan: What? Look, Tom, sit down and calm down. I don't get it.

Petrie: Listen, you dumb ox . . .

Callaghan: You're right, Tom. I must be dumb because why else would they assign me out here in the boonies?

Petrie: I'm sorry, I didn't mean that.

Callaghan: That's okay, Tom. You did mean it and you're right. So why don't you calm down and explain why you think Darth Vader is heading this way?

Petrie laughs, but his hand is shaking as he takes the glass of water. Some dribbles down the side of his mouth. A female hand, all bangles and rings, appears with a paper handkerchief. He dabs at his chin.

* * *

The President was biting a thumbnail. He glanced over at his Science Adviser. 'He's high on something, right?'

'No, sir. He just got more and more excited as he told his tale.'

'So he's a screwball?'

'No, sir. He's as sane as any of us.'

Bull shook his head as if to clear it. 'He's sure as hell blowing my mind.'

Hazel gave the President an arch smile. 'Wait till you hear the next bit.'

* * *

Petrie stands up again. He is pacing up and down and on occasion is completely off-screen.

Alice says, 'I'm getting a headache.'

'You said we're being invaded. They're already among us; maybe like *Invasion of the Bodysnatchers*?' Callaghan's tone is flat.

Petrie taps at his jacket. 'I have the advance guard right here in my pocket. But it's not a physical invasion. It's an invasion of ideas.'

There is a long, strained silence. Petrie, owl-like behind his round spectacles, forces a brief, nervous smile. Alice leans back in her chair. 'I'm sorry, but that's just off the wall.' She turns to Callaghan. 'I think we should turn him in.'

Callaghan is peering thoughtfully into Petrie's eyes. 'Keep talking, Tom.'

Petrie shakes his head in frustration, like a man lacking the words to get his thoughts over. He sits down again. 'Imagine a world where countries are always at war with each other. So, war is good. War forces change, drives technology, sweeps away dead wood and so on. But as technology advances it reaches a point where it's so destructive that societies crash if they go to war. At that stage things can go one of two ways. Either they keep going back to the Stone Age, or they get through the threshold by developing some code for living together.'

'Where did you get that from? Out of some CND pamphlet?'

'Now if you're on a planet that *doesn't* get through the barrier, you don't matter. You keep going back to the Dark Ages and that's that. But if you break that threshold, if you evolve a moral code which makes war impossible, there's no stopping you. You just keep growing in technology and knowledge. Survival of the fittest selects those civilisations. Until they hit the next barrier.'

'Which is?'

'Your first extraterrestrial contact. Then natural selection works just like before, only on a different scale of space and time. Now it's planets instead of countries but the same rules apply. On the long term the choice is still between mutual destruction or mutual sharing of some moral code which allows survival.'

'With you so far. The good guys win through.' Callaghan is humouring a lunatic. 'Don't quite connect it with this alien signal, though.'

'Right. Right.' Petrie blinks in surprise, as if he thinks the connection is self-evident. 'Okay, here's a question that bugged us from the day we got the signal. Why did they contact us? They don't need us, not for food, not for their test tubes. We're too primitive to be of any interest to them.'

'They just want to be nice to us?' Callaghan suggests.

'They want us to survive, for their own reasons. And to survive they want us to adopt a particular complex of ideas because that's our best chance of survival. If we don't, we become a threat to them, maybe a thousand years down the line, maybe just a hundred. They need us to evolve towards their values and morality because it's their best protection.'

'Otherwise we might turn into Vikings or something?'

Petrie nods. 'Exactly. And if we don't respond, we're a potential threat to the signal. Not now, but in the future. I don't know how they handle a threat.'

Callaghan is struggling. 'Excuse me, did I hear you say we could become a threat to the *signal*?'

'Yes, Joe, the signal. It propagates, it grows, it evolves

by natural selection, it communicates. By any reasonable definition it's a living thing. It's infinitely powerful because it contains all knowledge. And it uses life forms as its medium of storage. I guess that's why it wants us to survive and prosper. Life is rare and precious.'

Alice says, 'You're a nutcase.'

Petrie grins desperately. 'And I've been running amok with an axe. You know what Darwin said? He said the chicken is the means by which the egg reproduces itself. The egg has all the information it needs to make the chicken. The information is stored in the DNA but the storage medium doesn't matter – it can be molecules or silicon chips or paper tape. The knowledge is what matters. You can encode life in a string of letters, you could even reduce it to Morse code.'

'Now hold on, a musical score ain't music,' Callaghan objects.

'Excellent point, Joe, on the button. You need an instrument to play a tune, and the signal needs life forms to propagate itself. Signal and life need each other like the chicken and egg need each other.'

'The invaders are ideas? Not guys in spacesuits?'

'There's no point in interstellar travel because civilisations don't need it. With the information content in these particle flows you don't have to visit alien worlds, you could recreate them in virtual space. The signal outstrips any conceivable spaceship. At the speed of light, information can cross the Galaxy in fifty thousand years.'

'Still a helluva time.'

'Joe, it's a lot less than the lifespan of a primate species. Expand your mind. Anyway the nearest signallers could be next door. We're just four hundred years from Antares, two hundred from Betelgeuse, eight years from Sirius and four months from the Oort cloud.'

'Let me get this right – the invaders are *ideas*?' Callaghan asks.

'The life forms stay nice and cosy in their own planetary system or whatever. They might be organic life forms like us, or machines or computers or molecules, but so far as the signal is concerned, life is just a storage medium. The signal is the real living entity.'

'The *signals* have colonised the Galaxy,' Callaghan repeats. He is still struggling with the concept.

'Not guys in spacesuits, not even machines. The colonisers are imperialistic, all-conquering complexes of ideas and information bound together by a moral code which ensures mutual survival of life forms – organic life or machine descendants – because without life forms to transmit it, the signal itself would die.'

'Gentle Jesus, I'm just a Trade Adviser.'

Alice asks, 'Are we supposed to believe that this signal is a living entity or what? Is it a spiritual thing?'

'I don't know. It encompasses all knowledge. It evolves and reproduces itself and acts to protect itself. It inculcates its baby – life – with the moral code it needs for its own survival and that of life. It pervades the Galaxy.'

'Maybe even beyond?' Alice suggests. 'Making the Universe a living thing?'

Petrie grins again. 'You're getting into the spirit, Alice. Maybe our Galaxy has been seeded, maybe genetic material drifts around like spores, I don't know. Some of it takes, some of it doesn't. But just as soon as any garbage civilisation crawls out of the caves and learns the most primitive biochemistry, the signallers fire off a blueprint for survival.' His eyes are gleaming. 'There's a Galactic club out there. It's a paradise club, it's immortality. The signal is an invitation to join.'

* * *

The President put his beer can on a coffee-table, still unopened. He contemplated it for a few seconds, sighed, looked up and grinned. 'Yep, I've finally heard it all.'

The CIA Director said, 'Seth, if you were trying to beat a murder rap, would you come up with a yarn like that?'

43

The Oort Cloud

'Now just so we can get the complete background, Tom – why the murder?'

'It was self-defence. He was sent to kill us all.'

'Ah yes – "they're out to get me". You told me that. Who is out to get you, Tom? The Slovaks? The aliens?'

'Sneer away, Joe, but I have the evidence right here in my pocket.' Petrie taps at his casual jacket. 'I think my own government wants me dead, maybe the Russians too.'

'At the risk of asking the obvious . . .'

'My guess is they still have a pre-emptive strike mentality. They think we should keep our heads down. If we reply, it's telling the signallers that we're approaching a technological stage where we could become a risk to them maybe a few centuries down the line. They think the signal could be a lure to flush out civilisations like us in order to remove us.'

'But you don't believe that?'

'If the signallers thought like that, they'd have self-destructed long ago.'

'Tom, maybe my government will take the same line as your government. You know what I mean?'

'I know. I'm taking that chance.'

* * *

Hazel said, 'He's keeping something back.'

Sullivan looked sharply at the Science Adviser. 'Are you sure?'

'Can we run it back? Go to that bit about timespans.'

Petrie's soul-baring ran backwards, stopped, ran back again, and then settled on '. . . a helluva time.'

'Look at his posture near the end of the sentence.'

A frame at a time; Petrie's voice a low-pitched, robot-like drawl. *We're-just-four-hundred-years-from-Antares-two-hundred-from-Betelgeuse-eight-years-from-Sirius-and-four-months-from-the-Oort-cloud*. The frame froze. Petrie's mouth was half-open, intensity congealed on his face.

'A hesitation on the last phrase?' the DCI asked.

'Yes. And a slight shifting back in his seat. He wasn't sure about the Oort cloud.'

'Maybe he wasn't sure this damn cloud fitted his argument.'

'No sir, that's not what the body language is saying. Look at the way he leans back after he mentions the cloud. See how he puts his fingers over his mouth. He's thinking, *I shouldn't have said that*. He's said more than he intended.'

'What is this damned Oort cloud anyway?'

Killman said, 'It's a reservoir of maybe a hundred billion comets orbiting the Sun. They're so far beyond the planets that the Sun heats them to just three degrees above absolute zero.'

'How do we know this cloud is there? Can we see it?'

'It's invisible from here.'

'So how the hell do you know it's there?' Bull repeated.

'We see stray comets coming in from it.'

The President pulled a sceptical face. 'Surely three degrees absolute is too cold for life forms?'

'Three degrees rings a bell,' said Baxendale.

'Yes, ma'am,' said Killman. 'By coincidence the relict heat from the Big Bang is also at three degrees. We're immersed in it. So when the cosmologists thought they were seeing primordial ripples in the Big Bang radiation, they were actually looking at patches of dust in the Oort cloud. Fooled them for years.'

'Some of us don't have degrees in astrophysics,' Bull complained.

Killman put a fat hand to his forehead, horrified. 'And Petrie thinks the signal came from the Oort cloud?'

Hazel was shaking her head doubtfully. 'Does that make sense? Life on a deep freeze planet?'

'No, ma'am, not in my opinion. But it raises another issue.' The physicist raised a finger in the air. They gave him time, while he gathered his thoughts. Then he was speaking to himself. 'I think I see what this guy's getting at. He thinks there's a relay station in the Oort cloud.' He raised his head and seemed surprised to find that he had an audience. 'Could be it fires signals at us from time to time.'

'You mean they've been watching us?' Bull asked Killman in alarm.

'Maybe for a million years.'

Hazel turned to Bull. 'Mr President, if this Oort cloud story is right, then any contact you make may not just affect our remote descendants. The cloud's only three months away at the speed of light. If we replied to the signal, we could get a response within six months. Three or four weeks if it's in the inner cloud, which is even more stable.'

The DCI sipped beer. 'Maybe a response like a death ray.'

'All information about the galactic civilisations, all knowledge, could be stored in stations like this. They could be scattered round every planetary system with life, they could get updated every millennium or two.'

Killman was beginning to look wild-eyed. 'Dialogue with the relay station would in effect be dialogue with the Galactic club, but with a response time of weeks instead of thousands of years. If this guy's right – it's breathtaking!'

Bull sighed. 'I'd like us to keep our eye on the ball here. This Iraq business is filling my diary by the hour, and what am I doing about it? I'm sitting here listening to fantasy. All we have is this lunatic's word.'

Sullivan said, 'We have hard evidence.'

'Huh?'

'A compact disk. A sampler, this Petrie says, with knowledge centuries ahead of the present time. The main information is on another disk which he has with him.'

'Now that's what we really need. Hard evidence. So where is this sampler disk?'

'I have it on site,' said Hazel. 'At least its electronic contents. I'm having to call on outside help for analysis.'

Bull looked at Baxendale disapprovingly. 'That's dangerous.'

'I'd like to call in Fort Detrick with your permission, Mr President,' said Hazel.

'It's okay, Mr President,' Sullivan said. 'I'm handling the security angle.'

'We could have results by tonight,' said Baxendale.

Bull stood up, and the others got to their feet. 'I don't like this. Some knowledge is just too dangerous to handle. But yes, bring in Fort Detrick.' He turned to Killman. 'Thank you for your help, Mr MIT.'

Killman opened his mouth to say, '*Actually, it's Professor Killman*', but then he caught Hazel's look and left quietly.

She'd had enough trouble getting him into Shangri-La in the first place.

When the door had closed behind the MIT Professor, the President turned to his Science Adviser and the DCI. 'This is a helluva way to spend a day. Hazel, I'll hear your report on the guy's sample disk this evening. Use my helicopter to ferry in personnel. If this turns out to be kosher I'll bring in Paley and Flood. If it's not, I want to be back in the Oval Office tomorrow morning.'

Outside Aspen, the CIA Director glanced up at the low, heavy sky. Big snowflakes were materialising out of the amorphous grey. By tomorrow morning Camp David would be all but inaccessible by road. He turned up the collar of his windcheater to protect his neck against the freezing air and the big snowflakes, and made footprints in the pristine snow on the path.

He thought that his phrase 'handling the security angle' had carried just the right degree of vagueness.

There were some things with which you shouldn't burden the President.

44

Alien Solutions

A cold, overcast late afternoon. Snowflakes still drifting down, the sky darkening.

Bull looked through the slatted blinds at his old evangelist friend, in a blue windcheater and scarf as white as his hair. Harris was sat on a bench near the pool, reading something. From this distance it looked like a Bible.

Reading outdoors, in the snow!

There was a knock on the door, and Bull turned back from the window. The man opening the door was about fifty, stockily built, with short cropped hair and light blue eyes. He was wearing the uniform of an army Colonel.

'Colonel Rocco, have we met?'

'No, sir.'

'Time's very short, let's get down to business. Over here, please.'

They sat down on chairs set at a desk. The Colonel opened a laptop computer, and on its screen was a thing which looked like a dimpled sponge.

There was another knock. Sullivan and Baxendale crowded into the little study. Bull nodded indifferently and sat down next to the soldier. He pointed to the image on the laptop screen. 'What's this?'

'Well, sir, this is on the compact disk Ms Baxendale gave me. Happens it's one of the leukaemia RNA viruses identified only last year. Not the representation I'm used to, though.' The Colonel's brow wrinkled. 'It's not a simple C-alpha trace.'

'Remember you're talking to a layman.'

'Yes, Mr President. What I mean is, whoever obtained this construction is using a novel imaging technique.' The Colonel's finger traversed the screen. 'It's two hundred angstroms end to end, and wonderfully detailed. They must have access to some heavy CPU time.'

'Okay.'

'Now sir, here they've isolated a protein from an immature white cell. Happens it's the target of this virus. The virus gets on to that, screws up the immune response, you get an overproduction of cells, which is bad news.'

Another image replaced the sponge, this one made up of hundreds of tiny, multi-coloured balls joined by short sticks, the whole making an irregular, elongated hollow structure. It spun slowly.

'I'm more familiar with this type of imaging. I recognise it as something called the VP1 protein.' The Colonel pointed to a long, deep valley. 'And there's what we call the canyon. Dozens of research groups have been trying to find a receptor for it.'

Bull was patient. 'Colonel, if I could have it in simple language?'

'Sorry, Mr President. But now see what followed on the disk.'

The big protein stayed on screen, but another set of balls-and-sticks appeared, much smaller and simpler. Someone with a sense of drama had made this new image drift into view, approaching the protein like a little space ship returning to the mother station. It orbited the protein, hovered over the deep valley, distorted and stretched as it descended and clicked into place like a piece from a three-dimensional jigsaw, filling the canyon smoothly.

Now the dramatist sent in a flotilla of little ball-and-stick space ships. They swirled and orbited the mother ship and, one at a time, landed in other valleys, again filling them neatly.

The mother ship then tumbled, displaying its filled canyons. Bull glanced behind him. The CIA Director and the Science Adviser were absorbed in the image. Hazel was looking numbed.

'Colonel?'

The soldier came back to the present. 'My first instinct was to say that this is some sort of hoax. I mean, here we have fourteen hits, fourteen conformers to prevent receptor attachments, where *one* is a medical revolution.'

Bull was still being patient. 'Colonel Rocco, what does all this gobbledygook mean?'

'It means you can interrupt the lytic cycle – the virion can't enter a human cell.'

'Try harder, Soldier.'

'Mr President, the material on this disk is describing the molecular basis for curing adult leukaemia. These are small molecules, as you see, so we wouldn't have to worry about stomach enzymes. Meaning no injection, just swallow a pill. It might even be preventative. An anti-cancer pill, taken with your cornflakes every morning along with your vitamins.'

'Colonel, what I need to know is this. What can you say about the state of advancement of this technology?'

'Sir, it's the stuff of fantasy. It puts our chemotherapy in the Stone Age. It must come from some protein targeting procedure a hundred years in the future, maybe more. We have a hundred doctoral scientists at Fort Detrick and we pride ourselves on being state of the art. We're one of only two places in the States working at biosafety level four on account of we routinely deal with some mighty hazardous pathogens, and we're pretty clued up on what's going on elsewhere. But this – it's way beyond anything we've encountered. I haven't been told the source of this disk, but I surely wonder who has got this far.'

'Are you saying this is a cure for leukaemia?'

'Not yet. From genomics to commercial drug takes ten years and a lot of mice. But it's giving us the molecular basis. GlaxoSmithKline, Wellcome, all the pharmaceutical giants would kill for this.'

'Thank you, Colonel. This disk and any copies of it are to be erased. And that includes erasing its contents from your mind.'

The soldier looked blankly at the President as if he hadn't heard correctly.

'That will be all, Colonel.'

'Forgive me, Mr President, but the disk contains more than that, a lot more. Some of it we already know, most of it's new like the gene locations for polygenic diseases, and some of it's beyond anything we've even thought about, like . . .'

The President stood up and walked to the window. The Colonel was still talking.

In his morning walk, Bull had noted that cloud had already covered the cottages higher up the mountain. He guessed that come the morning he'd have to take a motorcade down to Thurmont to catch the helicopter. He'd give Logie a ride.

The President envied Logie. He envied his certainties. But a distance had grown between them; their life paths had diverged to the point where they were scarcely within hailing distance of each other.

'. . . seem to be maps for the flow of energy and biological information through the human body, and—'

'Colonel Rocco.'

The soldier stopped in mid-flow.

Bull was still looking out of the window. He spoke quietly. 'Kill it.'

This time the Colonel didn't flinch. 'Yes, sir.'

Somewhere out there, aliens reaching out to us.

Somewhere in Europe, fugitives with their message.

And hard decisions to be reached.

45

Brandy and Cigars

Now the cloud was enveloping Camp David like a white blanket, muffling sounds and creating a sharp, penetrating air. And it isolated the place, giving the guests in the cottages scattered around the mountain slope a feeling of intimacy, of sharing a village.

In Aspen, three men wore dinner suits round a table. Hazel was sitting, glamorous like an aging film star, in a long black cocktail dress. She wore a Mexican silver necklace and matching silver earrings which swung with every move of her head. Bull loosened his bow tie and swilled an amber-coloured brandy in a glass the size of a small goldfish bowl. He looked around at his guests.

Hazel Baxendale, my Scientific Adviser. A turbulent priest, highly capable, a wonderful technocrat. She'd been devastatingly right about the ET signal. She'll be pushing me to go for the new knowledge, to reach out to the aliens. But her background is academic, she's only ever worked with people like herself. She knows nothing about the range, scope and depths of wickedness on the planet, and thinks of the ET as saviours of mankind, like something out of a Spielberg movie.

Logie Harris, my spiritual mentor and old pal, all the way back to 'Nam. He's slowing down, and falling victim to a sort of dogmatism: he's turning into a man who's often wrong, but never in doubt. But he's still my moral compass in an immoral world, and the only individual round the table who shares my religious convictions. And the only man in America who knows about that little incident, long ago, with Miss Saigon.

Al Sullivan, the Director of the CIA. Now DCIs come and go with alarming speed but Al's been in the job for five years and brilliantly supervised the transition from remote satellite sensing to work in the field. Good old reliable Al. He won't have much to say about the issues, but if the defence of the country calls for sordid action in the dark alleys of the world, Al will be there with the knife.

Hazel Baxendale sat directly across from the President. From her end of the table she saw decisions which would affect the lives of billions and set humanity on an irrevocable course, being made over brandy and cigars. She wondered if Bull liked to see himself as another Churchill. Logie Harris, of course, was the big problem. He was a throwback to a darker age, a man who thought all problems could be solved by reference to revealed wisdom. He had a pernicious influence over Bull. Somehow she was going to have to lever the President away from him. She didn't know how. But it would be criminal beyond belief to turn down the invitation to a better future for humanity, doubly so if it was rejected because of this theocratic bigot.

Logie Harris, unlike many of his more calvinistic compatriots, enjoyed a good brandy. If the Lord was happy to turn water into wine, he wasn't about to thwart His purpose by refusing it. There was, he had now been persuaded, a message directed at us from something out there. But that fact had to be weighed against another message, the clear statement that we and we alone were the children of God. That being so, the message was coming from some alien creature which had no more right to salvation than Seth's Labrador, now under the table and sniffing at his shoes. The signallers – divorced from God's salvation – could only have malevolent intent. Their earthly spokeswoman in the form of Hazel Baxendale was right here, advising the President. *I sense great danger*, thought Logie, *and pray that God will help me steer the President on the true path. We must have nothing to do with these* entities.

Al Sullivan pondered. An issue like this needed a huge input of expertise, the wisest heads going. But there were no specialist advisers, there was no NSC meeting, no Chief of Staff, nobody outside this room. The Chief clearly saw this as a matter for the most extraordinary security. He wondered how Il Presidente was going to play this one. The man had some tough choices to make in a matter of hours, especially with those people running loose in Europe. *He's surprised a lot of us*, Sullivan mused. *He's turned out to be quiet, stoical, dignified even, and to have an open and reflective mind. I also know him as one tough-minded and obstinate SOB. Once he knows the right course of action, he'll pursue it relentlessly. The question is, what is the right course of action?*

The CIA Director took a cigar from the proffered box. The President nodded at the table. Stewards quickly cleared it, piled logs on the fire. There was a flurry of cold air as they left.

Sullivan puffed at the fine Macanudo. 'The situation has changed, Mr President.'

'Uhuh?' Bull gave an encouraging nod.

'When the Russians and British had a monopoly on the disk, we stood to fade out.'

Bull nodded again. 'I can see that. We'd have been excluded from the game.'

Sullivan said, 'But now we have this Petrie guy, and the disk. Now we can access the message.'

'Assuming we can persuade him to hand over the encryption keys, which are safely in his head.'

'That's not a problem,' the CIA Chief said confidently.

'Mr Sullivan, that has a sinister sound to it.' Hazel said it light-heartedly. She had settled for a cranberry juice and, in contrast to the men around the table, was sitting upright and tense.

Sullivan said, 'Relax, Ms Baxendale, we're not talking medieval torture.'

'I'm relieved to hear it.'

The DCI grinned. 'Not exactly.'

The President too was lighting a large cigar. 'I don't want to know, Al.'

Sullivan blew a flawed smoke ring. 'There could be overwhelming military advantages tucked away in these disks, even if they only let us jump fifty years ahead.'

Hazel nodded her agreement. 'Petrie's interrogation mentioned new force fields at energies beyond anything we understand now. They won't make practical weapons, not for a long time, but we have to keep a weather eye on anything that increases our understanding of subnuclear matter.'

'I'd go along with that,' the President said.

'So. Bring them over, let's analyse the material. You saw what was on the sample disk. It's just fantastic.'

Bull said, 'But the British and the Russians had their chance and turned it down.'

Logie Harris said, 'I praise God that they did, and trust our President to do the same.'

Hazel said, 'Their mistake is our profit.'

'These are not God's creatures, Ms Baxendale. They can only be motivated by malice.'

'Rubbish. There are strong selective advantages to the old-fashioned ethic of helping your neighbour.' Hazel turned to Bull, who was watching the exchange with careful eyes. 'Sir, you heard Petrie's interrogation this morning. Well, I took advice on the issue.'

'I know you did.'

'The opinion concurs with Petrie. If advanced civilisations hadn't evolved a code for living with their neighbours they'd have self-destructed long ago. The message is on the level. We'd be fools to turn our back on them.'

Harris said, 'Your argument is as false as the message because you base it on the idea of evolution.'

'Here we go, still stuck in the nineteenth century.'

'In the twenty-first, I assure you. Evolution is a story, no more. It fails to explain the irreducible complexity of even a single cell. Tiny evolutionary steps cannot have created it. From molecules to a living cell is a fantastic jump which no evolutionists have explained.'

'Hey, you've been reading up on this, Logie.'

'Indeed, Ms Baxendale. And what I also read is that the evolutionists believe mind was created from inert matter by mindless forces. They believe that all the complexity and structure of the world generated itself. They even believe that the Universe created itself out of nothing, a miraculous feat indeed.' Harris turned to the President. 'Your Science Adviser called me a backwoodsman, Seth, blinded by faith. But the evolutionists have their own faith, that of materialism. They will die rather than admit to design even when the evidence of design is staring them in the face.'

Hazel said, 'The fossil record speaks for itself. Life *has* evolved. And the genetic code backs this up. There's a ninety-nine per cent overlap between the genes of chimps and humans. How can that be if we aren't closely related?'

'You mean you'd let your daughter marry a chimpanzee?'

Bull grinned, and Hazel said, 'Oh Christ.'

Sullivan said, 'Mr President, perhaps I can bring some clarity to the situation here.'

'Al, please do.'

'We can remove this Petrie and destroy the disk. That way everything stays the way it was before.'

The President's cigar was well alight and he looked at the glowing end with satisfaction. 'We could just hand him over to the Slovak authorities. Let them, or the Russians or the Brits, do the throat-cutting. Our hands would stay clean.'

Hazel bit her tongue.

Sullivan sipped at an Armenian cognac. 'Too risky. We'd have no control over the situation. We'd have to do the job ourselves.'

Good old reliable Al.

The DCI continued: 'Or we could get hold of the disk and the encryption keys in his head. Make use of the knowledge already in the disks but just don't reply to the signallers, so avoiding the danger inherent in a reply. We could control the flow of the new knowledge, feed it through our institutes, make it look like a wonderful new renaissance of science or something.'

'Maybe we should be taking that route,' the President wondered. 'Now that this guy has walked through our door.'

Hazel said, 'That's unrealistic. Science doesn't work that way. Hundreds of people would have to be told the truth.

Hundreds or thousands of others would guess it. If just one individual susses out there's an extraterrestrial signal, we don't know what would follow.'

The DCI grinned again. 'Disinformation is my trade, Hazel. Don't underestimate the power of a good cover story.' Hazel shook her head sceptically and her earrings swung like little pendulums.

Harris said, 'This Petrie knows where the signal came from. He could talk. Some fool would then fire off a reply.'

Hazel said, 'We must go for it, Mr President. We'll never get another opportunity, not just for ourselves, but ultimately for the whole of humanity.'

Harris said, 'Join the Galactic club, huh? We become immortals, gods on Earth? Producing children in the image of little gods?' There was a smattering of uneasy laughter around the table. He continued: 'Who needs Frankenstein? The signallers are doing it all for us. And I've seen no more concern here about the moral issues of tampering with life than I suppose Baron Frankenstein did in the book.'

'If we have the knowledge we can choose whether or not to use it,' Hazel said. 'Sort out the ethical issues at leisure.'

Harris shook his head. 'That's pretty naive, Ms Baxendale. The knowledge would eventually be misused.'

'Or used. Even kept in reserve, to rebuild society if we were ever nuked or hit by an asteroid or blanketed with comet dust.'

Harris said, 'You're evidently a godless woman, Ms Baxendale, and I don't expect you to appreciate this point, but the fact is that God made Man in His image. There's nothing in sacred texts about extraterrestrials. And redemption is at the core of all Christian doctrine. But as I've explained to the President, there is nothing in the Bible to say that unearthly creatures have obtained redemption. That being so, they are not God's creatures. We are. It follows that we must reject whatever message they send, and make no response. We already have a saviour of mankind. All we have to do is listen to His message.'

The President, half-smiling, looked at Hazel expectantly. She controlled her temper and kept her voice even. 'Mr President, I have no answer to this Antichrist rubbish. If you believe it, there's nothing I can say.'

The CIA Director said, 'You know better than to question a man's religious faith, Hazel.'

'No, sir, I don't know better. We have a golden route to the future in our hands, the conquest of disease, unbelievable longevity, great wisdom. It's in our hands and from where I sit we're being denied it by one man's medieval superstition.'

Sullivan opened his mouth angrily.

Bull said, 'It's okay, Al, calm down. I'm not looking for Yes men.'

Sullivan strode over to a side table and poured coffees. The flames from the fire were now leaping up the chimney. He came back with a tray and distributed cups. 'If the disks end up in the wrong hands it would be a catastrophe. It could reduce our nuclear arsenals to the level of pikes and swords. They must either be destroyed or delivered into our hands.'

The President turned to his Science Adviser. 'Say we had to remove Petrie, Hazel. What's your view on that?'

Hazel replied tensely, 'Not my field. I'm just a hack doing my job.'

'If I thought that, you wouldn't be here. But I'm never quite sure what's going on behind those beautiful dark eyes of yours.'

'I just do my job, sir.'

'Uhuh. Tell me something. Would you kill a man for your country?'

'If I had to. Like any soldier.'

'Say some terrorist in Teheran needed to be stopped before he set out to spray New York with botulinus toxin? Me, I'd knife him in some dark alley and sleep like a baby after it. But you?'

'Pass me the knife.'

'But now suppose the man is innocent. That he just happens to know too much.'

'I'll pass on that.'

'See what I mean, Hazel? That's what I call an ambiguous answer.' This time the laughter was subdued, and had a nervous edge to it.

Bull finally dipped his nose in the brandy glass, took a deep sniff and swallowed half the liquid. 'Politicians have this in common with soldiers: they don't like ambiguities. It makes them nervous. We give a directive, we like to be sure it'll be obeyed.' He gave his Science Adviser a quizzical look. 'Having you around can be, let's say, uncomfortable.'

He looked across at Sullivan, who was eyeing the President speculatively. 'We've got this mathematician guy in a safe house?'

'The word "safe" is an exaggeration, sir. We haven't had much call for safe houses in Central Europe these last ten years.'

'What are you saying? That the Europeans could find him?'

'And soon. The Russians have sent in a team of specialists and the border is effectively sealed. They must know that this Petrie and his girlfriend might approach us.'

The President had been about to finish the brandy. He stopped, the glass poised at his lips. 'Yeah. The girlfriend. What do we know about her?'

'A young lady by the name of Freya Størmer, part of the team. She's a Norwegian astronomer, co-opted like Petrie. Our information is that they've become close.'

'And where is this Freya Størmer?'

'Vanished. But she must be at the end of her tether by now. She can't stay free without money.'

'Hell, Al, if they get to her . . .'

'Yes, sir. I've a team flying out there now. She was last seen in southern Slovakia, a few miles from the Austrian border.'

The President stood up. Light from the room was catching snowflakes just outside the window. Ford had used a snowmobile to get around the site and he wondered idly if he ought to get one in for himself.

He turned back from the window. 'Who do you have out there, Al?'

'A man by the name of Joe Callaghan. His file says he's third-generation Irish. Not what you'd call a high flier, but he has a reputation for reliability.'

'Christ, Al, we're talking about the vital interests of America, and an unsafe house, and specialist Russian teams looking for these people and the clock ticking away. And what do you give me? A footsoldier. Some third-rater out in the boondocks waiting for his pension.'

'As I said, sir, I have a team flying out at this moment.'

'A team? What sort of team?'

'Specialists,' the CIA Director said vaguely.

'Specialists.' Bull nodded thoughtfully.

46

Iced Logic

So far as Petrie could remember – or was it a false memory? – it had started at age four. He faintly recalled spending hours making patterns out of Smarties, sometimes constructing little regiments of rows and columns and eating the stragglers. Eating your prime numbers was a good way to learn about them. At school, he found that he was usually able to solve problems better than his maths teachers, and the same had often been true at university.

He knew, and didn't care, that it was an addictive drug. Sometimes his problem-solving was achieved through sheer logic, more often it came in an intuitive leap after hours or weeks of concentrated thinking. As he entered adulthood he found that the things which excited young men of his age left him cold. What did he care about who was dating whom or wearing what designer clothes? Why did the latest sports label on trainers matter? Why should he follow the progress of some team except perhaps as an exercise in random walk theory? Girls were interesting in a visceral way, but none of them could compete with Erdos's brilliant proof of the prime number theorem or Ramanujan's wonderful formulae for *pi*. Strangely, he seemed to attract the opposite sex. He had no idea why but guessed that they saw him as a challenge.

Of course, now there was that damned Norwegian female.

To Petrie, whose working days and nights were spent on the edge of the possible, problem-solving at the limit of his ability, the logic of his position was simple, indeed trivial, to handle.

Dozing on his bed, he heard low voices and footsteps, and then the click of a car door. And then the muffled sound of a big engine, and tyres crunching over gravel.

The little man on the wall, dressed in Wellingtons and sou-wester, was holding an umbrella and taking a tentative step out of a door. Next to him a clock showed twenty minutes to two. There was a trace of woodsmoke in the air.

Still floppy from the accumulation of a week's stress and the morning's interrogation, Petrie rolled off the bed and put his head in his hands. He went over it again.

1. *We're fugitives without money, false documentation or the means to obtain it.*
2. *We're in a strange land, without friends or contacts.*
3. *Two governments, British and Russian, are determined to obliterate us.*
4. *That being so, is there anywhere reachable on Earth where we'd be safe?*
5. *America, possibly. The Americans will go for it, or they won't. Lacking information on this, there's an even chance.*
6. *If the Americans go for it, and the signal goes out, and the celestial coordinates of the signallers become public knowledge, Freya and I will be safe.*
7. *If the Americans don't go for it, we're finished.*

8. *An even chance of survival is better than a negligible one.*

All this had gone through his head while talking to Freya in Roland's Café but he had kept his thoughts to himself, ruthlessly stuck with the decision that Freya and he should split, to double the chance of the signal getting out.

The logic might have been icy, but the prospect of being dead in a few hours was flooding his mind and threatening to paralyse him. He tried to relax his muscles, but with no success. His throat felt constricted. He knew, without looking in a mirror, that his face was white. At the same time he had the weird feeling of being disembodied, as if he was a separate person looking down on his anguish.

He wondered about Freya. What was her plan? How could she survive on air? Where was she heading? Would she be safe in Norway, or would she be arrested at some border control and then disappear?

Back to the Americans. If they went for it, they would somehow have to get him out of the country. Somehow they would have to get him through a hostile passport control at some airport, on to a transatlantic Jumbo.

They must have done stuff like that hundreds of times.

Or they might buy into the same logic which had made the heads of two countries, one of them his own, decide to kill the knowledge, and its carriers.

He wondered if it had occurred to Callaghan and Alice that, since they were privy to the dangerous story, they might themselves now be targets. He had a surge of guilt at having exposed them to risk; at the same time he knew that anyone exposed to the knowledge would be at risk.

The mobile was under his pillow, apparently unmoved, and it had a message.

You wouldn't believe what I've been through. Lift to Bulgaria took me to Varna, on the Black Sea. Now in Albena, a seaside resort to the north. Less than 300 km from Russian border. Will try to reach Odessa overnight and tomorrow fly from there to St Petersburg if Unur can get money to me. After that it gets hard but I have an idea. Reply through Unur if you are reading this.

Freya.

Freya, still alive. He heard her soft sing-song voice, smelled her perfume, watched the flow of her long skirt . . .

Cut that out. Concentrate on surviving.

Petrie walked on to the verandah. Clouds were straddling the peaks but the sun was riding above them. A car was descending the hairpin road, visible now and then through gaps in the conifer forest below. It was three miles away and Petrie couldn't be sure if it was Callaghan's. He breathed in a big lungful of fresh air before turning back into the room.

He stepped down the wooden stairs, meeting warm air coming up from the big living room. The fire was glowing red, and was too hot to stand close to. Petrie threw on some logs.

The kitchen looked new. Dishes piled neatly in the sink told Petrie that Alice and Joe had had breakfast. More exploration revealed a large cupboard which served as a study; it was cramped – 'bijou' in estate agent speak. The chalet was empty.

Petrie then explored outside. The house was built on a mountainside, in an acre of ground which had been sculpted from the rock. The property was enclosed by high fencing. He wondered about its purpose; he thought it was maybe to keep out chamonix or bears, but it seemed unnecessarily high.

Back in his room, he pulled out *Wildlife of the High Tatras*. The disk was still there, still between the marmot and the owl. In the bijou study, he fired up Callaghan's computer, and found that it was connected to the outside world. He typed in the address of Freya's Icelandic friend.

> *Urgent for Freya.*
>   *Overjoyed that you're still at large but don't send me any more details of your movements. Unless you're pgp-encrypted your messages can be, and probably are, being read.*
>   *Tom.*

Callaghan's e-mail system, so far as Petrie could see, had no inbuilt encryption, nor did he have time to download a system. His message had avoided the key words which would draw the attention of Echelon, but he thought GCHQ had probably extended the repertoire of trigger words. His finger hovered over the return button which would fire the message over a telephone line, into some paraboloid somewhere and then up into an aether buzzing with curious satellites. He thought the message would probably go down into one of the big ears listening on the Yorkshire moors, and from there to GCHQ and MI6. He wondered if its route could be traced back to this isolated chalet in the back of beyond.

He thought maybe yes, maybe no. If yes, the cost of warning Freya could be a visit from British or Russian specialists, and this remote, isolated safe house would become his execution chamber, and Freya might still be caught anyway.

The balance of the logic was clear: don't send the message.

He pressed the button.

Damn woman.

47

The Judgement

Half-past three in the morning. A stillness in the glacial air
blanketing Camp David, its paths now under two feet of
snow. Here and there, little oases of light in the dark,
illuminating the falling snow. One oasis around Chestnut,
where the duty officer sat at a quiet switchboard; another
surrounding Elm, little more than a hut, which a Secret
Service man was using to escape the Siberian cold. And
lights were burning in the lounge of Aspen, where the
President, Hazel, the CIA Chief and Harris were spread
around armchairs.

'Executive Order 12333 of 1981. Part two, section
eleven. "No person employed in or acting on behalf of the
US Government shall engage in, or conspire to engage in,
assassination." ' Hazel waved the document she had taken
from the library in Hickory, then dropped it on the floor.
She was on her fourth coffee of the night; hours of cigar
smoke were drying up her throat.

Bull said, 'Hazel, that's a presidential ban, not a law. I
can overrule it.'

'But article two, para four of the UN Charter confers
peacetime immunity of all people from acts of violence by
the citizens, agents or military forces of another nation.'
She paused. 'We can't seriously conspire to assassinate
innocent people.'

The DCI was starting on his fourth cigar. 'What do you mean by assassinate?'

'Come on, Al, you're not going to give me some legal fudge?'

'Hazel, the line between legality and illegality can be very thin. But these days we stay rigidly on the right side of it. That's why precise definitions are fundamental. The NSC, the Department of Justice and the army's International Law Division have all carried out legal analyses of domestic and international laws on assassination.'

'And?'

'The reports are all classified, but the essence is this: terrorist infrastructure is a legitimate target even if the infrastructure happens to be human.'

'And if the infrastructure consists of nothing but an individual?'

The Director's voice hardened. 'If he poses a threat to the security of our country there will be nowhere to hide. I think we demonstrated that in Afghanistan.'

'I see. So the legal niceties you mentioned, they go by the board.'

'No, they're more important than ever; they define us. They're the difference between the civilised world and the barbarians we're fighting.'

'Okay,' Hazel said. 'But these aren't terrorists. They're innocent citizens. Young people.' *It's going wrong*, she told herself. *This isn't turning out the way I wanted.*

Logie Harris said, 'You surprise me, Ms Baxendale. Why should you care? Since you believe we're all just animals then, to you, there are no absolute rules. Killing for expediency should be easy as falling off a log.'

Hazel flushed.

Sullivan said, 'An enemy soldier is an innocent man,

doing what he must. And he can be sixteen. It's down to definitions again. Are they bringing us destruction, does that amount to an undeclared war, and is bumping them off like fighting a pre-emptive war?'

Bull said, 'Logie, you got an ethical handle on this situation?'

The evangelist nodded. 'Practically all authorities agree that the Bible sanctions the taking of life in particular circumstances. Whether at an individual level, or at the level of nations, killing is justified in self-defence.'

'Self-defence?' Hazel said incredulously. 'You—'

Bull interrupted, 'But as Hazel says, these are innocent people.'

Harris's face was adopting the old dogmatic expression, the turned-down mouth, the fixed expression. 'They are not. They're emissaries of Satan and are only too willing to bring his message and insinuate it into our society. Consider the words of Paul in Ephesians six, verse eleven. "Put on the whole armour of God, that ye may be able to stand against the wiles of the devil." There are no half measures, Seth; nothing less than the *whole* armour. That's about as plain as you can get. In war you kill your enemy. And this is a war declared on us by the Prince of Darkness.'

Hazel was swinging her long earrings again. 'Logie, do you and I share the same planet?'

The President turned to the DCI. 'Al, say I wanted you to arrange for these people to stop breathing. Without fuss. Given all the internal and external scrutiny you guys are subject to, would that be a problem? There's my own Intelligence Oversight Board, and your internal one – the Inspector General's office – and then there's the congressional Intelligence Committee. And they insist on prior notification of all covert actions.'

'An assassination need cost no more than a few air fares, a few hotel bills and some bullets. Sure we can do it, hide it away in the rounding errors. But if it worries you, Mr President, there are other routes open to you. For example you could go through the Pentagon. They have authority to carry out "special operations" which bypass congressional scrutiny altogether.'

'Hell, that would bring in the Vice president, SecDef, the joint chiefs, the National Security Adviser and the whole damn NSC.'

'But as you know, sir, the rules for writing reports of an NSC meeting are strict. If you gave an assassination order there'd be nothing on paper. Eisenhower and Nixon both played the game.'

Hazel couldn't resist it: 'And of course there was the Castro farce, eight assassination attempts by the CIA, all failures.'

'That was the Stone Age.'

'And now? You're squeaky clean?'

'We're more efficient.' Sullivan's face was beginning to go pink. It might have been the heat from the flames leaping in the stone fireplace. 'Hazel, do we really need ethics to flush nasty things down the tube?'

'What about Callaghan and his assistant?' Hazel asked. 'Two Americans; and your own people. They know about this extraterrestrial signal.'

Sullivan looked uncomfortable. He glanced over at President Bull, who was leaning back in his chair. 'It's down to what the President wants.'

'What *do* you want, Mr President?' Hazel asked.

They held their breaths.

The President told them.

48

Execution

Petrie was on his second coffee when he heard the distant sound of a vehicle. From the bedroom verandah, he watched a white Transit van toiling up the hairpin bends, occasionally crashing gears. He felt a sudden surge of nausea, for a panicky moment wanted to run into the mountains, had to consciously go through the icy logic again.

He thought they probably wouldn't kill him here, in Callaghan's place. More likely they would string him along, tell him some story about transporting him through desolate routes to the safety of the States in exchange for the disk. That way they would keep him docile all through the desolation until the last moments.

The weather had worsened; the fluffy clouds over the peaks had reared up into towering black cumulus, and grey streaks under them told of falling snow.

The van turned into the driveway and pulled to a halt. There was slush under its mudguards. *Elmonet* was printed on its side, with a red arrow giving the impression that Elmonet was a courier service. However, the two men who stepped out didn't look like couriers and it didn't take two men to deliver a parcel. One of them, a man with a neat black beard to match his black T-shirt, looked up but gave no nod or wave.

Executioners aren't required to be friendly, Petrie thought. He took a last look at the mountains before turning back into the chalet.

'I'm Amos.' The man had an American accent and a neutral handshake.

'Of course you are. I suppose your friend is Obadiah. Do you want coffee?'

'No, thank you.'

Of course not. All that DNA left around.

'But finish yours.' The man wasn't trying too hard to be friendly but that might just have been tiredness after a long journey.

'Thank you.'

Petrie thought, *This is bizarre. Civilised conversation with the man who's about to murder me.*

'Well, Dr Petrie.' The man leaned back perilously on the kitchen chair. Tom could hear footsteps on the floor above. 'I understand you have a disk.'

'Uhuh.'

'And where is it?'

Petrie sipped at his coffee. 'Somewhere safe.'

The man grinned. 'Posted to a friend, maybe?'

'There's always that possibility, although that would just shift the burden. Not that a friend or anyone else could read it. We encrypted the message. The password is as long as your arm. Even the NSA would take centuries to get into it.'

'I see. And where is this electronic key, Doctor? Somewhere safe, you say?'

Petrie tapped his head.

The man's smile had a trace of sadness. 'I wouldn't call that safe, my friend, not at all.'

Petrie didn't respond. Vashislav had set up a duress

password, one which would instruct the computer to erase the disk. *For contingencies*, the Russian had said. *The disk's equivalent of a suicide pill.*

'The deal is that you give us the disk and we get you to the States.'

Someone was clattering down the open-plan stairs. 'And as I say, the disk is no good without me. It's both or neither. How do you plan to do that?'

'The High Tatras straddles Poland, Russia and Slovakia. Here we're very close to the border with Poland. There are lots of trails, this being a National Park. Some of the routes are used by Russian Mafia for drug-running into Poland. Assuming you have the disk here, the plan is to take you across the border to Cracow and then on to Warsaw.'

'What happens in Warsaw?' Petrie asked.

'You do have the disk here? It sure complicates life if it's in Bratislava or someplace.'

'Tell me what happens in Warsaw.'

'Don't fence with me, friend. We're here to help. In Warsaw I have contacts. You'll stay snug and cosy in a flat in the Old Quarter for a couple of weeks while we fix up documentation. After that it's a one-way ticket to New York.'

It was all reassuringly plausible.

'Okay, the disk is here. I'll get it.'

There was a tap on the door. A tall man in his mid-thirties was waving a silver disk. 'Is this it?'

Amos said, 'There's no time to waste. Contrary to anything Callaghan may have told you, this is not, repeat *not*, a safe house. People will be checking up on him and this is an obvious place to check out. Bad people could arrive here at any moment.'

'Maybe they already have, Amos.'

Amos gave Petrie a thoughtful look. 'Well, I guess you'll just have to trust us on that.'

'What about Callaghan and Alice?'

'They've been taken care of.'

Petrie slid into the passenger seat. The van smelled of stale cigarettes and the floor was covered with sweet papers. Amos took the wheel with a grunt, wiping a clear patch on the windscreen with his hand. Obadiah sat in the back, and slammed the door shut. He was clutching a black canvas bag. Petrie tried not to think about what it might hold.

The road levelled and joined another narrow one taking them north. The churning black cloud on the horizon had now reached the zenith and looked remarkably like a Plinian explosion from some volcano. Amos put his foot down and Petrie fantasised that they were fleeing from a pyroclastic flow. He'd have preferred that.

* * *

The High Tatras, Petrie was learning, consisted of forested tracks, chairlifts and ski slopes. Many of the side roads were closed. There was a trickle of cars and the occasional bus. From time to time Obadiah, his finger on a map, would issue some terse instruction. Apart from that he was effectively mute. Maybe, Petrie thought, Obadiah saw himself in the traditional mould of the Western hero; others gabbled, he rode god-like and aloof like Gary Cooper.

Following a one-word instruction from Obadiah, Amos turned left and was confronted by a track with a chain across it. Obadiah said, 'Road's closed.'

Amos gave Petrie a look. Petrie jumped out and un-hooked the chain. He thought that a closed track through a dense forest was the perfect place for murder. He wondered how long it would be before his body was discovered, whether it would be identified. He wondered what Priscilla and Kavanagh and his parents would think as his absence stretched from days to weeks and then to months. The snow was about three inches deep and light flurries were coming down.

The road was steep and the van slithered its way up through the forest track. More than once it threatened to leave the path. The pyroclastic flow had finally caught up with them and the falling snow thickened as they ascended. Amos was gripping the steering wheel and pushing his face up against the arc of visibility created by the wipers. Petrie looked into the forest but saw only darkness. He could easily have jumped out and run.

After about twenty minutes of climbing, a beep came from inside Obadiah's black bag. 'Message.'

Petrie had forgotten all about Vashislav's phone. Obadiah seemed to think the message was public property. He read it aloud:

> *Dearest Tom,*
> *Still in Albena. Quiet in winter, but have found a man with a boat. Am just about to sail for Odessa. If I can get to Norway I have lots of friends. Will try for Svalbard. Know the people at the Eiscat radar and will get them to fire a message back at the signallers.*
> *Are you alive? Please reply via Unur.*
> *Freya.'*

'You're just good friends?' Obadiah asked. Petrie ignored him.

'Who's this Unur?' Amos wanted to know.

'Forget it,' Petrie snapped. 'How can the stupid woman be broadcasting like this? I warned her.'

'Your friend won't last,' said Amos. 'Not more'n a day or two.'

And how long have I got? Petrie kept the thought to himself. They drove under a pair of thick metal cables. The trees were thinning and then the van was suddenly above the treeline, and the road was levelling out. There was a building with narrow slotted windows and a tall control mast studded with little antennae. The snow around it was pristine and there were no cars.

Amos said, 'This is it.'

Icy air blew around the van as he slid open the door. Petrie stepped out. His heart was thudding in his chest. They were on a plateau. Conifers fell steeply away on all sides. A single-file track led down through the trees, pointing to the north – he thought it was the north. On the horizon, beyond the track, he could make out a line of peaks, glimpsed through the snow flurries.

Amos caught Petrie's look. He said, 'Poland.'

The van door slammed shut. Obadiah, with his black canvas bag.

Petrie said, 'It's cold.'

'After you,' said Amos, pointing to the track.

There was nothing else to be done. Petrie headed down, snow getting into his shoes and wetting his feet. He heard the men at his back, their breathing heavy with exertion. He wondered when it would come, what it would be like.

Petrie wondered, and he thought, and he hoped.

He wondered about the signallers. Were they living creatures, human-like? Were they thinking machines, having supplanted organic life millions of years ago? Was he right about the probe in the Oort cloud and was the probe in it just an insensate robot, some super-powerful computer? Or by some trick of time beyond imagination, did the signal really come from the Whirlpool galaxy, sent to us before we existed?

He thought, what a way to end! To have been offered the interstellar hand, to have almost touched it, and yet to have sunk back into the slime.

And he hoped that, when they got to Freya, she wouldn't suffer.

* * *

The corpse was sprawled stomach-down on a flat, icy boulder, as if it had been kneeling before execution. It wore a black hooded fleece, heavy gloves, thickly padded trousers and furry, knee-length boots. Its face was expressionless. Its lips were thin and cruel, and its small black eyes stared unblinkingly ahead as if fixed on the Hardangerfjord far below.

The waters of this fiord were black and heavy, and speckled with little ice floes. Across the water, mountains glowed white under a sky dotted with stars and auroral curtains, dancing and shimmering, silent and awesome. Up here, on the roof of the world, Thor and Odin were a tangible presence.

In the Arctic cold, any corpse more than a few hours old would have solidified. Cracks would have split its internal organs and its cell walls would have burst, as the water they held expanded and turned to ice. But then, in the near-dark, something moved. It was a slow, careful, barely discernible movement, but it was there: a finger and thumb were adjusting a black, knurled knob. The corpse was alive after all.

The man standing next to the prone body was identically dressed, except that a scarf covered his mouth and nose. He was shivering violently and flapping his arms. The scarf muffled his voice, but failed to conceal its tension. 'Range?'

The corpse pressed a button and frosty breath drifted through the line of a red laser beam. 'Two kilometres. Just under.'

'Can you do it?'

'Of course.'

'Cold air's denser. Bullets have a different trajectory.'

'You live and learn.'

'Look, if you miss . . .'

'I don't miss.'

'. . . she'll run like a jack rabbit. You'll only get one shot.'

'Shut up.'

'I can't stand much more of this cold.'

The rifle, on a little tripod, was a precision instrument. It had been custom-built by the Tanyard Springs gunsmiths in Texas. From its origins in their Honey Grove factory, it had travelled in the boot of a car to Colombia, for service with one of the major drug families who had been having trouble with a judge. From there it had crossed water to Kingston, Jamaica, where it had seen action from the roof of a Trench Town slum. Then it had travelled back to the States where, for a few hours, it had lived in a large South Carolina mansion. In an attic of this house a fine lasergrip sight, product of the Crimson Trace Corporation, had been added to the barrel. Having been fired just once – its owner regarded repetition as bad business practice – the rifle crossed the Atlantic in a private yacht to Northern Ireland, part of a large consignment of rifles and pistols. Its trail then led to a flat in the Fifth arrondissement in Paris and at last, by train and car, to seventy degrees north, inside the Arctic Circle.

The rifle was loaded with a single bullet, reflecting the marksman's confidence. While the 300 FAB Magnum was a popular choice amongst his peers, the rifleman preferred a 173 grain HV. This was purchased from a source in Port Elizabeth, South Africa. It was a 30-calibre bullet, with an exit speed of 3650 feet per second, quite capable of stopping an elephant or piercing body armour. In a few minutes, if all went well, the powder in the bullet would be detonated and the shocked vapour would propel the soft-nosed head through the cold, dense air on a precise trajectory to the target's skull, spreading brain and bone fragments across the gritted road.

'Switch off the laser, you fool. You want someone to see it?' The man stopped flapping his arms and picked up his night-vision binoculars. A thin road, already gritted, led into the town below from the left. At the town's entrance was an open yard. In it, half a dozen big diesel trucks were throbbing, the noise drifting faintly up to them. Steam from their exhausts rose up to roof height and disappeared into the blackness. Over the door of a single-storeyed building in the yard, harsh lights illuminated the words *Henrik Hedstrom*.

There was nothing to say what business Henrik Hedstrom was in. For all the waiting assassins cared, Henry Headstrong was Santa Claus. What mattered was that the target had hitched a lift in a Hedstrom truck and was heading this way; that she would get off either in the street or the yard; and that for a few moments, while she was saying her farewells to the driver, she would be a static target.

The man said again, 'I'm going to die of fucking cold.'

He swung his binoculars to the right. Next to the yard was a post office, and then a two-storeyed timber house, glowing yellow in the streetlights. Pastel-coloured wooden houses lined the road, which hugged the fiord to the point where a massive rocky outcrop hid the view. At intervals there were boat-houses, and a mile away a pier jutted into the dark water. Smoke from overnight fires curled into the sky. In a few houses, chinks of light filtered through shuttered windows. One room had its shutters open and lights on, and it blazed into the darkness like a searchlight. The man peered into it, hoping to see something interesting like a woman undressing, but there was only shabby green wallpaper and a wooden dressing-table to be seen.

Somewhere below, a dog howled, wolf-like; answering howls came from around the little town. The noise died down. 'What if he takes her past the yard?'

The corpse grunted. 'Will you shut up? You want me to miss?'

'Not with what we're paying you.'

The marksman said, 'It's not enough. I'm losing my nuts.'

His nervous companion had no time to wonder if the statement was intended literally. His binoculars were picking up headlights, far to the left, where the road appeared round the edge of a mountain. His mouth was dry with fear and he could hardly get the words out: 'Here she comes.'

49

Endgame

The cabin steward shook him awake and Petrie was hit by his third surge of terror in twelve hours.

The first had been in Warsaw. At the check-in he withered under the steady gaze of hard-eyed officials. And again at Heathrow, the Special Branch officers seemed to have X-ray eyes which penetrated his mind. Petrie knew that a mistake at either of these key points, a tremor of nerves attracting attention, would have been fatal.

And now, on the screen showing the transatlantic progress of the jumbo, the aircraft was pointing south and practically touching Washington. He looked down, and glimpsed snow-covered ground through clear patches of cloud.

The endgame. A good one won't save you. It needs to be devastating.

In the Dulles terminal Petrie defiantly pulled off the wig and sideburns and the heavy spectacles, eased the plastic padding out of his mouth and the stupid little moustache from under his nose, and tossed the lot into a litter bin. He put on his usual round-framed spectacles from a case. Amos and Obadiah escorted him to the sidewalk at the front of the airport, where a stretch limousine was waiting, with another large black car behind it. Amos opened the door for Petrie and said, 'So long, Tom.'

In the back of the limousine, three people. Eau de cologne lingering in the air. He sank into leather opulence next to a strikingly beautiful young woman who gave him an open, almost naive smile. Her voice was melodious and tinged with a Scandinavian accent: 'What took you so long?'

For the first time in his life Petrie was out of words. He squeezed her hand.

The driver merged smoothly into the flow of airport traffic. A middle-aged woman sat across from Petrie, on the luxurious backwards-facing long seat. She pressed a button on the arm rest and a glass partition slid up between the uniformed driver and the passengers. She extended a hand. 'I'm Hazel Baxendale, the President's Science Adviser. On behalf of President Bull I'd like to welcome you to the States. Don't let Dr Størmer kid you. She arrived only a few hours ago.'

Her companion, elderly and white-haired, nodded at Petrie but didn't extend his hand. 'And I'm Al Sullivan. I run the CIA, for my sins. Glad we got you out okay.'

Heady company for a junior post-doc. Petrie said, 'I feel as if I'm inside a Bond movie or something.'

Sullivan managed a near-smile. 'We have a few guys like that on the payroll.'

The limo was now moving smartly along the freeway, the heavily tinted glass protecting them from the curious stares of other drivers. The CIA Director leaned forward. 'The deal is this. You give us the password to the DVD. In return we go public with the ET signal. We put everything into the public domain, all the new knowledge and all the material still to be decrypted. But all of us agree to keep one thing back.'

Petrie waited.

'The celestial coordinates of the signal, pending a decision from the United Nations. If they decide on a reply, we release that information too.'

Freya said, 'It's everything we've asked for, Tom.'

'But the moment I give them the password,' he warned her, 'they can do anything they like.' He looked across at Sullivan. 'You have the DVD, then.'

'Came in the pouch weeks ago. But we can't bust it. Neither us nor the NSA.'

'If I give you the password you could decrypt the message, use the knowledge for your own national advantage and keep the knowledge of the signallers to yourselves.'

'But if they did that they'd have to silence us, Tom,' Freya said.

'Seen the car following us?'

She glanced nervously out of the rear window.

'Don't be silly.' Hazel was smiling, but the smile had an edge.

Petrie said, 'How do we even know you are who you say you are?'

Freya attempted a light tone. 'It's the castle. It had an effect on everyone in it. We all ended up paranoid.'

Nobody smiled. She turned to Petrie. 'Tom, if they want the knowledge of the signallers suppressed they'll bump us off with or without the password. We're in their hands.'

The even chance. 'It kills me to say this, Freya, but we have to focus on getting the signal out. That matters more than us.'

Sullivan closed his eyes. 'Young man, there are people at the Farm who'd have the password out of you before the day's end.'

Petrie remained silent. *Yes, the duress one, the one that would wipe the disk clean.* Beside him, Freya had frozen, and suddenly the air was thick with hostility.

Hazel tried to break the tension. 'It must be the jet lag, Tom. May I call you Tom? You have to trust someone.'

It's not going well. Not the devastating game that Vash demanded. Petrie tried to unclench his fists, think carefully. The car was stuffy and he felt sweat down his back.

Freya broke the long silence. 'I trust you. You're nice people.'

There was a mystified silence. 'But before I knew you were such nice people, I made several copies of the disk when I was in Prague and sent them around to colleagues and friends, with instructions. If there was an accident, everything would go out, including the exact location of the signallers. To sub-arcsecond accuracy, if you understand that. Do you know how many backyard radio telescopes there are in the States alone? Hundreds! All convertible to answering devices.'

There was a brief silence as they assimilated Freya's bombshell. Hazel broke it; she threw back her head and laughed. The driver glanced in the mirror.

'There's another condition,' said Sullivan. 'A little rewriting of history. No mention must ever be made of the attempts to muzzle you people and suppress this discovery. The British and the Russians insist.'

Hazel said, 'And we're happy to agree. What else are friends for?'

Petrie asked, 'But what about our colleagues, Svetlana, Charlie and Vashislav? How will you explain their deaths?'

Hazel said, 'They're alive.'

Freya raised clenched fists, squealed with delight. '*Fantastisk! Hvordan ei all verden . . . ?*'

'All in due course, Dr Størmer,' Hazel said.

Sullivan spoke quietly. 'The password?'

Petrie looked out of the window. The facts were in and he had them analysed in a second. Freya, probably, was lying in her teeth. He glanced over at her. She nodded, almost imperceptibly; it was little more than a slight narrowing of her eyes. But Vashislav alive was like the *Bismarck* loose on the high seas; the genie practically out of the bottle; membership of the club all but guaranteed. This thing was beyond stopping.

He turned again to the window. '*Origin of Species*, chapter three, paragraph three, first sentence. "We will now discuss in a little more detail the struggle for existence." Join the words up and write the sentence backwards.'

The DCI scowled. 'This guy Darwin has a lot to answer for.'

50

Afterglow

His small fat wife was mouthing some words, but he couldn't make them out. Slightly irritated – he'd reached the climax of the thriller – the President of UCLA put down the book and took the proffered receiver.

'Professor Goldsmith? Would you wait for a call from the President's Science Adviser?'

He tried to keep the surprise out of his voice. He'd met the woman a few times, but a call at home, at eight in the evening, California time, which made it eleven at night in Washington . . .

'Professor Goldsmith? Hazel Baxendale here.' Her voice was coming over a background of chatter and clattering plates, like a dinner party or something. Goldsmith thought she was using a mobile phone.

'I have a favour to ask,' continued the Science Adviser. 'We'd be grateful if the University could take on board two young people – a British man and a Norwegian lady – for a few years. It would have to be in the Berkeley campus. Not to put too fine a point on it, the country owes them a favour.'

Wisdom and experience had taught Goldsmith that a White House whim was a University President's command. He didn't hesitate. 'Of course. Delighted to do so. What exactly do you have in mind?'

'Perhaps scholarships of some sort. She has a doctorate in planetary science and I understand he's a first-rate mathematician. Work permits and the like won't be a problem.'

'I'll arrange five-year appointments and fund them through the University. Have them call into my office whenever they're ready.'

'We appreciate it. Also, in confidence, we anticipate a little seed funding – maybe fifty million dollars to be going on with – to look into the ET question which I dare say you've been seeing *ad nauseam* on the box.'

Fifty million dollars. To be going on with. Goldsmith felt a light sweat developing on his brow. 'Ah, yes.'

'Would Berkeley be able to contemplate administering this money? It still needs Congressional approval but I'm told that this will be forthcoming.'

'I'm sure the University could manage.'

'Good. Good.'

The Science Adviser rang off. *A young Norwegian planetary scientist. A British mathematician. The country owes them a favour.* The clues could hardly be more direct. He opened a diary, skimmed over the telephone pages, and dialled a number. 'Dorothy? Henry Goldsmith here. I'd appreciate it if your Faculty could take on board two young people . . .'

* * *

The morning papers were waiting for them when they giggled their way into the Willard penthouse at midnight. A bunch of red roses on a dressing-table was accompanied by a handwritten card: *In appreciation. Seth Bull, President of the United States.* Freya slipped out of her new shoes while Petrie disappeared to the bathroom. By the time he returned she was under the sheets of the king-size bed.

They fell asleep with the newspapers untouched, the champagne in the bucket and the lights still on.

* * *

'Tom! Are you awake?'

Petrie drags himself up from subterranean depths.

'I know how Charlie and Vash and Svetlana escaped. They set the castle alight.'

'*What?*'

'Yes.' Freya laughs. 'That Melanie girl told me. The flames were a hundred metres high. Anyway, when the local fire brigade appeared, Svetlana was unconscious ha-ha and Charlie and Vash insisted on going with her in the ambulance to the nearest town, which is a place called Trnava, it seems. They had a police escort all the way.'

Petrie struggles into a sitting position. 'That would confuse the soldiers.'

'Most of whom were away chasing us over the Tatras. It seems one of the ambulancemen had a mobile phone. Vash borrowed it and got through to the American Embassy. Trnava's halfway between Bratislava and the castle, and people from the Embassy got there as soon as they arrived, and spirited them away. Like you, Tom, they were kept safe. "On ice", Melanie said.'

'That had to be Vashislav. Sometimes I think our Russian friend comes from outer space.'

Freya pulls a face. 'All that beautiful Hapsburg furniture.'

'I expect they spared the library.'

'Tom, why didn't he let us in on his plan?'

'In case we were caught, stupid. The less we knew the

better. By the way, his temporal lobe stuff. It won't get worse, and it can be controlled by drugs.'

She rolls over on to her stomach. 'Actually, I think Vashislav enjoys being on a permanent high.'

'He and I intend to meet up for a game of chess.'

'In Moscow?'

'In Stockholm.'

'What about you?' Freya asks. 'How did you get away after Roland's Café?'

'The American Embassy again. Vashislav and I must have gone through the same chain of reasoning. They kept me in a flat in Lodz for three weeks.'

'Who did?'

'Two Americans, Amos and Obadiah. I never knew their real names, never knew whether they'd turn out to be my friends or my executioners.'

'That must have been like waiting on Death Row.'

Petrie nods. 'It seems they're experts in exfiltration, that's to say, getting people like me out of hostile countries. And that, Dr Freya Størmer, leaves you. I loved your phony e-mails.'

Freya tickles Petrie's nipple with a strand of her hair. 'You knew they were phony? I wondered if you'd pick up my subtext. My message inside the message.'

'It was obvious just as soon as you said you were heading for Svalbard. Vashislav's friend is in Murmansk. Don't do that. Where were you actually?'

'Prague. Unur has a friend who has a cousin. I just stayed put for two weeks, looking up the internet for bad places to lead them and firing off false e-mails to you. Melanie told me I even fooled the CIA. They chased my electronic shadow over half of Europe. Then the real me flew to Paris with Unur's money while my virtual self was somewhere around Trondheim. After that it was Mexico City, then here.' Freya throws off the bedcovers and unwraps the wire round the champagne cork. The ice in the bucket has melted. She says, 'Vashislav and Svetlana are in Moscow, briefing everyone.'

'I heard. And Charlie's in London. They're holding a Guildhall reception for him around now.'

Freya smiles. 'Charlie Gibson, hero of science. The man who picked up the alien signal. I can feel his glow all the way from London.'

The cork pops gently.

Petrie asks, casually, 'By the way, Freya, did you really spread copies of the disks around?'

She gives Petrie a sly grin. 'That's for me to know and you to ponder.'

The last time Petrie had stared at a ceiling, it had swarmed with patterns which almost drove him mad. And now, almost against his will, the patterns are beginning to re-form. 'The bulk of the signal defeated me. Remember you asked about their poetry? Their art? Could it be there's nothing analytical in there? That it's some form of art – digital art, maybe, affecting them in a way we couldn't connect with, any more than a dog could understand jazz?'

'But what if the machines have replaced organic life? Could a machine enjoy jazz? Or poetry? Or sex?' Freya asks mischievously.

But already Petrie's restless mind is elsewhere. He is fantasising about his resignation letter. Something along the lines of *Dear Professor Kavanagh, The Institute has become something remote and unreal to me, like Ruritania. Your Department is provincial and your preoccupations are petty. My office is cramped, dismal and dull, much like you. I believe it's time for me to acquire a larger office, wherein I can deal with large affairs and high concepts. Time to become a high priest, an interpreter of the sacred text. My resignation is immediate and I will not require a reference. Yours, Petrie.*

In the distance, the faint wail of a police siren, just reaching the top floor of the Willard and penetrating the double glazing.

'Freya, I'm staying here. They've asked me to join the Mountain View team.' Casually: 'I don't suppose you . . .'

'Tom, I'd love to. But Olaf will have to join me.'

'Olaf?'

'My best and closest friend. Surely I've told you about him? On cold Arctic nights he's better than an electric blanket.'

'I don't understand.' Petrie experiences a dreadful sinking feeling.

Freya bursts out laughing. 'My dog, stupid!'

She fills the thin glasses and wriggles back into bed, holding them. Some of the champagne overflows and fizzes down a breast. She giggles and looks at Petrie expectantly, eyebrows raised.

Petrie sighs. He has read somewhere that Eskimos do this sort of thing all winter.

* * *

In the SETI Institute in California, jubilation over the announcement that an ET signal had been received was mixed in with a very natural human reaction: glumness that others had got there first. But government funding, long denied it by a myopic Congress, suddenly began to flow in. A cryptanalysis team was set up with links to parallel groups in Washington, Moscow, two centres in Europe and the United Kingdom.

There was a debate as to whether the long-running radio search should continue. One group argued that the Galactic club saw radio as too primitive. Presumably somewhere down the line humanity would, with help, develop the science and technology needed to make the return phone call. A second group argued that there were too many imponderables in that argument. There was also an unspoken consideration: too much had been invested in the radio search to stop now. The second group prevailed, and the radio search continued. But there was a pervasive, depressing feeling that it was all a waste of time.

Once the United Nations had sent its answering message, through the huge Jodrell Bank paraboloid in the Cheshire countryside, the location of the signal became public domain. Nobody expected a reply for years, perhaps centuries: only crazy people believed Petrie's idea about the Oort cloud.

Four months later, on a balmy summer's evening in California, the receivers at the Institute were flooded with microwave signals of incredible power. They spanned a broad range of frequencies and the computers were quickly saturated. Almost as astonishing as the signal was the fact that it was coming from a totally unexpected point in the sky, near the nucleus of the Andromeda galaxy.

Humanity had joined the club, and the SETI Institute got its reward after all.

From the *New York Times*, 12 January:

We Are Not Alone

SIGNAL FROM ALIENS

Scientists huddled behind closed doors in a secret location in the former Czechoslovakia have received a message from aliens. This sensational announcement was made to a packed plenary session of the United Nations by David Garcia Alvarez, the Secretary General, who opened the proceedings with the historic words 'We are not alone.'

A BRITISH TRIUMPH

A brief burst of high-energy atomic particles, detected on 3 January in an underground, British-run laboratory in a secret cave in a remote mountain range known as the Tatras in Eastern Europe, was found to contain an intelligent pattern. Decipherment of the pattern revealed that complex information, centuries ahead of present-day science, was being transmitted to Earth. Until this momentous event the laboratory had operated for twelve years without detecting a single exotic particle.

President Bull interrupted a vacation weekend in Camp David to telephone his congratulations to the scientists and invite them to the States. He has called for a full discussion between politicians, academics, scientists and the general public on the implications of this event. The signal, recorded on an ordinary CD, is at present with the National Security Agency and is being deciphered with the aid of specialists in many disciplines. A similar effort is underway at the British GCHQ and, reportedly, in Moscow. Tight-lipped officials at NSA Headquarters revealed nothing about whether progress has been made in decipherment, and if so, what the message contains.

'We are delighted that this fantastic discovery was made by a British facility,' said Prime Minister Alan Edgeworth in the House of Commons this morning. Lord Sangster, Minister for Science, said, 'Our warmest congratulations go to the team. Of course this finding, while made with a British facility, is made on behalf of all mankind, in keeping with agreed protocols and in the traditional spirit of scientific openness.'

A sour note was struck by Congressman Dan Shulman. 'This is the greatest scientific discovery of all time. And I think the American people are entitled to know why, with the billions of dollars which this country pours into its scientific community, we were second fiddle to a shoestring outfit in Eastern Europe,' said the 50-year-old Representative from Ohio.

But according to Professor Chris McCracken of Berkeley, 'We can't rule out that signals have already been sent to us and not recognised as intelligent. We laced a cubic kilometre of Arctic ice with light detectors five years ago and the experiment has been operating continuously since then. Many particles of uncertain origin have passed through the big ice cube. Some of them could have been from the aliens.' McCracken admitted, however, that this was just speculation at the moment. 'We will be re-analysing our data . . .'

NASA VINDICATED

'The finding is an amazing event, but it had to happen sooner or later,' said NASA Director Dan Tellman. 'Put water and organics together and you have life. Planetary systems are extremely common and most of these, in the so-called habitable zone around stars, will have water. In these circumstances we expect life to evolve, and intelligence to develop, throughout the Galaxy. This is why NASA has directed so much energy into the exploration of Europa and Mars. NASA's Origins program was designed specifically . . .'

RELIGIOUS LEADERS WELCOME FINDING

Religious leaders everywhere have welcomed the discovery. Speaking from his home in North Carolina, veteran evangelist Seth Logie said, 'This illustrates the bountiful nature of God. How can we imagine that He would create a vast Universe and yet limit life to one small planet?' Pope John declared . . .

SECRET LOCATION

A baffling feature of the signal is that it seems to

have come from an empty region of sky. 'This needn't surprise us too much,' said a spokesman from the Baltimore Space Telescope Institute. 'Many stars are faint and distant. The Hubble telescope is already staring at one of the two possible celestial patches of sky from which the signal may have originated.'

The location of these patches will remain a closely guarded secret until a carefully formulated reply has been composed, agreed by and sent on behalf of the United Nations. To be understood, the message will have to be in the form of easily deciphered pictograms until a common language has been built up. Depending on the location of the signallers, it could take years or even centuries for the message to reach them. Already, however, a team of . . .

MYSTERY

The finding is touched with a drama worthy of the pages of fiction. The castle where the data were analysed, near the village of Smoleniçe in southern Slovakia, was destroyed by fire shortly after the analysis was complete. Two of the scientists, Dr Thomas Petrie, a twenty-nine-year-old British mathematician based in Dublin, and Dr Freya Størmer, an astronomer from Tromsø, Norway, had just left Slovakia to bring the news straight to the United Nations building. The three scientists remaining in the castle were rescued by the fire brigade. The Russians, Drs Vashislav Shtyrkov and Svetlana Popov, are currently in Moscow briefing the Russian authorities. Dr Charles Gibson, the team leader, is in London . . .

Postscript

The Search for Extraterrestrial Intelligence

The question 'Are we alone?' is, at present, unanswered. Serious people deploy apparently sound arguments to reach opposite conclusions: these arguments, for and against, are given by the various fictional characters who populate *The Lure*.

The Galaxy is ancient. If civilisations were common there would have been adequate time for them (or even one of them) to have spread everywhere, including here on Earth. But they are not here, nor do we see any sign of them elsewhere. Therefore we are alone. This is consistent with the stunningly improbable series of chemical flukes needed to create life from dead matter.

The Galaxy is vast, and teeming with stars. There may be a hundred planets for every human being, many of which will be Earth-like. Given the speed with which life took hold on Earth, its development in the right environments must be commonplace. Given the selective advantages of a central nervous system all the way to a brain, intelligence must be found everywhere in the Universe where conditions are right. Therefore the Universe is teeming with intelligent life.

Both arguments are persuasive, but they can't both be right!

At present, the search for extraterrestrial intelligence (SETI) beyond our solar system consists of a dozen or so independent programs spread around the globe. Strangely, nearly all of this funding is philanthropic, in spite of the fact that the question touches on some of the most profound issues of human existence (p.85). There are two types of search program, namely sky surveys and targeted searches. In a project funded by the Planetary Society and the SETI Institute, whole-sky data from the giant Arecibo radio telescope in Puerto Rico are routinely analysed by about four million computer owners worldwide, running a 'screensaver', background program. Another major sky survey, Project Argus, consists of about a thousand amateurs operating a number of small, 'backyard' radio-telescopes. Project Phoenix, on the other hand, uses the world's largest radio telescopes. It is a targeted radio search, concentrating on about 1,000 nearby stars, that is within 155 light years of us. The project is well advanced, but so far it has met only the Great Silence.

Plans exist for a targeted search of 100,000 stars over an eight-year period. This may be a prelude to a search for signals from a million stars using the extremely powerful *SKA*, a square kilometre array of 500 to 1,000 radio telescopes yet to be built. Ultimately it is hoped to search a billion stars in the expectation of finding the strong, transient signal which will tell us that there are other sentient beings in the galactic wilderness.

These searches all take place at radio wavelengths. In recent years, however, a few searches involving small (again some almost backyard) optical telescopes have taken place for laser pulses coming from the nearest 1,000 or so stars.

As we go to more and more energetic particles, more information can be packed into a signal of given duration. This leaves one with the nagging feeling that, maybe, civilisations a thousand or a million years older than ours may not communicate with such primitive devices as smoke signals, radio telescopes or lasers. It is true that the energy needed to send a signal increases pro rata with the energy of the carrier particle. However, the energy available at the start of the twentieth century was dwarfed by that available at its end (compare the Wright brothers' Kitty Hawk with a Boeing 747), and it is reasonable to suppose that the huge energies required for particle beaming will be available to alien civilisations.

That there may be a subtle interplay between the Universe and the life it contains is hinted at by Freya (p.171). The fine tuning which she describes is real and baffling. It may imply that the universe we inhabit is only one of many, the whole 'multiverse' being an infinite ensemble of universes with different properties, only a tiny proportion of which have the properties to harbour life. Or it may be that our universe has arisen (if it 'arose' at all) as part of a process which allows new universes to grow within it, each with its own properties, some of them suitable for life. Or (unfashionable thought!) the Universe may have been created for the purpose of harbouring life. It has even been suggested that life itself structured the Universe to favour its own continuation. Whatever the merits of such ideas, we may well agree with Shakespeare's Hamlet that

> *There are more things in heaven and earth, Horatio,*
> *Than are dreamt of in your philosophy.*

The bizarre 'wheels of light' at sea are real, and the descriptions quoted are genuine. They have no known explanation. Petrie's apparently mad theorising about astral phenomena and altered states of consciousness in the *Book of Revelation* is in fact a respected opinion amongst Biblical scholars.

Bill Napier

*Read on for an excerpt from another
fascinating book by Bill Napier*

Revelation

*Coming soon from
St. Martin's Paperbacks*

Prologue

At the mention of memoirs, the Minister threatens me with everything from Section Two to the Chinese water torture. Naturally, since all I want is a quiet life, I back down. To his credit, he tries not to smirk.

'You can't stop me writing a novel, though.'

The Minister turns puce but then he's known to be heavy on the port.

So here it is. Of course it's only a story, and if pressed I will deny that it ever happened. And deny it I have done, consistently, in all my conversations with those people with polite voices and calculating eyes.

To me, as a polar ice man, there's nothing odd about a tale of fire which starts in an Arctic blizzard. The planet is an interconnected whole; I measure the burning of rainforests in the thinning of the pack ice I walk on, and of fossil fuels in the desperate hunger of the ten-footers which raid our camps. The Arctic, in turn, is biding her time, quietly stoking up her revenge . . . but I digress.

The key to unlocking the secret of the diaries was Archie. My old friend Archie was the fatal miscalculation of the puppet masters. They had correctly assumed that I wouldn't understand the material I was handling, that I lacked the arcane knowledge which was the key to the secret. But if this particular puppet cut its strings, if I didn't do what my manipulators expected me to do, well, I give the credit to Archie.

We went back to the Creation, Archie and I. As boys we'd wandered around Glasgow's Castlemilk district in the days when it was run by real hard men, not the sham jessies you see now. Young buccaneers in search of trouble, which we often found. And if that seems an unlikely start to a couple of academic careers, I could tell you some juicy tales about quite a few distinguished Glaswegians. In fact our current Scottish Prime Minister . . . but there I go, wandering again.

Then there were the ladies, and then I went to Aberdeen and we drifted our separate ways until we met by chance years later at a Royal Society dinner in London. Archie the buccaneer was now a respected nuclear physicist, renowned for his work on superstring theory. I was into Arctic climate, looking for signs of trouble ahead. New Age monks, we had disdained commerce, despised the worldly, and devoted our lives instead to the search for greater truths.

As to how this unworldly pair reacted when wealth beyond calculation came within our reach, well – that's part of the story.

The rest of it has to do with blowing the planet to hell.

1

The Shadow on the Lake

Thursday, 29 July 1942

Out-of-towners. Men with an intense, almost unnatural aura about them. Come from God knows where to the back of beyond. In his imagination, the station master sees gangsters, Mafia bosses come for a secret confab.

It is, after all, a quiet branch line, and he has to occupy his mind with something.

He has no way of knowing that the three men alighting from the Pullman are infinitely more dangerous than anything his imagination can devise.

First out is John Baudino, the Pope's bodyguard. His gorilla frame almost fills the carriage door. He is carrying a dark green shopping bag. Baudino surveys the platform suspiciously before stepping down. Two others follow, one a tall, thin man with intense blue eyes. He is wearing a broad-brimmed pork-pie hat, and is smoking a cigarette. The third man is thin and studious, with a pale, serious face and round spectacles.

The man waiting impatiently on the empty railway platform expected only Oppenheimer; the other two are a surprise.

'Hello, Arthur,' says the man with the blue eyes, shaking hands. He looks bleary, as if he hasn't slept.

'You could have flown, Oppie. A thousand miles is one helluva train ride.'

Oppenheimer drops his cigarette on the platform and exhales the last of the smoke. 'You know how it is with the General. He thinks we're too valuable to risk in the air.'

Arthur Compton leads the way to the exit gate.

The station master gives them a suspicious nod. 'Y'all here for the fishing?' he asks, attempting a friendly tone. It is out of season for the angling. His eyes stray to their unfishing-like clothes and luggage.

'No. We're German spies,' growls Baudino, thrusting the train tickets at him. The station master snaps their tickets and cackles nervously.

In Compton's estate wagon, Baudino pulls a notebook and a Colt 38 out of the shopping bag at his feet. He rests the weapon on his knees. He says, 'Do your talking somewhere quiet, Mister Compton. And not in the cottage.'

'Come on, John, it's a hideaway. Nobody even knows I'm here.'

'We found you,' Baudino says over his shoulder. He is already checking car registration numbers against a list.

Compton thinks about that. 'Yeah.' He takes the car along a narrow, quiet suburban road. After about three miles the houses peter out and the road is lined with conifer forest. Now and then a lake can be glimpsed to the right, through the trees. After ten minutes Compton goes down through the gears and then turns off along a rough track. About a mile

on he arrives at a clearing, and pulls up at a log cabin. A line
of washing is strung out on the verandah. They step out and
stretch their limbs. The air is cool and clear. Baudino slips
the gun into his trouser belt.

Compton says, 'You know what I'm enjoying about this
place? The water. It's everywhere. It even descends from the
sky. After the mesa, it's glorious. You guys want coffee?'

Oppenheimer shakes his head. 'Later. First, let's talk.'
He leans into the wagon and pulls out a briefcase.

Compton points and they set off through a track in the
woods. After half a mile they come to a lake whose far edge
is somewhere over the horizon. They set off along the peb-
bled beach. Baudino takes up the rear, about thirty yards behind the other three, to be out of hearing: what the eggheads
get up to is none of his business. His assignment is protection
and to that end he keeps glancing around, peering into the
forest. Now and then he touches the gun, as if for reassurance.

Compton says, 'Oppie, whatever made you come a thousand miles to the Canadian border, it must be deadly serious.'

Oppenheimer's face is grim. 'Teller thinks the bomb will
set light to the atmosphere, maybe even the oceans.'

Compton stops. '*What?*'

Oppenheimer pats the briefcase. 'I've brought his calculations.'

The studious one, Lev Petrosian, speaks for the first time
since they arrived. His English is good and clear with just a
hint of a German accent. 'He thinks atmospheric nitrogen
and carbon will catalyse fusion of the hydrogen. Here's the
basic formula.' He hands over a sheet of paper.

Compton studies it for some minutes, while walking. Finally he looks up at his colleagues, consternation in his
eyes. 'Jesus.'

Oppenheimer nods. 'A smart guy, our Hungarian. At the fireball temperatures we're talking about you start with carbon, combine with hydrogen all the way up to nitrogen-15, then you get your carbon back. Meantime you've transmuted four hydrogen atoms into helium-4 and fired out gamma rays all the way up the ladder.'

'Hell, Oppie, we don't even need to create the nitrogen. It's eighty per cent of the atmosphere. And we've already got the carbon in the CO_2, not to mention plenty of hydrogen in the water. If this is right it makes the atmosphere a devil's brew.' Compton shakes his head. 'But it can't be right. It takes millions of years to turn hydrogen into deuterium.'

Petrosian says, 'About one hydrogen atom in ten thousand is deuterium. It's already there in the atmosphere.'

'You mean . . .'

'God has fixed our atmosphere beautifully. He's made it so it by-passes the slow reactions in the ladder. The rates are speeded up from millions of years to a few seconds.'

'When does the process trigger?'

'It kicks in at a hundred million degrees. The bomb could reach that.'

Oppenheimer coughs slightly and stops to light up a cigarette. 'We could turn the planet into one huge fireball.'

'What does the Pope think? And Uncle Nick?' Compton is referring to Enrico Fermi and Neils Bohr, atomic physicists whose names are so sensitive that they are referred to by nickname even within the barbed wire enclave of Los Alamos.

Oppenheimer takes a nervous puff. 'They don't know yet. I want us to check it out first. We'll work on it overnight.'

Compton picks up a stone and throws it into the water. They watch the ripples before they carry on walking.

'Out with it,' Oppenheimer says.

Compton's tone is worried. 'Oppie, look at the big picture. The U-boats have just about strangled the British. Hitler's troops are occupying Europe from the North Cape to Egypt. Russia's just about finished and I'll bet a dime to a dollar Hitler will soon push through Iran and link up with the Japs in the Indian Ocean. The Germans and the Japs will soon have the whole of Asia, Russia and Europe between them.'

'So?'

'So then Hitler will be over the Bering Straits and through Canada like a knife through butter. By the time he gets there he'll be stronger than us. We have a two-thousand-mile border with the Canadians, Oppie, it's indefensible, and I don't want my hideaway to be five minutes' flying time from Goering's Stukas.'

Oppenheimer's intense blue eyes are fixed on the lake, as if he is looking over the horizon to Canada. 'That's a grand strategic vision, Arthur. But what's your point?'

'Ten minutes ago that grand strategic vision didn't bother me. So long as we won the race to build the gadget, we'd be okay. But how can we take even the slightest chance of setting the atmosphere alight? I'm sorry, Oppie, but given a straight choice we'd be better to accept Nazi slavery.'

Oppenheimer nods reluctantly. 'I've lost a lot of sleep over this one, Arthur, but I have to agree. Unless we can be a hundred per cent sure that Teller is wrong, the Bomb must never be made.'

There is just a trace of sadness in Petrosian's voice. 'I understand your reasoning, gentlemen. I'd probably think the same if I hadn't lived under the Nazis.'

2

Flesland Alpha

The new millennium

Death and destruction entered Findhorn's Aberdeen office in the form of a small, bespectacled, mild-mannered Norwegian with an over-long trenchcoat and a briefcase. He claimed that his name was Olaf Petersen, and the briefcase was stamped with the letters O.F.P. in faded gold.

Anne put her head round the door. She was being a redhead today. 'Fred, there's a Mister Olaf Petersen here.'

The red leather armchair had been purchased for a knockdown price at a fire-damage sale but it was all brass studs and wrinkles and it gave the little office a much-needed air of opulence. Petersen sank into it and handed over a little card. He looked around at the photographs which covered the office walls: icebergs, aurora borealis, a cuddly little polar bear, an icebreaker apparently stranded on a snowfield.

The card read:

Olaf F. Petersen, Cand.mag., Siv.ing. (Tromsø)
Flesland Field Centre
Norsk Advanced Technologies

'Coffee?' Findhorn asked, but he sensed that the man had little inclination for social preliminaries.

'Thank you, but I have very little time. The Company would appreciate some help, Doctor Findhorn.' Like many Scandinavians, the man's English was excellent, only the lack of any regional accent revealing that it was a second language.

'Norsk and I have done business from time to time.'

'This particular task is quite different from anything you have done for us before now. Something has turned up. The matter is urgent and requires the strictest confidentiality. We hope that you can help us in spite of the very short notice.'

Findhorn thought of the empty diary pages yawning over the coming months. Petersen was looking at him closely. 'I had hoped to take a few days' break over Christmas.'

Petersen looked disappointed. 'Frankly, I'm disappointed. You were perfect for this assignment.'

Findhorn thought it better not to overdo the hard-to-get routine. He said, 'Why don't you tell me about it?'

Petersen, smiling slightly, pulled a large white envelope from his briefcase. 'Do you have a light table?'

'Of course. Through here.'

By labelling the door 'Weather Room', Findhorn hoped to imply that further along the corridor there were other rooms with labels like 'Mud Analysis' or 'Core Sample Laboratory' or even 'Arctic Environment Simulation Facility. Do Not Enter', rather than two broom cupboards and a toilet. The light table, about five feet by four, took up much of the room. They picked their way over cardboard boxes and piles of paper. Findhorn switched on the table and pulled the black curtain over the window. Petersen opened the envelope and pulled out a transparency about a foot square. Lettering in the corner said that it had been supplied courtesy of the National Ice Center and a DMSP infrared satellite.

Findhorn laid the transparency on the table. Down the left, the west coast of Greenland showed as a grey-white, serrated patch except where sea fog obscured the outline. Someone had outlined the limit of the pack ice with a dotted line. There was a scattering of icebergs. Little arrows pointed to them, with numbers attached.

'Do you see anything odd?' Petersen asked.

Findhorn scanned the picture. 'Not really.' He pointed to an iceberg off the Davy Sound, just on the boundary between Greenlandic and international waters. 'Except maybe A-02 here. It's pretty big.'

'Unusually so, for the east coast. The big tabular bergs are usually found on the west of Greenland. They break off from the Petterman or the Quarayaq or the Jungersen glaciers, and drift down through Baffin Bay to the Newfoundland Bank.'

'So where is this one headed?'

'It's been caught up in the East Greenland Current. It may round Cape Farewell and join its western cousins or it may break out into the North Atlantic. But size and drift aren't the issue, Doctor Findhorn. Take a closer look.'

There was a little dust on the transparency, overlying the big iceberg, and Findhorn puffed at it. The dust didn't blow away. He brushed it lightly with his finger but again it stayed put. He frowned.

'Try the microscope,' Petersen suggested politely.

Findhorn swivelled the microscope over the big transparency. He fiddled with the knurled knob, brought the photograph into focus.

The iceberg filled the field of view. A pattern of ripples marked its line of drift through the surrounding ocean. It was surrounded by a flotilla of lesser floes, like an aircraft carrier surrounded by yachts.

Findhorn swivelled the front lens holder. He frowned some more, puzzled.

The specks of dust had resolved themselves into rectangles, man-made structures like huts. Other, smaller shapes were scattered around.

He turned the microscope to its highest setting and increased the intensity of the light shining up through the translucent glass. And then he looked up from the microscope, astonished. 'But this is crazy.'

Olaf agreed. 'Icebergs melt. Split. Capsize. No sane individual sets foot on an iceberg.'

'But . . .'

'But a large camp has been set up on this one.' Olaf, leaning over the light table, tapped the photograph with a stubby finger. 'Yes, Doctor Findhorn, this is crazy. These small irregular shapes you see. They're men. On an iceberg which could overturn at any time.'

Findhorn stood up from the microscope. The light from the table, thrown upwards, gave Petersen a slightly sinister look, like a mad scientist in an old horror movie. A vague feeling of uneasiness was coming over him. 'What exactly does Norsk want from me?'

Petersen gave a good imitation of a smile. 'First, we'd like you to fly out to the northernmost rig in our Field Centre.'

'Norsk Flesland?'

'The same. Then, from there, we'd like to fly you out to the *Norsk Explorer*, our icebreaker, which is currently about three hundred kilometres north of the rig, just on the limit of the helicopter's range. The *Explorer* will take you to A-02, which is further north again. We want you to climb that berg.'

And now it was happening again, the old, lurching sensation in the stomach. 'Why? And why me in particular?'

Petersen was still smiling, but he had calculating eyes. 'Perhaps I will have that coffee after all.'